THE MOSAIC
OF THE BROKEN SOUL

Branka Cubrilo

SPEAKING VOLUMES, LLC

NAPLES, FLORIDA

2011

THE MOSAIC OF THE BROKEN SOUL

ISBN 978-1-61232-058-8

Library of Congress Control Number: 2011922379

This novel is dedicated to my dear friend Dr. David Luke, who showed me the door in the darkness and led me out with wisdom and kindness.

As all my novels are dedicated to my daughter Althea, this one is, too. If I had to sum up the last seven years of my life in just one verse, it would say, *"She is the reason I survived."*

Acknowledgments

We measure our own worth by the noble deeds that we do and by the people that we call friends.

I would like to express my deepest gratitude to Irina and Aleksandar Dimitric from Mosman (Sydney) for their selfless, constant support and a deep, sincere friendship.

My love and gratitude goes to my kind parents: Milan and Milica Cubrilo, from Rijeka.

With special thanks to Dr. Paul Crea and to Dr. Elias Moisidis of St Vincent Hospital Darlinghurst, Sydney.

This novel is written for women with brains and men with a heart.

The events in this novel are not fictional; neither are the characters. Both are just slightly fictionalized.

The Mosaic of the Broken Soul is a contemporary, literary novel that has some darkness of texture. This is a novel that is impressionistic and metaphorical and a serious consideration of the relationship of art and experience to life. There is a good interior landscaping and description of situation. The prose is rich; it is a novel of the interplay of character and emotion. Branka uses language with effect: the images of internal alienation are integral to the entirety of the work. It lifts the text and takes the reader along with the flow of the narrative, although, the book is not primarily narrative driven. The environment that the author creates makes sense, and is graced with a good, controlled language. The writing is elegant and penetrative. The novel says quite a bit about the contemporary zeitgeist.

When the reader does enter this rather hermetic, introspective world that Branka has created, he or she will find themselves involved, and unable to leave. What on earth will happen next, we ask ourselves, and in fact, what has happened? Is it real, or are we in a book? *Penelope Plunket, reader, London*

…I have read Branka's translated work, *A Requiem for Barbara* and *As a River,* which tells the story of migration and place: Australia and Europe through the mysterious journey of a handful of characters. Branka's work has the great virtue of capturing the essence of place and of crossing the boundaries of time and nation with a seamlessness found only in the works of great writers who themselves have known displacement and separation. Her writing is beautifully evocative and captures this sense of place and atmosphere in a way which is transporting for the reader...

Despite many of the psychologically disturbing themes in her writing, Branka has a wonderful sense of playfulness and spirit for life. Branka Cubrilo is a writer to be cultivated. The Trilogy she is working on will bring to life Spain, Italy, Croatia and Australia in dramatic ways, which have yet to be explored by other writers.

Professor Penny Green, University of Westminster, London

...Branka, from comments by fellow Australian scholars fluent in the field of Croatian language and literature, contributes to the contemporary literary scene with an invaluable ability to succinctly and poignantly express complex and comprehensive issues within interpersonal relationships and historical settings into readable and flowing prose.

J.D.B. Williams, Historian, Sydney

CHAPTER ONE

I met Her on the long, sandy beach of Cadiz, down in Andalucia.

I have to say that She did not belong there, but it was a place where She figured it out Herself for the very first time. Years before Her going to Cadiz, She somehow believed that this visit would bring back the broken pieces together. The broken pieces belonged to Her Self and some to Her Soul.

The discovery of not belonging brought with itself a new feeling, one of total emptiness of the entire universe. It seemed as if it was a fake: made of nothing, for nothing, deprived of any meaning at all.

The pain obtained by that discovery was almost unbearable, it was sticky and gluey that made one feel it was impossible to get rid of it. She understood and accepted the fact that She was going to carry it all along, till the end of Her meaningless time.

Who am I? The answer never came; Her brain was wrecked like an old sailing ship that sailed unknown and unwelcome seas.

I dared to ask Her, *What meaning would an answer bring?* Then and there, She said that *Her soul was scattered all over the vast universe and it had pain of different origins and because of it, it couldn't be understood, not now or in some other times of Her existence.*

She would sit and let the waves answer, She would walk and let the echo whisper, She would close Her eyes and let the wind blow the answers ... yet loud silence dominated. No answer.

Am I the one who gives the meaning so my own emptiness blinds me?

Who said there was a meaning in my eyes, in the gentle movement of my hand, a meaning in the words still sounding as if they had never been uttered?

Is the breath the only meaning and purpose, is it dawn or dusk?

Is it the way or destination and what is the destination, and where is it?

She travelled to many faraway lands hoping they had different answers because of the different language they spoke. Different languages make different vibrations - maybe that creates different universes somewhere between two skies.

When She got there, She found nothing. Is this nothingness just a reflection of an empty soul trapped in an illusion of existence?

She kicked the stone to provoke the answer. *Is the stone mortal, the sky, the air we breathe? Am I more alive than the leaf; is the leaf aware of my question and able to argue to prove its point?*

Is Silence deeper than my thoughts, and as I travelled by myself, did I miss the point?

She would sit and let the river answer, She would run and let Her chasing wolf make Her heart beat, She would close Her eyes and hear the unbearable silence, the one which comes as punishment from the universe for Her curiosity.

Oh, Merciful Universe!

She was walking barefoot touching warm sand.
Where are my lost footsteps?
Will I ever gather them together and where can they lead me then?

She opened Her clenched fist and showed me Her tears on the out-stretched palm. They were still wet even though they looked like solid pearls (they become solid from many eons of hiding).

Then She told me *they left. All of them. One by one.*

Everybody took one of Her pearls and left without a word. That's why Her fist was tightly clenched.

She said She feared silence, it spoke of nothingness. Silence forgets time, it forgets events, words. It is so vast that it brings only fear.

Fear of what?

Back She travelled to the Last Land - the one you find the last on the map of the world. What did She hope to find in the vast empty land? Any little piece which could fit into the Mosaic of the Broken Soul?

Then the days dragged on and on ... repetitive days, they copied each other and people repeated their words and faces....

She used to sell words for a living. Her sharp tools long ago became blunt and heavy, words clumsy and fuzzy...

I don't want to sell my words any more, my silence is louder and my audience is illiterate, anyway.

Whatever I would say, would be wrong, I knew it!

She placed Her gifts on the altar of meaningless silence, the altar of emptiness of words and threw Her tools away, hoping the wind would carry them back to the Giver of the Gifts.

Fear of what?
The rage of the Giver of the Gifts?
Who cares, She could not care less, just hoped that punishment would be quick and final.

But it never came (but the one who came was named the Nobleman). The Giver of the Gifts brought her closer to the completion of Her work - completion of the grand mosaic She was working on.

The Nobleman.
Was He the missing link?
Does He know the answers - where to look for the pieces of a scattered soul?

There was something of me within Him, She told me.
He is the one who reads and heals misconceptions and lies. She was told He was skilled and a very learned man. He knows how to liberate little flies caught in the webs of illusions (he teaches how to recognize the invisibility of the web).
He is the one who tries to win against his majesty, the mind. The mind, which makes us believe in the genuineness of illusion, the grand manipulator.

I've got two sets of pearls, She thought, *how can I show them? Maybe he wants to break my necklace and let my pearls loose? Where will they end up?*
Her pearls were on a thin but strong yarn, two sets of them. One set She was holding in Her clenched hand, the white ones, and the other set of Her pearls were as shiny and black as a starless night and they were hidden from the world and from Her as well. So She really never knew how they really looked. She remembered as one can remember things that happened a long time ago, or verses of an old song heard just once. She knew She was in possession of dark blue pearls, shiny and murky at the same time, just to bring more confusion about them, but She feared them as if they had been programmed to bring misfortune.
She believed that each time somebody took one of her white pearls, the dark ones grew in number (another reason why She held Her fist as tight as She could stand).

When they met, silence filled the cracks. Everything has a crack: it could be to let the light come in, or let silence itself penetrate the banal loudness that keeps sanity away. She wanted to appear sane and silence was the best ally. It was Her shelter, so all the cracks were well filled and there was an impression of quiet contentment and wholeness. I said an impression.
After some immeasurable time had passed, She felt as if all Her well-hidden dark pearls started to produce quiet sounds, like gentle notes of music that came from another time.
Should I silence them?

3

How do you silence your pearls, by whom or what are they controlled, and as they are on a string are they just puppets in the invisible hand? What if the string breaks, am I ever going to find them?

But the most disturbing and mysterious question was: Why did She need them hidden deep down in the core of her very being?

Who gave Her the pearls? Why such an unexplainable gift?

She understood the origin and purpose of the white ones, but were the dark pearls just shadows of the white ones?

The dark pearl was found in Her right breast, I know She is not going to talk about it. In this order of the pearls, if She is willing to follow the hierarchy, there are ones that went before. Let's invite silence - it is worth millions of words.

After hiding Herself under the heavy cloak of silence, finally, She said, *Do you know that water from my eyes turns into white pearls? Do not make me water my eyes, please, we can smile gently at each other and that would be all. Ask no more.*

But She came back. She wanted to know, *Do the things or feelings exist if we just deny their existence? We can hide them in the obscure parts of our very body, not let them breathe so they become murky, and strange as if they had never really belonged to us. Some sort of aliens in our body. They feed off our blood and fluids, depriving us of vitality and youth. Such kinds of feelings form dark pearls.*

I see the wall and I am the only one facing the wall, even though the scene happened many, many years ago I can still see the wall, it has never left. It never occurred to me that I would be the one to leave the wall behind ... I was expecting it to leave me, and it never did. I carried my heavy brick wall with me all these years and it was always between me and life. I never knew that it was possible to jump over it or walk around it. I hadn't been told, and what was in my eyes was astonishment; later washed with a wild rain of tears, last innocent tears.

I thought, many years before, that walking with truth was a noble walk. Somehow I believed that the brave and honest would walk with me. But it is a lonely path and few are walking it... and then She said, *that's all there is to it,* and quietly walked away.

I knew what She was talking about; I have the gift of reading the pearls. The murkier and more mysterious they are, the easier for me to read them. I had never told Her that fact, knowing that She would shut down all the avenues leading to Her inner landscape. She thought I was neither a map-reader nor a pearl interpreter.

Well, that's why we could live together. She needed an observer, a quiet witness of Her existence, someone who could confirm to Her that She was alive.

Was I privileged or was it a difficult task for me?

I am not going into speculations because this is not my story. I shall keep it the way that it was intended to be told. This is why we need a third person, the Nobleman.

***

His face is smooth, eyes resting on Her silence. She thought, *he is never going to say a word. What am I supposed to do? What am I supposed to say? Should I look in his eyes or at the tips of my shoes where my eyes rest with more ease? Is he going to say a word or shall I be the one to break the silence?*

But silence stood in between them patiently.

When She opened a new chapter, I was afraid of Her voice.

Again he said he was going away, this time for good. No need for love any longer, no capacity to give or to receive. Throughout all these years I had collected various presents and did not know, right then, to whom they would be given if he went. When I really understood the meaning of his careless words, I felt as if the tip of a sharp knife was writing these words on the surface of my face. The scars were instant yet invisible but not unreal because of it. My face became one that I could not recognize any longer when I looked in the mirror. I did not know any longer what to do with such a face. Where to go and who would recognize me? Who would like me and listen to my numerous untold stories?

The broken flowers were lifelessly lying on the floor. Among them were pieces of my fragmented Self and they looked like little aquamarine marbles. If I watered lifeless flowers with my tears, it would be a useless attempt, I knew that. I did not say, "Stay," I did not say, "Go," he made up his mind many years ago. I read that in his dark, loveless eyes so many times. He was born to leave, to wander, to run away, to hide, to hurt. That was his restless destiny, just as mine was to be silent.

Her eyes grew darker. They grew bigger, so Her face looked thinner. Again She looked like a child who had lost the dearest thing and I knew She was going to word it this way.

I felt like a child who lost the dearest, most priceless toy. But hey, I hadn't told him just in case it would make him happier.

The decision to leave me happened a few weeks after my black pearl was taken from my breast. He did not need a woman with a black pearl. It was not about me, the fact that I nursed a pearl in my breast was the deciding factor. "What if the pearl regrows? And am I not the one with itchy feet and I never stayed and I never will. I've got to go, I never really loved you because I met many women and did not make them happy, so I cannot make you happy, let me go." And I did. What else could I possibly have done? I had no family in this Faraway Land, I had no money, neither energy for words, so I nodded my head and as I was nodding tears were falling up and down like the rain falling from two skies above and beneath me.

Before he made the final decision he read some books where he had learned about living. The books were his bibles, they were talking about how to live in the moment, here and now and not let anybody stand on your way to freedom. Not even the innocent kids you created years ago when you believed that would be great fun. The books were talking about your birth-right to be yourself, regardless of the harm you could cause other people. They would teach you how to be unscrupulous and selfish, all with the same good intent - to make you free from the world that is trying to tie you down.

The day before he'd gone for good he went to visit a grand master, the Astrologer. He came home, I was lying in my uncertain bed, and he explained to me that the Astrologer told him that he was a coward. That's all. "What does that mean?" I asked. He explained some more. "It means it is in my birth chart." That's all. What that meant I learned the next morning.

He packed his bags and explained easily that everybody had the right to live their own life the way they wanted.

Two children were inconsolable: one was within me and the other standing at the opened door, with an open mouth and eyes wide opened with astonishment. They both were left with deep scars as a gift from him to make him unforgettable. And all was about deep philosophy - how to live in the moment, here and now.

We were left to live in our moments, here and now, not knowing what each new day was going to bring. That day I heard a quiet whisper from my pearls, they reminded me they did exist. I did not know how to react, so I had frozen my insides, including my heart and got a new name, the Icy Queen. Only one compartment of my heart was alive and the label on that compartment carried the name of my fatherless child.

6

***

There was one more thing that She wanted to add, but I never knew if She told him that part of the story or whether She left it in Her dreams. I peeped into Her dream, which was rather a nightmare for Her, and the dream told me:

My beloved (that's how She was addressing Her child in Her dreams and out of the dreams) ... so, *my beloved was walking with a packed bag leaving their house. They packed in it her pyjamas, a pair of slippers, a pair of knickers and an old white teddy bear. At the bottom of the backpack they put three oranges and a fistful of tears. The tears were meant to be presents for her mother, as I had swallowed them many times before. I dined on all her tears and oranges, believing it would make her stronger. Somehow I believed she would never know to whom these gifts were given. But the child knew of her mother's sorrows coming from the bottom of the backpack that they gave her as a last present.*

I really wanted to tell Her to spill out the dream, because it could grow harder and darker, it could turn into a black pearl, but She had a will of Her own and was not the one you could easily, freely advise. She wanted that part of the story to belong to the dream. Maybe the reason was so that She could believe it never really happened. When Her gifts were unpleasant, She believed that they were just part of the Big Dream, and belief itself would keep them there - they would never surface as bright and shiny as a new sun.

When Her gifts were unpleasant, She did not want to unwrap them.

***

She was looking at the Nobleman's shoes. They were shiny, new. The room smelled of fine leather. It brought back memories, the leather. He moved his eyebrows up, asking Her, *"How are you doing?"*

She shrugged Her shoulders and let the silence answer. It lasted longer then She intended, She just did not know how to unlock it, which word was the key. And then She said that She *saw numerous butterflies flying off Her chest into the freedom as if they had been frightened in a pleasant garden.* When She smiled, it looked like butterflies' wings left Her with a new story.

I have lost the most precious gift I have been given - my soul.

7

She looked at the Nobleman's eyes as She was trying to find approval for such an invention of Hers - the soul. His eyes meek, full of compassion, a gentle nod of his head was a sign of encouragement. *Or was it? She wondered. What if he does not believe in the existence of a soul? He used to be a scientist - someone who knows the numbers, molecules, atoms, string theories ... in his laboratories there are no souls, just soulless machines and poor mice and guinea pigs being sacrificed for human good, as in some satanic ritual to please the invisible master.*

She said, *When we claim that we have lost ourself does that mean that we have lost our very soul? And what is the soul and what is the self? Are they the same, inseparable like a canvas and the paint? Is it so that the beginning of one is the end of the other? Or are they interwoven so finely that no scientist can separate them, no mystic can define them, and no fool can find the words to say which one is hurting? Is this grand malady of mine, and my fellow humans' who walk unnoticed with me, simply the loss of soul? And how can one retrieve the lost soul? Do you simply call for it; are there secret rituals for it so you can be initiated in this fine craft of finding it? Can it be the same, the loss of soul and loss of meaning? Which one led the way, which blindly followed? Does the soul prefer to be unanswered? Is it just a tiny voice that can tell you how to separate good from evil? Which tells you which way to take when in confusion? When it goes, the voice, where has it gone?*

Where does the soul live? Between understanding and unconsciousness? Is it married to imagination? Oh, sweet lovers, they cannot be separated! It uses the body to live in it and the mind to wonder but its instrument is neither the body nor the mind.

If I say 'my soul,' does it really belong to me?

One more question before I go:
Pain, loss, sadness, frustration, looking for meaning and personal substance, are they the gifts so that we can come face to face with the grand invisible?

As She cautioned him, She stood up, extended Her hand, still wet from Her questions, and quietly walked away.

She adorned Her living room with paintings caught in frames. Because of it they looked lifeless as they could not escape into freedom or add a new character. But each had a history of its own and She knew how to interpret their stories. That's why She kept them for so many years.

Get rid of the clutter, I wanted to tell Her so many times. She was of the disobedient kind but with a purpose. All Her paintings were Her past caught in frames and She was carrying this past as one carries heavy suitcases, with a back bent from invisible heaviness, and a distant look in the eyes spoke of a deep conviction that there was not a kind of healer or any sort of magic known to man that would teach how to let go of a heavy load. That's why the walls had cracks. Paradoxically Her house was only held together because of the paintings: they caused the cracks yet they held the walls together.

When I really met Her, it was on the long, sandy beach of Cadiz, down in Andalucia.

Even though She travelled there hoping to find Herself, it was I who found the first fragments of Her. She looked like She was made of fine, coloured glass, fine but broken and pieces of it were lying in front of Her very feet. Her legs were like wooden spoons unable to bend because they were tired from a long trip. As I can remember now I wanted to offer to bend down and collect Her pieces, but before I dared to say a word, She gave me a look of the terrifying certainty of imminent death - mine or Hers - if I only touched what was lying down in surrender.

The other reason for Her long travel was another illusion – to trade the pain for the beautiful scenery of Cadiz, down in Andalucía, *tierra de luz, cielo de tierra,* in a childish belief that this was the way things worked.

And that lovely game started right there. The pain had been traded. Who could feel the pain in Cadiz, far, far away from reality, where Her feet danced to the mysterious rhythm of flamenco, and Her stories took a different turn?

While in Cadiz, She wrote two love letters every day to two wrong men.

One never cared what was written in it so he gave Her the words back, not knowing that their sweetness turned into bitterness by returning them.

The other one was living only on the border of Her imagination, and he was brave and honest. He was the one who could make Her heart travel to the end of the world if he had only existed. The first one, the one who returned the love letters he never deserved, was the one who was never looking for love. He was looking for something hidden long ago in his past, and his emotionally undefined and unavailable mother had hidden it on the very first day of his birth, how sad, how sad. That's why he was cursed: on every birthday she would forget that he was born on that day, and that led him away, away from any woman and away from himself.

Do not want to talk about him, he does not exist any longer, not even as a shadow, why do you want me to remember him? They took him out of my breast where he found nourishment and shelter for a short time but when he sucked all the nourishment out, he turned his emotions into a black pearl. How fragile I was. How fragile.

The grand master, the one who speaks to the stars, told him he married a fragile woman. Very fragile. Go! Run, go! That's her pearl, not yours, go!

And he did.
Then, neither later, did he have any sense of moral responsibility.

She asked me if I knew what She would do if She could retrace Her footsteps on the Andalucían beach. As I did not have an answer, She repeated the same question over and over while it echoed in the corridors of Her mind and mine.

I never understood whether She wanted to rewrite the story but certainly She undertook the greatest departure from Herself. It looked almost as if She saw Herself waving to Her betrayed self with a gloved hand, as if the glove would protect Her from that icy event. She looked around Her, She looked above to the heavens. Silence was the name of Her home. She uttered, *Oh, merciful Heaven!*

She sat down on the sandy beach of Cadiz and put both halves of Her face in the palms of Her hands; each half in each palm and held it gently as if She was holding a world made of glass in Her hands. She looked as if She was crying, but Her cheeks and hands were dry, as dry as was Her thirst for new emotions. All Her emotions were packed in one suitcase which She had left behind in the past, right on the train station in Cadiz and believed that they couldn't escape the fine, leather prison and if they did, in any case, they would not be able to find the way to Her from the dusty station of Cadiz, down in Andalucia.

***

Each time She entered the room, I would sit quietly beside Her. Only he, the Nobleman, was aware of me. She had forgotten me a long time ago. Firstly, he thought that I was just a silent witness, and then, as time passed by, I understood that he was addressing me as well when he wanted any sort of clarification.

I read a book of kindness and rewrote it then. A long time ago I wanted to suggest kindness to serve as glue for broken fragments, but She would refuse it as nonsense, for She did not trust it was strong enough to hold.

Even though She was not aware that there were three of us, I can say that She started to co-operate with me - right through the kind, noble man. She believed him and once, She said, *Your words sound as if they are coming from inside of me, like there is a little hidden book which I wrote a long time ago and you are able to make me read it again.*

Yes, I was Her book.

Her eyes weakened: She believed the print had faded. She believed that book was very old and because of it, did not hold any good meaning, any right purpose. It could not help to liberate, just to imprison, and She was already in prison, but the Nobleman's words led Her back there, to Her own forgotten words that She had written a long time ago, reluctant to ever publish them.

Now is the right time to tell you the story of the Dishonest Man. Please, believe my every word, for I do not want you to doubt any comma or question mark I am going to impose. When I recollect this story in my mind, my dark pearls offer quiet rumours telling me where to go with the story. This story has never been told but was locked in the leather suitcase and left on the dusty train station in Cadiz, down in Andalucia. My dear friend, my kind Nobleman, now you have made me open the leather suitcase left behind that summer when I believed that you could lock yourself in the leather suitcase and stay forgotten on the dusty train station forever.

He brought with him a woman of little brain. She claimed that she was well schooled and a worldly woman, she claimed she was a psychologist, and yet she acted as someone who had never travelled and never attended much school. There was too much of everything: strong and unpleasant perfume, and strong sentences, as she was trying to convince herself that she was a learned psychologist indeed. Because of it, nobody felt at ease. Her personality dominated all the time and all the people there were sitting on the edge of their chairs, and knives and forks were louder than they were supposed to be while dancing on the surprised plates.

He was the only one who pretended to enjoy being right there among delicious dishes and her peculiar sentences.

I got to know him by accident. My dearest friend trapped herself in one of my stories and wanted the world to know it.

This is how it all started.

He read the story and sent me a letter. Sweet words wrapped in flattery smelled strange, as if telling me if the smell was not right, how could he be the right one when the smell was coming from him? I read that message, but was willing to rewrite it for the sake of my story. They took my story and sold it to four different parts of the world. Then they celebrated. They took another story and sold it to the four different parts of the world and celebrated. They took nearly all of my stories and sold my stories and when they had taken them all, nothing was left within me for the time being. When he learned that there were no more stories, he unplugged every connection. How brave, how brave and honest.

They ate and drank fine wines, they were telling jokes I never understood and when the feast was over, they got up, extended their greasy, but cold hands and left me sitting there with an unpaid bill. The large bill was looking at me with its zeroes, which looked to me like big eyes full of wonder - are you the one who is going to pay? The woman who tried to behave as a psychologist said that she hoped I had enjoyed her company because it was a rare gift she gave to strangers. Just because of my gift of telling stories, she allowed me to treat her with dinner.

It all happened in the place where people try to make themselves very important for no known reason and where women have been angry and arrogant for generations, believing that anger means independence and arrogance is a sign of nobility.

How bizarre, how bizarre.

Even though it is the finest craft, I ate from it sour bread. Is the money a mirror to show you dishonesty? He said, "No money" and he has discovered during all these years that I do not possess any craft and my stories are not read - nobody wants them, nobody. He said he never sold my stories, he never got any money or anything else, because nobody wanted to buy my stories in any part of the world divided in four.

I knew one thing for certain: there were my stories dressed in colorful covers, adorning the shelves of various libraries in the East and the West, and homes of people who wanted me to promise them more of it soon.

And this is all. I do not wish to talk any more about the loud woman who was constantly searching for someone who was going to pay for her dinners and learn about her achievements in all fields but psychology. The man who accompanied her, the one who sold my stories for no money, is dead anyway. He died many years ago, when he was jailed in some communist country for not very democratic ideas. When they let him out of prison, he was dead for good.

My dearest friend apologized many times when she heard the tale, but she could not read the crystal ball, nor did she ever know that his soul was still trapped in the communist jail and the shell we see is not really alive, all that explains the lack of money and him befriending a woman who claimed that she travelled the world. There is nothing more to add.

When She opened the door, Her gesture was lighter. I wondered, was the door lighter this Wednesday or just Her movement, or what else?

Next time She asked him, *Is there an explanation for this?*

When the Giver of the Gifts touches you on the day of your birth with a specially designed gift to give you to share with the world, why doesn't he warn you about the other side of human nature? Why does he not build somewhere in the body of the gift the same sort of shield to protect you from human nature - the darker side of human nature? To teach you from the start that there is an animal hidden in humans, somewhere between superficial words and the invisible hurt of deeper meaning of their own words.

They were like hound dogs. I still see their canine teeth; hear their barking, loud barking. I hear the psychologist's laughter, all with the same intent: bring her down to our table, let her dine with us, let her laugh at our jokes, let her drink and sink under the table where we can kick her with our leather shoes, let her pay the bill.

I paid the bill, that one and many others and then said to my whispering dark pearls - no more, I promised no more stories, they are not mine anyway, they are not mine any more.

The dearest friend of mine, the one who made me meet the Dishonest Man, the one who apologized for that many times, asked me the same question each time she met me: "Do you believe him? Do you believe them?"

I was as weak as the first rays of dawn. It looked like I had used up all my words. All I wanted to befriend was silence, so I sank beneath all the words and embraced silence with my arms and my thoughts.

She never knew whether this decision made Her pearls quiet and content or just the opposite - did they grow heavier, darker?

She wanted to know, *Can you escape?* Wanted to know, *Can you resign? Do we have free will and lead our stories with the sentences we choose to make, with the steps we choose to take? Can we choose? Is there some sort of heavenly menu where we look for what we want freely, or is it just a set menu and you eat what is on your plate? Is there a window somewhere in between Heaven and Earth where we can take our plate and give it back? Can we ask for a different menu, can we ask anything or is there some sort of hierarchy where you can't get to a proper one to ask the question and make remarks? Eat your food, whether you like it or not! Look at the pigs, they are pigging out, they wash down their food with wine, laughter and swear words, they want more and more, they take from other plates, while the feast is going on they laugh with full bellies, empty heads and hearts.*

* * *

I was a regular witness of Her dreams. The dreams were the gifts She gained from Andalucia. She came there with a heart that did not know to whom it belonged as it was not the heart She was once born with. But on Her first night in Cadiz She had a dream. This would be what She told me: *He came in my dream, the Giver of the Gifts and he said that I couldn't give him back what he had given me. There is no such thing as returning the gifts. I can choose not to use them but they will stay with me forever. If I choose not to use the gifts, they will rot my insides and they will eat my heart. Such was the nature of unwanted gifts. But if I cherish them, they will grow.*

Upon my waking from that dream, I did not believe myself that I dreamt it. I wrapped up the dream and tied a ribbon around it, then let it sink down into the sandy beach of Cadiz, down in Andalucia. That is how I started to bury my dreams in sand and one by one, they turned into little shells and waves carried them down towards Morocco. I heard in another dream that fishermen from the outskirts of Tangier made picture frames with my shells and sold them to young girls. Some of the young girls came to my Cadizian dreams and asked me nicely if I wanted to teach them what to do with my shells, but even in the dream I refused, because of the fear of taking the role of the Giver of the Gifts.

When She told me about Her dreams, She sank into silence again, and came from it with a question: *But what is a young girl without dreams? The dreams are like signposts: if we only know how to read them and follow their direction, they can take us where we are supposed to be. Dreams are like a shelter from daily storms, and they are messengers. Even if you turn them into shells, they can still reach young girls from the outskirts of Tangier, for the nature and purpose of the dream cannot be changed.*

Once She met the woman who had a mission to break other people's dreams. The woman was very small and had very sad eyes, as she was carrying many sad events hidden behind these eyes. Her eyes had that

Oriental look because she kept her eyes narrow, nearly closed, believing that was the way she would hide her sorrows. She believed that all other people, the ones she met and others she was yet to meet, were responsible for her sadness. She would shout at her son and daughter, believing that unkindness would make them like her more. That never happened. Fear is not a vehicle to love.

Fear is not a vehicle to love. She wanted the world and people in her world to model in her way. Everybody refused except her sorrowful son. She wanted me to carry a different name and different words, and even when she managed to talk you into what she wanted, all of a sudden she would ask for something new. She was never at peace, never at ease. We can freely call her a troublemaker, for troubles were all she was able to give. She carried her uneasiness as a second skin and knew the secret of how to pass it on to you instantly upon meeting you.

How strange - she was nearly a mother to the man I wrote the love letters he turned back unopened. I said nearly because there were never certainties, never certainties. Every day there were some new bizarre developments, twists and turns, and all members of that family were in a constant state of anticipation of what would happen next.

I had tried over the years several different techniques to help her to handle all her wild horses, but after a while my horses got loose. They nearly lost their direction and dragged me towards a huge pit of darkness and all I needed to protect myself from her and her world was a pair of dark sunglasses. How naïve, how naïve.

***

Next time She entered his room, She said She wanted to talk about the Other Man, the one who received Her love letters sent from Cadiz, when She was down in Andalucia. The Other Man never returned Her letters back, but in Her imagination he had written to Her the most beautiful words a poet can summon.

The letters She had written to both men were nearly identical, but the response was what counted, really. It was a mixture of deep sadness and extreme excitement, for at least She knew there was somebody somewhere who cared for Her letters. Even though sometimes She was aware that he was the inhabitant of Her imagination, She named him and talked to him on a daily basis as one can talk to one's very best friend, even more, their very best lover. Oh, how sweet, how sweet.

When She started to recount Her story, I was surprised at the turn it took.

It was paper love but not less real than the one of flesh and saliva. I thought I would never write a love letter to him, but he sent the first one. Upon my arrival in Cadiz, I sent him a note to express my gratitude, for he told me where to go and whom to visit in the mysterious streets of an old town. I took with me my written words, my ideas, all of the hurt from the man who never replied, and tightly clenched in my hand was a hand of my beloved child. It looked as if that was all that belonged to me. The rest was illusion. I was eager to let go of all illusions but willing to hold on to the last one, the illusion about my perfect lover hidden in the translation of 'Spanish Stories' which I commenced on the edge of reality and a very private dream. He knocked on the door, even though I had put up the sign "Do not disturb." When he entered, he knew there was no way back: we were going to tell the story that was written for us, but at the time I did not know it. I believed that he was just an inhabitant of my inner world, where all my heroes lived in harmony.

Then the Nobleman dared to interrupt and asked Her, *"Who are the heroes who lived in harmony?"* She paused and thought a little, then shrugged Her shoulders and said, *You are one of them.*

There are heroes and anti-heroes in every story, yes, there are.

Dear friend, we travelled to Andalucia by train. Five hours from Madrid to Cadiz. I felt so strange because of that feeling of belonging to this dry and avaricious land, which I believed I had never visited before. The land was gray and stiff, the grass yellow, lifeless, and out of those images, the voices and conversations were formed and I bet nobody in the train heard these voices. The voices lured me into a deep, profound, penetrating but strange sadness in the form of silence. I understood that language at once, so it became clear to me, right there and then, why I commenced my 'Spanish Stories' in Andalucia, which had lived in my memories for years.

I had lingered among the pleasure of the memories, listening to the complex stories that I took as reality - without asking whether the memories were true or false....

But whatever they were, these memories had been followed by others which were waiting to be told.

I loved being here and sincerely believed that my searching would finish here, because I was looking for the face I had before the world was made.

I sent the same letter to both men.
The other one replied.

"Do not thank me, there were never limits to my kindness for you, you ask and I will be at your feet, my feelings for you were well hidden but they are countless kisses deep...."

That was how we commenced our paper love, which lasted for many years to come, interwoven in 'Spanish Stories' with false names and titles, sweet as a forbidden fruit, bitter as a lie that needed to be swallowed after the last sentence.

As we could not proceed any longer, I decided to send him into a different compartment of my hidden world, right into imagination. Later I said to myself that I had never met him in any other part of existence but imagination.

On one occasion, he asked me where my words were, and I said that perhaps they fell under the table where we were sitting, so confused was I that day. Then we started to search for my words with our feet and, not deliberately, our knees were touching. We practised that game of the search for my lost words under the table each time we were sitting, whether we were alone or with thousands of others. Nobody understood the language of our knees. Our faces, up above the line of the table, were placid and calm, but our hearts were dancing a different rhythm, perhaps the one of flamenco as our feet and knees were celebrating their reunion.

She kept hidden from me some parts of this story, because I heard some of it for the very first time when She recounted it to the Nobleman.

Neither was I sure if any part of the story had any traces of truth in this realm. Maybe the truth belonged elsewhere. But I became aware that each time She delivered a little vignette about the Other Man, Her face would brighten up, as it does when we recollect the pleasant memories (regardless of where they belong). How cheeky, just cheeky.

When She said, the next time, that they *were dancing together that evening,* I put the entire story into a new file of the imagination folder. This is what She said:

We were dancing together that evening. There were many people around us but we lost touch with all of them, his eyes were getting deeper and deeper into mine and at that moment I experienced total fusion. Our knees were touching freely, cheek to cheek, my hand in his, his breath in my hair. He smelled of something that I never dared to name, but had the privilege to carry into my future and make my days in the loveless dungeon brighter. I never told him why my heart had many pieces and who was unkind to it, all that mattered were our knees touching on the dance floor or underneath the table.

There was a dark little woman, with short hair and short breath. Her eyes were on us (I saw how jealousy had changed the colour of both her eyes) and if I cared, I would be thinking she was hurting, but at that moment all I cared for were our knees touching freely as they should when two are dancing regardless of their feelings. How lovely, how lovely.

I wanted to ask Her when and where they *danced together* but I rather let Her disclose what She wanted in Her own time. I was looking at the Noble-man's face, maybe I could find some trace of suspicion in his eyebrows, but his face was placid as he was expecting the exact current of the words, his eyebrows combed with patience, waiting for more.

What She said was: *Keep your love as a secret. Once they know, their duty is to sour it. It is human nature to spoil beauty. Rare are those who stop to smell the flowers or to appreciate dew on the buds of roses. People's values do not lie in the unseen or simple, it has to be seen and grandiose to be appreciated.*

Then She kept on retelling Her paper love story.

I asked him what he thought about paper infidelity, and he softly laughed. Is there a thing as a paper infidelity? Oh, yes there is, said I, there is such a thing. Then explain some more, said he. And I did.
Your finest thoughts belong to me. I am your first thought upon your waking up and the last one before your retiring. This is what you have written to me. In your mind, where was the little woman with eyes coloured with jealousy? Was she making the breakfast while your first thought rested on my name? Was the breakfast tasty: sweet because of your thoughts or sour because of her hands? In your thoughts, where was she when your head was resting upon the pillow, still restless from the thoughts you were choosing carefully to put together in the next letter for me to like them? Because your words were always finely selected as one can carefully select the finest dress to impress on the first date. They were put together with the aim to

flatter, to provoke, and make my heart beat faster. Was your heart beating faster while you were writing me letters hiding in your study, with an excuse of preparing the cases for the next day?

You said when you drink with me, there is no such thing as sour wine: my smile makes all your wines the sweetest nectar. If it is so, is it so that you do not drink wine with the little woman with a restless mind? When you touch her, do you think of the pencil you tenderly touch when it dances on the paper when you sign your letter to me? Your sweet letter! Is there such a thing as - we are meant to be? What do we do when we discover that we are meant to be elsewhere? Do we go down to Andalucia and just write the letters, or what else?

The views and questions I imposed on you are not coming as the dilemma of a confused moralist. Rather, some sort of disguised jealousy colours my questions. Wasn't it a clumsy attempt to get your confession in a preferable manner; yes, there is no one in this world quite like you. My poorly hidden wish to be shoulder to shoulder with a goddess.
As I always had a natural inclination towards respectability, my questions nearly stayed behind my teeth, even though some of them came out, but significantly modified. I am free to say that I was fearful that more direct questions would upset the delicate balance of intimacy that I had so carefully modified, as I said.

But mind this: I have already taken the trouble of a broken heart; can it be broken into more pieces?

I knew a man who claimed that we can do whatever pleases us, regardless of the tears we can cause in our carelessness. He was born unhappy - even when he went all the way to the Far East in search of his freedom, he was not happier. He found a woman there, but then he remembered that he could not love a woman who was loved by many men. But freedom is not a location, neither a secretive love letter nor a woman who was loved many times before. Freedom is not a lonely vacation down in Andalucia when all you have is your heart in your pocket and the pocket is like a little but heavy bag full of marbles. When all you have is a soul broken by somebody else's wish for freedom, oh, sweet freedom, what a high price your name carries.

She looked at the Nobleman, then they both sank into the sand of silence. Her voice broke the silence, She sounded as if She had just come out of deep sleep (and right there She wanted to go), so She said:

I'd like to go now. I'd like to go home and have some sleep, my dreams are my islands where I am at home, there I take myself with me and only there I think I am whole.

How true, how true that was.

CHAPTER TWO

She went to hospital, then She came back one pearl lighter. Where the pearl was fear grew and stayed there for a while. At that time She believed that fear would stay indefinitely there and feared that fear of the fear could grow as a black pearl again. Then people recommended all sorts of different therapies but love. She tried this and that, in some of them She believed a little, in some a bit more, but was not aware that lack of love could cause the incurable.

I was a witness to one of Her dreams just days before the doctor told Her that urgent hospitalization would be the best choice.

Let me tell you about the dream that I witnessed.

The Giver of the Gifts came and said, *"You are not you, the one I created you to be. If you believe you have a free will, you can use it, but wisely."*

Lots of different things happened which accompanied his arrival. I saw Her head floating above Her neck and from Her head big and small letters started to fall down as stars from the tired sky. When I thought this would be an end of my astonishment, right then Her chest opened wide, and from there all Her colourful lorikeets flew towards nowhere, as if they wanted to be never found again. In Her open chest, I saw a reflection of myself -shorter than I ever was - and there I found and showed Her a black pearl.

Then a man came with an icy coat which was so very cold, for his chest had never hosted anything warm, and at that moment his eyes surprisingly grew tender while he said, *"I have tried, I have failed, let me go, I am nobody's man."*

It seemed to me that She was going to cry in this very dream, that's why I woke Her up. Later She said loud music had woken Her up. She said that in the dream Her heart stood up from her chest, sat in the living room and started to play the piano, loudly.

How odd, how odd.

I know I hinted that story on some level to Her and that was Her opening sentence the next time when She met the Nobleman.

I went to hospital, then I came back one pearl lighter. For many days to come my bosom was a home for the fear. It feared that all thoughts could lead back to where we did not want to be again. So I chose to get rid of all thoughts - but how is this possible? How can we forget our thoughts and choose which ones can reside in our mind and our bosom? People told me to think positive thoughts, kind ones, but I asked and haven't been answered yet: what lies deep down, below selected thoughts? Why, when we think forcefully kind thoughts, all of a sudden something wild and uncontrolled comes up and says: "Hey, what about me?" How easy, how easy, think positive thoughts.

Or how naïve, how naïve.

There is more to it, isn't there?

Posing that question, She gazed into the eyes of the man whose lips were slightly turned upwards at the corners.

I had a dream and the man in the icy coat told me that he wanted to break free. He told me that I had a strange pearl in my breast and he had nothing to do with it. I heard somebody's voice telling me that I was not myself, and later all my letters fell down from my head and birds left my chest, because loud music was the reason for all of this commotion. The loud music woke me up and then and there I knew my life was going to take a different turn.

She was only nine and her tears were different to mine. They looked like they were the sum of all the tears she ever had, and as they were rolling down her lonely cheeks, they were leaving a trace - as if they were tracing a new chapter in her life. The dolls on her bed tried to call her to join in with their tiny hands but, at that time, she could see nothing - her tears blinded her for many years to come. The dolls' times had passed after that morning.

Two roles were left to me: to console my child and to console my breast. What a task, what a task!

She matured quickly and completely. Her questions were too heavy for her age - not that they were too complex, but they were the kind of questions one does not know how to answer. That was exactly what I told her. I told her that the fact that I am an adult, that I am a parent, does not mean that I know all the answers. I told her that some answers never come because there are many things that we have to take into account in one event. Simply, I said, life is a mysterious journey and we do not know why some things happen to good people (as she put it). We do not know either if it is for good or bad. Sometimes, I said to her, very difficult situations help us to become someone we only read about in works of great writers. How about that? Then she said that she didn't want to be a hero, she said she was only a young girl, not a hero of a great old master.

I told her if she insists on answers that it can harm her mind; it can harm her body: some questions could be answered but many years later. How can one teach patience to a young girl who is forced to grow up instantly, fearing that all the responsibilities of the world are resting on her shoulders while her mother is still lying in her uncertain bed?

Some friends ran to me and some friends ran away from me. Only human, isn't it? What I would have done in the same situation I will not elaborate now because even then I knew that my measures were different and because of that, loneliness was always a good ally.

I haven't had time even to think about the dreams I have had in Andalucia. I haven't had time to think about the Other Man who stopped writing me love letters when he heard the story about my pearl and I thought, it is only human, isn't it? We all have fears and he feared my pearls and he feared my freedom because he believed that somehow my freedom was a threat to his own. How little he knew about me, how little.

When I think of him then and now, I have to put things in the perspective. After all, didn't I tell you that he was only the character created by my wild imagination? With that decision, he liberated me from thoughts about paper infidelity, morality and moral responsibilities. These were things that I inherited from my ancestors. I did not know whether these ideas have any meaning in today's world; the modern world. They were passed on to me as the appendix is passed down and we do not know the function and meaning of it. But it is there. I wanted to ask my Mother why she installed all that within my tiny brain many years ago, but what good would come of it now?

I know that my Mother's doings were acts of care and kindness, if she did not know any better, it is only for that reason - she did not know any better. She said to me that good people lead good lives, how simple, oh, how simple.

I had two different kinds of feelings at that time: one was wanting to be strong and brave to show my child how to act in times of adversity and the other was the feeling of being let down by a man I believed was trustworthy some time before. Because of that, I felt as if I was sliding down on some greedy slide right down into the dark, bottomless pit of depression. I mixed both these kinds of feelings on a daily basis and prayed to one of my own deities to keep me sane in the confusion I was imposing on myself.

When we place trust in the hands of the untrustworthy, the trust is going to be unpleasantly surprised, I can say cheated, to explain it better.

Anyway, life is about choices, isn't it?

And when She said that, the Nobleman repeated Her question: *"Life is about choices, isn't it?"* Then he said, resting his eyes on the clock, *"This is a good question to finish with."* She stood up and extended Her hand and left the room. Through the crack, I managed to sneak out and catch up with Her. Her walk was brisk, as if She was trying to leave Her memories behind - as if She believed that these memories now somehow belonged to the Nobleman.

As a natural way of unfolding one's story, the next time She continued where She stopped, with the very same sentence.

Life is about choices. Is depression a choice or a chemical imbalance in the brain? Does that imbalance occur when you are aware of various unpaid bills: medical bills, bills for the water we drink, the food we eat and the air we breathe? Thank Heavens; I haven't had a telephone bill because I cut myself off from the ringing of the phone. I took big scissors and cut the cord as I used to cut the dreams I did not wish to dream; those that would come as unwelcome.

Without telephone bills, I had the advantage of not paying an extra bill, but was in danger of cutting the world out of my living room and taking a risk of going mad; interpreting my own thoughts without any reflection, without a mirror.

Is it safer to go along with the darkness or to fight it? Simply to surrender? I wanted to borrow somebody else's language - the solutions of others, as if my mind was in the grip of the lord Asmodeus. Like him, I wanted to spy on other people's ideas, in the desperate hope that there would be a solution better than the one I was capable of finding in my own mind.

So, where was God, where was that God?

If I allow God to tell me where he was hidden in the dark hours, I can remember the light that shone upon me every time my daughter crossed the threshold of our home. It was as if God himself had come in with her, and I was astonished that all the dark clouds vanished as if they never existed. So, this is the question: where did they exist and where did they go, and who was once again pulling the invisible strings of my stability?

My mind, God, the presence of my daughter, or something else?

We would put up a little theatre and include all the characters that we needed. I would remember some of the people we met in various locations in the world and use their words and accents and expressions and gestures and all. She would ask a simple question and I would recite short or long poems I had learned off by heart in the years of my childhood. I remembered (maybe for cases like that) some of the funniest poems and they would come easily to me to my rescue. Her laughter was my remedy, just her laughter...

I would sing songs to the ingredients while we were making soup or another dish or ask for forgiveness the dead animals we were going to eat. I would speak in different languages, known and gibberish, while I was trying to keep her mind occupied with laughter and happiness. She would play the piano and I would dance, funny dances that I invented right there, right for her, because I longed to hear her laughter louder than the sounds of her piano. And she would laugh, she would laugh and I would heal.

Many years ago I carefully selected her name, Althea, which means a healer, or the one who brings wholeness, as if I knew we would be in need of healing of various wounds and pearls which we inherited from shimmering but silent stars.

There were times when I felt as if we were not two separate beings. It looked to me as if the same energy, the same soul, somehow entered two bodies and communicated with itself in perfect harmony. But I knew the time would come when I would be asked by life to let her go, to split the soul once again and let her choose her own path. For the time being, we were the bud and the fragrance, the instrument and the music, the breath in and the breath out. We were two kids sharing secrets and laughter. We were mother and daughter and I wished we could teach the world what love is.

And love itself is the biggest healer still known to the world, how privileged are those who know this simple truth and weave its threads into the fabric of everyday living.

After Her last sentence, it looked to me as if they were not going to utter a word, as if they forgot all the words which once belonged to them. It looked like they understood that meaning was beyond all the words and silently agreed and held onto that just discovered truth. As for me, I was thinking what was going to happen next - admitting to myself my inadequacy in articulating the workings of the mind.

And nothing really happened, they spent long minutes in silence and then She stood up as if She had remembered an important meeting to attend and with a quiet greeting She left the room. I never saw him after Her leaving, so I can't really describe his facial expressions or anything else in relation to his thinking, but never mind, never mind.

Next Wednesday She came with the same topic about choices. She said:
It is not a choice.
Firstly, life sends its messengers – some events that are too difficult to comprehend and handle, just one after another in a very short time to show

you how all can be crashed in one breath. Sudden or wild, or uncontrollable breath, that comes as a whim out of nowhere. I might ask you now: do we lay down our weapons in sweet surrender?

I did. I laid them down in front of an invisible but fierce beast because I couldn't see the cracks through which the light came in.

Then all what was there to be was darkness, deep as all wounds joined together in final peace.

No lights, no guides, all left, even those between living and dreaming. Sounds ran into themselves unwilling to share with me the melodies of life, that's why silence was at the same time the refuge and the enemy that tortured me with deafness. It was the feeling of a motherless child. When I think of it, my fear returns, looking me straight in the eyes and luring me back (I have never liberated myself from its grip completely).

And the enemy, the world out there, was not a part of me. It was clinical, making me question all the time the very meaning of life.

Was it a clear sign that I have to look closely at myself and find somehow that disturbing events can be valuable moments for my transformation? Our human life is made of light and darkness, thus isn't it only natural that after happiness, it is time to let sadness take its place in our garden? And you cannot hide in that garden, for it reflects all of your feelings and moods. I was supposed to swing and sway with flowers played by unpredictable winds. If only I had known...

If only I had known that there was something else that existed apart from my thoughts, I would have probably thought about these rhythms of moods. But when you are in the grip of unwillingness to participate, neither the world nor the words are supportive and pleasant.

I wanted to yell, to scream, to screech as a beast but it was only a wish that inhabited the unknown part of myself: the alien one. Neither was the other part of me, the one which was reluctant to scream, any friendlier. So many parts unwilling to communicate.

Who am I?

"Who am I?" I wanted to ask anybody who would glance at my face, which I did not know any more. The face, which was a face of my Mother's child lost in adulthood.

How much is too much? And what is the measure with which the incomprehensible merchant measures the pain for each of us? Does he consider the size or the build? Is the colour of the eyes, the skin or the nationality the deciding measure? Oh, how many times I wanted to tell him: I am quitting, resigning, please leave me alone ... but my strength was already taken and none was left, not even so little as to hold my pen. My very darkness became my guide; it took unthinkable avenues to lead me, wanting to amaze me as a gifted lover does.

I found myself in the place in-between and all whom I met there were in frantic search for broken pieces...

...But the music she played on her piano was coming through her from an invisible healer who wanted my soul to hear it. And she would play, she would play and I would heal.

***

Next time She entered the room, She said, *I have to look among the garbage and the diamonds for what I lost.*

He did not ask anything. I wanted to encourage Her but often was stopped by Her unpredictability. If I suggest kindness to Herself, to us, She can become suspicious and ask, *"Who is telling me?"*

She said, *Maybe I should have stayed in Andalucia. I could have written the letters there without further involvement with these two men. Maybe if I had stayed, I could have had a long correspondence, even with the one who returned my letters unopened. I could have told myself that he had changed his address and that was the real reason why his letters were coming back unopened. I could have told myself just anything to avoid the inevitable. Perhaps.*

Maybe I could have kept my paper love alive for many years to come, never fearing that the little lady was going to look at me with accusing eyes. I would be far away and she would anyway never come to Andalucia. I could have ... yes ... I could have....

But my thirst for the truth retraced my steps, I wanted answers even when all was laid down with a simple and quiet gesture, I wanted the words, the swords I wanted.

When I came back from Andalucia, heavy rain was beating against my windows. Wash my thoughts, heavy rain, wash my thoughts! But my pleading wasn't answered, the thoughts were heavier than the rain - all the rain could do was rhythmically beat against the windows. My dark hours caused by my, and only my, heavy thoughts looked as if they would never end, but would repeat themselves as if they were caught in some sort of 'perpetuum mobile.'

Was I aware of the need for urgent help? Often I felt as if somebody strong and well-meaning yet invisible was standing beside me and trying to advise me. Was I sane? I almost asked.

Both men fired my letters for different reasons. Maybe the beauty of the selected words exceeded their understanding, which lighted the fear. But one thing for certain they had in common: the pearl from my breast grew thick and dark in their minds.

And as if they cursed my vulnerable breast; yes, their fears came to life and the shiny pearl pressed again on my scar, telling me in the language understandable only to me that if I wanted to grow, I had to stop the pearl from growing.

What a rebus, what a rebus to be solved!

***

The second time around, I could not go to Cadiz to bury my pearl (neither pain) in the sand. Because the pearl had the story, I was meant to hear and understand it. I could not bury anything in the sand anymore. I wondered what the fishermen from Tangier would find as a rarity coming from foreign shores, as they were used to finding all sorts of wonders in their nets.

So, it looked as if I was left alone again: two men I had written to were lost in a jungle of words and could not find any suitable word any longer, just as the fishermen from Tangier could not find the right reason for their empty nets.

I knew what a lonely experience it was going to be for just the two of us: me, and my pearl, not knowing which God was to be asked for the strength.

We fear loneliness but we come to know it, really, when all of our plans have no meaning any more. I liked my lonely hours, for I had peace to weave my stories, but this was a different kind of loneliness. It looked as if the world had stopped just for me, and all the others were so busy with their daily life, in a constant rush. Only I was sitting with a pearl in my breast and this time I really understood that my phone was not ringing.

***

Sometime, somewhere, I read an article about a brave woman who never asked the question "Why me?" but silently suffered and accepted her destiny with dignity. Oh, how touching! She was well known, maybe adored by many and I believed that it suited her profile to show humbleness and bravery. But let me tell you something, my dear friend. You, the one who listens to so many stories about all sorts of misfortunes, you know better about human fear, despair, anger and helplessness in real stories, not the one printed in the suspicious press about a woman whose bravery should be celebrated. When you look at Death, eye to eye, you do ask, "Why me?" You are not willing to accept the destiny with dignity, you experience the anger, betrayal, despair, you go through all sorts of known and unknown feelings, through the kind of lows you could never imagine before that your soul could put you through. You question everything, you laugh at the premise of God's existence or of his benevolence. You ask and argue with him as if he were certain and alive and as if he could hear you and reason with you. The pain is so deep and precious and for both reasons you do ask, "Why me?" Bravery? It might come later, when you use up all your questions and there are none left to be asked. But before that happens, you have many, many sleepless nights, with millions of words buzzing in your head. Only tears are real. All else is faded like gone in some other world where you do not belong any longer.

The second time around, you do still ask, "Why again?" because by asking these questions, you are hoping that you will somehow start to communicate with your pearl, as if it is going to tell you the story.

Every dark pearl has its story. It is up to us to open to it, listen and act upon what was told.

It looked to me that not only God had forsaken me but that the entire world and all living beings, which inhabit it, had forsaken me with him. To whom do you turn in times of such adversity?

To Mother.

I needed her hands. I needed her voice to console me, to promise me to live a long and happy life, as she used to tell me many, many years ago when I believed that black pearls happen only in very bad, bad stories to very bad, bad people.

I did not need two men who betrayed me when I needed kindness and care, I did not need any man, nor did any man need me.

I needed my Mother's breasts to lean my tired head on. I wanted to be a child and cry on her bosom. I wanted to see her healthy breasts to not blame her that she passed faulty genes down to me. I needed her strength and her kindness, her simple wisdom, which came from the patience learned by raising three children.

I needed my Mother's bodily odour to bring memories back, to bring back a feeling of being protected - knowing that there is no God stronger than my Mother's will to make me feel loved and protected.

I can freely say - God's love is not perfect, as some try to teach us, Mother's love is unconditional. Yes, she came after many hours of long flight, with her legs swollen like over-pumped tires, with her fingers red from squeezing a handkerchief, she came with presents for both of us, with money my father sent for hospital bills, with her veins on her overworked, tired hands, she came with her mellow voice, with rose petals in her pockets (she smelled of roses); with her she brought a Hope.

That was all I needed, there and then I knew that I had used up all my questions and I could easily let any journalist write about my bravery and would confirm that I do not ask questions like, "Why me?" How noble, how noble.

And my house began to be alive again; flowers and plants started to flourish, the quiet rabbit became full of tricks and beans again, kitchen chairs were occupied all the time, dinner plates used and reused, all sorts of delicious smells ran out through our windows to water our neighbours' mouths with envy.

The windows were cleaner, the floor had a different colour, the clothes smelled different but just as in my memory, my child's voice once again became resonant with a careless flare and my eyes became bright and shiny, shinier than any pearl I have ever owned.

She wiped up one tear in the corner of Her eye and once again let the silence finish all the untied and loose sentences, then simply said, *I'd rather be going now, I'd rather be going.*

Mother brought us closer. She went to hospital again and I spent all the time next to Her bed, which was not uncertain anymore, even though a long battle was waiting for us. I felt that Mother brought cohesion and knew then for certain that She would be willing to co-operate. Without love, happiness cannot be achieved. Neither can good health, because love is the only ingredient that makes humans grow, flourish, aspire, achieve and heal. Life without love is a missed opportunity to make an ordinary human being into an extraordinary being. Life without love is never remembered by anyone, so you are forgotten before your time. You are not a part of a cosmic game, you are lost among your own rules and pearls, seduced and trapped by them at the same time.

She came to the land where She could not find love even though love was the reason for Her travel. The man She believed She loved was not raised for that reason. He was there, as he used to put it, to experience life. And all life was just one experience after another, that's all. He sailed shallow seas and his love was rather placed in lower parts of his body. Women with deep emotions and commitments were a burden, not an asset.

But I am not going to talk about him; She will say whatever She wants to say, because She surprises me as well with some interpretations of the events. I am here to be patient and wait for Her, She will understand - I know She will. She will remember, I know She will. One thing I know for sure, She trusts the Nobleman, which means that we have taken a gigantic but first step towards reconciliation.

Before She had left in search of love to the other side of the world, Her Mother said that She was not sufficiently strong to withstand the stress and emotional upheaval which life without family could cause. Mother knew of what She was made and feared that an irreversible fragmentation of Herself could occur in the vast, dry and empty land. *"Do not go!"* (She was not told but it lingered in the air). But She did.

In constant search of love a human being is capable of unthinkable heroic deeds. As any other being, She was born to love, though - She was born to think, but not to travel to faraway lands. Travels brought onto her all sorts of disturbances: physical and emotional exhaustion, unwanted companies and conversations, bad quality of food and severe headaches that lasted for days. Her Mother knew once She was gone, She would be gone for good, because She was the one who would not return. I can't say the reason right now but it could be fear and humiliation of admitting that She was wrong, that She had not found love there, that She had not found anything worthy of the story there, anything but the black pearl. Could be.

The only trip She had ever liked was the trip to Andalucia. Somehow it brought back Her dreams, and without dreams She was not alive. Long ago She had forgotten all Her dreams (or were they crushed by the reality She never wanted?)

She would sit on the long, sandy Cadizian beach and let quietness befriend Her, then let the waves answer, let the wind answer. She would wait.

I heard Her asking the evening stars, *Why did I cross the big waters? What was I expecting to find in the vast emptiness? It only imprinted itself into my soul, or left my soul unimpressed or betrayed.*

What am I supposed to do with all my questions? Shall I hang them here, on the beach poles, and wait for the next morning to find maybe somebody has answered them or somebody has stolen them? If they were answered, would it be that I would be the same old self? Or if they were stolen, I might be freed from me? I'd be free to dance the flamenco without inhibitions, because my questions make my legs numb while they are trying to catch the rhythm. The rhythm of my thoughts (questions) and the rhythm of flamenco are in disharmony. How can I learn to dance without thinking, just let myself dance and follow the natural rhythm, let myself enjoy my body, the vibes which are penetrating into me and threatening to take me to an unknown land? Fear of the unknown is within me. What would I meet there? To whom does it belong? Is it mine or have I inherited it from my ancestors or even from some other lives I have lived, who knows when and who knows where? Do my questions make me who I am? And if I just change them, do I change again who I am? And what about those who do not have any questions? Are they alive at all, or do they have any reason to be here if their questions have been answered? The universe continued unchanged regardless if the answers were given or not.

I'd like to tell all my stories stored inside of me to the little Andalucian fish, so when the fishermen from Morocco sell the fishes to the housewives, their soup would have a flavour of my stories, and their children would be fed by my stories. I'd rather choose this than the man who never pays for them, the one who brought the loud woman to eat the fish at that uneasy evening in a murky moral milieu.

The week had passed quickly and when he saw Her that Wednesday, he said that She appeared to be much more at ease. She said:

All my life I have been searching for answers. Everything had to have an answer, just as when little kids ask why the sun is setting and where it goes when the moon comes out.

But the second time around, I thought it was about time to stop searching for the answers. Somehow I knew that the answers would not come, or some would be revealed in their own time. As we all know, there are times for everything: for the rain to water a dry land as for the land to be dry; there is time for friendship and for farewell, time to grow and for stagnation, time for asking questions and time for acceptance. And I had accepted. No answers. Just me and my pearl. If the pearl wanted to speak to me, it would find the language, it would find the avenue to lead me. The answers cannot be forced. They run away when the time is not right and you never find them. My pearl taught me patience. Surrender. No, there was no place where I could go or hide, the pearl was within me and I was to carry it wherever I went. So I might as well stay wherever I was because probably this was the right place where I was meant to be.

Sometimes it looked to me that there was that other me, standing behind me and telling me to surrender. But that kind of surrender that leads to victory. I almost could read her thoughts as she was whispering that kindness and surrender were the answers for the time being. As if it was going to dissolve my pearl.

***

One warm, but disturbed by the levante, night, with the wind the dream was blown to me. I was not sure whether I was dreaming or just remembering something that was yet to happen.

The Other Man, the one who resided on the edge of my dreams and my reality, gave me one of his letters. It was a gift, more than a letter, for it was wrapped in a beautiful, colourful envelope and a red ribbon was tied around it. For some unknown reason I was surprised, as if it was the first love letter he had ever written to me. Contrary to what one might expect from such a gift, it was empty. Not a single word wrapped in the nice, colourful envelope. But yet again, contrary to all expectations, I heard his sentences as clearly as if he was lying next to me and whispering sweetness in my ear.

Following a few restless days, I tried to solve the puzzle of the empty letter, but then the man from the dream sent me, instead of the letter, a song; only one song, which repeated many times the sweet, same verse "...and what we forgot to do is thousand kisses deep...."

How sweet, how sweet.

I wanted to bury that dream into my reality and relive it, but I was afraid of not knowing the reason for it, because already the time had come when all my fears joined together and I believed that I had strength only in my dreams. The strength was taken by the man who promised to love me in health and sickness till death do us part, and when he discovered that he was meant to love many times, he broke not just his vows, not just mine, or our daughter's heart, but something much more tender and sophisticated, which left us to wander through the maze of old Cadiz veins. To what was left of me, every Spanish sentence I heard on the streets was "Regresa a mi" millions of times daily. Millions of sentences were calling out to my broken and lost parts: "Regresa a mi."

And then, there was another verse of a different song that my Mother took as her mantra during the long months while she was nursing me back to my health.

She used to whisper, "Let it be," holding my other hand, the one without the needle. I would lie as a broken-winged bird. All was broken outside and inside, and while I was reluctant every three weeks to get a needle and let the cure or poison course through my betrayed veins, she was sitting next to me, holding my hand, swallowing her tears and whispering as she used to lull me into dreams many years ago "Let it be...," "Let it be...," "Let it be...." And I did.

When I was lying without any strength in my body, she would ask, "What would you want right now?"

I would say, "I want to be your child; I want you to stroke my hair as you used to do when I was frightened or upset." And she did. She would stroke my hair, telling me, "You are my child, you always will be." She said many times that she had enough strength for all three of us. And she had.

Like a quiet, broken record, she would repeat over and over, "Let it be...," "Let it be...," "Let it be...."

I could not imagine how all that was for her, looking at my daughter's eyes full of peace and grace. With my Mother, hand in hand, peace and grace walked in.

No, I did not wish for anything but my health restored because nothing had any meaning. All was irrelevant and I did not care how many books I had published, or what people said about them. I did not care why the two men never asked about the state of my health, I did not care how much my bank account was worth, nor would I have been upset to learn the truth.

These days showed me what human beings could withstand, who my real friends were, and what it was really that mattered. My faith in human kindness was restored through the medical profession: all of the doctors and nurses were as perfect as those found on the pages of light literature, as if the universe conspired this time to bring me the best it could.

Thank you, Merciful Universe, thank you for just about everything I have learned in that year of uncertainties.

Needless to say, the pillars of my strength were two women: one was strong and courage could freely carry her name, the other one was tiny, full of light and undivided trust that her mother was going to be the source of her strength again. At these times, Rilke and Lorca were my refuge once again, because love and poetry were two essential ingredients in countering my tendency to depression at trying times of my life.

As for the friends, those who weren't frightened by new me used to bring me or persuade me to buy new, beautiful clothes. I was quite reluctant, thin from all of what the needles had delivered into my body, and my head was as shiny and smooth as a pearl (which in the first place, was the cause of that new look). Just my eyes were, somehow, the same: the eyes of a child who couldn't find the answer lost among the forest of the growing words.

Not knowing about my pearls, neither the black nor the white ones, my Mother bought me a beautiful, shiny, shimmering Swarovski crystal bracelet.

When I got that present, I could not hold myself back, so I cried a little thinking of immortality of the beautiful crystals and my own limitations. Then I read this gift differently and said to my tired mind, "Let it be a symbol of purity. Let it be." And I did.

Yes, my dear friend, I needed to learn to love my body again and not to see it as a traitor. I could not go on thinking that it trapped me and kept me as a hostage, counting my mistakes, my black pearls. I put my crystal Swarovski bracelet on my very tired hand, just below that sore spot where they used to insert a needle that could deliver either medicine or poison. Mother's bracelet whispered, "Let it be a medicine," and I did.

We started to treat aspirations and objectives as the same thing; that was our choice, initiated by my Mother's spirit caught in Swarovski crystals.

I do not wish to dramatize these events, which crowded the days of that particular year, but these days were packed with various emotions; coloured with different colours and shades. I believed that I had to believe in something - if in nothing else, then in the beautiful crystal bracelet, as I was raised in a house full of love but deprived of the trust in God. Historical and political events decided that this part of the world and its people did not need or deserve God.

As I was in constant search of God or meaning the majority of my days since early childhood, I perceived my Mother as somebody quite strong in body and mind and because of this, she perhaps believed that she was not in need of God. But watching me, lying without any energy even to talk, she discovered a new need that was born out of her pain - the need for God. She would sit and hold my hand, the one with the Swarovski bracelet, in her hands and silently send her prayers to Heavens, believing that there would be found the right messenger to deliver her prayers to the real and useful God.

She offered the frescoes of our daily struggles to the winged beings about whose existence she had never been assured, still hoping that they would do something, whatever it might be, but in our best interest.

She started to ask herself the questions I was asking myself over many years and these questions connected us like the umbilical cord once again.

She started to look for the meaning beneath the obvious. To me, to read her face, to know that she had engaged herself in that, for her, rather difficult but rewarding act, was both beautiful and painful. Painful because I knew it was her last resort. Was I looking as bad, I wondered? I knew I was.

I know that she asked God over and over the question to which the kind God never gave her an answer. Why he did not choose herself instead of me, and naively believing that things should work that way, she was offering to him her health and strength in exchange for mine.

How desperate she was, how desperate!

I wanted to tell her that God had more important things to do and more important people to look after and that he was indifferent to human suffering and pain. I wished I could say, "Mother, we are not an exception," but I knew it would sound cruel, for she just started to believe, she was just clinging to the last straw. I could not crush her belief because it would crush her strength and as she put it, she had it in abundance for all three of us. Wasn't only that the sign that God had heard her prayers, I wondered?

To deny the existence of God would be the same as to deny all her attempts to make any meaning out of this experience. I understood by her efforts, by her deeds, that she started to believe that every act of hers had been weighted from a cosmic perspective and that was the exact cause of her strength tripled.

We walked together through all the long forgotten streets of my childhood and her youth, and were exploring all the 'whys' and 'hows' of these days, which initially were coloured by many other events. But slowly and steadily, our remembrance joined together and grew clearer and clearer.

We understood each other as woman can understand woman. Our hearts were full of empathy as we entered the compartments other than mother/child labelled. While walking through the inner labyrinths, I felt that each time she told me a story, which was shadowed by time, one of the dark, nocturnal butterflies flew off my heart, freeing it from their grip. By talking only, she would untangle the knots of the past and she would talk. She would talk and I would heal.

I wanted to touch and talk to every pain I had ever encountered and collected in order to learn how they formed the pearls if they were not brought into the light of consciousness. She would say, "Do not go there, you are ill and tired, do not exhaust yourself" and I would say, "I will go there right now, because there is a right time for everything and going there doesn't bring either tiredness or exhaustion but this is the way how to heal myself. Talk Mother, talk as you used to talk when I was a frightened child."

And she would, oh yes, she would.

Her tea grew cold but regardless She drank it as if with the fluid new memories flew into Her dry mouth. She wiped the corners of Her lips and continued (I wondered why he didn't stop Her because more than a full hour had passed, but he didn't. No, he didn't.)

There is no such loneliness as loneliness in illness, but having here my Mother's courage, I wondered again and again which part is of human doing and which belongs to mystery?

When he heard Her dilemma, he said, *"Which part is of human doing and which belongs to mystery? There is something to think about till next time."*

CHAPTER THREE

He was not just a highly intelligent and cultivated man, but a man of good sense and sound principles. He was in his mid-forties, but little on him showed his age. His face was rather boyish, and his piercing blue eyes spoke of his innate curiosity. His smile was boyish, too, and quite often She would catch a little mischievous smile that quickly danced on the corner of his lips. Then he would swiftly bring his fist in front of his lips and pretend to quietly clear his throat. She would look at his, I can say, beautiful, eyes without blinking and they would rest in silence for a while, as their eyes continued with the conversation.

His gestures, the movements of his hands, were as measured and elegant as the selection and intonation of his thoughts.

There was more than respect, awe and appreciation that She harboured in Her fragmented heart for him. A different kind of love to what a woman feels for a man. It was deep gratitude and a feeling that She was understood, by a man, in a way that She had never been understood before. He was Her brother, the knight in shining armour, the brightest knight in Her novels or any other novel, which portrayed characters of finest virtues. He never saw a beautiful woman in Her but a human being with fragmented pain and was determined to help Her put all the pieces of the broken mosaic together. That's why She called him the Nobleman.

His empathy, his kindness and gentleness, his natural inclination towards art and poetry, his skill of listening and selecting the right words started the process She never believed would take place. She believed that Her soul had gone forever, somewhere in between two dreams and there had never been a road built in that scenery, so the soul was entrapped or lost.

She would talk and he would listen. He would listen and She would heal.

She felt indebted somehow and sporadically asked him if there was anything She could do for him, but he would smile at Her as one can smile at the naivety of the mind of an undeveloped child. He would say, *"Go home and write."* And She would.

She let him lead Her through the entangled and interwoven lines and threads of Her inner kingdom, showed him royalties, servants and ghosts; introduced him into forbidden rooms and beings who resided in hidden chambers. Each time She opened a secret place, the chain would break and would free the entrapped, invisible ghosts of the past.

The way he led Her through the hidden corridors of Her mind and remembrance was well planned strategically, as if it had come from the plan book of an experienced general battling the war of depression, not leaving the truce to chance and determined to win.

She asked him, *What is it that makes a person fragile, what is it that makes us strong? Is it a belief or determination? Where exactly is our strength stored, or is it the other end of our frailty? What is a common measure and does society approve only of strong ones? Is it the ego that makes us strong, or our good and noble deeds that we are capable of doing?*

Is it shameful to be fragile, because fragility does not make money?

But in the end we are all fragile, simply because this is the nature of human life. Can't you see fragility in the entire structure of the world that appears to be real? How easily does the strongest building collapse with the movement of the earth, known as an earthquake? How easy is it for solid matter to be moved or destroyed by strong winds, how easy is it for a strong character to be transformed into a fragile one by one illness, injustice or hate?

How easy, how easy?

***

There is just one little episode I'd like to add and then I promise you, I won't talk about the Other Man ever again. But there is something I owe him. It is again one of our dreams on the edge of his marriage and as we never crossed the line, the dream stayed intact and the marriage, too. But first things first. I will talk of the dream that happened down in Andalucia, in Cadiz full of blooms.

The night was warm and intoxicating, with smells of the ocean and music coming from the strings of a flamenco guitar, and my spirit was intoxicated with all that was there to be admired - plus I had a few little glasses of sherry, Jerez, as one has to have a sherry while in Andalucia - as from Cadiz to Jerez was just a few long walks, perhaps. The more I drank, the more I understood. The more I drank, the less I cared. How easy it was to let myself go with the sweet music of the flamenco guitar and even sweeter was the taste of Jerez or sherry, as the rest of the world calls it. There were many people sitting there, drinking their sherry and nibbling on tapas. The voices were loud to overtake the crying guitar. All were connected, all had something to share and to say to each other. Yet I was sitting there, all by myself, and wondering why I did not join in, instead of waiting for the letters of two men who might or might not send them anyway. All of my thoughts rhymed with the music and the loud Spanish voices and it seemed to me as if I did belong to the crowd and I did share something much more tangible than the language which often connects people. The waiter came to my table uncalled and asked me if I wanted another Jerez. I did not know whether I really wanted a drink or a dream, so I told him to come that very evening in my dreams, because I owed one dream to the man who sent me love letters.

After that he looked at me rather puzzled with one eyebrow high up close to his hairline and he left with no sherry and no promise to pass that very evening through the door of my other reality.

But you know what? The regular visitor of my dreams came, as he had promised before that he would be the visitor of my dreams for many years to come. Then in the dream he said that he wanted me to do something for him. How lovely - I was in a position to do him a favour, after the many favours that he had done for me.

He asked me if I remembered the waiter who served me no sherry this very evening but offered to bring one if I only wished.

Of course I remembered the young, handsome man with a little moustache, which I would say resembled Dali's moustache if only I was not afraid to say so, because it could sound like a cliché. So I preferred not to mention the moustache but told him that I did remember the waiter who came in that evening at precisely eight thirty, because when he entered, many young girls turned their heads towards him and giggled. I did not tell him anything about me drinking sherry and my offer to him to come to my dreams, but my visitor already knew about it.

He said things that would stick in my mind and at least in one piece of my heart for eternity.

He said that even though we had never crossed a fine line in our correspondence, in our dreams and marriages, he wanted to tell me that he loved me for all that I was. He said that it was much more important to have somebody's soul than body and he said he felt closeness in my presence, that it all looked as a dream, but he said, "Yet it was not a dream".

The favour he wanted from me consisted of making our friendship immortal. Oh, I asked myself, how is this possible? Yet, as always, he had an answer. He said that he wanted to be a waiter in my story, simple as that. He said that next time, when I write my story, he would be happy to recognize himself as one of the characters. Not the main one, but somebody insignificant - for instance a waiter who would bring the drink to my table.

And I promised him, yes, I did.

So now he has his place as a waiter in my novel and I have a broken dream, but what is a broken dream in exchange for immortality?

Then She fell silent and I knew She was turning the pages of Her memories. Maybe the Nobleman knew the same so he kept silent himself and silence filled up the room, reached each corner allowing the memories to come and go, leaving traces of their movements on Her face in a form of a little smile which sporadically came and went. It looked to me that She was not going to ever talk about him again, the Other Man, who really lived closer to Tangier when he was in his private space without the little woman who would ask questions that were never meant to be answered.

Then after a long absence of the words, She said, *I believe that this was a perfect gift for him, because nobody was able to exchange the gift and it will stay his forever - or as he liked to say, for eternity.*

I'd like to go now and bury the last memories and gifts in other people's dreams because they do not belong to me any longer. He is free from my memories, for I delivered what I promised, and there will not be a waiter with Salvador Dali's moustaches to haunt me after midnight.

***

I need to talk about my Mother a little bit more, for our pain was interwoven and I could not tell either then or now where my pain ended and her own started, or where the intersection was where they parted their own ways, only to meet again underneath my bed full of our joint fears.

When we grow up, we start to blame our mothers for all the mistakes we have made. How easy, how easy. But consider this: my Mother possessed the gift of inspiring friendship and loyalty from all the people she came in contact with while I was born with a different need, one of solitude and introspection, and this part of my personality could easily do predictable damage.

When I went down to Andalucia with my chest full of pain and unfinished and unresolved questions and answers, my Mother wanted me to come home instead. She did not know the origin of my pain and confusion, but she knew that I was broken, for I was not acting as the self she used to know. She said that I was partial in my expressions and sounded as if there were bits that did not belong to my chest. She begged but I wanted to go to Andalucia in search of other bits which possibly would belong to my chest but were scattered down there, who knows when, who knows when. Or, had I been less proud, I would have come and leant my head on her breasts, allowing myself to admit that I couldn't read the answers and needed her help, but at that time, the truth had to be kept at all costs.

I believed that the answers would come with the levante, but whoever has been in Andalucia knows that the levante brings only more confusion.

Because one man who was not capable of love said that he was not capable of love, I forgot all other people who did love me then and times before. I wanted the wind. I wanted the levante to blow my pain out of my chest and take it far away, beyond Tangier, beyond Africa, beyond the world, beyond understanding, just to take it off my chest, for I did not want to go to hospital again and have my breast cut, but no; it was all doomed to be a tragedy by the interweaving of my character and destiny.

I can't say what would have happened if I had gone home and cried on my Mother's chest, telling her of all my pain. Maybe we would have cried this pain out and we had our own local winds to blow if anything was left. Instead she came, but a few years later, as if I needed time to admit the truth to the bits of myself.

How easy it is to blame our mothers for our mistakes, how easy, my dear friend, and now you are telling me about your mother's passing and all the pain that comes with the knowledge that you can't call her, because there is nobody who can pick up the phone and answer, her voice resides only in your memory or in the dreams when she comes to tell you that she still cares. You can't say how sorry you are if you have done any injustice and it stays with you, it just sits there, oh, how unpleasant! For youth is selfish and arrogant and mothers are not there to be considered as more than cooks and cleaners; preachers and boring counsellors, antique in their views and too fearful to let you go and let you be.

A lot of water had to pass under the bridge, a lot of water....

So, finally, I understood the hidden meaning in her present: her Swarovski crystal bracelet was shining out the pure, crystal clear love my Mother harboured in her heart. Each little rounded ball, perfectly cut and polished, was almost transparent in its purity, as if they were a sum of all the crystal clear tears she ever wept for me; ever kept away from me. For the first time in my life, I saw not only courage but fear, for the first time in my life, I understood that she, too, had a little frightened child within her while she was holding my hand with a needle in it, moving her lips as she had summoned all the saints she had ever heard of to pray for our souls.

Pray, Mother, pray: it gives us not only shelter and hope, it brings us closer to each other, leading us towards a light. And light we needed in these grim days, light we needed!

Then She fell silent and looked as if She would shed a tear. There were parts of Herself that I never had a chance to approach or understand. But having the Nobleman as a bridge that connected us, my understanding grew steadier. I could freely say that I almost understood, that I almost understood, and his impact upon us was permanent. How promising, how promising.

Shortly after my Mother's present, I got another one, from the mother who lost her daughter. No, the daughter did not die, but quite late in her life, she understood that she did not need her mother, for reasons stubbornly kept to herself. St. Yvonne was her name, and she gave me a ring with a red ruby, the one she kept for her daughter for many years, but when her daughter told her that she didn't want her ring, her name, her voice or hands, she locked herself in a room, calling any kind of illness to come to rescue her from such a life. She started to visit various doctors and healers, but how can one heal somebody else's heart and mind, because her illness was in her daughter's heart?

She was a strong-minded, cultivated and self-assured woman, with knowledge of philosophy, foreign languages and western and eastern religions. When I met her, we could easily talk for hours about philosophical postulates and I could learn from her wise yet simple sentences. Because of being so wise and learned, she kept things as simple as they could be. I assume that highly intelligent and educated people come to that sooner or later. Pretentious ones need complicated words and expressions, while wise people are as easy as running water. Knowledge and wisdom pours out from them without any effort.

When the man who consulted the astrologer left us, astonished at the ease of his decision, I ran to St. Yvonne knowing that I could find wisdom, kindness and understanding under her roof. She offered more than that, because her family were people who were rich in their knowledge and souls, and as a result of this, their material world was comfortable and rich, too. I ran into some rich people years ago but met lots of fear in their hearts. They feared that people wanted to befriend them because they could gain some of their possessions or money or anything of material value. Some of them were very suspicious of the entire world, saying that nobody was ever grateful for their good deeds and that they were very watchful all the time. I would always run fast away from them, feeling somehow as if they were testing me - who I was and why I was and where I was...et cetera.

I was always drawn to people of knowledge or those whose spirit shines through their extraordinary deeds. But it looked like I could find all that in the house of St. Yvonne: knowledge, kindness, comfort, wisdom and lots of beautiful, expensive paintings on the walls; lots of rare books on the shelves; lots of delicious food. She would share with ease as she would talk with ease. As we used to share everything, we shared our tears, too - that is how I learned about her daughter. An only daughter, as mine is the only one, the brightest star in my sky, the motivation and the motivator, the reason and the cause, the joy and the fear at the same time. I would listen to her story with compassion and understanding the way she would listen to mine, days would pass and we would talk to each other, searching for each other the right words in the belief that the right words could heal the past and the present.

Because with the loss of her daughter, an even bigger loss took place: she lost her two only grandsons. They vanished from her life as if they had never been born, so often she would tell me that maybe all was just a dream, the same dream as my dream about perfect love with a man who wrote me love letters to Andalucia.

But what is the loss of paper love compared to the loss of two grandsons, who would colour her beautiful house with joy and laughter every time they crossed the threshold? For her beautiful house became a quiet prison and she felt like a caged bird who had forgotten her song, because her song was hidden in the hearts of her grandsons, whom she had never seen again.

How sad, how sad.

And out of that sadness was born a very rare and mysterious illness, which no doctor could find the diagnoses for, but when she would mention sadness as the root of her illness, they would dismiss it, because sadness could not produce such serious symptoms in her body, her brain and her mind. And her sadness, her pain, was something that bound us inescapably together, for in her pain and loss, I could read my own. We meet our friends to show us who we are and they are mirrors in front of our very eyes, for they are who we are - otherwise we would not meet them, for there would be nothing to say, nothing to share and nothing to learn. And good friendship is all about sharing and learning from each other and if you do not find your friends are sharing and you think that you do not learn from them, then look closer in your heart and ask what you are offering, for we get exactly what we give out. I learned from her about sharing, so we would share - we would share and we would heal.

When my Mother met St. Yvonne and heard the story of her lost daughter and two grandsons, she cried, for she said she did not know whether it was more painful to lose your child to illness or to some other malice of destiny.

And when it comes to destiny, I told them not to speculate about it, for we do not know what destiny is, just as we do not know if there is at all a benevolent or malevolent power that directs our lives. Acceptance would be the best answer, only if it were as easy as it is written in the wise but often not applicable books.

He would almost always repeat Her last sentence as an indicator to say goodbye to Her, so he said, *"Acceptance would be the best answer, only if it were as easy as it is written in the wise but often not applicable books... but anyway you think about acceptance till the next time you see me."* They shook their grateful hands and She left feeling lighter again for one butterfly, one story which flew off to the unknown, thinking whether this story was going to disappear forever or whether it would be out there where somebody could catch it with his mind and take it, and retell it as his own?

CHAPTER FOUR

I'd like to know what love is.

You might ask me now if I have ever loved and I can tell you that I have. Not many times, for I was not successful in that subject - hence I am asking you what love is. You are nodding, your smile is quite mysterious, as if you knew the answer, but yet you are going to keep it for yourself. It looks like, for those who know the answer, the formula is as if they have given an oath of silence in order to receive the revelation.

When love blows its horn, the sweet sound penetrates into unknown parts and particles and sweet blindness leads you through a mysterious rose garden. A rose garden full of thorns. As you are blinded, your sense of smell is so refined and you are intoxicated with the fragrance but cannot see the thorns. Once you have been through the pain, all your fears are the hidden swords, and the sweet fragrance of roses can't reach you any longer. But if you are afraid of the thorns and pains, how are you going to know the secrets of your heart? Is it that we seek only joy and sweetness to come as conductors of love? How do we grow from joy and sweetness? As we always say, love is a mystery because it doesn't come when you choose it to come, but rather it finds you when it knows you are worthy of its presents, its sweetness and pain; its roses and thorns. Love leads the way and gives the gifts that you cannot choose, for you cannot receive the roses without their thorns. We grow through love, but love itself doesn't come to us for our growth or our pain, it comes to fulfill itself. That's all.

You might ask me now if I have ever loved and I can tell you that I have. When your loved one gives you his heart, it is not for you to keep it, and that is what I have learned from the first lesson of love. It was my first love, the real one, which has stayed with me till this moment of telling you my story.

***

His name was Claudio Vincenzo Ferrara and I used to call him Claude, let's call him Claude because this is how it is written in the library of my memory. If I dive into an ocean of my dreams, I can still find him being the captain of every ship that sailed that ocean, for love always bears one name. And his name was Claude. I disguised his name in different stories, calling him Vincenzo K., calling him Davor, calling him Garcia, but his name was Claude. I can still find him being the captain of every love story I have told, for love bears only one name.

***

I shall retrace the steps of my memory and tell you the tale of my one true love. I am so grateful to my kind memory, what a privilege to have this story, what a privilege!

***

When I met him, I was tenderly young. Still a child. Almost seventeen. My fantasies were frequent and vivid, yet full of the fears and mysteries that real love could bring. I did not know at that time whether I was ripe for love, but love had chosen me right then at that tender age and with those tender looks of mine. I looked like a ripe plum and my eyes had the same colour; they were the reason for my early fame among my peers, the reason for my sudden and unpredictable luck and the reason for my pain and suffering. As they followed me all my life, all of that accompanied us along the way: sudden luck, pain and suffering were probably given in the same gift box.

Yes, my eyes made him speechless, yet they drew his fearful feet to me. I could not understand then: why would somebody's eyes make another speechless?

How odd, how odd, I thought, back then.

As I overcame my disinclination of youth to begin this story with my mesmerizing gaze, I can say now, many years later, that our first meeting was love itself communicating through our eyes. We said nothing, but just gazed at each other, as if we had forgotten that words are the tools of communication. Or is it so?

In his tender look and the little smile that danced on his lips, I understood every word he would tell me in years to come. I believed that all people who loved before us knew only a pale interpretation of love; but we, Claude and I, discovered the depths of love. We unveiled the mysteries of the heart and we knew that love like ours never existed before and never would again. To give it a special flavour, importance and romanticism, we would often eat our breakfast in Venice; our room would be full of roses, the sweet smell of love and roses made us feel chosen. I thanked my eyes every day, for they brought me my love and he had written little poems, which told a tale of a pair of the most beautiful eyes, of a colour which in reality never existed (not even ripe plums have that colour).

He treated me like a real princess and Princess was my nickname. The way he treated me, I assume, was the way that real princesses were treated by their fathers and grateful lovers.

Oh, Claude, many loved before us but we knew that love like ours could neither be repeated nor told as a story. The words did not exist for what we felt for each other and this fact made me search for the words and develop the skill to find the right words and put them together in a way that could take away Claude's breath.

Even though I inspired the lyrics for his songs, he was the reason I started my search for the heroes and my early stories were full of astonishing characters and lovers that resided on the edge of reason.

If you have a prism through which you already see things, it protects you from uttermost beauty. I did not have one, so I could easily give myself, and my stories, completely to Claude, asking nothing in return. I was happier to give than to receive and because of that, the cup of love was always over-flowing.

Claude would take his guitar and sing me love songs that were sung by others before and ones he had written in awe of my eyes and our love. As we never worried about anything, it looked like just everything took care of us. We felt like God's favourite children, made of love to be given back to love. That's all.

That sweetness lasted some years, we were self-sufficient in our world and nothing was missing. But all of a sudden, as if God was tired of looking at us, so perfectly independent and self-assured in our love, Claude suggested that he wanted me to meet his parents.

When his mother met me for the first time, after short observation, she said that there was nothing special about me, that my eyes had a common blue colour and all in all that I was just an ordinary girl, as if she expected an unearthly creature of undefined beauty ... or her intentions came from her fearful heart, as it is known that for an Italian mother to lose her son's heart is a time for great sorrow. To escape her sorrow she employed the old technique of exchanging it with me. She wanted me to take her sorrow and give her back her son's heart, which I kept imprisoned in my eyes of whose beauty she was never aware.

Because of my eyes and his love kept in them, she made me cry many times, for it was all I knew at the tender age of seventeen, eighteen and nineteen, when she tried to show me the price of my grand love. She believed that my crying would wash his love out of my eyes, and then it would stream back to her heart, purified by the tears of the sinner. Little did she know my crying could only upset his heart, not heal it, purify it and give it back to his she-wolf mother.

Every time she saw me, she would find little imperfections about every-thing: the way I spoke, the way I laughed, the way I combed my hair, the way I hugged her son - and she knew that "out there should be a way better young girl," the one she would like better.

How could I shed tears on his shoulder and tell him that his mother caused the pain, for he knew she had "good intentions," he knew she "liked me," that's what he said, but I could not believe it, I could not believe!

Quite often, quite astonished, I used to ask myself: "Is it so that when somebody likes you, they try to belittle you?" That was a new discovery to me. As I wanted her to like me for the sake of my love, I wanted to believe it to be true. What an ugly truth: liking means belittling. Did I want to live in such a world? Where liking meant belittling and bickering?

I wanted liking and loving to be of noble feelings and deeds. I wanted Claude to be my knight, but alas, she wanted the same and the question that was tearing Claude's heart in half was: how to be a knight to two women, do they ask of me to perform something superhuman?

When we were alone, we were again the Muse and the Hero of the tales. Only we understood the language of our hearts and eyes. We spoke of marriage and many children with beautiful plum-coloured eyes, we spoke of a house somewhere steep in the Alps where only the young and fit could climb to visit us, we spoke, we dreamt, we laughed anyway, and we loved as nobody loved before us. We swore to each other that our love would last for eternity and that there was not such a person or event that could tear us apart.

We would escape to the mountain villages and spend days roaming the beautiful fields, inhaling the cold air warmed up by our kisses. In the evening he would take his guitar, compose his songs and lyrics and I would write my first stories, which some years later became my first novels about great love, loss and sorrows.

The sorrow carried her name.

Oh yes, it did.

***

How odd: as much as his family did not like the way I talked, the way I laughed, the way I combed my hair or hugged their son, my family liked everything about him. My usually suspicious father thought him an honest and responsible young man, and even though my father used to be very protective, he approved of our love from the very moment he met him. There was something so likeable about Claude, and my Mother, whose house had always been open to good people, took him into her heart as her own son and spoiled him every time he came with the best dishes and the best wines she could find.

So we both agreed that the air was more pleasant, hence easier to breathe, around my home, so we spent more time there, which was only understandable: people tend to prefer to be around easiness and kindness. Because of it, Claude's mother liked me less (if possible!), she liked him less because of it. But do you know how difficult it was for me to come to her cold altar of judgment and place my pride there and turn the other cheek?

She labelled my inclination for writing as "nothing better to do" and my gift of wit and quick response as madness, telling him that he could find "the mad one anywhere, just about anywhere."

I was young and I loved Claude. He enhanced my creativity and when I was with him, I could come up with the most beautiful words, even though I never knew that they existed in my vocabulary and the way I would put them together sounded as if somebody much wiser and much more experienced arranged them together.

And Claude would sing beautifully, yes, he would sing.

While he sang, I knew that our love could withstand anything. When I wrote, he knew that my stories would win the best prizes in his heart.

Apart from his mother's sharp swords, it was not a complete truth that our love was an easy sail. No, we had horrible winds of jealousy and extreme attacks of the possessiveness that always accompanies first love. If I only looked with my plum-coloured eyes in a direction other than his, he would be sulky and snappy at the same time, and when it comes to my jealousy, I was not ready to hear any other name but mine, for his songs were mine as all my stories belonged to him.

I loved Claude with all my letters and he loved me with all his songs.

For my nineteenth birthday Claude bought me a golden ring with a small, white pearl in the middle. That was my first present of such kind. I believed it was a very expensive one. That was a sign of his pure love and promise of the same in the future. My first white pearl! The pearl from Claude.

Everybody liked my ring with a white pearl: my parents, my sister and brother and my girlfriends.

Everybody liked my ring with a white pearl except his mother.

She said that it was a ring rather for an old lady (herself?). She said that the pearl was not white but yellowish and that it was a far too serious and too expensive gift, referring the remark to the quality of our relationship.

With her words the white pearl turned into a dark one and hid itself deep within my heart. Every time I would look at the ring my love gave to me, the white pearl reminded me of her words spoken to me, almost in a whisper, and it whispered fear to my already fearful heart.

It was my first dark pearl. Its purpose was to teach me about envy and possessiveness; to teach me about the struggle to prove myself to be a good person, even though I was not the one she wanted me to be.

I would cry more often, yes, I would cry and he would not understand me. No, he would not.

Claude's eyes were as green as a deep river and as deep as a green river. I grew to know his river by just a glance and I felt like a master of its currents. I knew when it was calm and crystal clear and I knew about its murkiness.

I loved Claude's eyes as much as he loved mine, but his mother's fears would colour his eyes in the colours I would fear, so her fear and mine were the same - abiding in his eyes and reflected in his needs for more and more solitude.

We were only young, yes, we were.

I found myself trapped in my ability to express what I had undergone with the skilled Mistress of Intrigue, but my own Mother advised me not to exaggerate. So I did not.

All I wanted to say was - Mother, please believe me, for I have a black pearl in my heart and I do need your help to clean and polish it, so it will not eat my heart, for Claude's happiness is locked in it. But I did not say a word, for my Mother advised me not to exaggerate, and the pearl stayed to grow steadily with time in a good environment of warm darkness in a frightened chest.

If I look back to these events, it looks to me as if we played a slow and tactful game of chess.

The two queens: black and white, often changing their positions and colours with the intention of winning the prize, not knowing that the winner and the loser were the same.

Then She paused. On Her face I could see the struggle of internal dialogue. Was there something She was not ready to talk about or was She simply tired? Tired of the queens She had encountered during Her life and tired of Her own struggles to be a princess while the queens always ruled the kingdoms of their families.

She somehow always met the man who was in the tight grip of the Queen Mother and believed that a strong, intelligent and independent man existed only in the stories of old masters. *Do we need rulers?* She wanted to ask. *Can we lead a life which is unfolding according to our own needs, intellect and aspirations?*

When we possess beauty or talent, can we show it without being a threat to queens who can belittle almost anyone who dares to dream? A different and brave dream. I believed that the brave and honest would walk with me if I only dared to dream.

Before She left his room, She promised to finish the story of Claude, believing that just by telling it, somehow it would reach Claude, as Her letters never reached him because the Queen got them first, read them first and then cut them up into little butterflies, which sadly flew into her Italian rubbish bin.

She learned about Her unread letters to Claude many years after the Queen had won her invincible defeat.

***

My Mother was holding my hand. It looked lifeless, like an old, dry branch. Through the veins of that hand the poison was coursing instead of blood. I wondered if my blood would ever be red again - or was I going to die from that dark river which changed, some time ago, the beautiful eyes of plum colour? My eyes were the home of yellow clouds and I could not believe what had happened to them as they stopped to amaze people because of their unique colour. I even could not cry, for my Mother came to cry my tears and at that time I let her cry my tears because I never knew whether I would ever be able to let her do it.

Cry, Mother, cry, for to be brave and endure we have to endure the needs of a heart that knows how to cry.

I said to my Mother:

"Mother, if I want to cry, I swear to you I am not crying for myself, but I will take advantage of this sacred moment of your anguish and join you in crying. But my tears I shall weep for Claude, for this wound has never been healed. You said to me, years ago, that I had to learn not to exaggerate, but Mother, what if this is my nature, to exaggerate? You denied my need to understand my feelings and to exaggerate, let me cry now. I always wanted

you to let me cry when I felt frightened but you wanted me to be strong. Is it shameful not to be strong when one's heart is broken?"

Through her tears, she said:

"Do not think of Claude, it all happened so many years ago. Don't upset your frailty; don't talk about Claude now."

"Mother, it was not a long time ago. Everything still is as if it had happened yesterday. All these pictures are so vivid and alive in my inner chamber, I can hear the sounds of the sea, feel the breeze of the tramontana, hear his voice and the voices of the people closest to my heart. Mother, all is locked in my chest, nothing is gone, I have preserved the relics in the chest and you have been granted permission to untie its ribbons and unpack the chest's contents and look in astonishment at the treasures of my memories and my heart.

Mother, she said to him that I was mad, but I was still a child, in love with her son, in love with life, with a gift of telling stories nobody ever heard of, nobody ever told them."

The burning river of hot tears were streaming down my Mother's cheeks, she could not talk because tears and emotions were suffocating her, so she had to let me talk and clean the first black pearl planted in my heart by the woman who believed that I would ruin her son's happiness, but instead she did it and I wondered, while my Mother was crying, whether ever this woman was aware of what her possessiveness did to her son's heart. She wanted to hurt my heart by planting a black pearl in it but her son's happiness was locked in it, look what she had done!

I wondered daily whether her days were brighter seeing how her son's days grew darker.

And that trauma, I could freely say, shadowed my days to come and spilt over into the lives of our unborn children with the eyes of a plum colour.

What was going into my vein through the needle I did not know, despite the fact that doctors explained it to me in detail. But somehow that, I would say, poisonous liquid (the nurses looked as if they were astronauts as they were totally covered and protected), awakened some poisonous events that were dormant in the secret parts of my body. The formula the doctor gave me was the one that could untie these events. As motion pictures, they were changing in front of our eyes, for my Mother saw them as well, just by looking at my brow and at my not long ago plum-coloured eyes with little, but threatening, yellowish clouds as if the storm was coming, as if the storm was coming soon.

Look, I know all about words, for I have played with them all my life, they create the anatomy of the story, but these poisonous events stored inside

53

did not come in the words but in the pictures which were hung on the inner side of my brow, decorating and defining my insecurities. And their heavy frames were threatening, for it was uncertain how long my brow could sustain their heaviness.

***

We spent our last summer in Barcelona. I wanted to go to Andalucia but agreed to go to Barcelona, for I remembered my future and told him that I could go one day to Andalucia all by myself or with the child who was meant to be his, but in the grand scheme of things, somehow and somewhere, the cards were exchanged and that exchange determined our destinies. So in later years, the child we talked about would be only mine, and for him, in his loveless marriage, life would be reluctant to shine.

When I said that, he said that I was a little bit mad sometimes and how on earth I dared to say that I would have a child he would not father!

He would burn his sanity in the fire of jealousy.

We spent long days and long nights in Barcelona, roaming the beautiful streets of the old city during the day and dining and dancing to the first rays of dawn. We could sit in little cafés and charming restaurants where I would write my stories about characters I just saw passing by or talking in the language I did not understand completely. I would guess, sometimes I would catch just a shadow passing on somebody's brow and there the story would unfold. Claude used to call me "A Little Florentine Scribe."

While in Spain I would tell him, "Take me to Sevilla," and he would fire at me, "You will go there with your own child; I am not taking you, for you already have taken your fatherless child with you, you will not need me there."

Sometimes his jealousy would colour my mood dark and I would feel the pain of my future which I was destined to face without him, without love, I believed so. But look, nobody ever understood love and how would I, for love has mysterious paths and languages, it chooses when it wants and puts together sometimes what we would consider unimaginable. That's what love does; it does not explain anything, for it is unexplainable.

We are always looking for one person when there's more than one, sounds simple now, but back then all I wanted was to love Claude for eternity.

While we were roaming the narrow streets of Barcelona, we visited all the bridal shops and I tried on many beautiful gowns. He would laugh - he would laugh and I would glow.

Even though I fell in love with Spain, there was something quite disturbing in the air - something that would draw my footsteps back in coming years. I wondered, was that restlessness because of the coming events I was destined to face, or was it in the air itself? Or was it that my past would come with me from Barcelona to Cadiz and speak in the language which I could understand only there, for I acquired the knowledge which was needed to understand and unlock all the letters of that odd alphabet?

When I was in Andalucia, I was writing letters to two wrong men, but how could I write them to Claude when, by that time, I already knew that his kind mother had ripped up all my letters and thrown them in her Italian rubbish bin?
How heartless, oh, how heartless.

We came back from Barcelona coloured by the sun, richer for a few new wild, jealousy-coloured emotions, richer for a new novel and a few songs that were meant to be the biggest hits in the history of music.

But my novel was left unpublished and his songs never sang as life brought us to the crossroads, where we were given different tasks than writing songs and novels. All of this happened quite unpredictably, as often destiny comes unpredictably.

I found him on the verandah, crying.
My heart sank; my fingers started trembling as if they were playing the piano. My voice was between panic and uttermost care when I asked him why he was crying. He did not answer, nor did he look at me, he just cried and sobbed as I used to cry when Lila passed away. Not knowing what to do as I had never seen a man crying, I joined in his sobbing, for I feared something terrible was going to happen. I tried to hug him but he ran and ran through the astonished streets of his childhood, the same streets he walked proudly with his first love; but now he was running away from his first love, from me, and I was standing all alone on the indifferent verandah and all I could hear was the creaking of floorboards underneath my heavy, devastated shoes.

I heard her loud and sharp heels carry her back into the house or into the past to hide there her loud and sharp words and deeds. She went back into the pleasant darkness of the house to hide her triumph.
She would do anything to protect him from the false love, for only her love for him was perfect and everlasting.

Yes, she would do anything, for she knew she possessed a terrible power over him.

Then I learned that men cry, too, I learned that men are weak, too.

What did she say that day on the ashamed verandah? It stayed locked in the past on that very verandah which was watered with our tears that we wept for different reasons. But regardless of the reasons they led to the same outcome: he became a different and distant man and I remained emotionally unfulfilled and stuck.

His tears (shall I say, her tears?) changed him forever. These tears changed me forever and changed our love, yes, forever. It was never the same again. I was afraid to question him about his tears, I feared to tell him I heard her heels knocking on the floorboards towards the pleasant darkness of the living room.

She knew how to sow the seed of fear into our hearts and that very fear started to eat the liveliness of our hearts. Our hearts sank beneath the careless love and when I think of her, all I want to say is that God must have been very angry when he created her character.

She would lock herself in her room claiming to have a migraine and all the windows in the house were coloured with black curtains which protected her from life; which protected him from free choice, for mother might fall ill again, she might be upset or depressed again. She claimed she loved him best. I wanted to ask him, I wanted to ask her (and I did ask internally the same question many times) what kind of love it was? She judged everything, she judged everyone, as if all had to have some sort of usefulness to her and love needed to be earned by obedience and loyalty. I could say that he had never been sure whether it was good to be alive and happy, for it looked to me that answers to these very dilemmas of his were written on her never-pleased face. She could not understand that any other person, any other woman, could love him, for love was to her possessiveness and obedience and that was exactly what she feared; that he was going to be just an obedient puppet possessed by somebody he did not belong to. She could not expect anything else because what she knew about love was not what I would call by the same name. I never knew - was she giving of herself happily and freely or was this anxiety she showed easily and daily something she im-mersed him in from the beginning? Wasn't motherly love supposed to be unconditional, free from asking in return; and the only reward is just the child's freedom of choice, the reward would be his happiness? She feared his happiness, knowing that this was the way by which she would lose control over his life.

And how subtle, oh, how subtle it was.
Was he ever aware of her games, I wondered?
So, keep quiet, keep quiet!
She was determined to degrade all other women (including the one she had chosen instead of him), not letting him be a free, mature and independent man but dependent on her love, which was the only real love, which made him an emotional cripple.

She believed as she was the one who gave him life, she had the power to destroy it, playing her games and blackmailing him with her moods and depressions instead of creating miracles of love, by letting him be. Just to be who he was, or did she fear to see who he really was? Did she?

I thought of my wedding gowns in Barcelona's boutiques, asking myself who was going to wear them?

She abruptly stopped and it looked as if She had been suddenly awoken from a forgotten dream, She looked at the Nobleman and said, *I'd like to go home now and teach my daughter a new lesson. I was not tired when I was recounting this story to my Mother, but now I would like to go, I would like to go now....*
She stood up and without a handshake, without any word or smile She left his room, which looked to Her like some sort of a gallery where She had hung her paintings. That's why She suddenly came back and told him, *Do not let anybody in, lock the door.* Then She left as if She was leaving for good.

***

Next time She came with a few more questions: *Why do we betray each other? Where does this come from - my constant endeavour for understand-ing people, even those who were unkind and vindictive to me? Why are our human relationships so emotionally fragile?*
If the personal relationships are just a theatre play, a game or a school, who writes the script and on what are our scores, marks and awards based?
When we open the door of possibilities, different paths are leading to different experiences, but I always wondered, would the outcome be the same regardless of the characters we encounter on that path? Is it that we humans have to learn the same old stories of love, betrayal, pain, loss, and eventually in the end, again, love and compassion? How many times do we have to repeat the very same story, just with different protagonists? Is it all for one purpose: to be better humans? And then, where does that lead us? To a

greater love or a greater loss? For knowing does not necessarily bring liberation but more sadness, because it brings the truth about frailty and the illusions of life. In the end, life decays and destroys our bodies, by that time embarrassing bodies, and I am asking you now: for what, for whom are we better and wiser?

Or could it be true that bodies are, indeed, our temporary houses, and there is within them the essence of who we really are, for the essence needs schooling, not the body. I was always fascinated by the 'what ifs' of human destiny, but this fascination and unquenchable thirst for answers did not bring the peace that I was searching for through my questioning. It just led me from one misfortune to another, organizing them into stories with beginnings, middles and ends, and they lived only in my memory and all these fragments did not have any coherence till I gave them reality through the words.

She felt silent as if She was waiting for one who was going to answer Her questions today, but the Nobleman did not answer, he asked, *"So, what happened to the story of Claude?"*

We had never bought my wedding dress in Barcelona, neither in his nor my hometown. The one I liked the most stayed in the front window for years and got old and gray and I assume nobody wanted it for it was meant to be somebody else's dress.

How sad, how sad.

You know, people like me don't search for salvation, regardless of the depths of questions.

Even though she said that I was an ordinary girl, nothing special in my plum-coloured eyes, she changed her story, telling me that they needed just an ordinary girl and then I understood that when you marry an Italian man, you marry his family with his mother's permission.

Initially, I was just plain and ordinary and when she was threatened with the prospect of who I could become, then I was not a plain and ordinary girl. If I had not known her better, I would have said that she was confused, but take my word, she was not confused but rather the one who brought confusion.

You ask what happened to the story of Claude and I can tell you that we cried a few more times together. I got used to a man's tears and accepted the fact that men cry, too, but never accepted his confused words while he was trying to explain to me why it was the best thing for both of us not to buy the wedding dress in the front window of Barcelona's beautiful, expensive boutique.

All that was left of our love were tears now, the ones that his mother generously gave him on the verandah as a possible wedding gift. You can't keep your love alive with tears. Love needs different nourishment to thrive and be alive: laughter, spontaneity, care and kindness. How can it grow with tears? How can it?

She believed that she could, that she would drown our love in the sea of tears if we dared to go back to Barcelona to find a perfect dress.

When I understood his tears a little bit better, all I wanted was to run away, back to Barcelona and hide myself in the jungle of unknown faces, but I was afraid that I might meet a woman who bought my wedding dress. I wanted to run away and hide somewhere where nobody would read my pain but I came home and said that I did not love Claude anymore and that he didn't care at all.

That was all.

And nobody ever asked about Claude, about the wedding dress in the front window in the finest Barcelona boutique.

Nobody asked about my pains and sorrows because I buried them so deep down, beneath the inner hell and pretended to live my gray days as if they were the sunny, happy days of my youth. I denied my sorrows, believing that I would survive more easily.

I believed that without Claude I would never laugh again, I would never love again.

Anyway, it has passed, it has passed.

***

As She talked, with time there was less and less of Her and Me as two separate voices; but it looked as if we were merging through the memories which brought cohesion through words, and words brought us closer and closer. I could say that I recognized that truth even on the Nobleman's face, even in his voice. Yes, I did.

***

Ten years had passed and I met him again. I met the man who was supposed to be his best man at our wedding, cancelled by his mother's mysterious words.

Branka Cubrilo

I went to the conference attended by many people but recognized his face at once. We were very excited to see each other after so many years, he was careful in his words avoiding diplomatically mentioning the names, but I said, "How is Claude?"

He whispered into my ear, "He never stopped loving you."

That simple, direct sentence brought tears to my eyes at once, and it was the first time since Claude and I cried together that I cried in public at mentioning his name.

I said, "Oh, how silly, my eyes are wet with old memories, I suppose we are getting older."

As Claude was in France for his business trip, our friend rang him and when he learned that I was in Milan, he left his commitments and colleagues in awe, sat in the car and arrived in Milan for dinner; even though it was a very late one, the waiters served us just as if they knew that we hadn't seen each other for a long, lonely ten years. Last time we saw each other, we were crying, embraced, astonished and angry; he with an unnamed God and I with a well-known goddess.

We started our late evening with smiles and tender looks, our hands were in disbelief that they were touching again. We started our late evening with smiles, but tears were simultaneously filling our eyes and he said that my eyes had the colour of sweet, delicious plums and their colour coloured all his days, and I said to him that his eyes looked like green crystals lying on the bed of a deep river and that my days were coloured by a dark river since I saw them last time.

He said to me, "Do not cry," but I did.

I said to him, "Do not cry," but he did.

I loved Claude with all my heart all these ten buried years and he loved me, for he said that when he married an ordinary girl, plain and simple, the one of whom his Italian mother approved, he was thinking of me. When he said, "I do" in his mother's church, his eyes were full of wet memories of Barcelona's boutiques with lace wedding dresses. He remembered our laughter and the sparkle in my eyes; he remembered my stories and his songs that left him when he betrayed their rhymes. And after that day nothing rhymed, he knew that only our steps rhymed, and that was all there was.

He said that children did not come to loveless marriages and God knew that he wanted children with plum-coloured eyes. He asked me if I had ever visited Sevilla with a child who was not destined to be his, and I said that this

60

story might happen in the future, for I did not have my beloved child yet and my going to Andalucia was not destined to happen yet.

He loved, always loved the way I speculated about the future and its twists and turns and asked me about my stories and I have never told him that all my stories belong to him. No, I have never told him!

I could never stand in between him and his sacred, blessed-by-the-priest Italian marriage, for I knew better, I knew better. But I knew as well that his heart belonged to me, my heart was broken but the pieces were puzzles of his mosaic, and that was all.

When he started to talk about our possible future, I stopped him the same way his mother probably would do. I stopped him.

He took his bride, the one mother chose and approved, she wore the wedding dress borrowed from my dreams and in front of a benevolent God's face and all the relatives and our friends swore to love her and cherish her regardless of his thoughts floating through Barcelona's summer.

Tell me, is life about choices?

When he chose his mother's words, he chose a life without me. That was all there was to it.

He blamed the shameless, evil God of his and I knew that I needed a man who would not blame God but one who would be aware of the consequences of his own choices. I needed a strong man, for I believed that strong men did exist outside of my stories, too.

My heart was crying, but my head took charge, for it knew that it had to protect that vulnerable little bird which was quietly singing in my chest.

That evening I believed that the times of my heart were well behind me, and the times of my head were ahead.

I kissed my Claude goodbye that evening and he felt that he was betrayed, but the one who betrayed him always, he believed, was his evil God. I knew better but did not utter a word. We have the kind of God we choose to have.

When I asked him about my letters, he said that they never reached him, for he could not find my old letters in his drawer and learned that his careful mother had liberated the drawer from the heaviness of my letters now that his heart was beating for another woman.

Oh, how thoughtful, how thoughtful.

I wanted to say, "God bless careful mothers," but I did not. I bit my tongue.

As I could not change any facts of his reality, that evening I decided to change myself, to become somebody else, to learn there and then to be strong, stronger than I was, to be wise, much wiser than I thought I was.

***

When we met, we were very young. Still kids, yes, we were. We grew through teenage years to adulthood with lots of care, love and tenderness. We made some common mistakes, we cried, we laughed and loved and cried. We had a chance to love more or longer, I don't know, but we had a chance. And we did not take that chance, no, we did not. We were young and we were still not owners of our lives, far from masters of our destinies, somebody else decided instead of us, but we had a chance, we had a choice.

***

Even though it might appear to you that I have finished the story of Claude, I can tell you that that story never really ended. He lived in me all these years and the slightest thing, like an old song, a particular word, morning crisp or autumn mist made him alive within me and all these memories started to dance the dance of love. Every love has its name. Mine was named Claude.

My kaleidoscopic memories all have fragments of his words and many times I have tried to put them back together, but it was a useless effort, for once broken, the picture is never whole again because all these little pieces scattered around are difficult to find and fit into the right place where they originally belonged.

When I was on Andalucian shores, I used to look across the shimmering Atlantic ocean at Morocco and imagine myself travelling through the loud, full of life, streets of Tangier and meeting there three men: the two I was writing love letters to and then Claude, who would come as a rescuer. I believed in my imagination that he would cure me from false loves and promises but he could do that only in my dreams, for the only place where we could possibly be free and happy would be Tangier, because we knew neither their language nor their customs. We always dream that there is a place where people are happier and freer and our conviction is so deep because we will never go there to discover the sameness. Yes, the sameness, for human nature was created for the sameness and the same heart beats in the chests of all people regardless of their geographical points on the map of the world.

The same pain was carried in the chest, in the breast, of a betrayed and abused woman in Tangier, the very same pain as the one experienced in other stories scattered all over the rounded corners of our human home, the world.

But when I ran down to Cadiz, I did not know that, for I still believed that pain could be buried in the sand, not knowing that if buried, it would come in the dreams.

You may ask me now whom I loved; Claude or the two men to whom I wrote nearly identical love letters, and I can tell you I loved them all with a very different love, for very different reasons.

What happened was that all three of them had something they shared: the woman they feared. No, not me, for nobody ever feared me, as in love I was insecure as a little, wet mouse. But two of them feared their mother's moods and the one, nearly the perfect one who lived on the edge of my reason and dream, he feared a little woman with unusual facial features. I never said she was pretty, I never said she was not. But I could not read anything from her eyes, because where I lived in my own world, I never met women with such shaped eyes, so I could not read them. But I could read his eyes even though, sometimes, he would not let me, he would rather hide from me his real feelings; but the soul speaks through the eyes, so they can't hide its language.

When I was down in Andalucia, I said to myself that I did not need men's love anymore, for the men I met feared a woman, they feared a God, they feared commitment but paradoxically they feared freedom, too. I knew that I would never understand men, nor love, for love and relationships are mysteries of life which stay locked away from understanding, not only mine, but of many.

I said to my Mother, "Mother, I dreamt of perfect love, but we were fooled with fairytales and what am I going to do now with all these stories on which I have built my reality several times, just to discover that my grand cities and civilizations were built of sand and the winds of reality took them down, flattened them once again to belong to the sand."

In my own, inner room I heard the voice that reminded me, "Of sand you were made and to sand you shall return."

As I said before, I could not read her narrow eyes but I could read his: first I read that he was consumed by lust. What was gone from his marriage he never put into words, but nor was I ready to hear it. These lines could have stayed in his private possession forever, for his words would have made him smaller in my eyes and at that time he was big, strong and righteous and his eyes were burning with desire - why would I spoil the picture of perfection with words? Just by holding my hand he inspired me to travel to Andalucia and back into his arms one placid afternoon when the sun was setting behind the palm trees in his garden.

There he asked me if I had ever truly loved and I said, "Once," then I said, "Twice," and then I said, "Three times." He lit his big brown cigar and said, "Shall we dance?" and we danced and he kissed my neck and I did not know whether I was happy or sad because I was inclined to weave sadness out of happiness. He asked me why I was sad, and I said, "I wish I had met you a long time ago," and he kissed my neck and said:

"I promise, I will travel with you to Andalucia some other time. With you I would travel anywhere, with you I would travel blind, and I'd like you to know that I do travel with you in my dreams."

The whole of that particular late afternoon was dreamy, oh, how dreamy it was!

He told me that very afternoon that after he met me, my eyes were haunting him every night, and that every morning while he was tying his tie, he would think of the colour of my eyes. He said restlessness took home in his fingers, and his heart, he said he started to dream that one day he would dance me to the end of the day and that my eyes, together with its secrets in them, would find a refuge in his compassion.

I said:

"Let's bury this story in our dreams," and he said:

"You are my dream."

What could I have said, what could I possibly have said? For after naming me as his dream my words drifted, drifted away.

Anyway, we are all made of dreams, and when we lose our dreams we lose the reason to be who we are, for dreams make us to be who we are, unique and unrepeatable because there are no two identical dreams in the House of Dreams.

I shall never forget that dance of ours because its rhythm was a mixture of happiness and sadness; I was happy to be in his arms and rest my forehead on his shoulder, yet sad knowing that the man with whom I still shared my bed had danced me to the end of his love. I still wanted him to love me, but he said what he said and his heart would not consider any change, and I wondered, while I danced, why love went away when I needed it most, for deep down I knew that love heals, it dissolves stones, marbles and pearls.

While I was dancing that pleasant afternoon coloured with a touch of sadness, I even thought of Claude, and asked myself if our steps would still rhyme perfectly or whether he would be one step ahead or behind.

When he caught that look in my eyes he asked me, "Who are you think-ing of right now?" and "Never mind" said I, "Never mind," and sent back this thought about Claude to a different continent, where it would be more real than in his garden full of palm trees.

When I think now of Claude and the two men I loved less after him, I knew that he was the only one I let descend to my roots, shaking the very roots, the trunk, the branches and the tender leaves. So when the one who was supposed to be the father of my child shook my foundation, I was somebody else than the one Claude knew. I was a mother and the first, most concerning thought was my daughter. How was this earthquake going to reflect upon her frailty? I could drown in the ever-running river of her tears and felt helpless because once again, words betrayed me. We both were beyond words, we only had a pair of arms each to hug and to cling onto each other like there was nobody else, no, nobody else was there.

I wanted to give her my thoughts but knew that my thoughts belonged to me and I let her find her own, for life goes forward and I did not want to shape hers with my own experiences. She asked me about the meaning of pain and sorrow and, as I remember, I said that sorrow and joy were the two sides of the same coin. She said nothing. Nothing she said, but wept and I knew I had sown a little white pearl into her shell and with time it would grow, with time it would shine. For I had her to shine no matter what, because pain and joy, are two sides of the same coin.

***

All these little broken "I's" were merging, coming together liberated from the bondage of the different stories and She could almost feel physical-ly in Her body the fitting and clicking of the parts which would complete Her grand work – putting together the pieces of the broken mosaic.

***

I wanted to tell her of the seasons of the heart, but her heart started to beat just a few seasons ago, how could she be ready for the wisdom of grief?

How can it be true that pain is self-chosen? He said that there was no more love left in his eyes, that he wanted to see other opportunities; how could it be that her pain was self-chosen? What could she possibly say, what could I possibly say? I held her forehead on my wounded breast and her tears were the elixir I had to drink in silence and tranquility as if I was drinking God's sacred tears.

My Mother drank the same elixir of my bitter tears when I was lying in hospital and doctors were not willing to predict my future. They got needles into my hurting body and I wept silently, my tears were just rolling down easily from my frightened eyes in which could be seen little yellow clouds, which never before were seen in my eyes. On that particular day I wanted to be strong but I was in a stronghold of fear, because death was so close and I could not unveil the mystery of life, how could I possibly understand death? Maybe life and death are the same, or just two different sides of the same coin. I said:

"Mother, hold me, for I don't want to die. I know you came as an embodiment of a desire to keep death at bay, so just hold me tight and she will pass, never to return."

I wanted to be strong but I could not, and she drank my tears as I had drunk my daughter's pearls, which were burning our lips.

So, it looked to me, back then, that in all three of us there was an inconsolable, needy child looking for maternal love and attention.

My Mother said that morality had its own civil wars, and to witness his internal dialogue would not be pleasant and sooner or later his own ghosts would haunt him while asleep. I said:

"Let it go, Mother, let it go." And she did.

We never talked about him again because all he brought were tears and black pearls, and why would one want to remember only tears and hurt?

There are better stories to be remembered, better places and better people. When we lock the pain in the chest, after a while it feels imprisoned and does not know which door to open to go to freedom. So it is literally imprisoned and it is its own friend and enemy; its own leader and follower only into one direction, back into the past, the very place where it originated.

Why haven't I been told that love brings pain and sorrows but believed in the stories of happy beginnings and even happier endings? We have the right to know about pain, betrayals, weak characters and deep hurts which turn us into something we never wanted to be, or to experience, for our stories might be others' stories. Yes, easily they can be almost borrowed, but rather, listen to this story:

From London Mae Morris rang and said in a quiet voice, "The Prince of Darkness has left..." and choked on her trembling voice, and then quietly she started to cry.

The big revelation came to me at that very moment of Mae's grief.

Why was she crying? Why was she sad when she was supposed to cele-brate?

The Prince of Darkness got his name after many drunken abuses with which he generously showered his family. A long decade of sleepless nights, not knowing whether he was dead or alive, whether he was going to come back and how his mood would be coloured. The dark, or the darkest dark? Many times she ran to my home with a child covered with a thin blanket (as if it was going to protect her from the cold or the violence) and asked to stay with us. We would talk through the night as if we were night-shift workers. At that time I was writing my stories of love and thought that something really wrong happened to Mae, for she, in my opinion, never deserved a disturbed, lost alcoholic.

At one stage, I nearly said, "The pearls in front of the pigs," but I did not as if I had known that one day she would bitterly cry, for he had left, as I cried when I was left alone with a pearl in my breast.

I wanted to warn her that all that mattered was our soul and a healthy body but then she said that her late mother's illness came to haunt her, as if illness promised that it would take away all female members of that family. When the illness knocked on the door, the Prince of Darkness opened it and uttered the welcoming words: "If you come in, I am out, please take my place, for I do not have enough love for both of you." Then he left and she cried and I asked myself: "Why do brave, strong and intelligent women cry for weak and lost men who can only bring chaos and confusion?

Why are smart women trapped in stupid and abusive relationships? Why do smart women dumb themselves down in a relationship with a man who is threatened by their wit and intelligence? Why do we stay? Why do we cry?"

The Nobleman said, *"I don't have an answer, you have."* And She did. She knew the answer. She knew what to say to Mae, how to console her and lead her toward the obvious truth. I wanted to say, *"Lead yourself down the same path you led Mae,"* but I said nothing, leaving it to the Nobleman's skills and patience.

When I met my sweet Mae, we were two foreigners trapped in a strange country where we did not know whether we would ever understand the country, its customs or its people. We shared a common love for good literature and the written word and planned, for a long time, to publish a collection of short stories together. She had an intelligent and engaging mind and lovable English humour which sometimes would trick me so I would be put in between two possibilities, just to read in her eyes, after a short dilemma, how much she liked to play. I took that game of words gladly and soon we developed a very unique way of communicating, and anybody who happened to hear our discussions wouldn't understand what was going on, while our words, eyes, eyebrows and gestures meant something very significant to us. We had a secret code, a language locked in the language and our daughters, at that time, were delighted to join in, for they somehow understood all we wanted to say, they understood the game, the craft, for little kids understand all sorts of arts, only if they are exposed to them.

There was an aura of shyness and mysteries about her, for her memories were all laid in the misty Isle of Man, where every house has its own ghost or at least one story about it.

She told me the story about her mother. She passed away quite young, tired after a long and merciless illness, but before she passed away, she had passed the illness onto her daughter, not as a horrible, mean heritage but rather as an unsolved riddle which was left in the family generations before.

When she told me this story, she said that her body felt as if it was full of little stones and they navigated freely through her internal rivers like little boats which were not sure which destination they would reach or when they would reach their uncertain destination. All was more about 'when', because timing was important - the little boats could sink beneath reparation in their given time. But nobody knew when the given time was about to come, so her rarely sober husband feared this phantom fleet as one can fear a powerful naval army. Her army of stones was a good excuse for his uncontrollable drinking, which had its roots in his childhood, where he had lost all sense of belonging to the world around him. He strongly belonged to the world within him and from there the most beautiful paintings would come up on his astonished canvases. And we would all look at his paintings with open mouths and hearts and how difficult it was to comprehend that such inner beauty came from a verbally and physically abusive man.

How strange, oh, how strange.

He didn't have any friends, for he assumed that other people were the enemy. He tried always to win the argument, if not with words, then with shouting or physical force. He would come home from his walkabouts full of bruises and open wounds, not knowing in which war he earned them. They looked almost as medals on his ever-absent face, which clearly showed that he had no centre. Only once, I said to her, "Bear in mind that you are not his centre," and she asked me, "What does that mean?" and I simply said, "Figure it out yourself."

Every human being is a carefully crafted, individual creature with a unique formula to apply to their best functioning. So, nobody knows others' formulas, and I always wanted to say, "Refrain from advice, refrain from judgment and refrain from interfering."

For where I had grown up was a place where people were very quick to judge, to advise, to point a finger and to criticize. It was a place of immature pride and excess knowledge about life rules, so when I left the narrow streets of this city, I promised myself that in order to grow, I would never give cheap advice, or criticize what I did not understand. That was the reason why I never said much to my dear friend, for she was placed here to find out her own formula and apply it, just the same as me, just the same as anybody else. We are not above nor beneath, we are searching for our own answers to give us meaning. We all have different lives and different times to pose the questions. Even though some might wait many lives to get to the questioning, it does not mean that they will not get there when they are ready. As we all know, everything comes at the right time, only when we are ready.

When I told her that what had happened was for the best, she asked me, "How could it be for the best?" and I said that I did not understand it a few years ago, but now, clearly, I know that life worked out the best outcome.

"Let it be," I told her. I applied my Mother's simple philosophy and repeated soothing words several times.

I said to her:

"Embrace your golden solitude and just listen," and when she asked:

"How?" I said:

"I never knew the 'hows' of life, but trying out the ways will show you. Your deeds will show you, not my words, for all the wisdom is locked within us and the key to unlock it is silence. Embrace your golden solitude and just listen to it."

She asked me:

"Is the universe essentially meaningful and purposeful?" and I said that I did not have answers like that, though I asked the same question time after time. I covered myself with the golden dust of silence but lacked patience, for patience is the next ingredient to add. But patience is not something we are born with as curiosity is. We have to learn the lessons of patience throughout life. I want to say that it is a learned skill.

"Now is your time to learn," I said to Mae and that was all I could possibly say.

She said:

"All I want now would be to have you near me so that I can see your calming eyes and hear your voice of reason and wisdom."

Maybe those were her words or just the way she said it, but it made me remember all my girlfriends who ran to my bed when I needed them most. All the men I knew ran away, a million miles away, but the women stayed, offered their petite but strong shoulders, their kindness, their laughter and tears. So I said to Mae:

"I will come, for I long for one cold English summer."

And I came, we came. Yes, we did.

***

When I said to my Mother that I was going to go to London, she told me not to go because it was a long, exhausting flight and I was still not fit for travel.

I said:

"Mother, we are fit for life or we are not. Do not stop me with your words, for words often do not have the right meaning." What a paradox for the writer to say, what a paradox!

But I always saw the pictures and no words could describe them as words fail to describe the wind.

"Mother, life is here to be lived and friends are there to be hugged. We measure our worth by our noble deeds and by people whom we call friends."

My Mother said:

"I will say no more," and I said simply:

"Thank you for the respect," for there has to be a time when parents have to show the utmost respect to their children, allowing them to be who they are and taste life with their own mouths, even though sometimes it brings bitterness and the aftertaste lasts for years. They have to, yes, they do.

I was again in awe at the simplicity of life. I was aware that I was breathing, that I could touch my daughter's gentle face, comb her hair; I was aware of the warmth of the sun and could understand the language of thudding rain on the balcony. I was aware of all the different and beautiful tastes that food brought to my mouth. I was aware that I was alive again, for just one year ago I did not know which direction my life was going to take or whether there would be any direction at all.

I remember how happy I was to drive my car again.

The simplicity of life showed me how beautiful life was. The simplicity gave birth to appreciation and appreciation to gratitude.

"Yes, Mother, I will fly to London, for I long to see the beautiful pale-blue European sky. Whenever I think of the sky, it is pale blue on the canvas of my memories."

Fear was in my Mother's words.

What is fear? She looked into the Nobleman's eyes.

I want to know what fear is, for it blinds us and keeps us from experiencing all the beauties life and this world has to offer.

The Nobleman quietly cleared his throat, then She looked once again into his pale-blue eyes. They were resting on the clock, so he said:

"Think of fear and next time we will hear what you have to say about it."

Even though She talked about fear when She left the room, Her steps were free, maybe fear-free or something of that kind, and I wondered, and he wondered, where Her story was going to take us: to the narrow streets of fear or had She discovered yet new avenues?

Or had in Her heart much remained unsaid?

On Her way home She thought about her tools: pens and words. Oh, how She longed to marry them again. The Nobleman said that *part of the grieving process is to tell the story you have never told.* She translated the sentence into Her words and repeated it in Her mind, *part of the grieving process is to write the story you have never written.*

She asked, *Will I find the right words, for pain and grief have different letters? Do I already know all the letters of that language, all the words of this vocabulary?*

She told Her Mother the story of Claude, She told it to the Nobleman, but She knew that the story would be saved from oblivion only by writing it down. And to write it down She needed to call Her skills to come back, to take them from the dusty attic, clean them and apologize for believing those whose intentions were just to harm. For those who had neither gifts nor a noble heart, the only revenge on a selective God was to harm those to whom the same God was generous in his gifts.

She remembered the brainless woman, the one who claimed to be a psychologist and her man whose bitterness came from cold and shameless walls of a communist prison, two shadows that resided on the verge of kitsch and art; on the verge of lies and pretentiousness. We have all met people who dine on others' expenses, who laugh on another's account, who cut you short in your sentence because they have something more important or something more meaningful to say. We have all met people who promise but never deliver, for their cup is empty and they can't stand seeing somebody else's cup is overflowing. Because they have never understood that giving and receiving are the same, just two different sides of the same coin and only when you give of yourself can you truly give. We have all met those who give only for their own recognition and their giving is unwholesome, because their hidden desire makes it to be so. With those who ask of life only to receive, it is better not to sit at the same table, for this table hasn't been laid either for you or for them, for if they have to give, they will give with pain which will sit next to you at that very same table as it happened when She dined with the Dishonest Man and the loud woman who had a need to make others small in order to feel bigger. And bigger than life are only the humble, who give for the sake of giving, not asking anything in return.

***

But next time She came, She said, *I don't want to talk about fear, for you can't conquer fear by talking about it. You can conquer fear by developing the other side of it: bravery, and bravery is what you want to do despite what fear tells you. You look closely at fear and take a step forward. For fear is paralyzing; it keeps your legs anchored in illusionary security, but when you take a step forward, it is as if you have broken the spell of entrapment.*

I don't want to talk about fear but about bravery, for what we can learn from bravery is a lesson to be learned, and not from fear. With fear you do not grow, you do not fly to London to be with a friend in need, with fear you do not speak your mind but repeat somebody else's fear that talks through you.

The greatest manipulator of all emotions is fear. Claude feared his mother's moods as people down in Andalucia fear the mood of madness when the levante raises its wings. Often I would think that his fearful sentences were not made of his own mind. And they penetrated into his head from a well-known source, they smelled of her perfume. She played him as a game, using fear to keep him in control and obedience. She feared everything in his name: she feared that women (particularly me) would take advantage of him if she, the mother, was not in control; as if he was not smart at all, not sane! So he feared the same fear.

He feared to tell her that he was going to marry the one he loved, because she feared that his choice was wrong and would bring only disaster to the family. His fear smelled of her words mixed with a fragrance of expensive perfume and fine cigarettes.

I never really understood why I wasn't good enough or was all this game just an archetype, was it just a role we were playing: that of a never-pleased mother full of fears of what a horrible future was going to be bestowed upon her son, and the other of a young girl who discovered love and naively thought that love could conquer everything?

Naïve? Oh, yes, how naïve!

Once, I said to Claude that he had to make up his own mind, that he had to form his own thoughts and decisions. But alas, he accused me that I was set to tear a family apart.

What was I supposed to do and what was I supposed to say?

No, I did not know, nor do I know now, and I am asking you, my dear friend, for I was too young to know the answers and even now, years later, still when I think of him, think of her, I ask myself the very same questions, but there are no answers. They were buried in the chest of our past and got yellow and got grey and lost the meaning if the meaning was ever sowed into the answers.

Was it bravery when I silenced my heart, ten years later when Claude told me that he still loved me with the same, burning love, and I said despite a weeping heart that his sentences were not of his mind? Was it bravery when I admitted that I needed a brave man? The one who can distinguish between his own voice and the other one?

No, Claude, I need a free man. And you are not free and you've never been, not because of the one you married, but because of the one who had chosen the marriage.

So, what do you want me to do?

I can't be your wife, for we let go of that opportunity out of fear. I can't be your lover, for I am not a woman who is destined to be a lover, for I was your princess and this was the only place where I could be. It is not a moral issue; it is a matter of choice. You have chosen your mother's choice, you have chosen her fears and I assume you live a fear-free life now.

I can't be your mother and tell you what to choose and what to fear, for I need somebody who knows how to choose freely and the one who does not carry other people's fears like a pair of old, worn-out shoes.

Claude, I chose bravery. I chose to tell you despite the tears rolling down my cheeks, for you showed that without her decisions you were lost and I couldn't choose instead of you.

I had to let you go to live your mother's dreams, for she exchanged hers for fears which could come to pass, because she did not know who she was without her fears, as you did not know who you were without her fears.

Claude said through tears that he would do anything for me; anything for us. But then he blamed God, the wrathful creature whose only business was to make Claude's life miserable. In my mind I said to Claude that God had nothing to do with the way things unfolded, for they unfolded the way we chose them to be unfolded.

That's all.

He believed that no changes were possible, for he had no power to choose; but he believed that all that was some set-up and his hands were tied, his heart trapped in the past, his foot confused about which way to lead where he wanted to go, and above all, his head was full of somebody else's fearful sentences. As he spoke I understood that his language contained mementoes of his mother, the local priest and an unknown, confused poet whose verses fitted better in the past, where he lived, rather than in an uncertain future.

Their God was a God of fear and I left a surprised Claude that evening when we cried together on the grave of our grand love, to go in search of the God of Courage.

There are so many Gods, and I assume that the one that answers is the one we pray to. All our prayers are always answered, whether we are aware of it or not. We can be angry with God, but what kind of God can we draw to us when we pray with an angry and fearful heart? I wanted to say, Claude, choose a better God, yes, this one was wrong and, as you said, led you astray from your heart, from yourself. But listen to your heart and ask it what it wants and then act upon it. Maybe you will attract a God full of mercy and love. I learned that evening, eating a late dinner with Claude, that to play God has big, big consequences. I thought about my then-unborn daughter and promised her in my heart that I would not feed her with my fears, with my sentences, which would then belong to the past only. I promised myself that I would teach my yet-unborn daughter how to think for herself and to which God to send which kind of prayers, for each God answers each prayer.

Don't think, my friend, that that evening I knew all about God and prayers. I do not know now either how it all works, for what I could not really believe after the story of Claude fell into cold water, was that I would be ready to love again, to pray again.

These were the thoughts that I formulated into loud sentences and laid on the table among glasses of finest wine and finest china. But then, there were thoughts that I never articulated and kept away from Claude's inquisitive mind that particular evening. I never knew whether it was for better or for worse, for these sentences would come back year after year, telling me that they were supposed to be laid on the table without discrimination of my mind. I looked again as if there were two of us, or let me put it this way: the two of me. One was honest and brave, so willing to speak up; the other, the obedient daughter of my Mother, who was taught what a good girl was supposed to say. Why should I blame Claude for acting upon his mother's sentences or instructions when I was the one who would often obey my Mother's voice rather than be true to myself? Then, how does Myself feel?

How does it evaluate me? Was it ashamed or offended by not acting accordingly to what it thinks and wants? Was it, then, that Myself was betrayed by myself by choosing another voice than its own?

When I kept selected sentences to myself, it was as if I had turned the volume down, it was like censorship; as if there was somebody else who said, "Danger!" when there was really not any danger in being who you are, in telling what was there to be told. To turn the volume down was passed on, not only by my family, but the many families who wanted to raise good, obedient girls. Because they promised us that good girls would be rewarded. The ones who speak their mind are dangerous and not attractive. Wow, how frightening was that, to be a woman yet not to be attractive. We learn from a tender age that being direct, honest, strong or even powerful seems so undesirable, the same way that expressions of so-called negative emotions like anger are met with disapproval. And then we grow into 'lovely' women who simply cannot ask for what we want or need, for we learned that our role seems to be to please others. We learned that we do not have needs, for good women tend family needs, so if you have needs, then suppress them, be quiet, be quiet, and do not speak your mind!

How unattractive it is to be strong, how unattractive!

I said to my daughter when she was ready to understand:

Do not be obedient, but rather kind to yourself. Please, do question what I say, for I do not know all the answers, and those I know I do not guarantee will be true or relevant in your house of tomorrow. We are all walking carefully the Road of Unanswered Questions and often we stop and look back just to find that our former certainties were the stumbling stones on the same road today.

When I said to her that I do not know all the answers, the humbleness talked out of me rather than ignorance. For the more we know, the more we understand that there is not a final answer, nor the right one. They are all right; they are all wrong, it only depends on which angle and which perspective we are looking from. I said to my daughter:

"Listen to your heart, for all the answers there should be the right ones. If you tune in only to that tiny voice and obey it, it will always take you where you are supposed to go."

I said to my daughter:

"I will gladly give you love, but wisdom you will attain yourself, for you do not learn wisdom; you have to earn it. You can listen to my stories and parables but life is out there to teach you what there is to be taught. Embrace

life with an open heart and curiosity, for my mistakes were designed to teach me and you have your own tasks and lessons on your journey."

She would listen and I would see a twinkle in her stars, she would listen and I would know why I was here.

***

I've said to you several times that I am going to close the story of Claude and the book of longing, for it does not serve the purpose anymore, but how untrue it is! All stories, regardless of their fate, make the fabric of who we are, so without the story of Claude I would probably be somebody else. If I tell you now that the story of the man I loved by my letters perhaps never existed in reality, it is difficult to prove from both perspectives - whether it did or did not exist. His letters I sent back to the past with their ribbons and bows, for when I told him only one truth, he stayed silent for many years. To name the truth I told him: the black pearl was found in my right breast. When he learned that he swallowed, with excess saliva, all the words he could possibly have said. Maybe that silence happened because he feared my pearl but maybe he thought of the inevitability of our deaths.

As I can remember our conversations and our written words, I can surely say that he was one of those enlightened minds. Perhaps he wanted more than the consolation of words and philosophy? Was his silence governed by the denial or desire to escape the fact of the finality of death?

He promised to travel to Andalucia with me at some uncertain time, but we talked about it as if that had already happened and I wonder whether it was because we had talked, dreamed and imagined it so many times, that it became the reality of the dream; even though it was adorned by some frustrating gaps.

A few years after he fell into silence, he was given one of my books as a present from an old, mutual friend, and reading my words made him remember the times when we used to dance in his garden edged with tall palm trees. When he rang, he said:

"You are made of your words." And I said:

"We are all made of our own words, because our words create our reality, hmm?"

And he said:

"How are you doing now?" and I said, "Well."

I did not want to say more, believing that if he wanted to know more, he would have made an effort right at that time while my Mother was kissing my hurting hand and whispering, "Let it be...," "Let it be...," for she could repeat these soothing words over and over to calm our inner storms.

He whispered:

"I missed you," and I said:

"You missed the dream."

He said:

"I've been worried about you," and I said:

"You should not have, for worries cancel our dreams, and I always wanted to keep you in the dream."

He asked:

"And what about our reality, for..." I cut him short telling him that we never had a reality, that it was always a dream. And he asked:

"How can we make our dream come true?" and I said:

"By dreaming it, just by dreaming."

He said:

"When I think of beauty, I think of you." And I said:

"How kind, oh, how kind!"

He said:

"I'd like to write you a letter," but I said:

"I feel as if you already have."

Then he said:

"I have something special to say," and I said:

"Words are just words, nothing special about them."

I said this while I was thinking of his holy silence, which told me more than all the words he could ever summon.

I wanted to tell him that once lost letters could never be reconstructed again. If we tried, it could be only a vague interpretation of the original version, sort of plagiarism. When he said, "Now that you are free," I made him stop there, telling him that I was always free, for we are free as much as we allow ourselves to be free.

He said:

"Then all will be entrapped in the dream; all our words, all our letters and fine feelings?"

I said nothing.

So what if I had no words left? So what?

I knew back then when we were dancing that warm, almost tropical summer that we would dance to the end of summer, to the end of our dream. Our whole life is made of dreams. There are a number of little dreams which are constantly changing places on our screen, they come and go, some dissolve and we forget them as if they had never existed and some stay with us like a never-finished story, waiting to be taken again, lived again....

And when I was down in Andalucia, it was like a dreamland for me, and it was the only place from where I was able to write the most beautiful letters to both men who were visitors of my Cadizian dreams. And these dreams would come any time, they were not night stories, no, they would follow my footprints on the long, sandy beach of Cadiz and sometimes they were carried on the crowns of the waves to be taken towards Moroccan shores, or sometimes they would fly behind or above me towards the unreachable sky in an attempt to communicate with powerful forces that work beyond the reach of human understanding.

Was it real or not, I can't tell you now, for realism is a quality you look for in scientists, like you, my dear friend, and when it comes to my world, it consists of past dreams and future stories, built from liquid and transparent cells, and they float in the water of time where there are no barriers in between what was, what is, and what will be, that is why I do not know what belonged to dreams and what to reality.

If we speculate about moral issues, I can tell you this:
When I said I did not want to be his lover, Claude's lover either, this was a twofold statement. Morally it was not correct, for if someone loves you as much as he claims, then there is no fooling any of the three sides involved. I always had my loves all for myself, and to share the one I love with others was some sort of Communist approach to love: all belongs to all; we share and we are happy in our sharing. This philosophy could be borrowed from those who promoted 'the power of the flower,' the Children of the Flowers, but I did not belong to the Communist idea of sharing goods and lovers, nor were hippies close to my understanding. From what I understood from him, and my beloved Claude, would be: their love, their heart belonged to me, but they couldn't upset mother, God, family, children or colleagues....

How silly, how silly that all that came from two extremely intelligent men.

On the other hand, I said before and I will say again, apart from petty morality, I had always been treated as someone to whom all lights belonged.

And that was all.

You may ask what was in my heart. Sadness. Yes, in my heart sat deep sadness.

Aren't we all on our journey to find love and more of it?

But when I was lying in my bed made of withered rose petals and thorns, I was lonely and as dark as a tunnel on the country road and my Mother gently but consistently encouraged me to plug the world into my lonely heart. I plugged the wires of the world into my home and love started to pour in and I had never really been aware how much love I could get if I was only willing to open the doors. Yes, I said before that my heroes deserted me but my heroines were there, gathered as some sort of a beautiful love army ready to combat the opponent with me. They reached out daily in different ways: the constant presence of my Mother brought me strength. St. Yvonne's wise and philosophical words and approach kept things in perspective. Another saint was Santa Barbara, always coming in with an invincible smile and a pile of books on different but relevant topics to bring more understanding and clarity. A reserved yet warm approach from a deep, English soul, Mae, would tell me to remember who I was and what strength I always possessed and then my dearest friend who studied human troubles simply said, "I will come," and she did.

She sat on the plane together with her daughter and came after many hours of flight over wide oceans to teach me what the human heart, what human love, looked like.

My friend Joanne we called 'an emergency unit,' for she was there for us 24/7; she came with me for the hospital trips, she bought flowers and cards daily, she brought food, games, magazines and tickets for different shows, plays and operas for all of us, regardless of numbers and costs, she brought laughter all the time and if she could not perform some task at a certain moment, she would engage Linda, and I believed that they were angels sent from New Zealand's skies to be with us in the time of need.

There were other women; my dear women who could not be with me, but in their hearts they were and from different parts of the world I would get the most beautiful get-well cards and inspiring e-mails.

And the most strength I gathered from the most fragile one: from my daughter. Her small, almost bony hands were touching my face daily, each touch from her finger was as if heavenly drops were falling down on my face, and people would tell me how peaceful and collected I looked, of course I did, I had a divine healer, the love which came through her fingers when she played the piano or when she would touch my face, or just with a simple gesture to put aside a strand of my hair.

Love was pouring to me from different avenues: through telephone and internet wires, through cards and flowers, through the carefully selected books and words, through doctors and nurses, through touches and kisses, laughter and tears.

And love heals, oh, yes, love heals.

***

She ended Her monologue and lifted Her eyes wet with Her memories. He said quietly, more to himself than to Her, *"And love heals,"* then She said, *This therapy is a form of love,* and when She said that, She stood up, looked deeply into his, as I said before, quite beautiful, blue eyes and all She saw there was beauty in the form of compassion and understanding. Yes, it was there, looking back at Her silently. And in the room was a sense of absolute stillness, with a feeling that something fantastic might happen.

When She met him, Her inner landscape looked as a beautiful but frozen field. When I said beautiful, I think of all the flowers that had the most beautiful colours and scents, but as they were covered with an icy dust, it was not possible to see the colours, to feel the scents. It was a long, long winter and it looked as if Her warm being had fled that country in search of eternal spring, but how real could it possibly have been? How can we escape the winter of the soul and live in everlasting spring? Then we would not be aware of the goods spring offers.

When She went down to Andalucia in search of Her everlasting spring and warm weather, the Andalucian sun could not defrost Her inner kingdom. Yes, love keeps us warm and alive while hostility forms icy stars which show us a path to the Frozen Land whose lords take a strong hold of us, unwilling to ever let us free, whispering with their crystal voices that there is not love out there and the only real kingdom is one of frozen hearts, for if the heart is warm, it is going to be broken again. You can't break a frozen heart. No, you can't.

But then, what is there to be lived for in such a cold, icy, infertile land?

These pictures of Her inner land I described, the pictures of Her private collections, were in their original frames, well preserved, and they used to be of great beauty but the chance to see them was rare.

When She opened Her inner gallery and showed the Nobleman in, She knew little of his skills, She did not know that he had a skill to unfreeze the land or the gallery and restore the collection to its former beauty and glory. He was an artist in his field and I was deeply grateful, I believe on some level She was deeply grateful, too, to this gifted and courageous artist, who took so much trouble and risk to give us both the strength and courage to step into the frozen land and out of frost to weave the stories of warmth.

Her frozen pictures came to life and were again filled with colours and shades, the field of flowers started to smell of various fragrances, Her pain took on a new form, for understanding softens the pain, softens the heart, and tears were rolling down Her cheeks, and it looked to me that Her white pearls became liquid and alive like a river which runs and runs and never stops.

***

After our last conversation, the man who easily could have become my lover, had I never cared about anyone else but myself, never rang again; nor did he send one of his pale letters. His fingers grew tired and timid, especially the one with the wedding band on it. But when there were no more yellow clouds in my bright eyes, I sent him a letter. I assumed that his eyes and even eyebrows were pleasantly surprised; I assumed that he had a little smile on his masculine face, and I assumed that his fingers were too quick and clumsy while he was trying to open the letter and let the words out. But nevertheless, how he felt I only assumed, but how I felt when I had written the last letter to him was another question. My eyes were bright and cloudless, but which kind of clouds were still held by my heart was difficult to say with certainty. Because certainties are not real, they are illusions of the mind as well. We know how easily reality can be changed just by a torrential rain or unexpected storm.

I wanted to give him back his words, because they did not belong to me any longer, so I told him in my pale letter that I was willingly but gently giving him back all his words. I said:

Here are your horses, and here are your medals, and here are your flags and titles, I am willingly but gently giving up the dream carefully sowed by all your belongings, by all my belongings, which both were stolen underneath the table where our knees talked the language of belonging together. I am giving you back the unfinished dream and if I only dare to think about what might have happened that almost tropical summer in your garden edged with tall palm trees ... if I only dare to think ... but the dream ended on the fine line in between my collar bone and my iron jaw. You were the one who could have softened it, almost melted it, but you knew that that iron jaw held the pain which was given as a gift from the man who said that he did not love me anymore and that he did not belong to anyone.

I said to him in my last pale letter that we would never go together to Jerez and ride one of his white horses, which he promised in our dream, and on top of all that, we would never go to Barcelona, for there was a beautiful bridal shop which still held the dress I wanted to buy in another dream which suddenly came to the end.

I told him that I was supposed to be married twenty years ago and six-teen thousand miles away. I asked him what would have happened then, and whether we would ever have been dancing in that Far Away Land, holding our hands and our hearts on the palms of our hands. The letter was a sort of gratefulness to the chance that brought us together to dance two consequent, warm, almost tropical summers.

Maybe the dream ended because we did not want to accumulate too many feelings of guilt. Keeping it on the edge of the acceptable and explain-able added a sort of incomprehensible, painful joy each time we dined alone or with others, but around the same, kind table where our knees and eyes met the pleasure of a gentle touch.

I told him that there was no expectation to understand the real basis or to understand the origins of our relationship as long as we left it where it belonged - to the dream. But I will always remember the ease with which the natural movements of life occurred when I was with him: the rhythm of my dancing feet, the rhythm and music of the knives and forks, the cricket's song somewhere in the garden, the sound of the clock in the spacious dining room....

I had a feeling that time had stopped, that I was primevally loved and the man who said he did not know what love was never uttered these very words.

With my aching heart full of cracks, I did not know what to do or what to think, so I had chosen to end the sweet dream while nightmarish impressions entered through the cracks of my heart.

The letter was much longer than I intended it to be, it was warmer than I wanted it to be; but while I was writing him my pale-blue letter, it seemed to me as if I had no one to tell my sorrows to. The sentences were put together with no apparent logic and while writing, I felt as if my soul was escaping through the white lines in between black-inked letters, arranged in a particu-lar order as if to please him visually, if not by its meanings.

His last sentence was that he'd like to see me in Dubrovnik and all I said was that I didn't like the crowded city with narrow streets.

That was all there was to it.

***

Then She looked at the Nobleman and asked him, *How could I walk the narrow and overcrowded streets with a man with whom I danced that warm, dreamy summer when we already waved goodbye to Andalucia, which was waiting for us with its gifts hidden on its laced shores?*

I said to him, "No, I could not go," and I told him the truth, for I really couldn't.

Was I brave to wave goodbye, or was I scared of being really brave and letting it be?

When I told this story to my Mother one pleasant and free of nausea afternoon, sitting on the balcony and drinking afternoon tea, she thought, and thought and then said, shrugging her shoulders as if she was defeated by the story itself:

"Am I really entitled, and to what extent, to make retrospective judgment of your situation, thus of your decisions? I am not here to judge you, but to love you, for I am your mother, and so concerned about your, and only your, good."

She said no more.

I said no more, for that was all I wanted to hear.

Yes, I always feared my Mother's judgment. I still believe that we all do, as Claude did. Within us, there is still that little child willing to please the mother, searching for approval and love.

And after all these stories and letters exchanged between us, I heard that his aging had been hurried and I never thought that it had any connection with my very last letter. Do not forget that we shared our Andalucian friend, to whom I was still writing letters that would be returned to me with much delight and details about Andalucia, Cadiz, the levante and him, our dear, mutual friend.

Even though it was my last letter to him, even though I knew, knowing him, that he would respect and obey my wish not to write letters any more, somewhere in the hidden part of my unsettled heart I still believed that he would find different ways to express his thoughts and tender emotions. Yes, I did care, oh, yes, I did.

And I can tell that I needed a very steady soul to stand behind my final words.

I felt alone in spirit, but still I had chosen that rather than to live in unpleasant anticipation of a disaster, which was brought on by thoughts of my loneliness and his long silence after I told him that my breast was ill and tired.

Telling him that and looking at his dark, at that moment emotionless eyes, I had an unexplainable presentiment that something within him took a step back and that something was about to happen - whether it be verbalized or retained in the chambers of his mind.

But look; now all of that really belongs only to the very distant past.
"So what?" I said.
"So what?"

She stood up and extended Her hand and repeated once again, *So what?* and the Nobleman smiled with only one corner of his lips and he repeated as if it was some sort of magic mantra, *"So what?"*

Then She said, almost laughing out loud, *I am going to wait until God shows an interest in me or wills otherwise,* and then, as if She was a seductive visitor, She came on the tips of Her toes and planted a kiss on his very surprised cheek.

I thought it odd.

It was completely out of Her character, I thought it odd.

***

Do you know what happened when Claude and I agreed 'mutually' that to end our love 'would be in our best interest in days to come?'

I spent some years locked in my inner, lonely garden, hoping that there I would find the real reason for the failure of our love, to learn the lesson the failure was hiding in itself, and I was eager to understand how to love better when and if love called again. Otherwise, in that lonely garden, I would go insane if I did not try to unite again with the world outside of me.

There were still lots of fears locked in my inner book and the bare fact that love itself was uncertain and indefinite kept me locked in my book of fear, not letting me open myself to the world out of its covers.

I was young and I had the capacity to give and to receive love, and without asking me whether I was ready or not, love walked in. As it walked in once again, I understood that it asked for courage and a brave heart. I understood then that if there was love, fear did not exist any longer, for fear was the other side of love. We do not hate, we fear. When we allow love to take possession of us, fears disappear like the morning mist when the sun comes out.

The first few years after we said goodbye, I was extremely disappointed with love, but youth is sweet and forgiving, youth repairs hurts and it demands new experiences. Youth does not know and does not allow a prolonged, unbearable sense of aloneness.

I believed that fear was the opposite side of love, but I feared love itself, knowing from the love I had for Claude that loving meant giving myself completely to the person I did not know well and just hoping that my love would meet the love in his heart. To conquer that fear I needed courage and faith but the beauty of love is in this: when it comes, it comes accompanied with courage and faith, and gives you a feeling that you can conquer just anything.

Yes, I loved again, but the love was different. It was not deeper but it was more mature, I believed.

I was starving for love, as all humans are, and was eager to pursue the meaning of love. I wanted it to be mature, responsible and meaningful, not some superficial version of it. The difficulty of the task I put in front of me, in front of us, was not the reason to doubt a successful outcome in the form of the always last sentence in fairy tales, 'they lived happily ever after.'

I understood that without burying my fears, and without being myself again, I would never achieve love, so through new love I discovered new ways of loving others and myself. When I started to speak the language of love again, my stories flew more easily than ever.

Once again, I met a mother who feared for her son's wellbeing, as if I was appointed by an invisible, dark master to ruin men's sanity or health. I found myself soon, with a son and the mother who played a play on my stage, pushing me behind the curtains.

So, I became a shadow.

The shadow of my former self.

This shadowing, this disintegration did not happen in one part, nor in three, but over the years his weaknesses and her strength overtook my stability and I did not know whether love could save love itself, but I tried to love for both of us, for his mission was to make his mother happy and it was mission impossible, I can tell you it was, for her unhappiness lay elsewhere; in the long past, when she decided that control and obedience were confirmation of love and she asked for it on a daily basis from all around her that she claimed she loved, just as any addict needs her source of temporary happiness.

What a strange kind of love, I thought, what a strange kind of love.

I understood that these two mothers could not comprehend that there was a young woman drawn to the activities that could not make money or put bread on the table; activities like writing, reciting poetry and study of the religious texts of strange religions. What could one possibly do with this kind of a woman, and not understanding brings only fear and hostility, and how bad that was for my tender chest, still not accustomed to human hostilities, how bad it was for my tender chest!

I didn't have anybody to tell my sorrows to. I had the most beautiful little girl and did not want to knit the sorrows into the fabric of her childhood; all I wanted for her was to see my brightest self, the carefree one, the world-loving one, but you know, sometimes it seems like the world doesn't allow you to be what you want to be. I said it seems like it.

In my stories he became 'the other character,' for Claude never really was dethroned from being the leading man; so I named him David Goldberg, and I named him Ted O'Donaghue and some other names, but none of them was his name; just his vices and weaknesses were represented in these names.

I believed that you could sustain love by loving, that you could give strength to love by obeying its rules. When love goes out through open windows, all you can do is to close the windows, for the frost is coming in, just the frost.

***

When I said to my Mother that I was going to the Far Away Land for the sake of my love, she fell silent. Her fears were battling their battle on her face. There were many little muscles that I never noticed before, which were trying to fight in order to stay together and present a picture of cohesiveness.
I said:
"Mother, there should be a time when you have to learn to step back and let life flow."
She thought more, I saw the other picture sculptured on her face when she said:
"You are not emotionally equipped for such an extravagant deed of courage. I am your mother and I know you well. You were a fragile child, you were, and you still are."
When I said to my father that I was going to the Far Away Land for the sake of my love, he expressed worries asking me how responsible and stable he was, knowing that he'd got married hurriedly and divorced even more quickly the woman he barely knew.
When I told my friends about my going to the Far Away Land, they told me that he was known for his art of easily falling in love and the art of quickly running away after a while, for love was not lasting and deepening but an ever-changing experience, as he would claim later.

The strongest impact on me left the sculpture on my Mother's frozen face, but how shall we find what we long for if we listen to our mother's voice after time has allowed us to listen to our own voice?

She did not say "Stay," she did not say "Go," but I went.

I believed in love even though I remembered that once I was eternally disappointed, I was grateful that I did believe again.

I did not care what all of them had to say, for his eyes were dark, coloured with secrets and mysteries, I thought, but then there were lots of sad events which coloured his eyes in reality, for mysteries were only in my wild imagination, in my wish to see the beauty, to see the love, as love is the biggest of all mysteries.

What I can tell you, my dear friend, all love stories start like that: we see a reflection of our own self in the darkness of somebody's eyes and from that we weave different stories for all loves, as they can seem to be similar, but are different in their making, for all the souls are different regardless of the same need, to be loved.

He used to say that he felt caged, for his heart longed for yet another strange and far-away land and his sentences were the bricks in the wall of separateness and nothing was there which had the strength to penetrate into that wall.

Love took the form of disintegration and he claimed that we grew different in thoughts, feelings and actions, he longed to be the other self, not the old one before he met me, for he grew out of that self, long ago. He just said he wanted to be somebody else and try new things and new people, as if each thing and each person had fixed worth, for all that was old lost its meaning and worth.

Before he said that, I had already a nice and long necklace of shiny, black pearls around my neck and as they started to suffocate the life out of me, they started to penetrate into my body. When he learned that, he simply said:

"I do not love you anymore; you are a very fragile woman who appeared to be strong. Let me go, for I need somebody strong to carry my weaknesses."

He went to his mother's home and leaned his tired head on her breasts as if all nourishment would come from there.

How weird, oh, how weird.

***

I didn't have anybody in the strange Far Away Land to tell my sorrows to, but I had a friend who loved my stories and I told him that my heart was heavy and he took my hand and kissed it. I still remember the timid, wet kiss on my hand, but his voice was soft of sorrows for me, yet it was strong to convince me that he was my friend in the strange Far Away Land where each individual had his worth measured in money only. He always knew the right, soothing words, he never asked for more than I wanted to say, he sat next to me and listened attentively, or held my hand, the way Claude did the first time when he summoned the courage to hold it, when we were still only kids, when we learned together the simple language of love. He never asked for anything, he had the patience that adorns a mature, cultured man who knew himself the aches of the broken heart.

When I thought of the 'whys' of my failed love, I understood that I had never been certain of the reliability and unchangeability of his fundamental values and attitudes, as my father feared years before and dared to say:
"Only one kind of man is able to be trustworthy and faithful to others: the one who has faith and trust in himself."

You may think from what I said that I believe I was a perfect or ideal woman. Let me tell you to remove this fallacy now: I was aware that there was not such a thing as perfection and people who are trying to reach perfection are chasing yet another illusion. So, I was not a perfect woman, but what I surely was, I was ready to give as spring gives - continually and abundantly nourishing those who came in thirst.

When I think of him, I just think of my child's tears, streaming down her mellow, innocent cheeks, ploughing deep furrows on before an intact field. She used to ask me, eyes full of uncertainties, coloured with deep fear, the deepest one - the fear of losing her mother:
"Mum, are you going to live?" and I would search for my most certain voice telling her:
"Of course, I am going to live, what else?" and she would ask:
"Are you going to live forever?" and I would say:
"As long as you need me. If this means forever, then yes, I am going to live forever."
I ate my fear of death, but instead, I gained the fear of living, for I could not grasp the meaning, if there was any, or was the meaning what we alone give to it?
But what I said to her was quite opposite to what I was feeling, for I said that we could not invite fear into our house, but lay the throne for bravery. If

we let fear lead our thoughts and decisions, it would lead us into a dead-end street, but bravery was going to show us how to build a future on all four corners. For we were holding two corners and only bravery could hold the other two. Instead of asking questions about uncertainties, we decided to certainly let go of them, for we wanted to build a new, strong house that would shelter us from strong and moody winds.

What I learned from her was how easy it was to mould young minds, for children believe what they are told and when they give the power of youth to their belief, it can rapidly lead them into great success or sorrowful failure.

Believe, my beloved child, that I am invincible; believe it, for your belief spills into my firm matrix of knowing the exactness of the things and it makes the matrix liquid and then it flows as if it had never been solid, it shows me even the illusion of the matrix itself.

Believe, my beloved child, only your belief makes me invincible. And who said that childhood had to end, I said to her, for mine was still hidden in our house and we could be innocent and loving, without permission, in that House of Innocent Hope.

***

I said of him that he was my paper love; that our love was constructed of delicately selected words even though he always apologized for his "boring, administrative style," wanting always more of my "unusually coined sentences, which had to be read several times to grasp the real meaning as they had several meanings blended together."

As I was writing two letters to two men, nearly identical but with some distinctions, to address the one for whom it was meant to talk, I often wondered whether I was writing them, my love letters, because I loved both men or I just needed to write for the sake of writing, exercising my skill in daily written letters.

I would sit, somewhere in the quiet corner of the beach (if there is such a thing as a quiet corner of the beach of Cadiz), the wind in my hair, and I would search through my soul for what would suit it best. It was almost as if I was writing it to myself. I would read my letters addressed to two different men several times and would be contented only when there was nothing more to say for that day or I could not find any other polished word or expression to adorn my letter with.

That was my daily duty and pleasure, and sometimes it would take from early morning till late afternoon, about the time when the levante started its restless dance, carrying the little, mixed seeds of madness and depression in itself, that I would read the letters for the last time and would suggest to my legs that they carry me to the post office before it closed.

One of those days I met Nicholas on the sandy beach of Cadiz.

The wind blew off my scarf and I did not even bother to stand up and get involved with the levante's cheeky dance and chase my scarf around the beach. But I sat minding my numerous sheets of paper which would turn into letters as the day approached towards more tiresome hours for me.

He approached from behind, I never heard his footsteps, for the sand was a silent road, nor had I caught his very distinguished odour of strong spirits, for the wind was blowing it away from us. He said:

"Your scarf."

I grabbed my sheets of paper as if I was guarding them with my life and did not know whether he came as a rescuer of my scarf or whether he was an intruder keen to interfere with my tided-up sentences. I had had enough of the levante's interference, for with it my sentences were somehow less obedient to my mind; but I did not need any interference, either from any other natural source or from a man who came as a rescuer, who caught a freed bird I tied below my suspicious chin. Honestly, I did not know whether to say something or just to take the scarf he was holding, for I was holding my letters tightly to my chest and both hands were full of my conversations with my men. I was very hesitant, for if I wanted my scarf, I needed to let go of my letters and it would be more of a disaster to lose my pages than the silken scarf I bought in the bazaar down in Cadiz town. He read my dilemma in my trembling hands and as he came closer, he simply asked if he might tie it around my head.

I did not say "Yes," I did not say "No," but he came closer and tied it around my head and tied a little bow on the back of my neck. I said "Gracias," I said "Thank you," and was looking at my feet which were keen to go; but he said that we could speak English, for he was an Irishman who came here, and just like me, was trapped by the wind and delicious food and he never went back to Ireland since, and he never finished his novel, but he said, "What's the hurry?"

I said to Nicholas that I was not the easiest person to talk to, and not the best company for the rest of the day, for I was quite a troubled soul who was most comfortable when I was alone with the wind. He said he would never trouble me, for his troubles were numerous but quite well hidden behind a friendly façade and cultured attitude. He said he saw me writing every day and expressed his envy for my passion and dedication, for he said his pages had remained blank for a number of days, which altogether had already leaked into a year.

For this or that reason we humans open up more easily to people we know we are not going to see again, so Nicholas sat next to me and I told him about the broken pieces of my troubled heart, and told him about the two men I was writing love letters to every day.

Nicholas was a gifted listener; he kept his eyes on the little shells and his ears on each of my words, nodding his head speechlessly. He suggested I keep a copy of my letters, for I might need them one day, but I told him that one of the men did not read the letters, that they came back, returned unopened, for he did not care about my words anymore. I told him I had all my letters, they were still in a sealed envelope, tired of the long trip around the world, twice.

Nicholas asked me which one of the two I loved better, and I told him that I did not know, for both of them were wrong, as I had a gift of choosing the wrong, sometimes troubled, man, but I said as long as I could write my letters I loved them both and Nicholas nodded his head as if in agreement, saying, "I see, I see..." from which it appeared to me that Nicholas understood exactly what I wanted to say, as if he had grasped the real meaning.

The sun was getting down, looked as if it was pouring ochre paint into the ocean, the shadows grew longer and darker, then I turned my head to Nicholas and saw his face for the first time and he looked so young and sinless, and I told him he looked so young and sinless, and he laughed heartily and said that no Irishman looked sinless, for they were all troublemakers, even though, he said, it sounded like a worn-out cliché, in clichés always a good part of truth was held. I asked him about his sins and he said that he knew all the sins humans invented or were tempted into, for his learning consisted of one after another episode of extravagant choices. He said that he looked young because there was a needy little boy still caught inside of him, but he was often in bitter dispute with a domineering master who asked that his will and wants were instantly satisfied. Nicholas asked me if I thought that it was easy to make peace and live a trouble-free life between the two of them. I said that I assumed we all had a little needy child locked in our subconscious mind and we all had a tyrant that asked for instant perfection and gratification. Then I told him not to take what I said too seriously, for I was not really competent in the field of psychology, but where I was at my best was writing love letters, even though it might appear that they were not appreciated, at least from one of their recipients.

Nicholas asked me out that evening or any other to get drunk together, but I told him that I couldn't for several good reasons and did not feel obliged to list to him all my reasons. Instead I took one, which looked the most appropriate and told him that I did not drink, for then I did not know who I was, and this could be a very frightening experience. He said that he never knew and never would know who he was, but when he drank he thought he didn't really care.

I said I had to go to the post office to send my letters and Nicholas asked why I didn't send my letters by wind, for it would be the same, but without any cost.

***

Two nights after I met Nicholas on the beach, my sleep was interrupted by loud knocks on my bedroom window. I was frightened at first but as I remembered where I was, I got up with a feeling of curiosity rather than one of fear. I opened the window and with a warm, Andalucian summer air Nicholas's drunken voice came in. He asked me out to have a few drinks with him, for he wanted to talk English - since he came he had been fighting a battle with awkward Spanish words. He said that all the waitresses were laughing at him and when I asked him why he didn't find more learned companions, he said that was the exact reason why he was knocking at my window. Plus, he said that when he asked about my address, people he considered might know me asked him if he was looking for the weird woman who sat on the beach all day alone, writing and talking to herself in a different language. Even though I did not want to drink, he said that at least I was weird and what a fantastic glue to glue us together this warm and sweet Andalucian night. He pleaded with me to forget my two men just for a while and get out and sit on the stairs of my house and listen to his stories.

Somehow I felt indebted to Nicholas, for I told him what brought me to Andalucia and I wanted to lend him my ear, but first I asked him to promise me two things before I sat next to him: first, not to insist I share his drink (the bottle was in his hand), and not to be too loud, for my daughter was sleeping in the other room and I did not allow anybody to interrupt my daughter's dreams. When he promised he would try his best, I put on a light linen summer dress and sat next to the uncombed Nicholas, thirsty for his drink and as he wet his mouth, his story started to unveil.

The night was warm, the sky full of little shimmering glow-worms, there were voices in the distance, a dog's barking and women laughing. It looked as if I invented the whole scenery, unreal; only Nicholas's voice was too close to let me believe in the illusion of a perfect friendship of two perfect strangers caught on the same page of a picturesque picture book.

He said he came to Cadiz following his beautiful but commitment-free Andalucian woman who cared only for physical pleasures like dancing, drinking and love-making, and when she said that the Irish sun was more like the moon than the sun, she took her bag which was always half-packed, half-unpacked for both cases: if she stayed or if she went away.

He said a very absurd thing happened; when he fell in love, he was nei-ther inspired nor urged to write, but quite the opposite happened, all his words were stuck, as if kept on hold while he was only thinking how to stop other men's lustful eyes chasing her movements when she danced, when she walked, when she accompanied her talks with her hands. She was an artist of movement and her perfect body was her instrument and he would go mad with unexpressed jealousy when other men touched her body in their minds.

When she took her half-packed bag, he stopped her at the door, but she said that she was a free spirit, free to go wherever she wanted to go, and whenever she wanted. Nicholas said that he smashed his world as if it had been made of glass: he smashed the kitchen - plates, vases, stools and the table, then the living room - the pictures on the walls, the glass on the table, the vases on the side tables and in the end, the tables themselves. He said she was looking at him quite amazed at his rage: for her the extent of jealous rage equalled the depth of his love. When Nicholas smashed all what was there to be smashed, his hands were bleeding and as he said, "The bitch came, took my hands and kissed them, and as a conspicuous display of her loyalty she cleaned the rooms and made love to me while my bloody hands left marks all over her body and face."

"Oh!" I told him.

"How disturbing, how disturbing, keep this story locked in your Belfast flat, for I do not want to know about such a violent and weird story."

"Oh, yeah, you want sweetness? You said I looked young and sinless, aren't you the one who wants to appear to be young and sinless?"

"But sins are meant for humans, for who are we without them, and what flavour does life have without them? You grow old, righteous and bitter, for sins teach us how to do better; they are like the steps we climb towards Heaven."

Nicholas looked at me with his drunken yet provocative eyes and said:

"How sweet, oh, how sweet."

He said that what we had in common was that we were always falling for a wrong or unsuitable partner, but wasn't that the reason to feel alive, to be engaged with big questions, rather than live a peaceful life on the calm shores when all what could come from there was death from boredom? Even when we felt utterly alone, we were not part of the crowd, the same crowd, he said, I would avoid on the sandy beach of Cadiz, covering my identity with a silky scarf. He said that we never stayed in one place long enough out of fear that we could get too sad or too angry, and I said to drunken Nicholas to tell the child inside of him that childhood had to end. Then he asked me:

"How mature is it writing letters to the man who will never open them?"

The next day I told my Cadizian friend, the one who befriended my Other Man, about my encounter with Nicholas. He laughed a little, and then quickly said "Sorry," for he did not want to appear as someone who laughed at the less fortunate.

He told me that Nicholas came with a dancer sometime before last summer; he said he thought Loreto was her real name. Loreto was known not just as one of the best dancers but as a woman with an endless string of lovers. From each of her trips, she would return followed by misfortunate men who each naively thought if only he came with her, he would calm her restless feet and she should not long for travels any more. But in reality this was not the case and when men would come to Cadiz, she would pack her always half-packed bag and run away, leaving men behind, not knowing whether she was going to come back or whether she would come alone.

He told me that Nicholas was just one of Cadiz's tenants who came with Loreto, but the last one, for she had not yet returned since she left the last time. He said:

"We have here an actor from Madrid, a very young man from France, a German count, who could be the French lad's father, a writer, who as rumour has it, has published ten novels and three won a Booker Prize. But to tell you the truth, all of them stayed and claimed that the levante made them mad, but I think they carried the seeds of madness in their hearts or under their hats. They all are now well integrated into Cadizian society and I heard they do not communicate with each other, except when they are drunk."

***

Even though Nicholas claimed that he could not stand the boredom of a meaningless life, he spent his days walking the beach, chasing young women and his nights drinking all night long. From my window I could not see the meaning in it and when I said that to him, he said that my window was too narrow and my tower of righteousness too tall to read his pleasures.

I thought that Nicholas would never knock on my window after midnight, for I pleaded first, then forbade it, but he could not understand why I was "a pretty cold fish when, actually, nothing stopped us from building a casual friendship in the moonlight."

I met him sober one windy afternoon and he greeted my daughter, telling her that he met her underneath her bedroom window while she was asleep, but he said he thought she was even prettier when awake. He gave her the origami he was playing with and suggested that we all eat some churros down on the Paseo Maritimo, where all of the tables were always occupied with young kids and tourists as confirmation that the best churros were served there. My daughter clapped her hands and an origami bird flew off carried by the wind towards the ocean. She said:

"And what now?" and Nicholas said:

"You know, there is a reason why it flew away."

"And what is it?" she asked.

"So I can teach you how to make paper birds," and looking me in the eyes with a cheeky, childish look, he slowly said:

"It is better to make a paper bird then to make paper love."

He took her hand and led her towards the Chocolateria and I followed. Yes, I did.

If I hadn't been so broken and lost, I could have had some sort of friendship with Nicholas, for when sober, he was pleasant, entertaining and an incredibly informed companion.

A few nights after we met him on the Paseo Maritimo, something strange happened. You do remember Mae and her story, for these two stories somehow are connected, as you will hear now.

Yes, he promised he would never knock again on my window after midnight, but when he did, he said that he promised that while sober, but drunk, he never kept his promises. The loud knocks woke me up and I knew that I would hear his drunken voice but when I opened the window, two voices were coming in.

How delightful, two drunken men were standing next to my window with two bottles of different spirits. Their spirits were high and Nicholas said that he could not wait till morning to introduce to me the best painter of all times and his best pal from Belfast and London pubs.

Oh, how honoured, how honoured I was. But when the moon came out from hiding behind a cloud, I saw his face and recognized him at once.

"How peculiar," I thought, "how peculiar!"

He extended his hand while trying to keep the balance and the bottle in the other hand at the same time. He said his name and I said:

"Do I know you?" and they laughed, saying that all the best-looking women on Earth claim to know them. How entertaining, oh, how entertaining!

When I understood that he was as drunk as a Russian soldier and did not recognize me at all, I joined them and sat on the steps in my light, white linen dress.

They tried to amuse me with their stories about the great time they had when they worked together in a London newspaper, one as a journalist; the other as an illustrator, and I learned about their drunken excursions around the country and about the women who accompanied them in search of excitement and freedom from boredom.

They were laughing, and I was thinking of Mae, I was thinking of her sleepless night tonight, I was thinking of her body as a home of wrecked little ships, of the aches, of her tears. They were laughing, drinking and talking about their adventures but I heard almost nothing, for all my thoughts were on the island of Mae's pain and when the first rays of dawn dawned on us, they realized there was no more spirit in their bottles and the spirits in their bodies were about to leave as well.

The Painter was talking all the time about a young and untamed Moroccan beauty he was going to visit the very next morning, if only he were not late for the morning boat.

When I asked him where he lived, he said wherever his spirit took him, and I did not know whether he referred to 'spirit' as the booze or the one he believed lived in his heart; the one I believed left his heart a long, long time ago.

Even though I was such an intimate and close friend of Mae's, I can say that I met him only a few times and he had never been sober. That was the simple reason why he could not recognize me that evening when they paid me an unexpected visit under my window and Andalucian stars.

I slept in, so my daughter was late for school and I told her that I felt 'somehow tired.' I spent nearly the whole day recovering, not only from a sleepless night but from the Painter's unexpected visit and his story about the young, untamed Moroccan beauty as well.

When I got back to my, let's say, normal self, I rang Mae. She was planning to pay us a visit in Cadiz while we were in Europe and we were talking about the right time. But when I asked her about our plans to get together that summer, she said that she did not have any money, because her husband took all the money from their bank account again and she heard that he was last seen in Amsterdam. And I thought, what a distance from Amsterdam to Cadiz, but I kept the truth to myself, fearing that her boats might sink beneath the wisdom. I said to her that I met an Irish writer, Nicholas such and such, and she said that she knew that he was somewhere in Andalucia

and that I would be better off if I had never met him, indeed. I stopped my story there and asked her when she might come, she only said:
"You know my life, full of uncertainties."

How angry, oh, how angry I was with the two drunken men and at the same time grateful for women like Loreto to exist and torture the kinds like Nicholas and the Painter, for they have to taste their own medicine.

Next time when I met Nicholas, he greeted us with a song, but I said to my daughter:

"Stay here and do not move," and came to Nicholas and whispered in his ear:

"If you come once more close to me or my daughter, or you knock on my silent window at any time, I will call the police. I will tell them that you are a pedophile or something else and your reputation here is fragile anyway. Leave us alone!"

We left puzzled Nicholas on the Paseo Maritimo that quite pleasant afternoon, free of the disturbing blows of the levante, which smelled of freshly washed clothes.

She asked:

"What did you tell him, mum?" and I said:

"Never mind."

***

Days after their visit, I was thinking of Mae and my moral dilemma was haunting me daily and interfering with my nightly sleep. Finally I had resolved it, finding an excuse for not telling her: she was not strong enough to keep the fleet, and the lies on the surface of her stormy ocean sailed alone, for the lies were stronger in weight and number and they could drown her spirit beyond repair. What good would come from telling her? But what good came from hiding it from her, anyway? I knew that she would learn the inevitable.

As if he had never walked the Paseo Maritimo before, I never met him again, he never knocked on my window with his trembling, drunken fingers. Last time he said that I was "common but snobbish," how wrong he was, how wrong. He was so self-absorbed that he could not read anybody else and the child within me answered that he was a "perverse, greedy alcoholic." In the variety of human endeavors to insult others, I said things I might be ashamed of in some less fragmented times, but what brought us together also drew us apart; it was that nameless anxiety which lingered above us as one of the stars in the mellow sky of Cadiz. We have the right to tell stories to an unknown audience, but to tell it to each other was not what any God would recommend, and when he claimed that we had undergone "a unique and intense friendship," I told him, "In your dreams, only."

It struck me as odd that I let myself into that kind of argument, but when I think of it retrospectively, I believe that this argument was an attempt to make it even for all the wrongs his best pal put my Mae through. Insulting him, I imagined that it would harm the other drunken bastard, who was on his way to Morocco with all the money withdrawn from Mae's account. Was I vengeful?

Oh, yes, I was!

***

Next time She walked in, She asked, *Of how many selves are we made?*

She stared into his eyes, and he said without any change in his position or expression:

"What do you think of how many selves we are made, or shall I say, you are made?"

All of my life I was in search of Myself and the further I went along in my life travels, the more and more of them emerged. It was not that they emerged, it looks to me now that the original Self was broken into more and more little pieces and each of them took on their own life and fought and battled within me for their own space, their own truth, identity, their wills and whims.

I feel like an exhausted battlefield of my disintegrated fragments that tried to rule the land, each of them wanted to rule rather than live in co-operation and tolerance. I feel as if they were enemies, they carried the voices of my enemies and the more I pleaded, the more I became defined by the obvious conflicts of these occupants.

But I assume that all of us are to a different degree aware of the contra-dicting wishes and ideas, unexpected decisions and unpredicted acts of whims. Some of my selves, which were fighting for their voice in the field of my inner shores, have already been given their names as characters of my narratives, and some of them are still residing in the waiting rooms, armed with impatience, nagging and arguing and pushing their way towards the freedom of their expression. I feel exploited. Used and exploited!

He repeated, *"You feel used and exploited."*

She quietly said, *Yes.*

After quite a long silence, which cooled the temperature of his pleasant room, She said:
I believe that we are never one, never really at peace knowing where to go and how to respond in each situation. What are we made of? Are we the sum of all our thoughts, all our deeds, dreams and remembrances; the real ones and the false ones, which we cannot distinguish as such with a passage of time?

Am I less of me when I talk of myself and expose all my inhabitants, or am I less of me when I keep them in the dark room and never develop their characters?

You remember my three men; was I robbed of some pieces of myself when they left or enriched in some future that my eyes couldn't see on the horizon of the misty Atlantic Ocean? As I carried them inside of me, did they become an indissoluble part of me and if I want to let them go, what process should I undergo to perform this uncommon and invisible, yet desirable and effective surgery?

No, I do not want to cut my body again; I do not want to cut my body!

I want this separation to happen on the invisible level, where the results of causes are beyond my intention or control.

And the belief that we do control events in our lives can come only from a young mind.

How childish, oh, how childish.

When I heard that he'd got married, I wasn't happy, I was not sad. I just could not understand how easily we made decisions that would reflect on our entire life and sometimes for the rest of our days. But you know we have to make decisions, even when we do not make one, it is a decision in itself. When we avoid making a decision, frightened by its heavy load of responsibility, often others decide instead of us.

And that was the exact source of my anger: when somebody else decided my misery. I could have chosen the extent of hurt, but how easy in theory it is, in the fine books where we are taught to choose a happy attitude. Please, do not sail shallow seas. What we see on the surface is controllable from the depths underneath, and if you decorate a sentence, you do not change what lies underneath, for underneath is what gives depth and governs, not the décor of the shallow mind dipped in sugarcoating.

When I heard that he'd got married, I did not know whether a part of me died or whether a part of me was born. For something new emerged underneath the apparently placid façade.

Antonella came back from Trieste carrying with her a box of Bacci chocolates and news that she did not know how to deliver - with concern, a smile or with chocolates. She smelled of Trieste, as if she was carrying the bora in her hair, and her cheeks were pale pink, which only emphasized the darkness of her chocolate eyes.

"Have a chocolate," she said, and I did. The sweetness of the chocolate transported me at once to Trento where we, Claude and I, could spend days eating nothing else but our sweet love and Bacci chocolates. How weird, oh, how weird it was, for love was feeding itself and my body never experienced hunger, just a few sweet lollies could carry me through the day.

When she asked me, "Did you meet somebody?" she tried to sound casual. I looked straight into her dark eyes with a penetrating gaze to disperse any attempt at shallowness and stupidity in them and said, "I did indeed. Every day I met somebody."

She lowered her eyes and I saw hurt mixed with compassion in them and she whispered, "Do not be cynical," and I said, "I can't help it."

After a few more minutes of silence coloured with the redness of her cheeks and a few more Bacci swallowed by my bitter mouth in my attempt to sweeten my sentences, she abruptly said:

"He got married last month."

I said nothing but was concentrating on the texture of my lolly and was very intrigued with the fact that its sweetness turned into sourness after Antonella's unexpected announcement.

He got married last month.
Oh, how nice, oh, how sweet, he got married last month!

But I did not say a word, toying with a sour Bacci in my mouth, tossing it with my tongue from one side to another and in the end I glued it onto my palate. In the room I could feel the reality of her sentence, I could hear the tick-tocking of the clock on the wall behind us, I could hear her unrhythmical breathing whose rhythm was caught in her phrase, I could feel minutes tapping on my forehead as little drops of water dropping from the roof hours after the rain, I could see Claude's face forming out of thin air, I could see the bride's veil tying itself around my neck as if it was going to suffocate me, but when I finished sucking my unusual in taste lolly, I said, "Never mind."

Never mind, I said.

So, ten years later, when he told me about his marriage, I faked surprise and said, "Oh, did you?" but I knew in both cases; when Antonella told me so and when he said it almost apologetically, I appeared calm and collected but the noise inside me was unbearable, and I am asking myself today what kind of artist was required to perform this task of placid and calm surface, while the depths were shaken with screaming and crumbling? But I was not acquainted with the concept of being in accord with my real emotions. I thought if I only denied them, they would go somewhere else in pursuit of expression. I would allow anybody to own them and express them if that was only possible. But me? No! I am not hurting, why and what for? So stuck and unexpressed, fairly and truthfully these emotions lay in their silent bed, patiently waiting for new events to be expressed and heard.

If this attitude was an example of how easy it was to pretend that some-body else was hurting, not me, I am asking you, then, with this attitude do we integrate 'somebody else' within us? Or what?

As I never left evidence of my real feelings, it almost looked to me that with that attitude I opened the door for somebody else and welcomed her in.

***

She was the one who communicated with the Nobleman. If only I had had my voice, I would have said that it took Her more than twenty years to discover this on the long, sandy beach of Cadiz, when She went down to Andalucia after all Her marbles were spilt and Her mosaic broken and it looked as if She would never find the pieces to put them in the right place to complete the picture.

***

People say that only time heals the wounds. I would say the truth heals the wounds. When I understood that Claude was going to justify his weak-nesses by blaming a capricious or malevolent God, I knew that this time I couldn't pretend to be blind. Yes, it was the moment of integration built on the integrity of my understanding and deeds.

The truth really liberated me and the time that passed gave the impres-sion of wholeness, the wounds were as fluid as a river, but I never said they were not there.

101

CHAPTER FIVE

She sat there without a word. It looked as if She was turning the pages of Her inner book, searching for the untold or just selecting a new story in an order known only to Her mind. She said, *I have been down in Andalucia wearing my sunglasses and pictures of the three men in my mind, pocket and heart. I told you their names, their deeds, fears and sorrows, and all that belonged to me as my fears belonged to them. But I kept one story from you and intended to keep it deep down and put a lid of shame on it because this story really was never meant to be a part of me. I never wanted to integrate it into my tales, for it was funnier than the theatre of the absurd and more confused than clumsily presented lies.*

Apart from the love I felt for these three men, it was a deep friendship that coloured our days together. At least in the fragments of our separate, yet interrelated stories, I felt deep human care at different times.

There are always two sides to the same story, and I can tell you if they narrated the story from their hearts and minds, they could easily be quite different, I assume.
I'll say now something about friendship, for friendship is a voluntary act of kindness usually between two beings who merge their souls in a sincere attempt to make each other's lives richer or more meaningful. For we measure our own worth by our noble deeds and by the people we call friends. I never wanted to fall into a trap of love disguised as friendship but I am asking you now - how couldn't I when everything I believed that I had deserted me? He said he did not love me anymore, oh, how easy, how easy to say it to someone without strength. He said that there was nothing left in his heart, even friendship was out of question, for real friends did care and all care was stored in an Empty House of Nothingness, charted out by his astrologer a few days before he said he was going for good, a few days after he understood that I was weak, ill and needy.

And there, in the shadow of all of these events and others that led to them slowly but surely, I knew a man who offered friendship, kindness and understanding. A man with knowledge of this world and many others. The one who had refined manners, the one who understood his people, their needs, happiness and sorrows as a good king would. The one who read the right books and mingled with grace and beauty, the one who would dance with me in his beautiful garden with tall palm trees which were touching the skies, just as our brave, hidden wishes while we were dancing and whispering kind, soothing words which found their way to our hearts.

I could not believe that he feared my pearl, too. I could not believe that he could fall silent, but he did.

Can you believe, my dear friend, that I kept hidden the story of Erwin from you, as if he was the one who belonged to the fields of dreams (but I could not dream of him, for the fields of my dreams were already densely planted with various plants)?

I had never intended to enlist him into the seriousness of my struggles, but St. Yvonne convinced me, or nearly begged me, to talk about him because in her words, there were not many characters quite like him populating this planet. I gave it a little thought, then said "Let it be," for it looks to me now that I am fulfilling my promises to other people, so I have to talk about him, for I have promised it to St. Yvonne to stay honest to my promises as I stayed honest to the promise to my Other Man, turning him into the waiter with Salvador Dali's moustache who brought a drink to my table down in the old town of Cadiz.

* * *

That particular year I started to practice tai-chi in order to bring my spirit closer to my body. Since I moved to this Far Away Land, my spirit was rather restless and often, when I was asleep, it would travel to my hometown and roam the kind and pleasant streets of my childhood. It would knock on my Mother's house door or the windows of my dearest friends who never left their spirits and bodies apart. But I did.

As I said before, I was searching for love all my life but I never knew how far one had to go in order to find it? Later, much later I learned that in order to find love you do not have to go anywhere, for it can only be found in your own heart. That simple truth I had to learn by separating my soul from my body.

And what a difficult lesson, oh, how difficult.

I am asking you now, among all my choices: why have I always opted for the most difficult one, as if the difficulty itself would confirm that my life is a reality but not a dream that will be forgotten when it all ends?

I really didn't believe that this Eastern practice brought my spirit closer to my body, but certainly it did bring closer Erwin to where I was standing. I

103

was still walking around with my plum-coloured eyes and that was precisely what he said drew him to me as a magnet a few sentences after he introduced himself.

He extended his big but warm hand; he showed his big, healthy teeth and said:

"Erwin Von Konfusioux."

I told him my name and he said that he was very pleased that I came here, because the room lightened with elegance and beauty.

How brave, I thought, how brave.

He asked me whether I was married and when I said I was, disappointment was written on his broad brow. He shrugged his shoulders and apologized twice, saying that the most beautiful women were already taken, but I reassured him that there was no need to apologize, for no harm was done.

And that was all.

Later, from a friend of mine, I heard the story of Erwin and his ill fortune, for he lost his young and quite beautiful woman to a dreadful illness, the one we all fear when we talk of illnesses or dying. She left behind two little inconsolable girls, how sad, I thought, how sad.

At the time of meeting Erwin, I was in good health, only my spirit was restless at night and it travelled back to where it belonged every night while my body was asleep. I knew little then that the body can start to wither away if the spirit wants to be elsewhere.

When he said to me that there was something special in my eyes, I had the same thought about his pale-blue eyes, filled with deep sadness for his lost woman.

For me, that story written in his eyes made for sad reading, and every time I climbed up to our tai-chi room, I would stand quite apart from him, as if I was afraid that this story could somehow brush against my shoulders. It was more some sort of intuition, some little voice, telling me to go to the back of the room and stay there, away from his eyes where I could read, as well, that he was lacking any fixed purpose, for his eyes wandered around the room, they were going around like an inviting merry-go-round waiting for someone who would hop on and have a ride.

At that time I already had a restless husband and a restless soul because of it, which would often travel back to my Mother's garden while I was asleep; I had a loyal friend who danced with me in the garden with the ocean view edged with tall palm trees and our dreams, and I had uncertain pain in the right side of my body and I could not determine its origin: whether it came from my heart or somewhere else.

Erwin knew nothing of it, just as I never knew that he liked to change his moods and his promises quickly and easily when things weren't going the way his steering wheel was steering.

I did not know how the events of my life were going to unfold soon, but I can tell you that on some level, which I do not have a name for, I knew that the men I loved would discover their passions or callings for yet another different country, and every morning upon my waking up I would check as follows: was my husband still sleeping next to me, was my soul back from its travels to the Mother's garden, was my pain still there, stubbornly refusing to go away?

When Erwin told me after the session finished that my husband was the luckiest man on Earth, my smile was rather sour with the truth that was lying in my subconscious mind waiting the right moment to rise up. As it was portrayed with an aura of nostalgia, I ran quickly down the stairs, as if I was running away from his and my own past.

Eastern practices could not prevent my soul from its night journeys into a happy land, as they could not prevent my body from the aggressive invasion of my black pearl.

As we know the story by now, I went to hospital and they both went away, never to be heard of again.

When I felt better, a bit stronger and brighter, I went back to practise Eastern wisdom, for a supple and happy body at least, for my soul was elsewhere and none of the Eastern practices could call it back to my aching body, which was left to live alone with my accusing mind.

I never knew which God was the real one or how many of them were out there for all of us; I did not know whether we could speak and negotiate with him and as I was multilingual, I did not know in which language he was the most fluent and benevolent. But I swear to you I needed help, I needed God, I needed more than the image and the book, the pleasant Bible, but I did not know how, nor did I believe that clapping my hands and stamping my feet while practising Eastern movements would bribe the Almighty to come down and speak to me.

He never came, but my Mother did.

***

When Erwin heard of my illness and the 'strange and unexplainable' deeds of my then husband, his pale-blue eyes were filled with tears and wonder, asking me, "Who would, in their right mind, leave a woman like you?"

I said He would, and Erwin said, "Please, explain it then to me," and I said that it couldn't be explained to others, maybe he was the only one who could explain but not to us, only to his God, who approved and supported such a decision.

I was appalled at the thought of explaining to Erwin his deeds and because this story was the one which would not return, why should I call it back just for the sake of Erwin's curiosity?

All loves, regardless of their grandiosity, are of a transitory nature, and that was what I said to Erwin as a possible explanation from my side.

Erwin was soundly and broadly educated and there was an aura around him of a consistently focused and grounded person, which was the exact reason why I was attracted to him. I had always been attracted to strong, intelligent men but the paradox was that I would always end up with a luminously attractive one, the one with clear signs of a neurotic and fragile personality, and because of this he was often more aware of his own needs and wants.

Erwin said that I resembled a little bird that had fallen out of its nest and that I needed broad, strong shoulders to lean on. Don't you think that I did not appreciate what he said; it resonated with the truth within me. But my wounds were deep and bitter and salty, and their roots reached beyond his understanding and beyond my admission.

All I could say to him at that point of my life was that I was a very troubled soul; that my heart was in a thousand little pieces and my dreams were left on the lazy shores of Andalucia. He held my hand and stroked my hair, saying, "We will heal your wounds, we will!"

How soothing was that, oh, how soothing.

If I think of luck, I would say that it is not something you are born with, but rather something you create along the way, with the right choices and attitudes. Be it so or not, his biggest stroke of luck was being born into a noble and privileged family with prominent ancestors and a number of vast properties in the most beautiful locations of the world.

God knows I needed a friend more than any therapy, for I have already said that when love deserts one's life, then such a life is a fertile soil for any kind of illness.

Compassion and kindness shone through him and I was glad to give the same in return, for what else a grateful and wounded soul can give in exchange.

But soon I noticed inconsistencies in his attitude. I would say I noticed that there were two Erwins there: one whose words and promises were textbook perfect - how a real, noble gentleman talks - but the other one was made of his deeds that never matched his kind words but were rather in complete opposition to them.

Look, I know that I am not the easiest person to handle, for I observe without much comment, which leaves a feeling of uncertainty until I speak my mind. You know, I liked the truth and liked to say what I wanted to say, but how high a price was attached to it! That attitude drags loneliness with it but I was prepared for such a life. I learned that if I wanted to be myself completely and truly I had to be alone, so I pardoned him in advance for all his inconsistencies and conflicting words and deeds.

We all have two lives: the one of public persona and the secret life. In our secret life we are often very different from our public persona life, but somehow we all manage, some better, some not so well, while with others, to maintain the public persona life and to keep the secret life under the surface. These secret lives for some people are real burdens, for they are so different from what is presented out there on the cover of the public persona book. It is like a secret diary where you are able to write not only selected thoughts but also brainstorm brave and peculiar plots which in public persona life have no place at all. Sometimes there are some hints about people's other lives, sometimes the public are shocked by some public persona's secret lives when it shows them in a completely opposite and shocking light. But we all protect our privacy, which is the Land of Secret Life.

To enter the Land of Erwin's Secret Life was not easy, for nobody had a valid passport, but to me to come to the awareness that he belonged to his secret life, first I needed to pass the guard of the perfect gentleman.

The first few months I was quite at ease knowing that there was such a caring soul and our friendship instantly made five people happier than they were before. He appeared to be a person blessed with a lot of optimism and brightness and whenever we would spend a day together with three little girls, I would forget all of my troubles with the two men and the scar which I was left with on my right breast after the black pearl was taken out of it. He would take us out on the ocean on his yacht, we would make a picnic and the girls, all of them, were so happy because there was an illusion of family, for all three of them missed a missing part. It looked as if we were all more complete and laughter was the proving fact of our newly-found completeness. Their laughter was so soothing, so healing I wished I had met him a long, long time ago - but knowing that wishes, particularly those about the past, can blur the present, I just accepted the things the way they were.

He showed me the portraits of his noble ancestors and told me when he was a child, they used to invite descendants of Prussian and other kings to dinner. For me, an ordinary woman, but curious writer, these stories were gladly taken into my memory, for I believed that they would, somehow, serve me sometime in the future.

Finally my restlessness took a holiday. I had a friend who understood my troubles, who cared, offered kindness and compassion and all he asked in return was to make his house into a warm home.

I asked myself, was it real? Can I breathe more easily, can I trust? What was that little voice inside my head making an unwelcome noise? The voice asked me why his eyes were so restless, as if they were searching for something else still not found. The voice asked me why his face was so red when the girls would not obey his words. How much anger was his chest bearing and would he colour my days with the redness of his angry cheeks?

God knew I needed kindness and I would not settle for less. Not this time, not after I loved the three men honestly but was left with a scar on my breast.

***

He said honestly that he loved me and that he believed that he could make me happy if I gave my hand in marriage to him. I said to him, honestly, that I had been broken like a glass and that I had to collect all my pieces, for only whole and glued could I start again. I told him that to collect my broken pieces could take some time, and that time was uncertain, for that craft of collecting my pieces was rather a detailed and slow art. But he said that he was a patient man, that he would wait, he said that he understood what I was telling him and that time was on his side. We kept our friendship.

I was thinking of the man who left me. I was thinking of the Other Man, the perfect one who always knew the right word. I was thinking of Claude, the man who bore the name of love. I said no more, for as he believed that time was on his side, so I believed that time would show us which course our friendship would take. I had no one to write my letters to and what I was writing in my head belonged to my secret life, nobody could enter it.

All of a sudden She got up and said that She didn't want to talk about him, and the Nobleman said that it was OK if that was what She wanted. She left the room as if it was Her last visit.

But it wasn't. She came a week later and continued with the story exactly where She stopped last time.

***

The first time I noticed that something quite strange happened was when I already thought that I knew him well.

We were sitting and sipping cold drinks on his big balcony under which a much-cared-for garden lay edged with tall, elegant trees, the kind of trees that were edging all the gardens in that affluent part of the city. Some neutral music was playing, we could hear the children's loud voices while they were splashing each other in the swimming pool, the afternoon sky was already reddish from the sun which quite lazily was heading towards the water, there were home-made cookies on the plate, the papers carelessly folded, there was a sweet, homely atmosphere around us, we were dressed in loose and casual clothes and maybe because of that or something else, he approached carefully, he knelt on one knee, he took my hand and said that I was a perfect woman for him and his children, we looked into each other's eyes and when I was just about to say something, he abruptly, quickly got up, ran into the garden, hid himself behind some shrubs and locked himself into a hard shell, acting as if he had done something very, very shameful.

What was I supposed to say?

What was I supposed to do?

I sat on the balcony quite surprised, looking at the sun which was lazily heading towards the ocean, the entire sky was red with it now and the edges of the water were coloured with the same redness.

I thought that we would talk about this unexpected event, but we never did. When he came back from the garden, he was dragging his two girls by their hands and yelling at them, my daughter was dragging her feet behind them.

I said:

"We shall go now," and we did.

And a long silence fell between us. I really did not know should I call him or should I wait for him to call me first, and when some time passed, I gave up the idea of calling him, I sank into my memories and it looked to me that this was precisely the best place for me to be. I could linger in the comfort of my memories for days and talk to the protagonists of my past as if they were my guests at my dining table. But whenever I would recall this episode on the balcony, I would think "How bizarre," oh, how bizarre it was.

***

A few months passed and he appeared on my doorsteps with a smile and flowers. He looked relaxed and fresh, as if he had come back from a long and pleasant holiday. He had his boyish smile, his white, big teeth adorning his broad smile. He reminded me of a little puppy, he hugged me, kissed the top of my head, he said how much he missed us, how silly were the days without us, worthless and empty. I was standing in disbelief, not knowing what to say and I just said, "I haven't heard from you for so long, where have you been?"

He never answered this question but kept on smiling and hugging my shoulders, telling me how much he missed us both and that the girls couldn't wait to see us. He rang his older daughter and gave me the telephone to talk to her and when I heard her sweet voice, I understood at once how much I missed these two little, kind girls and promised her that we would come the coming Saturday.

And we did.

When I asked him again where he was hidden all these months, he said, "You wouldn't want to know that," and I said, "I would," but he kept on laughing, full of contagious optimism and brightness.

But soon after that I found out where he was hiding all these months. We went out on the boat and his daughter was wearing a bright-coloured, pretty little hat. I said to her that I liked her hat and she said, "Daddy's girlfriend bought it for me." I said:

"Oh, where is she now?"

"She was very mean to us, so daddy broke up with her."

"When did they break up, a long time ago?"

"No, the other Saturday, thank Heavens!"

I started to tease him about his girlfriend but he got quite angry. He was denying it, saying that he did not care about women; that he was a father and that was all he cared about. He said that he cared about me, but when I laughed, he went red in his face and I knew that I'd better not laugh any more.

We kept our friendship, from my side for the sake of the children, for the girls really liked each other, which was quite rare, for single parents often can't find a partner because children do not like the other person, or they do not like each other.

But he never gave up proposing, never gave up the idea of us being a family, and never gave up his mysterious disappearances. There were times when he would tell me that he played golf on that particular Saturday and his daughter would say something completely different, like he had gone to another town on a business trip.

Look, I had enough of worries with my three men in the last twenty years, I had enough of worries with my pearls, I had enough worries with my daughter's feelings of being abandoned and had enough worries about how to pay my bills, knowing that there was somewhere else in this world the Dishonest Man who kept my money for himself, and as a defence, he said that my stories were boring and shallow and nobody wanted to buy them.

I understood that I liked Erwin's public persona, which was a made-up one, and the more I saw of the persona of his secret life, the less I desired to be called his friend.

For his public persona was really what one might desire to call a friend. He was so polished and clean, both in his body and in his mind. He knew so much about everything, and was so interesting that I could easily fail to notice that an entire day had passed in our conversation. Bear in mind, I always preferred intelligent dialogue to anything else, so our discussions could easily cross the border of late afternoon and spill into the hours after midnight. I confess, I did enjoy it, but every time I would learn something new, it was like a page was torn out from the book of his secret life and I would witness weirdness. Yes, weirdness I would witness.

I was happy to keep our yacht in the bay of friendship, but every time we saw each other he would try to convince me that we would be ideal for each other, and when I would ask him what he would do with the other women he was seeing, he would ask me faking surprise:

"What women? Are you paranoid, what women?"

I would give him the look you give to the child caught in a lie; I would just flap my eyelids in disbelief.

I grew to be fond of him, to like him, as one can like and grow fond of a mentally undeveloped child. I learned that he would not keep his promises when he said that he would go with me to the hospital for the very important check-ups, the ones I dreaded to go to alone. I learned that he would not turn up as he promised to pick up my daughter for a tennis match, so I was always ready to go in case he had forgotten. I learned that he was not going to do anything what was asked from him but that he would ask for favours and kindness, for it all naturally belonged to him, he was born into almost a royal family.

Oh, how noble, how noble.

I've got so many entertaining and funny stories that came from that unique friendship and he acted as if he had never understood what was strange and unacceptable in his behaviour. Because of it, he would often disavow his words and regularly justify his deeds.

Later I discovered that he suffered from unknown and unseen ills caused by different forms of boredom which often nobilities were regaled with as a heritage. The ills were not of a physical nature but rather a delicate balance of his mind, and emotions would be put on an invisible seesaw and played him as a child. I could have easily been the master of his moods if I had ever wanted, but I had my own troubles and moods and was learning the art of balance for myself, for the sake of my wounded self and my daughter's, to give her that gift for her future.

I had a troubled man before. If you wish to stay balanced, do not take the other's troubles because their heaviness will weigh you down, that's what I learned, yes, that was exactly what I learned before I met Erwin.

What I believed was that all of his ills were just there to cover up his numerous fears: fears of his mother, fears of his daughters, fears of love and a loveless life, fears of death and fear of life itself. Oh, how fear can dictate our moods, our levels of energy and zest for life. If we only let the fear climb the throne, we have the monster whose slaves we are going to be following orders blindly and faithfully.

Because of his background and very sound education, initially I compared him with the Other Man, my paper love hidden in Andalucian letters. I thought that I had met a kind, sophisticated man and there were no boundaries to our friendship and no disturbing thoughts of sharing his attention, or even worse, stealing his attention from someone who might be hurting somewhere in the dark corner of a sun-lit house.

How could I have known? Only time could tell; only time, and I decided to let time answer his mysterious and most ambiguous disappearances.

***

When I learned more about his strange and unbalanced decisions and moves, I decided one thing: I am not going to call him, and I did not. My telephone was mute, as if I never talked through it. But rather he was the one who would ring or pay an unexpected visit. He would be the one who would be very angry with me for never a clear enough reason, but after some time of silence from his side, he would call again full of joy, optimism and more eager than ever to see us again. But I can confess now that I was neither innocent nor honest myself, because I encouraged his mad behaviours, knowing that one day he would serve as a base for a rare character of my novel.

When I was talking to his public persona, he would remind me in his intelligent conversation and gentle approach of the man with whom I had lovingly danced two warm summers, hugged like two children who were about to discover something special in their arms. He had the capacity of the Other Man's brain, the same sophisticated manners, the same softness, but it was of a short sigh, for after a while he would turn into something else, while my dancing partner was always elegant and true to his word.

***

The Nobleman was scratching his head. I wondered what he was thinking, for there was nothing to read in his neutral look. Next time She came She wanted to entertain him with the story of Erwin:

He proposed a trip to Europe. All of us. I told him that I did not have such money and he offered to pay for the fare but I refused, which, as you can assume by now, made him angry. He said that I was a very self-sufficient person, which was not true, especially at that period of my life. He came to visit us, believing that seeing him would change my mind. I made chicken soup and herring salad, and we ate with much gusto. He was in quite a good mood until he came to my study and saw all these pictures of Johnny Depp and in disbelief he asked me why I would have so many posters of Johnny Depp. I simply said that I loved him. His face was coloured with the same colour as the Mateus in our glasses. When I thought that this might hurt him, I said that it was just a piece of paper, and Johnny was a man I had never met and never would, so it was harmless by all means. He said nothing, just nodded his head. Soon after that they left; the girls wanted to stay longer but he insisted on going, and after that day I did not hear a word from him.

Six months later I heard from him. He was in a very good mood and told me that they visited the Greek islands with some old friends. Great, said I, knowing that he could travel wherever he wanted and whenever he wanted.

We were invited to his daughter's birthday party and there were other people there and through some conversations I understood that they believed that I was more than just a friend. Then I talked with his older daughter who was, I always believed, an old soul and she told me about their holiday in Greece. She did not like it, for the woman who came with them was only looking after her son, not paying any attention to them. When I asked him, "How was the trip to Greece?" he said, "Fine," and when I started to tease him about his old friend, he said that she was just a friend and nothing more, and when I asked why he needed these stories, he said that every writer had a wild imagination.

Once he said that he hated Johnny Depp, "A lousy actor with gypsy looks," but he really hated the man who hurt me by leaving me ill and penniless, who had dark eyes and olive skin and looked free and desirable to women.

I told him earlier not to burden his soul with hatred, for I did not harbour such emotions for the one who left me. Maybe that was the exact reason for his dislike of 'the man without any virtue,' as he used to label him. I told him that separation or divorce was a very traumatic event and when you stop living with a person you loved, it does not mean that you stop loving this person at that very moment. It was not a matter of the head but rather the tangible matter of the heart, and I wanted to ask him because he was from that icy land by his origins, how can one control one's heart? How?

To stop loving is a process, the same as falling in love. Who's the one who has found the answer to the broken heart, whose advice or remedy can repair it, put it back together with a glue of understanding? With a broken heart you run away, whether down to Andalucia or the Far East, but you have to go with all the pieces, and only in the land where they speak a different language can you try to concentrate on the language of the pieces, which are just a rumour in your pocket.

But his game of hide and seek continued.

As he flew twice a year to Europe, he asked again if we wanted to go with them to Paris. His best friend was marrying for the second time and as he missed his first wedding fifteen years ago, he would not miss this opportunity.

As I always was a very practical person, I asked him where I would stay in Paris and when he said, "In a hotel," I asked him why he thought I could afford two plane tickets plus a room in a luxurious hotel in Paris? He fell silent knowing that I did pay my bills alone.

A few days after his departure, a very strange conversation took place between us. I believed then as I believe now, that the whole conversation was his little pathetic comedy, just a sketch for his Parisian audience, so let me tell you what was said:

He said that they had arrived in Paris and how misfortunate we were because we could not make it this time. He said to me not to be so sad, for he would stay only four weeks and after that we would be together again. My eyebrows nearly touched the ceiling in my study, he really left me speechless, but it was rather a monologue for his audience than a call to me, so he continued without intervals and I could not squeeze a word into his rhetoric. He called me 'my beloved,' he called me 'my beautiful, talented girl,' 'my sweetheart' and 'my dearest' while the wild river of his words was pouring from his heart, through the wires, then the receiver, right into my very surprised ear. In the end he said that he would call me from Rotterdam, for he was going there in a few days and said with much care, "Take care till I come back" and when he had hung up, I did not know what to think. Was he sane or what?

Do I have to tell you that he did not ring from Rotterdam or any other city, for I hadn't heard from him again for several months, except for some time around the Christmas holidays?

***

I said to my Mother, "Do not accuse me of anything anymore!" and she nodded her head. When I told her the story of Erwin, she said that I was difficult and demanding all my life and I really never agreed with that. I know that no one is ever entirely in the right, but being difficult and being aware of the nature of the relationship is an entirely different matter. Was I supposed to be tolerant, patient, understanding and loving? What was I supposed to be but myself, so I said to my Mother, "Mother, let me be myself, for I don't know whether my days are numbered or whether I'll live longer, let me be these days who I am or at least be the one I believed I was and never fully experienced. All my life I had authorities over me: Mother, father, sister, brother, husband, bosses, boyfriends, publishers ... Mother, so what if I am difficult, so what? Do we love difficult people or do we punish them? Do we try all our life to change difficult people into non-difficult ones? And what is the difficult one like? Is the difficult one the one who has her own values, opinions and ways of experiencing and expressing life?"

I said to my Mother, "Mother, 'they' do not exist! 'They' are just voices in our head. Voices we fear as to what others are going to say about almost everything. Let me be different, let me be difficult, for life expresses itself within all of us in different ways. I can't be what you imagined me to be, nor can I live the modus of happiness which was written in your mind, passed down by our respectful ancestors."

In her believing in goodness, she tried to say that if only I was compassionate, patient and obedient, he would gladly be my knight. Mother, I do not need knights and when it comes to obedience, I can only be obedient to my mind, and as I experienced before, whenever I was not obedient to myself, my soul felt like living in an empty shell.

I had days when I would tell my Mother my troubles, my sorrows and fears, there were days when I easily accused her of just anything and she would patiently listen, nod her head and sometimes she would hold me tight while I was bitterly crying, telling her that I was in the tight grip of fear of death. The fear would come at night. It would sneak into my dreams and colour them dark. I had dreams populated with demons and beasts and they promised to take me away, to ride my soul to their kingdom and when I asked what would happen to my child, they would laugh with an incredibly loud laugh and it echoed through my frightened body, I would scream and my Mother would run into my bedroom and hold my heart in her hands till dawn, till the sun rose, till my daughter rose to greet me with her smile.

I perceived myself all my life as a dignified person, whether it was a fallacy or not I understood this truth and said to my Mother, "Mother, there is no such thing as a dignified death. We fear death, we dread it, even the bravest of us, when faced with the fingers of death, are trembling."

Mother said numerous times:

"Do not talk of death, do not think of death!"

She would take me down to the beach and we would walk barefoot and collect little shells. It reminded me of my childhood, but it reminded me of Andalucia as well and I told her how lonely I was there, bearing in my broken heart all the words and deeds of the two men I believed loved me while I was well and giving.

She said:

"Let's talk about something else," and then I told her the story of Erwin, and she really could not understand why, he would behave in such a strange way and I told her that we were all mysteries to one another and we really

never understood others, for we could never understand ourselves either. She agreed.

***

Erwin lived just down the road from St. Yvonne. The road was beautiful, circling around the bay, all the houses were near the water and the view was breathtaking when seen for the first time. As we humans take things for granted, we fail to see beauty when the eyes become accustomed to it. As the outside beauty doesn't necessarily bring the inner out, I knew that even there, in this beautiful bay road, lived people who failed to see, appreciate and experience beauty. The houses were enormous, the trees in the gardens big, tall, wide-spreading, the rows of flowers ideally organized.

St. Yvonne expressed her wish to meet Erwin, for she was genuinely happy that I had met "a man of the same age and the same intelligence," as she put it.

We had dinner at his house; it was in the early days of our friendship when I believed that friendship with one woman would satisfy his persona. When I mentioned that we were invited to St. Yvonne's house for a cake and coffee, we went there, all of us.

He was as kind, elegant and charming as a character from the finest movie, where all were rich, successful, honest, and beautiful. He was in a capital mood once again, and he transported the same onto St. Yvonne during our stay there. He treated her with extra care and emphasized dignity and paid many compliments to her beautiful house and expressed his deep gratitude to God for meeting the kind of woman I was.

It was all so sweet, oh, so sweet: it looked unreal because of all this sweetness interwoven into his sentences and manners.

As one may anticipate, St. Yvonne rang the following day, saying that he was a delightful, old-school gentleman, just the kind I needed....

St. Yvonne was the person I respected most, but I said to her that there was still something about him that made me wonder; made me indecisive.

"What is it?" she asked and I said that I did not know, for it belonged to the sphere of the unidentified field within me.

When I slowly started to discover more about his inconsistencies, I would tell them to St. Yvonne and she was puzzled, too.

"Hard to believe," she said, and

"I know," I said.

***

I have so many colourful episodes that could portray his richly unusual and complex persona, but let me tell you this one:

When we came back from sailing one Saturday afternoon, he stayed to wash the boat. I felt that the wind from the east had changed his mood suddenly while we were still on the boat but I did not say much, as I did not know what there would be to say. He grew more and more silent and distant, and to help to get him out of that particular mood I offered a helping hand to wash the boat together. He did not answer, so I repeated my offer and to my astonishment he said in a very harsh voice that sounded as though it knew only how to issue orders:
"Get into the house!"
Then he repeated:
"Get into the house at once," not looking at me at all, and those words and this attitude were like one we have towards a mischievous dog.
Look, I might have been hurt, abandoned and bruised, but I am not the one who is going to obey commands. No, not me.
Kindness is the way to a woman's heart.
I took my car keys and my daughter's hand and left with no explanation.
Do you think the story finished here, as I believed that very afternoon, in his seemingly peaceful lagoon?

I saw him some six months before my Mother came, and it was the first time I willingly made some plans with him, regardless of the story I told you.

We were sitting on his balcony drinking tea and talking about neutral things. I learned that with him, it was the best to talk about impersonal things. There was a lot of anger towards his mother, so I never really liked to witness how much suppressed hatred he harboured for her in his heart. We agreed that we would not talk about my ex-husband, for I would not allow him to dirty my memories.
Once I told him that I did not live with a primitive villain and never would, but I said that my then-husband had his own weaknesses and demons, as all of us had them hidden, and we were not gathered together to judge him on that nice, calm day which could bring harmony if we talked about something less personal. So we talked about boats, marinas, sailing and all these summer leisure activities and then we talked about the possibility of

spending a few days together in my hometown, for I had planned to travel home for the coming European summer. He travelled all the time, every summer he went back to Europe, every winter he went to Canada skiing. By then I knew that he would never give up his polygamous life, whose existence he would never admit, but I did not care, for I kept our relationship exactly where it belonged: on his balcony, occasionally sipping a cup of hot tea, regardless of the season, studying his character, his behaviour, his gestures and his mood swings.

And a cup of tea I was holding while he was holding his glass of wine. From the neutral theme of boats and sailing we moved on to a more personal arrangement: the possibility of travelling together. We talked for a long time that afternoon about the places, islands and food of the country where I was born and, building these possible future memories, some sweetness entered into his glass with the rim coloured with a red colour, so he became as sweet and mellow as his wine, and intoxicated with the moment he kneeled once again and said that he wanted to be with me for the rest of his life. His pale-blue eyes were wet from excess alcohol, I would say, and I said just a short "C'mon," trying to lift him up holding his arms as if he was a little boy and pulling him up.

He asked me what was wrong with him and what kind of a perfect man I was looking for, and then I told him that there was nothing wrong with him but he knew well himself that he would never let go of his womanizing ways, and he acted as if he was genuinely surprised, or shall I say, shocked when he said, "Which women? I am a single man; I struggle as a single father as much as you do. There are no other women, I am a man of integrity," and once again he ran down and hid himself in the garden.

I can't tell you now if I regretted what I had said, I can't tell either if I was sorry, for it was all truth, but I never understood whether he thought that who he was, was really not obvious, or that he really thought of himself as a man of integrity.

You could ask me why I kept that strange kind of friendship, but to tell you the truth: the truth is never black or white, for he had lots of other shades of colours. I felt sorry and again, it was a twofold sentiment: first, I was sorry I could not deliver more, for when it comes to a man, I was looking for a stable and predictable person, let's say, a mature one; and secondly, I was sorry that he could not be what I wanted, for he was just the opposite of this. But as a friend, I would have kept him forever, if only he had not lost perspective and underestimated my capacity to read people.

How bizarre, oh, how bizarre.

***

Even though we planned our trip together, I travelled with my daughter alone. After that afternoon when he hid himself in his windy garden, we left earlier than what I had promised my daughter. She was still wet when I suddenly said that it was time to go. They came to me, all three wet and surprised and hugged me, wetting my dress. They pleaded with me if she could stay longer. Nobody knew where dad was, so before we left, I told them to tell daddy we needed to go.

Needless to say, he did not ring.

So there we had a man who was optimistic and enthusiastic, yet with a sudden change of the east wind, all his optimism was blown away and replaced with a dark, introverted, speechless mood. Sometimes his silence would last six months and with a sudden change again, he would knock on my door, accompanied with two little angels asking me to forgive him his 'forgetfulness.' He altered from that mood to another according to which persona he presented; the public one or the one of his secret life.

As I said before, within me, a curious writer was born to see who this man was and what he really wanted, as he claimed that he was genuinely happy being our friend. But he had never been a friend in need, for I had tested him many times asking of him some favours or tasks (as real princesses used to test their suitors).

Oh, yes, he would promise the world, and then these promises would slip through his weak character, as if promises were just vacant words easily served to fools.

If I would mention any male friend of mine, past or present, he would angrily change the subject or stop talking at all. He said on one occasion that he hated the fact that I was so strong and a self-sufficient woman; he said he hated the fact that I was even stronger than him.

I knew that there were many men who could not pardon a woman for being strong, intelligent and self-sufficient.

But I told him what I thought was the truth at the time. I told him that I only appear to be strong and self-sufficient and that, on the contrary, lately I felt more fragile than strong, quite lost rather than self-sufficient, and for my feeling of being lost, he held responsible the man who left me ill and he said, "You laid your pearls before swine," and when he said, "You deserve much better," I did not say a word - I just changed the CD and the sounds of a quiet Spanish guitar softly changed the atmosphere.

From some very strange sentences of his I understood that he wanted to see my weaknesses and tears, and he hated the fact (he even told me so) that he never saw me crying and I told him that I considered my tears to be heavenly drops and shared them with selected people.

It was obvious now that we lived in opposed dimensions and bridges were not built by anyone's intelligence. All we could do was to wave to each other's image as they started to get smaller and weaker and we knew they would diminish very soon into nothingness.

But still it was not the final step in the history of our friendship and I will get back to the story, for it finishes after my Mother left, soon after our irrevocable last supper.

***

That summer I spent at my Mother's house, and it was a long and easy summer. That summer brought me lots of dormant memories, which I easily relived with my family and close friends. These memories were stored in the places within me which could come alive only at this geographical point and only with the sounds of this country and the voices of the people with whom I felt the most at ease, so my soul quietly sang, "Stay, stay," but I did not. If I ask myself why I did not, I really cannot come up with the right excuse. There is only one place where our soul soars, for it knows the language of the wind, it reads the messages in the clouds, it understands without words the land, the stones, the shores, it gets messages from the smells and sounds ... but the narrowness of the streets and its people kept me travelling and searching for wider expressions, for narrowness brought all sorts of misfortunes to people of the country of my birth; they fought invisible, invincible enemies over the centuries and their stories were full of blood, tears, and childless mothers whose kids were killed in wars and raped in narrow streets. I needed wider streets, avenues where the soul could stretch. But as my soul was being fed by these smells, these sounds, these seasons, it longed for the particles of what it was made of before it knew my body. So, my body could be anywhere, my inquisitive mind could search for the new, wide avenues, but my soul was at peace at the place where it entered my body for the very first time.

Now She stopped and looked at the Nobleman as She always would when She talked about the soul. She was looking hard into his eyes as if She was going to find agreement in them, then She murmured to Herself, *Scientists do not talk about souls, they talk about numbers ... they talk about numbers....*

She shifted Her focus from his eyes to the table, took the cup and started to drink cooled tea, and after a short pause, She continued:

While I was at my Mother's, I got a call from St. Yvonne. She asked about the state of my health and I told her that the soul knew where it belonged and that the land, the wind, and the sun talked to it easily, I said, "Yes, I am well, for where love is, health beams."

What I learned from her was that Erwin came a few days before to her house and expressed his deepest concern about us. He said he had been calling for days and nobody answered the phone, nobody returned left messages. She told him that we went back home and he wanted to know whether we were coming back or staying for good. She said that when he was leaving, he asked her to pass on his deepest concern and love for both of us.

Jokingly, he would call me 'a heartless woman' but my heart was beating in fragments and there were fragments of him as well in my fragmented heart, but it was far from what we experience when we love a man.

When we love a man, we travel across the seas and the continents to be with him. When we love a man, we dance in his garden regardless of the dangers the garden hides in its bosom. I danced that summer in the Other Man's garden, I saw her eyes, I knew I could hurt him, could hurt myself, the little woman or others, but love is selfish, so I danced, yes I did, my feet shamelessly, fearlessly, followed his.

I followed his feet, for they led to the higher peaks where there were new possibilities for further developments on different levels and God knows how my soul longed for these high peaks which could be climbed at that time only by following his feet.

I knew that if I were ever to follow Erwin's feet, it would be a road to humiliation, following him through shady streets where women he never admitted he knew lived. I read in between his lines and a big sly smile in one corner of his lustful lips that he would not be capable of ever leaving his erotic friendships of a short sigh. Would you ask me if I was appalled at that thought?

Probably I was, but you had better listen to the end of the story, for I have only one episode left to close the tale.

I had a child who needed sound foundations and if there was nobody who could dance me to love through commitment and fidelity, what would be there then to enjoy?

***

When it comes to Erwin, I often thought how many parallel lives he had. I even asked him once, for I was interested from a rather psychological perspective in that question, but he would always turn the story around, telling me that my imagination was fascinating, but harmful as well in its attempt to penetrate into his rather uninteresting reality, which repeated itself in the daily, boring routine he called his life. To defend himself he would blame the man who left me, telling me that I believed all men were disloyal and unfaithful and giving me friendly advice to widen my horizons and not look only through the prism of my experiences.

But through some sketches of his inconsistent memory and his daughters' little recollections, I could always see that the stories were overlapping in time, little holes were unfilled with a logical order of things. Even when he would tell me the tales which were in his happiest days, I overheard parts of the sentences that carelessly slipped through, for to tell different stories you have to be the master of the plot, you have to know the names, the dates and hours, the locations, sometimes the food you said you ate, the clothes you wore according to the season when it happened, what you said, et cetera. If the story doesn't meet these requirements it is highly suspicious.

To look for all of that in one's story you do not have to be a writer with a wild imagination but rather an intuitive woman who knows both: how an honourable man talks and behaves, and how he does not.

***

I hadn't told the entire story to my Mother while we were walking along the long, sandy beach collecting little, pretty shells. There were just bits and fragments of the story, as I tended to tell all my stories in fragments. My style of telling stories was directed from my fragmented soul. So, not knowing the whole story and believing that she knew me best, she said that I was always quick in my judgments and unwilling to offer a second chance.

I would not agree with her but I needed to conserve my energy for the next day, for I would walk a long path to the doctor who knew where to insert the needle and deplete my energy, so I left her remark hanging on the beach, waiting for the wind to take it to some other shores, for all I wanted that particular afternoon was to collect little, pretty shells which would be placed on the window-sill of my bedroom so that they could smell of the sea, of the beach, of Andalucia, or of my youth while I was lying tired after seeing the kind doctor.

CHAPTER SIX

We came back from Europe and because of Europe this city where we lived looked to me now impersonal, cold and hollow. People were in a constant rush because money had no time to wait for anybody; it would easily and gladly exchange hands, pockets and wallets only if you were not in a hurry to grab it first.

As I left my soul that summer on the steps leading to my Mother's house, I thought I would never climb the stairways to heaven.

Whether or not it was because of the way I phrased it, hell, rather than heaven, entered again into my fragile mind when I was told that my pearl was slowly but steadily growing in my breast again.

What a silly, useless question, "What have I done wrong?" What a childish question! But regardless of the naivety of the question, it played with my frightened mind.

Again: How shall I look in my daughter's eyes? What shall I tell her? There was nobody else to tell her what was in store for our future. Was there a future at all?

By now, my dear friend, you have put some pieces together, you know that my Mother came only six months after a seemingly easy and certainly warm holiday, with her bags armed with love and hope.

Before she came, St. Yvonne was my pillar of strength and she said with a calm, but firm voice:

"Do not panic. Sometimes it happens more than once and life goes on. You will go to hospital and you will do what the doctors tell you to do, and you will be fine, for you are young and it is not true that you are fragile. You are a very strong woman, for what you've been through with elegance and patience will get you out of troubles again. Believe in yourself, all will be fine. We are here when help is needed, you are not alone."

***

While I was nursed by my Mother's and my daughter's love, I can honestly say to you that I spent quite a lot of time thinking of the past and the three men I loved and I had forgotten my unpredictable and disloyal friend, for I hadn't even had time to think about useless relationships.

I can say that I believed that it was better to have one more friend than one more enemy, but under the name of friendship all sorts of masked needs could be hidden.

***

On my easy days I would take my Mother around the city, we would visit galleries and museums or meet friends for lunch.

Just the day before Erwin mysteriously appeared again (both were equally mysterious: his appearances and disappearances), we had some guests and instead of being tired that or the next day, I felt like they filled me with extra energy.

The telephone rang and I heard the joyful voice of my forgotten friend.

When Erwin heard that my Mother was visiting, he insisted on taking us out to dinner, and all of the conversation with him failed to surprise me. I could not accept it without reservation and when he felt some hesitation in my voice, he said, "We'll come to visit first, we really missed you," and he was on his way. My Mother was very keen to see who this man was, whom I portrayed as a character from the theatre of the absurd.

But he never failed to impress!

He came with a gigantic bunch of flowers for my Mother and for all of us he brought a chocolate cake and a bottle of sweet wine.

How sweet, oh, how sweet!

My Mother has a likable personality, nothing like me. I took some bits from different ancestors (as legend goes), but I have always firmly believed that I am the way I am, full stop. Mother is a kind and patient woman, she does not talk a lot but she knows exactly when to talk and what words to use, even the colour of her voice is always in accordance with her words. She always met respect from anybody with whom she would come in contact. She claimed that she was a good judge of character even though she did not like to judge people, she would say, "Let it be" instead. If I have to describe her, I would say that she rather floated than lived. When we live we breathe, we walk, talk, eat, sneeze, argue, we judge, we like and dislike. But I always had a feeling that my Mother floated, for everything she did was with minimal effort: while she was breathing you could not see her chest rising up and down, while she was talking there was no change in intonation, she walked slowly but steadily and in the same way she has eaten every meal, every day since I remember her.

Whether she is a good judge of character or not, I know for certain that she was grateful that there was a good-looking, well-educated and well-presented gentleman with manners and style coming to my door with flowers and cake, for her pain, caused by the fact that I was left as a burden by the man I loved, was less bearable than for me.

It was summer. It was hot. I had a little wig that I never liked and when I took it off, my Mother's eyes widened. Yes, I took it off, for I could not stand the plastic hair and was wearing it only because she pleaded with me before he came in.

I said to my Mother the day before:

I love my baldness, I love my eyes and my narrow face, I love my slender shoulders, I look like a child again, and my Mother's eyes would be moist and so blue; they had the colour of a ripe plum, and for first time I understood how beautiful her eyes were and for first time I understood why Claude said that it all happened because of my eyes, I understood why the Other Man said, "Just because of your eyes." On my face I was wearing my Mother's moist eyes and when I took my wig off, Erwin stood up from the armchair, came to me and kissed the top of my head and said in a really humbled voice, "You look prettier than ever."

When he heard the story about my pearl, his pale-blue eyes had the same moistness as my Mother's ripe-plum coloured, glassy eyes had. The very same moistness in their eyes connected them in seemingly long moments of silence, which gracefully filled the room. As a particle of tangible evidence that something which deeply connected them had just happened, each of them had one tear rolling down their cheeks. As I know that all of his life he longed for a mother with moist eyes, I felt like an intruder, regardless of the fact that my baldness was what connected them and I fell silent to let them experience this moist moment.

***

She fell silent.

She looked at the Nobleman's face. He did not say a word nor did She. I saw unavoidable melancholy in Her eyes. She said She was tired. The Nobleman made a gesture similar to the one the Pope makes when greeting his audience. She said She'd like to bury these stories somewhere where nobody could dig them out, but the Nobleman said that these stories had to be told. She shrugged Her shoulders. Melancholy was accumulating like dark clouds on an unpredictable sky, which was a good sign to go home. She wanted to ask, *"Where is home?"* but She did not, for She knew that *the real home was elsewhere* and after a short pause said, *"or nowhere, for we are just passengers through the time which is set in the frame of nature which is transient in itself. Even though we live in the same cities our ancestors lived, and walk the same streets they walked, the trees had grown and later died, the stone of the houses will eventually turn into sand, the bridges will corrode and collapse, what will be the evidence that we have lived? We will pass as if we had never been brief visitors, we will pass taking nothing and leaving nothing, for memory wears itself out, too."*

She looked at the Nobleman's eyes once again and said, *Could you tell me, am I strong or am I really fragile? For when I think that I am strong, I face my frailty and when I believe that I am too frail, somebody strong enters my mind or heart and I can perform tasks I never believed I could ... how confusing, oh, how confusing.*

In his measured manner and his sober voice the Nobleman said:
"We are all fragile and strong at the same time. We live in opposites and one does not have to contradict the other. Your frailty is the shadow of your strength and everything has its shadow: when we switch on the light, the shadow does not disappear but rather it merges into its opposite. But when the light is on, you know when to use each quality of the merged entity, while the light is off we fight opposites believing they are not the same, just as the coin has two sides everything has its other side."

She said, *Then I am neither fragile nor strong* and the Nobleman nodded his head. She said, *Then all that is there to say is simply - I am* and the Nobleman nodded his head. She repeated *I am*, and then She left the room.

***

Oh, they loved each other! When he asked us out for dinner again, my Mother agreed at once. I was as easy as running water and I was as curious as I had never been before, so I agreed, too. I wondered where they were heading in their mutual understanding, respect and agreement about everything.
When he left, my nonjudgmental Mother said that I did not understand him, for all he could be was a genuine gentleman, so I was proclaimed by no intention as one who saw what others couldn't see. That meant that I was wrong in my judgments, it placed me once again in the inferior position of a quick and impatient person whose observations were rather too subjective. My Mother wanted to study him for the second time with 'an objective eye,' the one that I lacked.

I thought, "Let it be," so he took us to The Boat, a very posh restaurant on the water with a nice view of expensive yachts and even more expensive houses.

On our way down through the park and a little, private marina to the restaurant of his choice, we met a pretty, young American woman who gave him a provocative look and comment: "Not alone again, nice big company." There were six of us: three adults and three children holding hands and skipping.

He looked at me and said that she was his neighbour and there was a little peculiar story attached to this adventurous American and he promised he would entertain me with the story later that evening, and I said that it was not necessary, only if he felt obliged to interpret her cheeky greeting.

The table in the corner was waiting for us with a big bunch of red and pale-pink roses in a crystal vase. We didn't have one, but two, waiters treating us in a way that made me feel uncomfortable. When we sat down, I took off my little wig and my Mother's eyes widened, her mouth opened wide and her hands started to dance, trying to fiddle with the cutlery as if she was putting it in a straight line, but the cutlery played music out of tune, I took her hands and I said, "It's me, all is well, it's me," Erwin stood up and kissed the temple of my head, just as he had done a few days before in my tiny dining room. My mother could not contain her tears. She excused herself and went to the rest room.

I loved my baldness… and… I loved my boldness.

The girls came in from the deck and when they saw me sitting without the wig and with a big grin, they ran to me and hugged me. One of them said:

"You look cute," which made me feel even more relaxed and ready to accept the challenge of the evening.

It would be easier to write a biography of Alexander the Great than to slalom through the conversations and moods of that evening. It started with my act of baldness, spiced up with my Mother's tears in the rest room after Erwin graciously planted the kiss of loyalty on the temple of my bare head. I will take out the bits that added colour and texture to that evening and put some light on them, for they were contradictory in tendencies. The themes were nonsystematic, we were jumping from one subject to another, for he was at one moment chatty then irritated, one moment high-minded followed by frivolous, then changed again to wise followed by absentminded … and I was bald, yes I was.

My Mother loved him for his gestures; roses on the table, a kiss on my bare temple, squeezing her hand when she came back from the rest room, in her view these gestures were the evidence of his undivided love.

One good thing was that they could not communicate freely even though they used several languages as an aid; they needed my help to translate when they couldn't grasp the real meaning. When he wanted me to translate to my Mother that a man who abandoned a sick woman was worse than an animal, I refused. That angered him. Nevertheless he managed with the word 'barbarian' and my Mother's eyes were filled with tears once again when she excused herself and went to the rest room.

I asked him, "Why don't we change the subject?" and when my Mother came back, he took her out to show her his yacht. He told her he wanted to come to our hometown to see if he could find a place in the local marina, as he wanted his yacht to be there for his European holidays.

When they came in, we started to plan our holiday to Europe together when I got well. My Mother invited him to her home and said that she would be more than happy to see him and the girls for a nice Mediterranean supper of fresh seafood and local, homemade wine. As it was Christmas time, they calculated that by July I would be as good as new, so that was what they agreed and all were happy; the kids overjoyed, but he and my Mother were more excited than the kids. I was sitting there, the little wig in my lap, with a smile of compassion on my lips. I was thinking of summer, of the Adriatic sea; of my youth. I was thinking of Claude, he used to take my Mother out to dinner ... how strange, how strange.

He caught my look and asked me of whom I was thinking and I said nothing, then he said:

"You will never get over him," and I said:

"I am thinking of Claude." And he asked who Claude was and I said:

"He was my first love and he used to take my Mother out for dinner. I suppose she sees Claude in you."

He asked me:

"Did you love him? And I said, "Very much."

"How many times have you loved?"

I said "Once," then I said "Twice," and he nodded his head. I never wanted to mention the Other Man for he was not real anyway, but somehow after a short silence I said, "Three times."

He gave it a little thought and then he said:

"So, you loved Claude, you loved your husband...and...who was the second love."

I said:

"My husband was my second love," and after he gave it a little thought, he said:

"You loved somebody after your husband?"

"I did."

"You tell me. Please, tell me who the third person you loved is. Do you still love him?"

"I do."

"Who is he?" His curiosity could not be stopped at his smiling lips, it spilled all over his face and gave the face the colour of the pale-pink roses on the table. He had the expression of a little child whose anticipation was both sweet and torturing, he said:

"Tell me his name; tell me who your third love is."

And I said:

"Why would you want to know it?"

"Yes, I would like to know it, please, please tell me."

"I do not want to expose him."

"What does that mean?"

"He was married and still is, I was married...."

Oh, yes, his mood changed, quickly and dramatically.

He summoned all his skills and might to control the intensity of his voice and dance of his muscles, and with an apparent look of disgust said:

"You had an affair with a married man?" and I said, "This is not correct. We never had an affair, we just loved each other."

"Like in cheap movies, who would believe this story?" and I said:

"There is no need for anybody to believe this story. It was the way it was and I do not need a believing or trusting audience, you asked and I answered honestly."

He did not add a word but was deep in his thoughts, some shadows flew over his face and I knew that he had a passion for assessing people, men in particular, and I was not willing to know his current thoughts.

But what I saw was the opening of an abyss of misunderstanding between us; I could see cracks dividing the table in two and was afraid in which tone this evening would end, which persona would prevail; the Public Gentleman or the Master of Unpredictability with his secret life.

My Mother intervened, asking me in the language he could not understand what we were talking about right now, and when I told her 'about the men I loved,' she said that I did not have to list all of my previous boyfriends and flings, and I told her that if he did that, the list would make the road of sixteen thousand miles to Europe.

We changed the subject and we talked again about my hometown and boats, yachts, sea and salt, seagulls and the tramontana and easiness entered our hearts again as we sailed calmer waters. He drank his wine and took care of my Mother's glass and the choices on the menu and when my Mother told him a little history of some well-known places in our country, I added that I had a friend here who had been visiting my hometown for twenty years. I said that he was a German man and what connected us was the name of my hometown, for when he heard where I was from, he said he felt as if he had entered through the doors of his childhood and youth.

Erwin's remark was, "Is he married as well?" and I laughed, oh, I laughed.

When a little bit of alcohol was shared and drunk, the promises followed easily. He promised my Mother he would come in summer to have dinner on her verandah, I promised I would travel with him to Rome prior to visiting my Mother, and he promised us that this was going to be the best summer we ever had.

My Mother promised to bake a cake, hoping the name of the cake would be a 'wedding cake.'

When the cake was mentioned, he insisted that we take dessert to his house, for he wanted to show the house to my Mother. We took six pieces of cake and walked slowly back to his house.

Some houses speak for themselves. It was not just the matter of the size, but the house spoke of real wealth, of old money caught in the heavy frames of original paintings of the world's most renowned artists, who caught the youth of Erwin's ancestors in the frames for future generation's pride. The house looked like a big gallery, a collection of real art and antique furniture combined with the ultra-modern style of contemporary designers. I knew that my Mother had never seen a house of that kind, for it was a real rarity. He sat my Mother on the comfortable armchair, brought more cushions and told her to make herself comfortable. I lay on the sofa, lifting my legs up and they told me to sleep if I felt tired. He took my Mother on a tour around the house and in his study he showed her his family tree, the books they had written, the prizes and the medals they had won. I fell asleep, yes, I did, I was tired, so tired that evening.

When the tour ended, he made coffee and they put the cakes on little, porcelain plates. Once again we talked about light themes, he was in a good mood and when my Mother went to the bathroom, he sat next to me and said in a curious but tender voice:

"So, your heart does not ache for your ex-husband, but for some other man?"

I was tired, I thought of the Other Man, I thought of my ex-husband, after which I smiled to him, his face looked kind but I knew that this was not his real face, I said to him:

"It aches for both of them."

"How could you...."

"How could I what?"

"I never thought of you in this light...."

I was tired, too tired and I said to him, "I am tired" while he was drinking sweet wine from his crystal, elegant glass, I was looking around asking myself what these beautiful and expensive things could or could not change in our souls. I was looking at expensive art with the eyes that demolish myths and my memories were like these paintings on his walls. My Mother entered the room and the cake was eaten accompanied with light conversation.

The persona from his secret life was looking at me from the other side of his eyes. He had one more glass of wine and when my Mother went down to the children's room, as she was called to be the fourth player in one of their board games, he sat again next to me and said:

"I owe you the story."

"Which story?" I had already forgotten the little American friend.

He said: "The story about my American neighbour."

"Well, I am listening," I said, for my curiosity was stronger than my tiredness at that moment.

Before he started to talk, he emptied a full glass of wine. Honestly, I did not count his glasses down in the restaurant nor in the house, but just looking at his eyes and listening to his stretched sentences I knew that he did not need a drop more of wine. And he did not take more wine, but he stood up, took a round, big cognac glass and filled it half with Martell. Then again he sat down next to me. There was a little mischievous smile on both sides of his lips, there was a mocking sparkle in his eyes, he cleared his throat and took a good sip of drink, wiped his lips with a serviette and started his story, which somehow I anticipated would be the final step in the history of our friendship:

"Actually, she is a little American slut, wouldn't you say so, just by looking at her?" That was not his public persona talking; the other one took the lead. For his public persona was, as my Mother pointed out, "A civilized gentleman whose company was a real pleasure," and we all know that a civilized gentleman does not talk about women that way, particularly about those with whom he shared intimacies, as was already obvious from her little smile and from my gift of hypersensitivity to others' feelings, as in this case,

the feelings of the narrator who looked like my friend but just invaded by some alien entity.

I learned that actually, the little American slut, as he called her, was the best friend of his former girlfriend. I was curious to find out who his girlfriend was at the time, but he told me that he had this relationship a year before he met me. He was almost overjoyed when he observed that there was a hint of jealousy in my question. But it was not a jealousy. I said:

"But a year before you met me you were married."

He said:

"I met her a couple of months after my beloved wife died."

His mourning did not last for eternity, but I had no remarks.

I said:

"Fine, you lost your wife, you met your girlfriend two months later and an American was her best friend."

He asked:

"Do I feel jealousy in your voice, do I?"

I said:

"Curiosity, rather."

He emptied his round glass and poured another drink.

"I came to the party with my then girlfriend and she was a woman I was not really fond of. You know - the kind of woman to soothe your troubles at the time. She wasn't even pretty. As I was sad, I was not really choosy at that time. But then the American walked into the room and all eyes were on her, you saw her, isn't she, if nothing else, pretty? And what had happened between her and me was a fatal attraction. She walked straight to us, for her girlfriend was there, but the reason she came, you know, it was me. As she was approaching I knew that we were irresistible to each other and that feeling changed the flare of the evening. Everything became as easy as a game, and the we started to play the game with our eyes, hands and words, and my then girlfriend was not willing to lose the game, so she invited us to her house at the end of the evening and it was the strangest evening in my entire life. I was there caught as a little fly in their web of perversities but we continued our game which we started earlier that evening."

Then he started to throw the obscenities in my face and I said:

"Stop it, it is disgusting. It is sickening!"

He said:

"We continued with our games for several months, the three of us, so close to each other, nearly house to house, and the little American slut persuaded her even younger husband to join our friendly, neighbourly games. Whenever she could, she would run to my house and she would look

from my bedroom window at her husband reading a book in their bedroom while she was...."

"*Why don't you stop it, you are just sick or too drunk....*"

He laughed.

I got up and called my Mother to come up, he stood up and said:

"*It was a joke, you know I was joking.*" *And he took my hand, which I pulled away full of disgust, and he said:*

"*But you were the one who had an affair with a married man, didn't you? You are the one who has a German boyfriend while you are making plans with me to travel.*"

Then I understood that he was sick. I was a bald woman, with a little wig in my purse, I weighed just a little bit more than my daughter, I was kind enough to accept his invitation to dinner even though it needed lots of energy. I called my Mother and called my daughter and told them that I was too tired and needed to go home at once.

***

While I was driving back home, my Mother tried to say something, possibly something affirmative, but I said:

"*I'd like to drive in quiet. I do not feel like talking right now. I am too tired.*"

My Mother kept her lips sealed together with a little smile, my daughter fell asleep on the back seat, and I was driving them and a thousand thoughts in my head.

I was thinking of Claude.

I was thinking of his mother. Even though she never liked me, and I never liked her because of that, silently I thanked her for bringing him up to be a kind and gentle soul from whom I learned what kindness was and what love should look like.

I was thinking of my husband who had left. The years came back and the pictures were changing on the screen of my memory: while I was driving my car, it seemed to me that I was driving through them: how many beautiful moments, how much care, how much giving, how much laughter, how many dreams and support, how much comfort when in distress or battling my depression brought on by uncontrollable creativity and restless determination to put it in some sort of order. The joy we shared being parents to our daughter. I was thinking of our dreams and his weaknesses, I was thinking of his mother who feared my creativity more than I did. Maybe she feared that creative people were not stable or sane ... who knows.

I thought about the Other Man and how much kindness and support he gave me in my endeavours, in my travels and personal struggles. I thought of our dance, of his insecure yet honest hands, they were trembling while he would touch the little strand of my hair.

I thought about my breasts, about my youth, about my travels and about the ultimate destination of my travels. I stopped the car, put my head on the steering wheel and cried. My Mother did not ask why I cried, she put my head onto her breasts and pressed it tightly, I could hear her heart beating fast. All I could hear was the beating of her frightened heart and the breathing of my child while she was carefree in her innocent dream.

I said to my Mother:

"Mother, I do not want to die, for I have not lived long enough, I haven't loved enough, I haven't laughed enough, I haven't travelled enough and haven't seen enough of the world and its people, I haven't written all the words I wanted to write. Mother, I do not want to die young, for there are so many people out there I want to be with; you and my daughter, my siblings and my friends, I do not have time for sorrows and wrong choices ... I can see the world right now in its original form, I can understand right now why we are here. Just to be, to experience, to share, to love. My heart was broken because it needed to be, to let more love in, more love for the world, more love for life and all forms of it."

Mother held my head without a word.

***

A few days passed and Erwin called. His voice was apologetic yet playful. Teasing. Just to call me at that time, this idea was sacrilegious to me, for he knew that I had now my daily visits to hospital and was quite exhausted. He knew that my Mother was going home in two weeks, so he said something like, "Now that your Mother is going back, you will need me more than ever" and as I had never initiated our friendship or any of our meetings, I had never considered our friendship to be more than what it was, nor did I consider it to be a failure, for failure occurs only when we do not meet our expectations, and knowing him well enough, I did not expect anything, for his life was very different to mine and his values were the values of the people I did not meet in the circle of my friends. He said that I was far too serious a person and did not recognize jokes. He said he joked that evening to make it funny and light. But I told him that that evening was neither funny nor light to me and he blamed me, telling me that it was like that because I was the one who did not play either funny or light notes on my internal instrument.

When he said that he knew that I was bitterly disappointed with him, as I was hoping for a more serious relationship, I told him to stop such nonsense, for I understood what he wanted to achieve. He wanted to see me hurting. He wanted me to tell the world not how much I loved him but how much he had hurt me. But neither happened; I never loved him the way a woman loves a man; he never hurt me, for the quality of our friendship was not worth mentioning. He called my former husband by all the names that hatred can summon, but may I put it this way: he hated him because I loved him.

I understood that all he wanted from me was to remember him as the one who hurt me, and I told him he never did.

This was the reason why I never wanted to tell you this story, for it has the seeds of sickness in it, and when I told the complete story to St. Yvonne and my Mother in the end, they could not find the words.

That was all.

That was all for me, but not for him.

CHAPTER SEVEN

When we had packed my Mother's bags, we put them in the middle of the living room and all three of us fixed our gaze on different points to keep our tears at bay in our eyes. The words ran into the past and we could not find any word, so my daughter sat at her piano and started to play. That was her way of coping with the moment of silence caused by three heavy bags in the middle of our living room, their heaviness indicating that the inevitable would happen in just a few moments, as we were waiting for a call from the taxi service operator. The music was pleasant regardless of a few wrong notes caused by her intense restlessness.

I feared going to the hospital all by myself, for I thought about how cold, impersonal and indifferent the events, relations and people in that building would be from now on. I knew I would not have her hand to hold me while we were walking in, while we were waiting and while she helped me to dress and put my little wig on. I feared that she would take all the colours of my soul with her, for my soul became so colourful when she landed six months ago.

I feared the words, she feared the words and my daughter played her piano and the wrong notes were flying around her head. Usually a very skilled and critical player, she could not care less about the notes now, she just played. Yes, she just played.

With the sharp sound of the ringing telephone, the awkward moment was broken, like a thin glass. The taxi, we all thought, and I headed towards the ringing phone, my Mother towards the three bags and my daughter was still playing.

Erwin said that he wanted to talk to my Mother. He wished her a 'bon voyage' and told her that we would visit her that coming summer. He said to my Mother not to worry about me, for he was there for me whenever I was in need. She thanked him and the second time when the telephone rang, we took the bags and walked out. These bags and my legs were among the heaviest experiences in my life.

We kept silent in the car.

We kept silent at the airport. I checked the ticket and meticulously had done all the things which had to be done, we were free of luggage, free to hold our hands, afraid to look at each other, I knew I could not be a child again and say, "Do not go, Mummy," but it was exactly how I felt, yes, it was exactly how I felt. Our eyes looked like glass eyes full of moistness and sadness and my daughter hugged my Mother and started to cry. With a solemn voice, I said:

"Please don't, we will see Grandma in a few months," but I was not sure, how could I be?

We saw her back, she turned once again before other people covered her body, but what I saw last were her eyes and tears streaming down her red face. We were holding our hands and crying. I said:

"All is well, this is the nature of life, when we greeted her here six months ago, we knew that we would have to wave goodbye, all is well."

But we were dragging our feet, fearing the emptiness of our living room, for all her life was packed in three bags and there would be no evidence that she had been here at all.

She turned to me and said with a different expression on her pretty, curious face:

"Where is my father?"

"Somewhere in the Far East, isn't he?"

"Yes, but what I wanted to say was where is he when I need him?"

"I can't answer this question, sorry I can't."

"He is never here when I need him," she said, and she started to cry different tears now, and my chest was full of fire from the daily visits to the hospital; nevertheless I pressed her little head onto my wounds and I said:

"Cry, my baby, cry, you will feel better after a good cry."

I kept my tears in my burning chest and said to God:

"Your ways are mysterious, oh, how mysterious."

And the other voice said, "There is no such thing as God, no, there is no God" but I, in any case, did not want to be a consequence of his cosmic joke. After this thought, I could not be bothered any more, but said to my daughter that we needed a good breakfast.

I was thinking of her father. I saw him with a woman three days after he had left. He brought her home to his mother and said she was a friend. I saw him with a different woman at the local café, toying with her hand.

Then my daughter got a call from the Far East. He said he would buy her a big house. She said she would be happier in a little house only if he lived closer. He came back with a short woman with narrow eyes and hid her in the house, how peculiar, oh, how peculiar.

He came with debts and he was not talking any longer of buying a house for my daughter. What he wanted was to sell our house to pay his Far East debts. He was a broken man, but I did not know whether he knew that or whether he was still chasing what was written in his birth chart, as The Wise One told him to do some years earlier.

She said that he was useless and I said that he was sad, and when she asked how I knew that he was sad but not useless, I said that happiness came from usefulness, hence, that his uselessness was rather a sign of deep sadness.

She said:
"Mum, you are my hero," and I said, "You are mine," and when she finished her breakfast, she was in a better mood. She said:
"Shall we go home now, or would it be better to go elsewhere now?"
I said, "Elsewhere," for I did not want to come to the empty house, which did not contain any evidence that my Mother had lived there for six months. While we were planning to go to the city, the mobile rang and St. Yvonne invited us for lunch.
How thoughtful, how thoughtful.

***

When Mae rang from London telling me that he had left without a word but with an empty bank account, I wanted to say, "I saw this coming," but I did not, just as I did not say a word when I met him a few years earlier that warm Andalucian night, full of sweet smells and sounds coming with the light wind down from Morocco where he had left his young, untamed Moroccan beauty. I did not tell her that I had put my white linen dress on and joined them after midnight in their drunken rampage, even though I had an excuse for joining - curiosity.
I heard from the tremor of her voice that her inner being was shattered into tiny splinters and because of it, and partly because I felt guilty for not telling her, I promised that we would come to London as part of our European wanderings.

In as many airports as we had landed, the crowd everywhere looked the same. The airports are the world in miniature: the colours, the costumes, the languages, the features. The huge buildings are busy and noisy but amongst everything, one emotion prevails - excitement. You can see altered moods; hear high-pitched voices, exchanging warnings. There are hugs, kisses and tears in abundance.
Heathrow is the busiest and because of it, the one that holds the most excitement, regardless of the fact it is set in the British capital. Even though

my daughter was tired from the long trip, Heathrow's atmosphere and the anticipation of seeing dear friends kept her alert and chatty.

I spotted her at once. I gently smiled, seeing the kind but quite serious face she had when in public.

She always used to say that I was her sister, as I say that you, my dear friend, are my brother, for real sisters and brothers are seldom born under the same roof.

The girls had grown much and could not even remember each other, apart from the little stories we told them and kept repeating them. When we embraced each other, I saw all our years connected in a little quick movie that was running through her hair and as we could not let go of each other, the girls started to call our names. As we walked, we held each other's hands and our daughters walked a few steps behind, for young girls are easily embarrassed by the gestures of adult tenderness.

When she said, "I love your hair, you look like Annie Lennox," I said, "I love my hair, because it is real."

We were walking the streets of London impatiently, for all we wanted was to sit somewhere and talk, and talk and talk, the way we used to talk many years ago when we shared our secrets, pains and joys together.

With some friends we are connected with an invisible cord and the freshness and authenticity of our relationship is always the same. It looked as if we had never parted. The warmness I felt when with Mae was the same warmness I felt when I was with my daughter; something very genuine, simple and ever-present. These were even more reasons why I felt like a foe when I was thinking of her drunken husband, who paid me a visit not knowing even who I was.

I decided I would tell her this story on one of these days we planned to spend together, for it had really started to walk behind my back as a shadow, and the shadows in our friendship were nonexistent and when my hair fell off, I promised myself that I would never have the shadows behind my back. Never.

***

When she told me he went down to Morocco, I said to her, "I know," and she said, "Oh, how spooky, you always know the unknown," but I said that my knowledge did not come from the 'spookiness,' the unknown or from my oracular talents, but rather from the very known fact, which made my friend surprised. But we hadn't finished this story, for there were more important ones and as I assumed that the story of the Moroccan untamed beauty was still painful for my little Mae and the silent flotilla in her body, I deliberately avoided it, as she liked to avoid cruel, windy, winters of the Isle of Man.

When all the stories were told, I was ready to tell her the story of how I knew he went down to Morocco, which by the third day of our stay in London had become my nightmare, threatening to leak into reality and sour my new, otherwise pleasurable day. I started to dream about drunken Nicholas and his painter friend, and their visits to my London dreams were displaced. Even though I asked myself a number of times whether it was a crucial piece of information, I felt like I was obliged to tell her out of sheer loyalty.

I took a deep breath in and was ready to tell her the story without pausing for breath, but the telephone rang and after a short conversation she told me that we were invited to dinner at a French restaurant by her friends, who were curious to meet me, for as we were the mirrors of our friends they wanted to mirror themselves in different cultural settings. So I kept the story that had occurred under the Andalucian stars for 'better times' - I did not want to spoil her dinner talking about the man who nearly sank her boats beyond repair.

When we walked into the restaurant, it was already three-quarters full of dynamic people. Nearly all of her friends were there, and to be precise in number, there were nine adults and three children, excluding us. Mae's daughter and mine were just two years apart and they spoke the language we could not understand, for today's children speak in the language known only to the experts of the technological era. They talked to us only when hungry or when there was a need for any sort of short information. There were another three children about the same age and after a while they were sitting with their heads together, looking at the small screen.

Mae's friends were more English than Mae, from my position of objective observer. Mae was a warm and soft soul with a calm, inoffensive tone, with big dark eyes that easily could be moist, often for an unknown reason, but she blamed her Celtic soul for expressing itself in this way through her eyes. They were extremely polite and considerate, I was thinking of some characters from the English classics, and laughed internally, for they really behaved this way.

I sat next to a man; Tom Boyd was his real name, a former friend of Mae's ex-husband, a writer of short stories well known by a famous pseudonym. He wanted to know more about my writings. I could have had one of the most enjoyable evenings but something happened which changed the tone of the evening.

Somebody called out his name:

"Tom! Tom Boyd!" and a thin man, with a wobbly walk, hurried towards the table. Expressions on the faces changed, the faces now had an expression of annoyance, as if a hailstorm of shattered glass was approaching which would cut sharply and at random.

"Where have you been, you bastard?"

And he sat nearly on my lap.

When drunk, his Irish accent was as sharp as glass, and even I was in the same state of uneasiness as others were, but they could not grasp the deeper meaning of my feelings, for they believed that I had just met the misfortunate drunk. No, no, dear friends, I wanted to say, we were friends one long, warm, Andalucian summer when I had my crushed heart in my pocket, when I could not wait for the night to come to hide my sorrowful eyes; then he would knock on my low window and ask me to come out and share his drunken evenings under the pleasant sky. There I wanted to say to Mae that I owed her an untold story, but it was too late, Nicholas was sitting on the half of my chair, drinking the wine from Tom's glass.

How exciting, oh, how exciting.

Tom said:

"Look, Nicholas, we have here a friend we haven't seen for a long time, how about giving me a call sometime next week and then I'll see what I can do for you."

"Yeah, but you do not return my calls, do you?"

"I promise I will ... plus the woman at your table is sitting there all alone."

"I can call her to join in or tell her to go to hell."

Mae, sitting on my right-hand side leaned over me and said:

"Nicholas, you are sitting on my friend's dress."

He turned and looked at Mae, then looked at me.

He said:

"Do I know you?"

I smiled. He said:

"I know your smile."

I smiled again. He said:

"I know your eyes."

I smiled. He said:

"Do not smile; say something, where did I meet you?"

Tom said:

"I think this is rather a matter of a mistaken identity. Nicholas...."

But Nicholas cut his sentence in half, and said, touching my hand which was resting on the table:

"Have you ever heard that there was a woman who was writing two identical letters to two different men?"

Mae protested:

"Do we really need his theatre now?"

Nicholas said:

"You see, I have never knocked on your window again."

I smiled.

Tom apologized, Mae apologized, but when the others joined together in an attempt to silence Nicholas in his, as Mae said, theatre, I said:

"I met Nicholas several years ago in Cadiz, down in Andalucia and yes, I was writing my letters when he met me, and he chased my scarf as the levante took it off my head, he brought it back and that was how we met."

I did not say that when I met him, I learned that he was drawn to stories of a miserable outcome. When he followed that woman down to Andalucia, he already had disappointment tattooed on the bicep of his right arm. The bicep of the other arm was bare at that time; reserved for the future disappointments which would be taken gladly, for his behaviour was dictated from the depths that he was not aware existed, but to which he was as obedient as a little powerless wooden soldier.

That sentence was permission for Nicholas to stay, for he said that he was overjoyed to see an old friend. Mae whispered:

"I remember you told me you met him there, how bizarre, how, bizarre."

Even though he brought his own chair, he literally glued himself to me. He sat next to me, excited to tell me how that summer ended and how he found himself again in Belfast, then in London again.

He said to my friends that down in Cadiz people thought me to be mad, which made us all quite surprised and I asked him again, *"What did they think about me?"* and he said, *"That you were a mad woman,"* and when I asked by which criteria that was brought to conclusion, he said, *"Mine, for I told people down on the beach, down in the tavernas or on the streets that you were quite mad for writing identical letters to two different men and the letters were never answered."*

I said:

"One lot of the letters was not answered, only one, but from the other recipient I received letters almost every day."

"Why did you send the letters to the man who never replied? Why would you do that? I can understand that you exercised your skills, but I always

*wanted you to answer why you insisted on sending him letters which would
never be opened?"*

I said:

"I don't know, I simply do not know, Nicholas. That's all I can say."

"Have you ever published them?"

*"I have published 'The letters to Ted,' but they were quite different, even
though Ted was one of the recipients of my Cadizian letters. Though, Ted
was not his real name."*

*No, Ted was not his real name, I smiled and Mae showed her little sad
smile.*

*It was only a few years earlier that I met Nicholas and told him that he
looked young and sinless. He had the face of an angel at that time, but the
habits of a demon, and I really believed, judging just from his face, that he
was very young. He had green eyes with little brown squares in them and
these squares looked to me like little dormant piranhas swimming peacefully
in that green ocean, but when the winds of Nicholas's moods would change
the waters, the piranhas would come alive, threatening to swim into his brain
and eat it all up.*

*His dark brown hair was never combed and looked as if it was seldom
washed. He had freckles on his nose and underneath his green eyes, and
these freckles made him look boyish. He had straight, long teeth darkened by
cigarette smoke. His breath was unbearably unpleasant, so when he talked to
me, I would tilt my head backwards while trying to keep my body straight.
Even though he was tall, his frame was boyish again. Lean muscles and a
thin frame made him look fragile.*

*But what I could see a few years later was that he also did not carry his
years well any longer, because of the abuse of alcohol, perhaps other
substances as well, and late nights made him age before his time.*

*Do you remember when I said that rumour had it in Cadiz that he had
written some ten novels and won no less than three Booker Prizes?*

*Mae said that he had written two novels and they were rather of moder-
ate success. He tried to publish short stories but he was not skilled in
expressing himself in short stories, so he never found a publisher who would
be willing to publish his wicked stories about women he met on his travels to
other lands and realms.*

*When he got drunk, he started to mix places, names and stories and no-
body could make any sense of what he was talking about. When he said to
Mae that her ex-husband visited us in Cadiz on his way to Morocco, Mae*

said, "I see, I see, " and then I decided that I would not tell her that story, for what would be the use?

What would be the use?

Nicholas drank our wine and ate from each of our plates, deaf to the protests and comments, and I can freely say that I had never met anyone closer to the idea of doing what he wanted in each moment. The most free-spirited child could not match his freedom from the opinions and comments of others. But that evening I saw something else as well and never was able to name it. Whichever name it carried, it left him often in self-contradiction and confusion.

Suddenly, with a conviction that would not allow a second of delay, he said in the end that somebody was waiting for him at the pub around the corner and he needed to go urgently.

What if I tell you that he planted a wet, smelly, greasy kiss on my cheek?
Mae said:
"How disgusting, oh, how disgusting, " and I said:
"There are all sorts of misfortunate people out there, still, they are people. In some, we can clearly see ill health, while with others, it is hidden, but whoever has been ill learns not to judge. For our own sake, we must learn to lift ourselves out of judgment and condemnation. Who does not have faults? Who is the one who wants to perpetuate them? Nobody is proud of their own limits and flaws. If we lift ourselves from the burden of other's errors and mistakes, we experience lightness in our inner world, and more and more I do believe that the inner world is more real than the outer, or shall I say, the inner creates the outer?"
Mae looked at me and smiled, she said:
"How much I missed you, " and I said the same, looking down through her eyes into the light and the darkness, which she carried in her heart, at the same time.

As Mae and I renewed our memories over the past three days I dedicated myself to Tom's stories; the real and the fictional ones. We never mentioned Nicholas again, I did not know what had Tom done with him, but I sent him back to the Andalucian beach, hoping that the levante would carry him out of my mind, out of my way.

That evening in London, Andalucia looked so far away to me. Not because of the geographical point but rather from the state of my inner being.

With my suitcase and my child, I carried to Andalucia lots of pain hidden in various parts of my body and in various thoughts and memories. I carried my heavy heart and believed then that there was not a healer known to this world who would be trained in the art of healing my broken heart. I would dream the most vivid dreams, which I could never distinguish properly from the unidentified reality I lived these days. I learned the language of the wind and the whispers of the sand and was conversing fast and quietly with both; the wind and the sand, and that was what Nicholas was referring to as being mad.

Was I mad at that time?
What makes us mad?
The pain? Unanswered questions? Lack of understanding? Lack of trust? Loneliness? Suddenly revealed truth? Longing for home? The fear of vastness of the universe? Or just our own mind?
What I had experienced at that time deeply grieved me, it deeply grieved me ... and I sincerely hoped that in this unceasing, vast, meaningless or meaningful universe my words would find their place.

***

Now She was looking at the Nobleman as if She was waiting for the answers. This time She looked to me as a passenger who travelled many roads and read many maps and because of that mastered the knowledge of patient waiting. There was no other way for the answers to come but through patience, or otherwise they never come.

Next time She came, She was wearing a light, linen dress. She had selected it carefully as if She was going on a much-anticipated date. I dare say that She looked prettier than ever, counting from the time She met the Nobleman for the first time.

She thought about the many changes that had occurred in Her inner world since She met him. I saw how these changes reflected in the selection of her clothes; the colours were brighter, the materials were lighter and Her trademark black jeans, black skivvies and black boots slowly were exchanged for light-coloured dresses.

***

When we came to my Mother's home, the first night I had a dream that made me restless for the rest of the week.

146

I dreamt that I read in the local papers a rather disturbing piece of news which said that from such and such date it was forbidden to write untrue stories, which meant all fiction was to be destroyed and authors of the same punished for causing and inflicting too much pain to their fictional characters, as God himself did not approve any longer of writers taking his role and deciding people's fate.

I found myself among other gathered protestors and when I was about to object loudly, I heard a loud voice addressing me:

"My will be done, not yours!" and I asked him where he was when I was ill and he said in a loud voice again:

"Who killed Barbara without my permission?" and I was speechless.

That speechlessness made me wake up in a cold sweat. My heart was beating as if it was attacked by a pack of hungry wolves, for I knew that I had recycled my words, reprinting them some twenty years later, and all the feelings of that time followed, as if in those words those particular feelings were encoded.

I could not disown my words, my stories and their characters.

I remember, I asked God in that dream wasn't he the one who told me in yet another dream to write the stories and let the characters out of their cages? But he said that the new regulations and rules had been voted for by the majority and all I had to do was to obey.

I entertained my chewing with the morning newspapers and I found there the article whose author assumed what I meant and felt while portraying a certain character, and it was not even close to my feelings and intentions, but on the contrary, it was quite the opposite.

I remembered his name vaguely from the already forgotten narrow streets of our youth, the streets he never left, but walked confidently, for often confidence accompanies narrowness. This might sound conflicting to you, but a second deeper thought widens this statement.

After that dream and the article in the local papers, I made a vow to the creative part of my mind to write next time a story with real characters and events.

After this resolution, the Almighty, who earlier visited my dream, came back as if my vow to the creative part of my mind was exactly what he wanted when he visited unexpectedly.

It was just the beginning of the summer, the days were long and warm, I was wearing a light, linen dress, I would sit in one of the numerous cafés on the main piazza in the town and in the rumour of the town's rhythm I would listen to my past, present and hear fragments of my future. Life looked so easy while I was breathing a calm, familiar atmosphere (which was as welcoming as the beautiful young waitresses) into my mind for future references.

Then another dream came to my easy night and the visitor of my dream appeared to be a waiter from the flamenco taverna, the one with a little moustache that resembled Salvador Dali's. Hard to say if I was pleased or not, but I knew for certain that I was pleasantly surprised, and he said to me:
"You can keep it here if you wish, for not only dreams are dreams, but our lives are as real as dreams are, and as unreal as dreams are. You can keep it in the dreams."

What I was to keep in the dreams was not clear to me, but when I was at my Mother's home I never cared about interpreting my dreams, only when abroad, I would listen to my dreams, begging them to reveal their symbolism to me, telling me what was going to happen, whether I could escape unknown catastrophes or whether there were any.

***

Listen to this now:

Some might say it was early in the morning, but as I got up with the song of the first birds, ten o' clock was almost midday for me.
We were sitting on the sun-lit verandah sipping our second cup of coffee.
The day started lazily as all days do on this earthly quota. I decided to stroll down to the main, cobbled piazza where I was familiar with the sounds of my heels and my heart, and start my search for inspiration in the quick and changing slides produced by casual protagonists.

The doorbell rang.
My Mother asked:
"Can you get the door?"
She always gets up first. She always gets the door.
I looked at her again, as if I needed to confirm what I heard, and the doorbell rang again, and again she said in her calm tone:
"Get the door, please," with the clear intention of staying right where she was.

Knowing her ever-accommodating attitude I hesitated a while, then she said:

"Hurry up."

She had a strange expression on her calm face, the one of secret conspiracy - that was what I thought while I was going to answer the door.

I opened the door and a tall man, with dark but mellow eyes, was standing in front of me.

When I recognized his face, or shall I say, his mellow eyes, I thought it was a mirage, for the day was bright and hot already and the air was tremulous and I thought of his tremulous fingers that would gently put in place a strand of my untamed hair.

All my words deserted me at once, especially those that would best accompany my feelings, so he was the one who said:

"Will you let me in, or...."

"Of course, of course," I said, and he walked in.

I took the lead and walked him to the sun-lit verandah where I was sipping the second cup of coffee with my Mother, but as if it was just a dream, the verandah was empty, the table was bare and all I said was:

"Shall we sit?" He sat down and crossed his legs.

He crossed his fingers and I crossed my heart.

He smiled.

I asked:

"Is this a mirage?"

He said:

"I told you, you were my dream."

I said:

"So, we woke in the same dream this morning."

All he said was:

"We did."

We did not need a lot of words. He looked at the calm surface of the sea and said, "So peaceful," and I repeated, "So peaceful."

I forgot to offer him a cup of coffee, maybe a piece of cake, or maybe breakfast, for my Mother was like a ghost in her own house and I believed that the house was enchanted; unusually quiet this morning, for in my parents' house mornings were spiced with inviting smells and impatient voices - *my father wanted his coffee, my daughter wanted her pancakes, the radio played the music and Mother listened to the local news.*

It wasn't the same house that morning. I was young again that entirely different and profoundly meaningful morning which left me short of words as youth can be short of words when confronted with sudden, deep feelings.

Some time had passed in this atmosphere of sweet uneasiness when I realized that we had to say something or do something, for it could not be a permanent state where we placed ourselves among silent thoughts and irregular heartbeats.

"How did you know?" said I.
He smiled.
I asked:
"How did you find me?"
He nodded his head barely noticeably.

I knew that a man with his possibilities and his access to any kind of information could find me any time anywhere only if he wished to do so. And that was what made me speechless, that he wished so.

My Mother came in, after what seemed to be an eternity and without any introduction started to talk to him in a different language (the one which was compulsory, years back when she went to school.)

How odd, I thought, how odd.

Again all of that resembled a dream, and I really did not know whether I fell asleep on the warm verandah or was I just daydreaming and mixing the other reality, when I used to dance with him in his garden overlooking the ocean, edged with tall palm trees and our poorly hidden yearnings?

I could not understand what they were talking in that language which was compulsory in her school days, so I said to my Mother:
"Mother, what are you talking about?" but instead of her he spoke, asking me to take a little walk on such a beautiful, sunny day.
I put on my light, linen dress and black leather sandals, took my bag and without combing my short hair headed towards the main door. He followed, then turned back and thanked my Mother. They shook hands and we found ourselves walking slowly through the narrow, cobbled streets of my youth

and all I thought was - how unpredictable, oh, how unpredictable life could be.

He transported me into this slow-motion reality I had experienced when I was with him. Everything was slow, meaningful and in the right place as if touched by grace: I heard the noise of the traffic as if it was in yet another faraway dream, I heard his soft voice mixed with birds singing, I felt the hardness and softness of the cobbled stones under my soft leather shoes, I felt the breeze on my cheeks and his fingers trying to keep the little, short strand of my hair away from my forehead. I said:
"You cannot win, the tramontana always played with my hair." As we walked these familiar streets, he held my hand in his and I felt at the same time whole and displaced, for neither of us belonged to these cobbled streets while hand in hand.

We sat on the sun-lit terrace with little, round tables and he said:
"I hoped to see you last summer in Dubrovnik," and I said:
"I do not like that crowded city with narrow streets."
He said:
"I like your hair," and I smiled.
He said:
"The thing is, I do not have excuses now for touching your hair or your face. Looks like your long locks were my ally."
And I moved my face next to his and touched his lips with my frail fingers.

We talked about my health, about my letters, about his new duties and new placements. We talked about his children, about my daughter, we talked about a few Hispanic writers, we talked about the ice-cream that we ate, about food, about Andalucia and again about my letters, for he said:
"I miss your letters," and I said:
"I miss them, too."
"Re-reading your letters I understood that I never really knew you well."
"Neither did I, neither did I."

When I think of that I could have said that all my life I tried to understand who I was, for there were within me all sorts of conflicting emotions and needs, even though I dare say that the main patches of my personality were sewn with a thread of melancholy. But all I chose to say was, "Neither did I."

I learned that he heard from his Andalucian friend that I was coming to Europe, but not to Andalucia this time, for when I was there, I carried with me lots of pain and hurtful memories and I was afraid if I went there again, they could haunt me, for as I said before, they were buried in the sand on the long beach, there where the Paseo Maritimo stretches.

I learned that he was going to Vienna and when he heard I was home, at my Mother's, all he wanted was to see me again, to see my eyes, which had left him restless since the first time he saw them. I said:
"They were a sky for yellow clouds...."
And he said:
"Let's not talk about the past, you know better, I know your letters; let's talk about your plans and your bright future."
And we did.

A short time after the church bell counted twelve, we agreed to have lunch.
The birds flew off the cathedral.
We walked again hand in hand and between us was a deep peace, the one experienced by mystics and seers.

I chose the restaurant, and it was odd to walk in with him hand in hand, for I first walked in some twenty-five years before, so I felt as if I was young again, as if the past and present merged together and gave me a new, sweet feeling.

There was a white, linen tablecloth covering the table, covering our knees, which started touching and dancing under the table and I said:

"Do you remember our last dance?"
"Should it be the last?"
"We do not know the answers; it would be brave and foolish to pretend to know the unknown."
"But we certainly can decide, we can choose."
I smiled.
He said:
"When are you coming back?"
I looked out, through the narrow window, onto the narrow street.
He said:
"What keeps you there any longer? Why don't you come back to Europe ... to me?"

I said:

"Look at my hometown, how beautiful it is with its cobbled streets and old buildings which resemble the pages from an old picture book. Look at the sea, so peaceful, can you feel the tramontana, can you hear the birds? When you ask me whether I miss it, I can freely say I do. What keeps me there? Look at these narrow, cobbled streets and listen! There is something beneath the perfect picture-book image. This is a little town with many rules and its people are quick in temper and judgmental, and because of it, in this beautiful land we had wars for centuries. In these narrow streets many were killed, women were raped, the flags were changed but nothing new came. People in authority always had and will avert their eyes from crime and corruption. Common people never learned what tolerance and democracy was, and probably never will, for there is a lot of hidden and open anger and hatred in this little country and the little neighbouring states, and I do not have time for anger or for hatred.

I discovered new, wide avenues and left these narrow streets behind many years ago, all I need when I come here is to remember my past, for I do live in the past, as all writers do. Writers are like historians - interpreting the short history of human existence set in the frame of time and a certain ambience. And how shall I live apart from my past when it made me who I am and placed me exactly where I stand? I have a child born in a country where democracy was written and has been practised over many years; when she comes here, even though she is very young and inexperienced, she notices that what they lack is tolerance. Everyone, from the shopkeepers to the bus drivers, is short-tempered and quick to insult without thinking, because this is their first impulse.

And nothing really ever happened in this small country that would bear significance in the intervals of sleepy repentance of its days between two wars. The wars would awake the dormant beast and the little that was done to advance the civilization there was ruined and humiliated by raw impulses of suppressed hatred. No, I don't think I will be back ever, for all my needs are met; for all I need is to put my laptop on the table and answer the phone when my daughter needs me."

He said:

"You don't have to live here. Come to Paris, come to Vienna."

He was silent, for his thoughts sank among the pictures of what might have been possible.

I smiled, thinking of Paris, thinking of Vienna, I said:

"I have been to Paris and I have been to Vienna. I have been to Venice and Rome; and I have been to Turin, Toronto and Sydney. I have been to Andalucia, all by myself writing love letters to you, I have been to Madrid,

thinking of you, I have been to Cadiz and Landon. And none of them is home."

And he asked:

"Where is home?"

I said:

"Nowhere and everywhere."

He kept looking at his plate. I was looking at the window and the shadows of the poplar tree on the window's glass. It reminded me of Madrid, of the day we arrived at the airport and a taxi took us downtown and we were delighted at the sight of all these tall, leafy and elegant poplar trees. That day I had written in my diary that I loved him. He said:

"I hope we'll stay in touch. I hope you'll write me your pale-blue letters...."

I said:

"On the day we landed in Madrid I had written in my diary that I loved you."

He said:

"Perfect platonic love...."

"But not less real because of it. I had always dreamt of idealistic, platonic love, fearing if it came to life, it would lose its sweetness."

"You never really told me that you loved me."

"No, I never did."

"Because...."

"I did not want to cause any harm, to hurt anybody. I was already deeply hurt and you were there like the stone of wisdom."

He said:

"Come back to Europe. Settle down in Andalucia, for it looks to me that you loved it there the best."

"It only looks like it, but all I want to do is to write."

"You can write wherever you are."

"Listen to this. Last night while I was sleeping, God, the Almighty, visited my dream and told me to stop making up my stories and its protagonists, but to write about real people and my own experiences."

He asked:

"Will you write about me?"

"I dream about you," I said and he smiled.

The waiter came, he called me by my first name and I was quite sure that I had never met him before, but what I liked was that lost feeling of closeness with people you barely know. I was not an expert in matters of closeness, so all I could offer to the waiter who called me by my first name was an uncertain smile.

He was called because my friend suggested a dessert and after a short discussion, we decided to take only one cake, made of seasoned fruit, to be precise, of different wild berries. It came on an enormous white plate edged with melted chocolate. The cake had on it a thick layer of cream, which reminded me of an intact layer of snow, and how odd, I was thinking why it did not melt, for summer was hot and humid at the same time.

The cake was made of brown flour, which reminded me of earth; the little, colourful berries looked like the hats of dwarfs covered with a heavy layer of snow and I almost felt pity for these little people, wondering how they were going to withstand that heavy blanket of cold snow and icing. When he caught my eyes fixed on the cake, he was puzzled and I told him how sorry I felt for these little trapped yet innocent people.

And he laughed, he laughed.

And I laughed with him.

He fed me with little hats and a thick layer of snow and while I was carefully eating the little people's hats, he said that the way I saw things was always different and always amazed him, and I said it was because I looked beyond the outer appearance. And he said:

"How do you do that?" I just smiled and then said that images and the intellect must be transcended, for subtle things were only accessible by intuition.

I told him that I had never eaten from the same plate with anybody and he asked me if he was privileged, but what I did instead of giving him an answer was to dip my index finger in the snow, then in melted chocolate and painted these sweet creams onto his lips. He had a boyish look in his mellow eyes and I simply kissed his chocolate, delicious lips.

When it came to dessert that was all.

Later I said to him that he had to feel our local wind, for in these late hours the tramontana came down from the mountains bringing freshness and ease, and I took his hand and led him along our lungomare and told him stories of my youth while we were walking towards the sunset.

He said that he had a very important meeting in Vienna and he asked me to join him for a few days, but I said that I would rather stay at home and keep him in my dream; he looked into my eyes and said:

"How difficult, oh, how difficult."

I said to him that I knew I was difficult, but I learned that a long time ago and I accepted it was the way it was, for I needed to live with myself for the rest of my days and the only way to live in harmony was to accept all that was there.

He said:

"How complicated, oh, how complicated."

And I shrugged my shoulders, and he asked:

"Are you cold?" for the breeze was coming down from the cold mountains.

He offered me the light, pale-blue cardigan that he was casually carrying over his shoulders and when I put the cardigan on, it smelled of him and I told him that I loved this smell, for it smelled like our dream, years ago when we were dining and dancing in his beautiful garden edged with tall palm trees.

We found an empty bench and sat on it, for the sunset was, in his words, "The most spectacular," so we watched the sun slowly melting down into its own wavy image in the sea. When the sea swallowed 'the most spectacular' sun mirrored in it just a few minutes before, it suddenly grew dark and cold. I moved closer to him and he kissed my nose and my lips and said that he was grateful for the sudden, unexpected coolness, for I pressed my body onto his.

When it was dark enough, enough to hide my pride and frailty, I said:

"I went to hospital and you never rang."

He kissed my hair.

After a long silence, he said in a quiet voice:

"I thought that it was the time for your husband to be by your side. I believed that this misfortune would bring him closer to you. I did not dare ... but do not think that I did not care. Please, do not think that I did not care."

All of a sudden I felt as if I was breathing with full lungs, deep fresh breaths and wondered: was it because of the tramontana or what?

Still, silence prevailed, for we did not want to disturb such a perfect, idyllic picture, his voice was still quiet when he looked into my eyes and said:

"Do not think that I did not care."

I said:

"Will you walk me home or what?"

"I can walk you home, for I have a few hours before leaving for Vienna ... but if you wish to stay a little longer...." and I said:

"Yes, I do."

And I stayed.

He took my hand and walked me to his car and we were driving around listening to quiet music, listening to our own thoughts and our own heart-beats, for their little drums could be heard in the short sequences of silence when softer notes were played.

He stopped the car and then we watched the big yellow moon, proud and full like a pregnant woman, and I asked:

"How is your lovely wife?"

"She is well. Her practice is always full and the list of her patients is long. She has no time for other things but work, she loves her work."

And I said:

"Do you love your work?"

And he said:

"I love you."

"Wow," I said. "Wow."

We were sitting in the car and I felt the same old unease when he said that he should be going, I did not say, "Stay" and I did not say, "Go."

But I hugged him.

Yes, I did.

I knew he would never leave his wife and I would never wish for that. I am asking you now, what was I supposed to say?

She looked at the Nobleman and repeated Her question, *What was I sup-posed to say?* The Nobleman said, *"You were supposed to say what you felt, obviously you felt something ... you felt a lot."*

Yes, I did. I felt I again gave my heart to the wrong man. By now you understand that he was a sophisticated, kind soul, but knowing that he belonged to somebody else did not make me feel that I made the right choice, did not make me feel good about myself. Let me tell you this, I do not believe that people 'belong' to others as things might belong, so I can't even say that he belonged to the other woman. I knew that his love for her had gone through the open window many years ago, all they shared was care for their kids and mutual respect. I knew his background and I knew how traditional he was, for when I told him that my husband left after the pearl was taken out, he said, "Say no more."

He said that an honourable man would stay for the sake of the past days and the sake of the children and give a chance for a good recovery.

I knew what the honourable man would do, and I knew what the honour-able woman would do, so I kissed him goodbye, yes, I did, and when I saw his car in the distance and heard his horn, I knew that I would never see him again.

***

It was rather late when I walked in. Both my Mother and my daughter started to talk at the same time. I apologized to one; I apologized to the other. They asked me where I had been the whole day and I said that I needed to finish one of my stories. I told them that it was actually a dream that I brought in my suitcase and rewrote it, giving it the closure it never had. They wanted to know more about it, but all I said was that I was sitting in the restaurant downtown and had a good lunch, and for dessert a delicious berry cake with a thick layer of snow and melted chocolate and that I met a waiter who called me by my first name.

Mother said:
"You look pale, go and have a rest now," and I said:
"Mother, I do not look pale, I am not tired, let us watch a movie right now with a happy ending."
And we did.

***

When we came back from our holiday, the letter was waiting for me. My letter-box was crammed with various papers from advertising companies and the bills, but when I saw the letter, I knew it was his straight away: neat writing and the colour of the envelope perked up my tired body.

I did open it straight away. It said:

"My dear, this long, warm summer I had a very vivid dream. I dreamed of you. As I heard that you were in Europe I simply rang your Mother's house and when I told her who I was, she told me that you had arrived a few days ago. If you only knew how I longed to see you in that dream, after some troublesome years for both of us, and a missed opportunity last year because of your disliking of the old city of Dubrovnik. I knew, otherwise you would have come and seen me. I knew you would.
Even though I hadn't done something like this before it would not present an obstacle, for which obstacle would be so real as to prevent me from seeing you?

158

In my dream you walked me downtown holding my hand, for the streets were paved with cobbled stones on which simple walking was quite demanding.

We talked about our past with lots of warmth and a sort of sweet nostalgia, but on the future we could not agree, for your writing came in between us, I never understood whether it came as an excuse or you were so far away already.

You told me you intended to write a new novel with real characters and when I asked if there would be a little part where I would recognize myself as a part of your life, you said that I would be a waiter with a little moustache which would resemble Salvador Dali's moustache, and if you can remember, once I asked to be a waiter in your story.

I laughed in that dream, yes, I did, for it was so typical of you, it was you, and all I wished that summer dreamy day was to keep you in my memory forever, keep you in my book which had not been written yet.

We ate the cake from the same plate and you said that you had never eaten from the same plate with anybody; I understood that as some special gift you gave me, one which could not be exchanged or stolen but would sit in my memory forever.

I begged you to come to Paris or to Vienna but you said something quite uncertain, some definition that I could not quite understand. I did not want to be intrusive or pushy, for I know that your decisions seldom change, all I could do was to ask and hope that our dream would come true.

I saw you in the rear mirror, the wind lifted your white linen dress and that was the last image of you. I took this image in as one takes the last breath and exhaled slowly, letting my mind create a different reality for me. While I was driving, I imagined that you happily accepted my offer and went with me to Vienna, I opened the house where I was living and carried you into my bedroom. While I made love to you, you told me that you would stay in Vienna longer then I hoped for, longer than you intended....

It was a dream.

Next morning, when I woke up, I thought about the unpredictable events and people that enter our lives and what impact they have upon us.

I hope your melancholy was not a part of the parcel that you were given on the day of your birth; I hope you will read between the lines. If not, then let me put it in simple words:

I hope to see you again, to touch you again, and to love you more. "

I wanted to read it again, and again and again.
I wanted to, but I didn't.

I put that letter with the others and tied a little ribbon around them, and when my daughter asked who all the letters were from, all I said was:

"Let's go and have some sleep, we are tired after a long, long trip."

***

She fell asleep at once. I was thinking about the letter, about my dream.

I was thinking of my confused Mother, who asked me the next morning, after the evening when I came back from the town in my light linen dress, where we were. I asked, "Who, we?" and when she said his name, I said to my Mother:

"Mother, all my life I carried my theatre with me wherever I went. I carried with me all of my characters, whether they were the characters from my dreams, Andalucia or any other place or realm. I always had them all under my tent and needed not an audience.

I am asking you now, Mother - Was I the loneliest one? Was I?"

That question made her puzzled and confused. She shrugged her shoulders as one does when surrendering for having no weapons at all.

I wanted the story to be anonymous, just as the dream was, for in dreams, characters could be anonymous and often are displaced, confused, unrealistic in their expectations, or shall I say, surreal?

She heard the voice, which woke Her up from Her dream-like state. The Nobleman said:

"You wanted the story to be anonymous, just as the dream was."

She said, *Yes,* and he said, *"There is something to think about till next time...you wanted the story to be anonymous."*

They shook hands and She walked out. She walked slowly, as if She did not like the destination where She was heading. She walked slowly not knowing whether Her stories were made up or real, for if She remembered them, it could mean that they had happened.

While walking slowly, She asked Herself, *Is reality just an interpretation of our memories by which we remember past events and deeds, and could it be different if told from somebody else's little window, for each window has a different view and angle even though it could offer an outlook on the very same scenery?*

So, what if we change the angle?

CHAPTER EIGHT

She was wearing an old pair of jeans, torn on the knees. When She was a child, Her knees were always bruised, pants torn and arms scratched by the branches of the trees She climbed. Without waiting a second after She sat down, She said: *Is reality just an interpretation of our memories by which we remember past events and deeds, and could it be different if told from somebody else's little window, for each window has a different view and angle even though it could offer an outlook on the very same scenery?*

So, what if we change the angle?

So, what then?

The Nobleman did not know what to say, for knowing Her he waited for more words to come to form a new story. And even She did not wait for him to answer, but after a short pause She said:

Last time we were at Mother's the telephone rang often.

Susanne rang every day.

She just rang to hear my voice, for she needed my voice and I needed hers - they led us right into the days which we would often consider to be the best days of our lives, years later. Maybe they haven't really been 'the best days' but certainly they have been the easiest ones.

We grew up together.

Susanne was a little bit mad, that's why I loved her, and I was a little bit different and that was why she loved me.

Our 'madness' came from our own philosophy, which we created to be exclusively ours and completely opposite to other people's rules and views - and that philosophy gave us the strength and freedom to think about the future and develop in a direction which pleased only us. We were so strong in our unity of independence from thoughts and rules of the society we lived in, believing that society called upon you only to endorse it, and we were determined that we would never exchange our dreams to work for 'theirs' and to exchange our philosophy for 'theirs.' Even though we could not understand a line of Nietzsche's work at that time, we would read it and quote him regardless of whether or not it made sense or had any relevance.

We would soothe each other's broken heart with Goethe's or Schiller's poetry. We were at some time during our youth in very unique telepathic communication; one would start the sentence and the other would finish it, knowing exactly what each one wanted to say.

*We would sit on the deck of her house overlooking the calm sea, intoxi-
cated with the strong smell of pine trees and clean, fresh air and talk of
philosophy heavily spiced with nonsense the whole afternoon. I was so
skilled at making up stories that she would say to me, "C'mon, stop lying,"
which would make me turn red with rage, for I could not stand to be called a
liar, but a storyteller.*

*We shared a lot: we liked the same music, the same authors and the same
boyfriends. We went to the same school, the same holidays and the same
disco clubs; we were even driving the same car when we were a little bit
older.*

*We had very different ideas from our peers, so in order not to be teased,
bullied, or simply laughed at, we hung out together all the time for quite a
long period of our childhood and youth.*

*We were drawn to western philosophy, and with equal zest to eastern
thoughts, to mysticism and occultism and often we would read each other's
future in the empty and dirty cup of coffee, where images of the future were
very clear to us.*

*What I would read in her cup was that she was going to be the successful
manager of a famous band, for at that time she had a drummer boyfriend,
whom I had fancied a year earlier. I prophesied that she would have a lot of
money and no kids, for who would want kids to ruin your perfect career on
all these exciting locations in the world?*

*What she foresaw for me was an equally exciting life with a famous mu-
sician, and when I met Claude and fell in love with him, she was convinced
more than ever that she was a real clairvoyant.*

*We slept at each other's houses, we ate at each other's, and we shared
the clothes, the long-play records, the posters and the books. We shared the
secrets, the heartbreaks, tears and laughter.*

*My nickname at school was Proust, for my literary achievements were
read at school events and printed in school papers, and I called her the
Doctor, for her 'exceptional' skill of looking into the future.*

*We believed that we would always live 'around the corner' to pop in,
when in need.*

But life had written different scripts.
For both of us.

*The first time when I faced a totally unknown aspect of my personality
was when Claude and I decided that it would be the best to go our separate
ways.*

Instead of running home for comfort, instead of running to Susanne for comfort, I said, "Never mind."

She met me one autumn morning and I ran into the corridor of my house to hide my tears and she ran after me. After she had used up all her questions, I said that I'd like to be left alone and she walked off, telling me that she respected my wish.

If out there, somewhere in the universe of our mind, are other worlds, then they should be numerous: each world for each mood we enter.

Time passed and I was self-sufficient in the world created by the particular mood of my mind until one day she knocked on my bedroom door. I was listening to some blues and she took the record off the gramophone and said:

"So, your pain is untouchable. Divine in its origin. It lifts you where the rest of us can't reach by mortal emotions. You can't cut me off, for you owe me the rest of the story, weren't you the Storyteller? Has my Marcel Proust gone into hiding? How can we reach him?"

We hugged, we cried and after all we laughed.

She looked at the bottom of my coffee cup and told me that my future was going to be even brighter than the one I imagined to have with Claude (but it was not, looking retrospectively). She said to me that anyway Italians talked too much, promised too much, but in her opinion they were weaklings. All men were, she said, and I agreed and we listened to the music till the late hours.

Her nickname was the Doctor, but later she studied medicine and became a real one, the medical doctor who married one of my best friends but years later when I was not any more part of her daily life.

*** *

When I decided to leave my family, my hometown and my country, Susanne was the second one to hear of this decision.

She stayed silent for quite a long period of time.

She said:

"A part of me feels that this decision holds a potential for the great adventure which would give you unseen possibilities and unfold your numerous potentials, yet part of me feels that all the nourishment you could find is right here. I would like to say - do not go, but that would be dictated by my inner selfishness, for I do not want to lose you. But I am not going to tell you anything, for if your happiness lies elsewhere, you have to go and search for it. Do you remember our philosophies? Be yourself, be different."

When I saw her the last time before my leaving, she cried, as if she had known that there would be several long, hostile years before we would sit again together on the terrace of her house overlooking the calm sea in the peaceful gulf our childhood.

When we met again we were mothers.
She was a doctor and I was an author, so it looked as if our own nicknames had fulfilled their prophecy.
She looked in the bottom of my coffee cup where, by now, in the new circumstances instead of our future, our past was written.

***

We rang each other regularly, keeping each other posted.
I loved the fact that she married one of my best friends, for there was no need for learning about the other person, weighing him, liking or disliking, which would have had an impact on our friendship. I just loved George since the time I met him, and I can say that he was one of those people who got better and mellower with time. Each time I came, we would have a long dinner under the mellow, starlit sky on the terrace of their house and we would talk about the past with nostalgia and sweetness, with a strong mixture of irony and satire.

Susanne would ring me early in the morning. She knew that I was up early, for that was the best time to write my stories. If the telephone rang that early, I knew that it was her, for who in their right mind would ring at five o'clock in the morning?

It was a gray, dull morning, I was not sleeping when the telephone rang, for he took my sleep with him and left me to stare at the ceiling.
Susanne said that I sounded strange, and I said that she had woken me up.
We talked a little and she insisted that I was sounding strange.
I said:
"He left."
"Who?" Her voice was altered by anticipation.
"What do you think, who? Who else?"
I did not tell her that I had an operation, I did not tell her anything about my black pearl, for she had two ill children and I would not want to create

more distress for her. I thought if life gave us one sick child, what a difficult task it was, but two?

When she heard about my tired, cut breast, the doctor started to talk, not my friend.

After that day she rang even more regularly, always armed with new articles from medical journals, new research and new findings. She would read it to me; she would give me numerous pieces of advice and tell me about my forgotten strength.

When I told her how frightened I was, she reminded me what a fearless child I was, how easily I climbed the highest trees, crossed the busiest roads in town, learned to swim just by throwing myself into deep water at the age of six and telling the teachers how pathetic they were.

Every time she rang, she would find a little story about my courage and rashness and I would listen. Yes, I would listen and I would ask myself: "Where had the person she was talking about gone? Was she ever going to come back if I survived?"

She told me that I was her strength, that I was the voice of the weak, and that I was different, free and ever reinventing.

I would listen; yes, I would listen and ask myself where this person had disappeared, and I would think, if she was killed, who committed the crime?

To my mind none of this was agreeable, my mind searched in the wrong places for the pieces of me, and it looked to me as if some sort of censorship from a hidden source had been bestowed upon me, cutting out the strength, the light and the lightness.

What I understood later was that she was consistent and persistent in her attempts to make me remember who I was. In plain words, she would say: "Please, please remember who you are." And I could not. No, I couldn't.

Every time I came home, we would go for an evening walk along the lungomare, hand in hand, as we used to do when we were children. The walk was long and the evening endless, for we would sit in every little café on our way, and to each of these cafés a little story was attached, and to take the stories from the past I told her the story of the Other Man and how much I cared for him and she said: "Let him love you, just let him love you."

165

But I did not.

When I told her that the main parts of my personality were sewn by the thread of melancholy, she rejected this thought at once, saying:

"Not true at all. Why would you label yourself? Why would you put a sentence on you and give it strength by believing in it? It was quite the opposite before, you were the one telling me about the freedom of being whoever you wanted to be, don't you remember? You used to say that there was really nobody who was going to give you permission to live your life the way you'd like to live it, isn't it so? You said that there was nobody great out there; neither a celestial being nor one of flesh and blood who was going to give you permission to live, to love, to share and to be happy. Don't you remember?"

And I did not remember.

I went down to Andalucia in search of my broken pieces and all I found there were the words which would form the letters for the two men I loved at that time. One never replied to any of them, the other wanted more of them, but I never knew what my letters could achieve in terms of healing myself from the belief that I was weak, melancholic and lost in the wilderness of Andalucia, in the wilderness of my life.

I asked myself over and over if life was worth living without love, for emptiness could be experienced anywhere.

Once, when I was better, she asked me what I was doing at that time and I told her that I was working at the local radio as a producer, so she said:

"Hmm, hmm, pays the bills" and I agreed, then she said:

"The time will come." And I asked:

"The time for what?"

"You figure it out yourself."

I did not want to figure out anything anymore, for I never wanted to write a word again. All my words were undervalued or dismissed by one man, or underpaid by the greed of yet another one, so I decided to keep all my words for myself only, and when needed, share them with selected friends.

But life does not ask for a sudden and complete change, a great quantum leap. Rather, it asks for a gradual change that would allow adapting to new circumstances or new levels of understanding.

166

To learn that I needed to wait. To wait to meet you, my dear friend, and learn new steps as a dancer learns new steps, progressing from simple ones to more complicated and demanding ones, yes, as a dancer who met a master of the steps. Now I can say what I learned was that life was a progression through different tasks, starting with the simple ones (like a dancer beginning her steps) to those more demanding in complexity on a visible plan to the unseen demands to change the mind; to affect the soul. And to fully participate in this process, which is life itself, we should look at that gradual process of change, acknowledging the process in each step (as a dancer does) willingly, calmly, kindly, as if we were leading our child by hand to teach it an important lesson, lovingly.

Susanne said:

"Remember your words some twenty years ago, would you like to say that you knew more back then than you know now? That you were wiser, stronger? Do you want to say that I always looked up to you just to understand that it was all fraud? That you were wise and strong only while supported by agreeable life circumstances? Weren't you the one who told me that adversities build heroes?

Build your bridges! Let your wild river overflow, you might have been the one who searched for the meaning, but never the one who searched with fearful eyes.

Do you want to tell me that I never really knew you?

That you were somebody else?"

These were my conversations with Susanne while the poison was coursing through my burnt veins, while my Mother was holding my hand and overhearing Susanne's words, nodded her head in silent agreement, knowing that these words were coming from a woman worthy of belief.

As all these memories were waning as if they had never been a part of my personal recollection of reality of strength and freedom, I would talk with Susanne as if we had met a long time ago, just once, and as if she had made up her story, made up my personality and image to her own liking, as we do with people we meet once who impress us gravely.

But she never failed to call, never failed to talk and convince me that there was a hidden being within me she called a friend and loved her for being free, strong and honest and above all loved that being, for she had the courage to be truly independent.

Where was She?

(Weakness looked to me like a miserable but acceptable disease, too difficult to overcome, the door through which I entered into the kingdom of the Princess of Darkness, the holy depression.)

***

The Nobleman asked, *"What have you done with his letter?"*
She said, *Tied around it a pale blue ribbon and put it aside.*
"Did you answer him?" He asked.
Oh, I did not. I feared love as one might fear hatred, how strange, oh, how strange!
And the Nobleman said:
"How strange. Why would you fear love when you said before that you were starved of love?"
She said, *I feared that my dreams would stop if exchanged for love, and when there is just love alone, without dreams, it cannot survive, for love needs dreams to thrive and flourish.*
The Nobleman asked, *"And why does love have to be exchanged for the dreams?"*
The pause was short, and then She said, *For it happened before. While I was dreaming all was easy and flowing and when love entered, my dreams were reduced to the reality. If only I had been free to love the Other Man, if he had been free to love me, we would have stepped out of our dreamland and entered into unknown reality. My dreams brought me the men I loved, but then my dreams became controlled by them, slowly but surely they changed into different ones and eventually disappeared into nothingness like a mountain haze or foam of the ocean.*

And I know that I am not the only one who fears love. All humans ache for the same, and we fear the same, which is the most powerful and the most noble feeling of all and I dare say we fear that the price for that magnificent feeling of love might be too high, the price could be one of broken dreams.

The Nobleman said, *"The price of love could be one of broken dreams."*

She said that if She wanted to make changes, it was almost as if all Her thoughts had to be used up or worn out, for they would return as ghosts when it grew silent and dark. She said She wanted to exhaust Her own thoughts before they exhausted Her.

She did not say any more to him, but I was there to observe Her thoughts which travelled effortlessly and easily like a train without a destination and without an arrival time; *When it comes to the memories and the mind, the instrument by which I enter into the field of my memories, I feel that the mind remembers past experiences, called memories, and then the mind leads me into so-called future events which have already been modelled by the old patterns of my mind.*

Loudly She said to Him, *I always wanted to know the 'hows' of my mind's working. I wanted to know its subtle manipulations in order to break free from the fears which were only the repeated past experiences created by illusions of my mind. And as I said to you sometime before, whether the universe was meaningless or perhaps meaningful, in both instances I always demanded that the hidden meaning of human existence in it should be revealed to me, not gradually and slowly, but all at once, as it was revealed to old seers, if indeed it was so.*

No, I had never replied to his letter or anybody else's, for I was done with letters. I heard that he was waiting for my letter for quite a long time; I heard he grew older than he should have. I heard this story from my friend who knew some little vignettes of our dream, and I heard this story again the year after, even though I am not able to attach any date to it right now.

I might come back to the theme of moral issues again. I would talk again of sharing love with others and tell you that it was not in my nature, and that was the sole reason why I did not give in, for I knew that solid flesh demand-ed physical, earthly love, but I kept that story on the level of finer energies and in the book of soul-longing, for only from that book could our love enter into the big book of eternity. And this is why this love was special and different, for I loved Claude more than him, but with Claude, love was the one of flesh and sweetness, and higher energies of the soul were mixed with the lower energies of the body, they produced lower feelings mixed with love; the feelings of jealousy, possessiveness and suspiciousness ... while with the Other Man, love was like one summer dance, danced to the subtlest tones of our souls, danced in his warm and beautiful garden, without demands, without expectations, without plans ... just a beautiful dance to the pleasant music heard only by our hearts which rhymed perfectly.

She said, *Next time we will start with the reading.*

He said, *"Looking forward to this."*

She left with a little smile on Her narrow face.

***

Next time She said, *I started to remember....*

He said, *"But you did remember all the time. You told me so many stories, all of your past, all your kaleidoscopic remembrances ... what the mind does is to remember all the time."*

She said, *I took the pain and locked it in my breast and nursed it many years while with him. He took my dreams and threw them out through the window of our fragile house, which was built on shaky lands. The reason why he threw my dreams out was that we could live his dreams only, yet the problem was that he never knew which dreams were his and which belonged to other members of his family. So it looked to me now that even the pain I locked in my breast originally did not belong to me, but I inherited it from his ancestors the day I crossed the threshold of his house. Though, I could, of course, be mistaken regarding the origins of the pain, for sure I can say that I was nursing it as if it was my dearest possession and belonged to me only. It felt almost as if I had found a beautiful, rare, black pearl and kept it in the shell of my chest, for fear of losing it by exposing it.*

We had different needs and values and he was always endlessly surprised by my choices and conclusions which were diametrically opposed to his and he always opted for the simple and easy solutions, telling me that I was too complicated and too deep, and who needed a deep and complicated woman in such a warm climate where everybody was so simple, so easy, oh, so simple to edge with brainlessness.

I wanted to ask my Mother:

"Mother, why was I not a simple and easy soul?" But I gave up this thought, for how could she possibly answer that kind of question, which was neither simple nor easy for her to answer.

You remember Susanne's and my philosophy that we established and lived for many years? It started to wither away and with it, some deeper aspects of my inner being started to wither away, to disappear, to hide in different parts of my, by then, already tired body.

One day he said:

"All I needed I learned from you and there was nothing left to learn, and life itself is all about learning. Thank you, I shall go and learn more and teach some of my knowledge to others."

So, as easy as that.

Simple and easy. No complexity, no philosophy, no extra wisdom, just simple simplicity.

Oh, God, please, let us start again somewhere else, for the rules are as simple and easy as breathing itself is; just breathe in and breathe out.
And that was all. The rest was just a cosmic joke!
What a joke, oh, what a joke!

I saw him, a few days later, with a young girl on the street. She looked simple, uncomplicated in her polyester, simple dress, with a simple smile, the one that adorned the faces of utter simplicity, oh, how touching, how touching!

I had my X-ray on that particular day; they searched throughout my body to find more confusion, but there was nothing left, as it seemed on that day. Confusion was only in my mind, for I did not know whether the results were good or bad. The doctor told me to repeat it in a few weeks. It all looked to me as if it was happening in some slow motion pictures, the clouds were more distant, the trees were taller and they were swinging slowly and leaves were dancing and I heard their whisper but could not decode their language. I thought that there must be some message in their whisper, but the sentence that I had to repeat my X-ray was louder than the leaves' whispering, anyway. As I didn't have anybody to tell my fears to about repeating an X-ray in a few weeks, I looked at my brown patent leather shoes and it looked to me as if they knew where they were leading me, for some dark clouds entered my head and I had woken up when I saw him with a young girl in a simple, polyester dress.
In my head, I saw the film, I saw myself approaching her slowly, telling her that he was still my husband, who left just a few weeks ago, and she did not have the right to walk with him this street, in her simple, polyester dress, where my daughter walked to her school and back. I told her in my mind that I had wounds in my breast and I needed him to walk me home, to make dinner for our daughter and talk to her while I needed to hide my eyes, for my child might read something disturbing in them. I told the young girl in the simple, polyester dress that he wouldn't stay; I wanted to tell her to run away, run away.... But they passed by without noticing me and I assumed that my dark cloud consumed me completely so nobody could see me, recognize me, not even him.
It was a long walk home, I did not remember whether the day was bright or rainy, the slow motion pictures were now unclear and hazy, I felt as if I was walking on the surface of an unknown and hostile sea which could open

any time and swallow me with my fears, wounds and pains. A part of me wished for it, the other part knew that I had to go home and make a delicious dinner for my daughter.

I came home and cried freely, because of the need to repeat an X-ray in a few weeks, because he simply passed by without noticing me, with a simple girl in the simple, polyester dress, and while I was crying I made dinner for my daughter and when she entered, my black cloud disappeared and all I said was - Shall we eat? And we did.

My daughter said: "Mother, why are your eyes red?" And I said that I bought new mascara and probably not the one of the best quality. She came and kissed my eyes and said to me: "Mother, please do not cry" and I kissed her back; her eyes, her hair, her fingers and her soft cheeks.
I never told her that I saw him walking with a young, simple girl in a polyester dress, for how can you tell that to a young child? But he walked the street she walked to school and back every day, with that simple girl ... oh, how brave, how brave.

She took my hand and led me to the living room and said: "I will play for you and all your troubles will be gone."
It looked like that for a few minutes, for I listened to her voice and her music and tried to forget the world.

***

A few days after I saw him smiling while strolling down the street my daughter walked to school and back, with that young girl dressed in polyester, he came in a very good mood and brought me the document written by his lawyer.
I read it and signed it without protest. I wanted to ask him if he could take the child to the piano lesson for two consequent Saturdays, but I hadn't finished the question for he said:
"Don't always ask for something. You are such a needy person. We are not together any longer and learn to be self-sufficient. You can't lean on me, I have my life, you have yours now."
And he walked out with a signed document, on a bright day, lighter for two commitments of two coming Saturdays, for he wanted me to be self-sufficient and teach my daughter the same lesson. I could not drive the car

yet, so we took a taxi, and she played these two consecutive Saturdays, yes, she played and I sat on the sofa, closed my eyes and listened to her music.

That sentence of self-sufficiency had determined our lives on some subtle level that I became aware of only when I looked at it retrospectively.

As his motivations were always hard to fathom, the mystery remained to this very day why he left the country, his job, his responsibilities and his child and went yet on another adventure – to the Far East.

She told me that she felt betrayed for the second time, and I did not count any more my betrayals caused by his freedom to be himself, as he learned in the simple but popular books on the topic of human freedom.

I said before that I started to remember but did not define what was different in my remembrance. I started to remember the stories my friend Susanne was telling me over the phone, over the past several years.
I started to remember climbing the highest trees, stealing the first cherries in the suburban gardens of my hometown, which was dreaming peacefully in the azure blue gulf on the shores of my childhood.

But now it is time to go, and I shall take with me these last sentences and I shall call more memories in these lines to come, and eventually next time I shall have another story which could be dormant in the hidden alley of my mind.

Before She walked out, the Nobleman said, *"Shall we start with the reading next time?"*

We shall, She said and closed the door as if She was closing the hard cover of Her as-yet unwritten book.

She was thinking of Her as-yet unwritten book, She was thinking of the Nobleman, of empathy, of friendship and what in the "ideal world" the relationship between people should look like. She knew there was not such a world as an ideal world, yet She was absolutely aware that they had undergone a unique, sincere and utterly open relationship and in order to write Her as-yet unwritten book She needed this unique friendship, for his presence strengthened Her sufficiently in Her creative endeavours. She knew that She had the strength to face the emotional upheaval of writing the stories, initially solely tailored for his ears and possibly Her liberation.

As he was able to grasp the aspects of Her inner life and experiences, they laid an unshakable base of empathy which allowed the stories to unfold without interference of false emotions, shame or guilt, to unfold in the safe environment of empathetic understanding.

***

The days used to be so long; summer days would stretch in endless, slow events, sometimes coloured with boredom, for summer holidays were long and after the first few weeks, the whole summer looked like one long day traversed with short periods of rest. When they are bored, children tend to invent all new mischievous ways of being, just to entertain themselves. We used to steal young cherries on the outskirts of our town and then run, run fast when they yelled at us.

One of these summers Susanne and I were roaming the streets in search of any kind of adventure. The day was lazy, too long and not eventful at all. It was too hot to go to the beach, the beaches were crammed with fat Germans and we liked to go to the beach when all the tourists were gone, giving us back our shores, cafés and our streets.

You can't imagine if you have never seen the mixture of these colours: the blue of the sky, the redness of the earth covered with bright green grass, the redness of the big, round cherries, and the azure of the sea at short distance. The cherry tree could be quite high and Susanne lifted me up, but regardless of it, I could not reach the lowest branches. She interlocked her fingers and leaned on the trunk of the tree and I climbed the first step, formed of her interlocked fingers, then I put one hand on her head and reached with the other hand the fork in the tree. From the first step, which were Susanne's interlocked fingers, I climbed to the fork and then she put both her hands on my rear end and started to push me up, and as I climbed the first branches, I started to break them off fast and throw them down to her.

The feeling was awesome; a mixture of excitement, fear and achievement. So, armed with these feelings my confidence and zest for adventure grew and I climbed higher and higher overlooking the little fragmented picture of the sea through the leaves and the dark red cherries. I felt invincible climbing higher and higher and little inner butterflies in my stomach accompanied me while climbing. I was breaking the branches with luscious cherries and throwing them down to fearful Susanne, who started to urge me to climb down, for she heard the voice inside the house behind the big, strong cherry tree.

She said they heard us, she said the dog was barking and I did not hear, and I did not care, it was not for the cherries, it was for the view, for the bravery, just for the story of my brave heart which would be told years later.

Susanne pleaded, I climbed higher, intoxicated with the view, the song of crickets, the beating of my brave heart and the tickling of the little butterflies in my stomach.

What brought me back to the moment was the loud barking of an enormous dog standing next to Susanne and showing his sharp teeth, while saliva was dripping down on her shoes. The dog was held by his owner, who grabbed Susanne's shoulder with his other hand.

How could I let go of my bravery at once?

No, I could not, so as bravery still lingered around me, I said from the high branches with a firm voice (the height gave me more courage, for only The One can talk from the heights):

"Let her go or I'll jump. If I break my legs it will be your fault."

He said he'd call the police.

I thought of my father. I thought of Susanne's father.

Probably she thought of her father, probably she thought of my father.

She started to cry, and I, above all of them, had the voice of the omnipotent negotiator, so I said:

"Let her go and I will come down, you can call the police on me."

Susanne had joined the negotiations by now, for she did not want to leave the crime scene and let me take all the credit by giving myself in to the police.

He was holding his dog, but when he let go of Susanne's shoulder, I yelled out, "Run, Susie, run," and she did. The man held his dog, for it really looked like a fierce beast, so I saw Susanne's back getting smaller in the distance. And from my height I climbed a few branches lower and from there I jumped onto the mulberry tree, scratched my hands and forearms, tore my jeans and scratched my knees, jumped down from the mulberry tree, and praying to God that the man would not let his dog after me, I ran, ran, trying to catch up with flying Susanne.

When I came home, on the kitchen table was a large bowl of big red cherries, and my Mother said:

"Wash your hands and have some cherries."

When she saw my torn jeans, she said:

"So, what happened now?"

"I fell off the tree."

"Nice." She said, and I said "Nice," too.

Later, we would turn this story around, adding the elements of bravery when arguing with a man, or extract some details of embarrassment.

I said to her:

"Who cares, I'll go again."
And I did.

I was a fearless child.

She said She was a fearless child!
The Nobleman said, *"You were a fearless child."*
And She said, *Yes, I was.*

***

He learned from his astrologer that to be a coward it had to be written in your birth chart. All he could possibly do about it was to accept it, first himself, then let others accept it, and a new life would open up.

I needed to deal with several issues after his announcement: betrayal, illness and my child's shattered reality.

For the first two I believed I was equipped to a certain extent in given circumstances, so I would find ways how to cope on a daily basis, but when it came to her tears and moods, I did not know how to respond. All I could do was to hug her tight and hold her endlessly.

The questions she used to ask me were the same questions I am asking you all the time, about the meaning of our existence and why our destiny reveals itself the way it does, for how could she believe that we chose our destiny when she never made a choice to live without a father, to live with a mother whose health was as frail as a snowflake in the spring. When I did not know how to answer her questions, I would say exactly what my Mother said to me: "Let it be," convincing her (without firmly believing in it myself) that something good would come out of it. She would ask:

"What good could come from a broken family and broken health?" and I told her to never repeat that we were a broken family, for we never were. I told her that we were mother and daughter going through life as if we were walking through a maze, but the maze itself was made of beautiful flowers, bushes and little trees, there were shiny pebbles on the paths, there were birds singing, and little benches were there for us to sit on and have a rest while enjoying the bird song and the fantastic fragrances in the air. I told her to remember the beautiful gardens in Alcazar of Jerez de la Frontera and imagine that we walked these gardens again, hand in hand, supported by the warmth of the summer, by the wind, by the fragrances, by the kind people, by God reflected in all of it.

She would listen to the soothing words as to the dearest melody, she would listen and would whisper to me, "Mum, you are my hero" and I would say, "Of course, I am your hero, and you are mine."

And she was.

***

When we came back from Europe last summer, it looked to me that all my troubles were behind me.

The mellowness of the sky, the greenness of nature, the blue of the sea, the smells and the tastes of the known, the melody of the language and the love that came expressed through it strengthened me.

I met the Other Man there and kissed him for the last time and there was no sadness in the decision at all. I could take his image with me, in my thoughts, wherever I went, as we take a lucky charm on our travels. But I left him in that very restaurant where we had eaten our lunch and had a delicious cake made of forest berries with a thick layer of snow still on them. I think I will remember the sweetness of that cake for the rest of my life, just as I remembered Claude's first kiss by the weakness of my knees.

I got his letter and did not answer it but he knew, as we agreed before, that if I did not answer he would read it from its silence. We talked about this silence and then agreed that we never knew each other as more than passing acquaintances (even though this passing acquaintance graced our lives), we never knew each other's handwriting and we questioned in the end whether we had ever met each other, but it had all happened in the dream somewhere far, far away, where reality looked like a big lie.

But he promised me, I promised him that we would relive the dream once a year, no, not on a particular day, no, not simultaneously, but once a year we would think of that dream where nearly he became a waiter somewhere in Andalucia's wilderness and I would think of the dream where I nearly loved the man with a moustache which resembled Salvador Dali's moustache.

That was the last that was defined by the words. The rest was put behind the domain of the words, behind the mind and behind reason.

***

When we came back from Europe last summer, it looked to me as if all my troubles were behind me.

My health had stabilized and there were no more black pearls found in my body, as the doctor advised me soon after our arrival. I could look for more work again but I was reluctant to write, for what was the use of the words, anyway? It looked to me as if the only person who could communicate with me, or just join my silence, was the Other Man. We never needed too many words - a little smile was sufficient, or a gesture which would say more than a thousand words. I took all his words and put them into a short story that was downloaded into my memory, to use their beauty whenever I doubted the beauty of the words.

***

When we came back from Europe last summer, it looked to me as if all my troubles were behind me.
As he left in a hurry, he did not take a lot. He said that he did not need the old clothes but wanted to buy new ones. He did not take the books, for he took the knowledge from them, he did not need anything, since where he went all was provided for his needs.
His lawyer made an agreement and I signed it. We agreed to pay for the house together for the sake of our child's frail stability.

Stability is just another illusion of the mind.
But she had a place she called home, she had a place where she would return and hide from the world behind its, for her, warm and stable walls.

She never exactly knew where he was; whether he was in Europe, Asia, Australia or any other exotic place.
He would come unannounced. Sudden appearance. He liked to surprise equally by sudden appearance and sudden disappearance. He thought that there was no harm in either of these. He liked spontaneity, simplicity. And it was usually brought about by unexpected whims.

When he used to come from far away destinations, in haste, he would look good, younger in his appearance: carefully selected clothes made him look dandy, the haircut was fashionable, the shoes light, for his light feet, and he would bring presents which often were of no use. Some of the clothes he would bring would be too small and he would be surprised by how quickly she was growing.

She never knew whether she was happy or sad when he came, so she learned to marry the two opposing feelings and would be at one moment extremely excited about his unexpected arrival and at another deeply sad, knowing that with the change of the invisible and unpredictable wind, his light feet would fly off again, who knows where.

He moved to the Far East. Found new friends, new women.

We heard he loved it there and I was wondering how long this love would last, for all he agreed had meaning and worth was change itself. He had big plans and said to my daughter that 'one day' she would be very proud of him.

In the meantime, I was mother, father, friend, counselor and storyteller.

I never wanted to label myself as a patient.

I never said I was brave, but I never said I was afraid, either. I always said to her that I was her storyteller and that whatever happened in our lives, which were so intertwined and in tune, was just a little episode in our story.

Not long after we came and unpacked our luggage, he knocked on our door, with the smile on his face darkened by the sun of the opposite season. He brought her little presents and she was not certain what emotion she harboured in her heart, nor was she certain what emotion to express. After a short time, he asked her to go to her room because he wanted to talk to me.

She went to her room.

I looked into his eyes for the first time. The dark brown eyes, almost black, the eyes I fell in love with the first time I saw them, for I believed that they were hiding deep mysteries in them. But later I learned that what I saw were not mysteries hidden behind his eyes but troubles.

When he started to talk, his eyes changed their colour, they became mellower, I would say sadder.

He said:

"How are you doing?"

"I am doing well."

"How is your health?"

"I do not want to discuss my health with you."

I never wanted to. If he had ever cared about my health, he would not have boarded the first plane and flown away, so far away from us that this life could look to him like a lie. When I was in hospital the second time, he pretended not to know. Whenever he asked about my health, I would say, "Do not go there."

And he would shrug his shoulders, or he would say:

"You are such a difficult person."

He asked me if I could offer him a glass of water, so when I brought the water, he said that he did not have a lot of time, that he was in a hurry but there was one last thing he wanted me to do for him, the last favour.

I said:

"Let me hear it."

He said:

"I have to sell the house."

"What do you mean, you have to sell the house?"

"Literally, I have to sell it because I need the money."

"You need the money ... where are we going to live?"

"Can't you be self-sufficient? I am not your husband, I am a free man, I had a bankruptcy over there, I lost all my money, so I have to sell...."

"Hey, it's not about me, it's about your child. You are not my husband anymore, I agree with that, but you are still her father, you want to take the house and where will she live, I am asking you? Where?"

"Well ... why don't you go home?"

"Home? Where is it now? This was my home, my child's home...."

"Calm down. I will pay my debts and I will go into another enterprise with a friend of mine, I will help you in a few years' time...."

I did not want to respond in this way but all I could do was to let go of all these uncontrollable emotions, let them run down my cheeks, and I was sitting on the sofa sobbing like a child, for the first time really aware of what St. Yvonne meant when she said, *"In the end this man brought you only chaos and tears."*

He knelt down and wanted to touch my hand. I pulled it away. He looked at me with a deep sadness in his eyes and I was aware that I was crying for him. I cried for all his misfortunes, for it was all he could carry and freely give to others, even when he wanted to give different gifts, all he could give were misfortunes.

While I was crying, I heard his voice telling me not to cry, telling me that he never really wanted to hurt me, telling me that he used to love me but he stopped when he understood that he was not able to stay with one woman, in one city, with one job, he apologized several times, he touched my head before he left and he said, reaching the door, that his lawyer would send me the papers.

My daughter was standing by her bedroom door looking at me; she ran to me, hugged me and wiped off my tears. He turned to us one more time, he

*just wanted to say something, maybe "goodbye," but before he uttered a
word, she said:*

"Just go, go and close the door."

And he did.

*I said to my daughter that we would not cry again but that I would go
tomorrow to see my lawyer, for I was sick of signing the numerous papers
where I would say that I did not need or want his properties or his money.*

*When it came again to frailty and strength, when I was in extreme situa-
tions, unexplainable courage would fill every cell of my body and that was
why my daughter would say, "You are my hero." I would act as if in a
trance, focused on the strength, not on my weaknesses, and when it all
passed, I would feel exhausted and weak, almost broken.*

*When I recollect our last conversation, I could say that he was a broken
man when he came back. From a distance, I could say that he looked
different on that day, that his voice was different, as if he was ashamed of
something that I could not name at that time. His gestures were different
from the usual and the way he carried his tall body was different; he was not
as straight as a dancer, like he used to be, but bent in the upper back. His
shoulders were pulled in as if he was hiding a pain or shame in his chest.
And this was a brief description of what could be seen in terms of what lay
too deep to be seen even by those who knew him well.*

*Yet when we came back from Europe that summer, it looked to me that
all my troubles were behind me.*

They had just begun.

*Lawyers like long, exhausting battles, as if they were some sort of army
generals: their strategies are slow, the documents are often confusing,
schedules often cancelled, they call you for explanations and clarifications,
and I was asking myself: was that all that was left behind after two people
who loved each other went their separate ways?*

How sad, oh, how sad.

*I said to my tired mind, "Do not go into battle," for there was the battle
for health, the battle for the house, the battle for peace.... I said to my mind,
"Let it be" knowing by then that I did not control the outcomes of the*

lawyers' papers or my doctor's findings. Let it be and be patient with yourself. Be forgiving.

From that day we hadn't heard from him. We heard that he brought a little woman with him from the Far East. We heard that she was very short, stubby; with very dark, short hair and small narrow eyes on a rounded face. We heard that he was hiding her; it might be that he did not want his daughter to know the reason why he needed the money. From some other people I heard that he wanted to buy a house somewhere, in some exotic place where people work little but enjoy a lot. We heard, but we never knew for certain whether he was in the country at all.
And we did not care, no, we didn't.

Several months later that woman was heard crying loudly in the house for hours, and she was neither heard nor seen after that loud cry, that loud 'goodbye' again. She went back to the Far East, for she could not understand the language nor the people, what a burden, oh, what a burden.

I tried to fix so many stories in my memory and I do not want to do that any more. I want to tell the stories exactly the way they happened, as a reflection of my inner state. For we try to make the past look mellower and sweeter through the crooked glass of the passing time, that's why nostalgia has that sweet pain attached to it. Even when the past has bleak and terrifying images, nostalgia paints them softer, changing their reality, so that it looks more as a lie than the past.

***

Long before my going to Andalucia, he started to come home later and later. He would say he was tired of his work, he was tired of wearing a suit, he was tired of the routine, and he needed a drink after work. He used to come late, and every week an hour later. Initially, he would come armed with excuses or explanations. After some time, words were not needed.
I read something different in his eyes.
He was seen with a woman who liked to tell vulgar jokes. The more men were there, the more vulgar jokes she would come up with. She came from the country of steep mountains and her tongue was as sharp and shameless as the peaks of the mountains of her native country.
He said I was serious, he said I was complicated and demanding. He needed simple company. If it was a woman, then let her tell the jokes. He said I never joked. He said he needed a light woman, not a structured or

182

demanding one who told stories he was afraid of. Was he afraid of my stories?

I told him that when he met me, the lightness of the world was what frightened him. He said then that he needed substance, meaning, structure and deepness, for he saw the world and its people as empty and shallow structures in the universe, where there were better opportunities for knowledge and growth. He said to me that he was tired of the simple women he loved or married - he said he needed somebody who was drawn to different needs and qualities. I did not think at that time about what he was saying; I was fascinated by his big, dark-brown, almost black eyes holding hidden mysteries while he was explaining to me what his soul searched for.

But when it came to jokes, I can say I joked, yes, I did.
He had forgotten.
Yes, he had forgotten.
The illness stopped the jokes.
It stopped the love, how strange, it stopped the love.
Or was it the illness?

The Nobleman repeated, *"Was it the illness?"*
She did not have an answer, but She took Her handbag and left the answer unanswered, believing that She would never know it anyway. Did it matter? Did it matter at all?

***

How many boats have we unanchored and let sail down the river of my remembrances? Where will their destination be and what will be there when they reach this, for now unknown, murky end? Will my river be boat-less and hence lighter for their load?

The Nobleman said, *"By telling me each of these stories, or as you said, untying the ropes of the little boats and letting them down the river, you are actually grieving. You are calling up one little picture at a time, you are reliving it by telling it to me and then you are letting it go, as you said, down the river of your remembrance.*

Part of the grieving process is to blame others and yourself and then you learn to live without the person you loved and the learning is difficult, for you have to learn and accept that that person is not there anymore, almost as if he didn't exist. It is difficult to accept that you cannot rely on him again. It is almost like when you learn to love, just now it is a quite opposite process; you have to unlearn to love that person."

***

One day I was sitting on the pier with Pablo. We were looking at the anchored boats while they were dancing on the waves, awakened by the first but light blows of the levante. I liked to listen to Pablo, for he had so much knowledge about everything. I heard from him so many stories about Andalucia; the women of that land, the costumes and tradition ... we tried local wines together and ate food on his patio made by his little, plump maid. In his house we never felt like guests but rather like a part of his large family. Each day, late in the afternoon, he would call me or knock on my window and we would walk down the Paseo Maritimo towards the pier and if it wasn't too windy, we would sit and tell each other different stories. His life experiences were rich and many, for he was in his seventies and served his country as a diplomat in many foreign lands.

While we were sitting on the pier, I was full of uncontrolled anticipation awoken by the rising levante and fascinated by a dance of the boats wondering if their destiny was predictable and safe with the rope that held an anchor?

I said to Pablo that these boats resembled the certainties and uncertainties of our lives, for we never knew when the levante was going to raise its wings, how strong it would be and whether it could blow the boats away in the wide-open ocean. What was an anchor? There was not a rope strong enough to secure their tranquility.

Where was my anchor at that time? What was my anchor?

I said to Pablo:

"I'd like to let my boats down the river and never search for them again."

Pablo told me that he couldn't always understand to what I was referring when I talked in metaphors and I said to him, "Never mind," and he said that regardless, he enjoyed very much our late afternoon conversations and walks.

Once he told me that I had to eat more and drink a little bit more of good wine, for life went too quickly and there were not too many enjoyments apart from physical love, eating delicious food and drinking the finest wines with the dearest people, and after all what was the point in being too ascetic in my approach? So I told him that I was not a forced ascetic but that I was doing what my nature told me to do. I might have sounded childish, quite immature, but I have always had a need to create a powerful sense of goodness within and around me, as if that was exactly what was missing in my adult life by making awkward choices.

When he told me that my husband was a 'blessed man', I said to him that things often appeared quite different from what they were in reality, and he said yet again that he was confused with my answer. "Let it be rather philosophical to avoid confusion," was what I told him.

Looking at the boats with Pablo, every late afternoon regularly brought back the memories of our summers before our daughter was born.

He said that I did not joke, that I was serious and demanding, but he had forgotten our summers when we would take the boat out and sail to the little islands, scattered in the gulf of our youth. All we needed was some food, some wine, his guitar and my book.

He would sing to me to make me laugh and I would read him plays; funny ones and all would be spiced up with a little bit of good, locally made wine and a few chords from his guitar.

Once we were too drunk to get out of the boat and we laughed so hard that we rocked the boat and it turned around, tossing us into the water. It was an instant sobering, but we laughed, and I recited a wet little poem with my arms around his neck, nearly drowning him.

The food was floating on the surface of the sea and he was biting a little sausage with his drunken mouth like a greedy, silly fish, and we were laughing, oh, we were laughing....

Then the tramontana came, raising its wings abruptly. So that's why the levante reminded me of that summer, why the pier and the boats were ringing with the laughter, the one we forgot to take with us that summer on the open sea. That laughter, which I could still hear on the pier in Andalucia, was the reason why I would walk with Pablo down the Paseo Maritimo towards the pier that held little boats tied up to its rocks.

That laughter was the reason I was sending him my letters from Andalucia, always hoping that we would laugh together again, yes ... hoping that we could laugh together again.

***

When I met him, he was very different to all the men I knew in my hometown. Even though it is one of the most beautiful regions in Europe, just the beauty of the land was not sufficient to feel contented, for the majority of the people were righteous, angry and pretentious, after all. The men were domineering because of the mere fact that they were men. How simple, how arrogant that attitude was.

My first experience with a man was with a soft and kind man and by Claude I measured later all those who wanted to impress me with arrogance and pretentiousness. In that land in men's blood was inbuilt the need to belittle a woman, to dominate her and to keep her obedient, but it was subtler than that, for they divided women in only two categories: the real women, who were good, obedient, and kind regardless of whether it was a genuine personality or the one adapted by the rules in an attempt not to fail. These women could be controlled as easily as the story in the making. The other kinds were women who wanted to be authentic regardless of what was asked of them. But the problem was, because of a long period of historical repression of women in these regions, those who wanted to be genuine and authentic were actually aggressive, self-obsessed and righteous themselves and resembled the men from whom they wanted to liberate themselves.

That was why I knew immediately that when the woman who came with the Dishonest Man, the one who claimed that she travelled the world, the one who said in the first sentence that she was a learned psychologist, we could kiss goodbye to a pleasant and easy evening. She called her boyfriend by his second name, as if she wanted to show, possibly, her independence, her strength, her hidden need to belittle him, that man, and any man whom she had ever encountered in her past. That was what I read when she addressed him by his second name all the time. She said to me that she was a very respectable and learned woman, and she travelled a lot. She said when she travelled to other countries she could wear blue jeans and sneakers, for she could not afford that commonness in her own hometown. With her gestures, the tone of her voice, her too-strong perfume, the complicated structure of her sentences, she wanted to show what an independent, modern and worldly woman she was. How wrong, oh, how wrong.

The men of my hometown used to call young women by very spiteful names, too spiteful to be repeated. They told the stories in local cafes about who they slept with, which one was good in bed, which one was skilled in which technique.... The stories were mostly made up with one aim: to humiliate women, especially those whom they could not possess and control - at least they could humiliate them.

With Claude I had a genuine love story, tender and caring and I considered myself to be lucky, for I escaped the difficult task of finding a decent, loving man in an environment where decency and kindness were not virtues.

After Claude I did not want anybody. All I wanted was to remember our times together and to dream that one day we would be together again. When the pain subsided and I was ready to show my face to the world again, Susanne and I started again to chase the wind and laugh together once more.

We were young and we were pretty as youth can be. We were different, for we were free. We laughed at all this petty pretentiousness while having our own rules and we were self-sufficient in that 'better world' we had built for ourselves, and the only voice we were listening to was that tiny inner voice which always knew the right answers. When I was listening and following that small voice, I was led by wisdom to the right choices and to the right actions, knowing that I was doing only what that voice would whisper.

The first time I had betrayed this little voice stayed in my memory till today but I never gave it full acknowledgment. And as we know, the first time is always the hardest, after that, my own deafness to the inner voice followed more easily.

He married quickly, divorced even more quickly, all in the same year.
I did not care, for youth never cares.
When I asked him how come he had married a woman he barely knew and then after a few months he divorced her, he said in his deep voice that that marriage was "an experiment." My eyes opened wide like an umbrella and I repeated it letter by letter: "E-x-p-e-r-i-m-e-n-t." He laughed, hugged me and said he was joking.

But the little voice said, "How wrong, oh, how wrong!"
But I covered it with other thoughts, with thoughts that we read the same books, that we listened to the same music and that he sang almost as well as Claude did - and it looked to me at that time that he knew the art of kindness towards women, as a man who had many experiences with women usually knew. If we add to the picture the colour of his mysterious dark brown, almost black, eyes I am asking you now: how could you listen to the little voice? So I did not listen to reason, I did not listen to what others had to say, and I thought I was following my heart.
Yes, I thought so.

So, I followed my heart to this faraway land where I could not read the dawns and sunsets for a long, long time and they left me puzzled and fright-ened by their colours and birds' screeches, for we are frightened of what we cannot read, oh, how brave I was, how brave.

Sometimes we misread kindness, for it masks weakness, but to know other people truly we have to walk with them many miles and exchange many shoes, and I walked many miles and lent my strength whenever it was needed, until it grew tired, used up and quietly my strength deserted me.

This change did not take place at once, it was rather slow and I was unaware of it, just as we can be unaware how quickly our own child grows and changes, for our eyes have been fixed on the child all the time. So my changes were growing slowly but steadily under the southern sky, where days had a different colour, words a different meaning and nights were frightening, for he was never at home at night-time.

I would write at night-time and imagine that I belonged to my stories, set in a different ambience, and the people I met in my stories were supportive and virtuous. I wrote about what I didn't have, compensating for the reality.

The experiences which followed for many long, lonely years, sailed into my brain, modelling it to fear and I started to fear that they could sink even further, down to my genes, and I feared that this fear could poison my daughter, too.

She grew silent for a long time. He was silent, too. You could hear their breathing. After a long silence, She said, *How many restless stories could be woven from these long, lonely years? These were the stories I wanted to bury in Andalucian sand, to hide them from my parents, from my friends, my daughter and me. I wanted to disown them, give them to the wind to carry them above the ocean to other lands, whose customs and languages I had never heard of.*

When I got ill, he said that he did not need me any longer and after that I completely lost all sense of self and became plagued totally by self-doubt, not believing in the world, in goodness, in health, and so fearful that I believed it would take me an eternity to recover trust in myself and others.

***

I said that I had always had a need to create a powerful sense of goodness within and around me, as if that was exactly what was missing in my adult life by making awkward choices.

But when I think of 'goodness,' what exactly would that be? Does it come from the mind, the noble heart, or from the deeper levels of our soul? How much does one need to immerse oneself in the soul in order to understand it?

How and to what extent do others affect our own goodness? What would be the visual representation of 'goodness'?

How good can I be to others if I am capable of betraying myself, betraying this little voice, which speaks in the name of my own goodness?

I can say that I was often interested in doing the decent, good deeds, but let me tell you this: nothing can be created out of nothing and when I think of his last letter, I am asking myself why would he be saying that he carried me across his threshold and laid me on his bed if that was not what had exactly happened in that dream where I tried too hard to be decent and honorable, and said that I waved while his car got smaller and smaller? I said that I waved and he said that he carried me in, in his arms, and he said that I smiled and was happy, and he said that I promised him I would come back to live in Paris or Vienna, wherever, just to be closer, where our letters could reach us more quickly.

I created this ending out of feelings of guilt, but can love be painted by guilt or shame? If it was fear, I am still asking who I feared, for he noticed my fears and said to me that I knew that only goodness could come from him and that I did not have to fear, for he would never do anything to hurt me.

So yes, I sat in his car and we drove to Vienna, holding hands all the way while listening to soft music.

When we walked in, the dogs ran to him, jumping and licking his face and then they came to me and licked my hands and he said that they remembered me well, for they never forgot the people who were soft and kind to them. I knelt down and took each Labrador's head into my arms and talked to them as one talks to little children. They wagged their tails and rocked their intelligent and grateful heads.

He quickly talked to the maid and when she came back, she carried enormous bunches of red roses and somehow I thought of the berries that were buried under the thick layer of snow-cream. She placed them in white vases made of fine porcelain, she put the vases on the table, on the side tables and on the little tables next to the armchairs and the room lightened, it came alive with red colour, alive with coursing blood, alive with the redness of love he demonstrated as he demonstrated it a few years before when I had walked into his house full of people and red roses, and while welcoming me at the door, he whispered into my ear, "The roses are because of you," and nobody knew, no, nobody knew why the roses were there in abundance.

We were slowly drinking coffee, then I stood up and came to the window. It was an old, beautiful, big Viennese house, we could see pine trees through the windows and I said to him that the scenery had changed, the pine trees replaced the palm trees but the rest was the same and he said, "And a bit better," and I agreed, for I nodded my head, saying, "A bit better."

He put on some soft music and took my hand, saying, "Shall we dance?" and we did.

My hair was wet with his kisses and my soul forgot that it cried, it forgot for a while why it cried. With our steps once again we danced into a perfect dream.

After we had danced a little, he walked me to the sofa where I sat down and he went to the open library, coming back with a book. I recognized the book at once by its red covers and that recognition made me soft and mellow; he opened the book and started to read while sitting down next to me:

"Her hands were full of flowers and books. He approached her from the back and in a soft voice, the way a voice softens when yearnings accumulate, whispered:
"I'd help, if you'd allow me to."

(While reading, he was looking into my eyes and continued, not looking at the page):
"He took her books; she carried the orchids. He said:
"You smell like an orchid."
(I said to him without looking into the book):
"I am carrying orchids."
(He continued reading and looking into my eyes):
"You always smell of orchids. Even when you are not carrying them."
(Now he sat closer, he closed the book and repeated the sentence which followed in the perfect order):
"He approached her from the back and in a soft voice, the way a voice softens when yearnings accumulate, whispered:
"I'd like to carry your books, your orchids and you ... you are prettier and more tender than all these orchids, the very sight of you makes my blood race...."
He told me that he knew I was reading this citation to him even though it was a brave thought, for there were more than three hundred people there while I was reading. He said he knew I addressed him, and I smiled.

Yes, I just smiled.

After a while he said, looking into my eyes:
"It looks like there is still sadness in your eyes."
"Why would you say that?"
"For you look like all these experiences sadden you ... do you still love him?"
I shrugged my shoulders, for I did not want to talk about him.
He said:
"Is there anything I can do for you to make you feel better?"
"Yes," I said, "Can we dance again?"
And we did.
And with us the whole room was dancing: the red roses in the big white vases, the big leather armchairs, the chandelier, the orchids from the red book ... the Persian carpet was swirling around, dissolving and mixing its colours and patterns into big perfectly rounded colourful circles, the pine trees were dancing out in the big garden, and the stars in the evening sky were dancing with us and all looked like images from the dreams.

If I had been at home, I would probably have whined that I was tired at that hour, but dancing with him in this calm, warm Viennese evening, I was filled with lightness and easiness; the room was swirling, the stars were shimmering, the dogs were happily barking, the roses smelled like orchids, I was not tired, no, I wasn't.

He opened a bottle of wine and led me into the garden. The evening was unexpectedly warm for a Viennese evening or was it that I was warmed with dancing, conversation and sweet anticipation for the first time, aware that our dream might be reality as well?
He said with an uncertain melody in his voice that my eccentricity always took him out of the life of ordinary rhythm and in these rare and short moments it took him out of the common run.
I took his glass and while sipping his wine, truly surprised, asked:
"Do you really think I am an eccentric?"
"No, I really don't," he said and took his glass from my hand and brought it to his lips to cover his smile.

191

CHAPTER NINE

For a long time I was not aware of the love that I was surrounded with by many people. How selective in memory and thought depression could be. When he said he stopped loving me, when I felt just emptiness in his heart, I stopped loving myself and could not recognize love any longer. It was because I wanted him to love me, and it looked like others were not capable of giving me what was missing.

How selective depression is when it chooses stories. All are black and bleak, with no room for colours at all. My selective memory, painted only through depression, nearly cut off all the people who wanted to help me. All my stories were dark and I allowed only Susanne to remind me of the stories which we had painted together on the canvas of our childhood and youth.

Can you believe I have beaten a boy? He was even older than I was, he was taller and he was the bully of our street.

Susanne rang and said that Marco came from Trieste and sent his regards. She said:

"Do you remember when you beat up Skunk, because every day when he would pass by, he would call Marco 'Marcolina'?"

It was true.

Marco was a few years younger; a friend of Susanne's and a friend of mine. Particularly, he was fond of me, for apparently I was strong and free and Marco was a very timid, introverted boy who liked to be in the company of girls.

When I met Marco, he was with Susanne and they were smoking their first cigarettes in the little park, hidden behind the wide trunk of the oak tree. When I came and saw them smoking, I took the cigarettes out of their mouths and broke them in half, then in half again. I took the packet of cigarettes and took them out one by one and broke each of them in half and this was accompanied each time by the words 'bloody shit.' They were speechless, Susanne tried to protest twice and I gave her a terrifying look and she looked at Marco, nodding her head, which really did not have any particular meaning. Marco looked like a girl and I thought he was one when I saw him for the first time, but soon I found out that he was some sort of a boy. But what a beautiful young boy he was, I thought that he was the prettiest boy I had ever seen. Susanne was twelve, Marco was two years younger and I was the oldest, thirteen.

Marco had the biggest black eyes edged with long, dark eyelashes and the eyes were set in the middle of a longish, thin head adorned with dark, so black, almost ink-blue, thick hair. But in his eyes was seated never-seen softness, when he looked at me with his big moist eyes, I choked, I nearly cried out of tenderness. His lips were more the lips of a girl than a boy; not too big, but full and red like the late summer cherries, the ones Susanne and I were stealing regularly some summers before from the gardens on the edge of our town. His lips were pouted out and when he spoke, I had a feeling that he whistled rather than talked with such shaped and full lips. When he smiled, he showed perfect, white teeth with little bumps on the edges, a reminder that he was still only a young child. He looked older because of his colours, the blackness of his eyes and hair, and his olive skin. He even had a little, just visible dark mole, the size of a rice grain, on the left side of his lips. When he smiled, he had dimples on his cheeks, and when he looked at me with his moist eyes and when the dimples showed on his cheeks, all my anger ran out of my head and I told them:

"What's wrong with you both?"

I learned that he was a distant cousin of Susanne and a family friend and he lived in the neighbourhood and I wondered why I had never seen him before. He was sort of grateful for my abrupt arrival, for he really did not want to smoke and it was Susanne's idea. She never told me, for she feared exactly the same reaction from my side.

Marco became my friend, too, and he started to follow me like a faithful and grateful little puppy. As he grew older, he showed more and more interest in the things girls do and like, and he was considered more like our girlfriend than a real boy. As his eyes were soft and kind, his soul was made of the same softness and shone through him the way an aura shines out of the saints in the religious paintings. The three of us shared many moments together: we shared secrets, clothes and the mascara when we started to use make-up.

When I talked, he would look at me and hug me timidly, saying, "You are my hero," for I dared to do and say what he would not dare in his wildest dreams. Susanne and I took care of him because he was younger, and he looked like a little, perfectly crafted, porcelain doll, and we feared he could be prey for others with not-so-noble intentions.

Oh, yes, he was teased. The older he became, the more teased he was.

I would catch myself sometimes looking at him while undressing on the beach and thinking, "What a pity," what a pity, that was what I thought. But I loved him as we can love somebody who is fragile, dependent yet so beautiful and faithful. When you knew him better, you could understand that he was not so timid, but that he had a great eagerness for life. Naturally, he was drawn to all sorts of art and fashion and when he dressed up, it was obvious that he had a better dress sense than any girl.

When Susanne asked me if I remembered my courage, which often edged with madness and reminded me how I had beaten the older boy, I said that I did not remember. Why would I remember such a silly episode when I acted "rather as a boy than a girl," as my Mother used to put it? However I acted at that time, I knew that I had to experience the things and emotions first-hand in order that they would acquire real meaning for me.

But it looks to me now as if some hidden chapters had opened in my inner book and I am able to read the past more easily; with more clarity and sympathy.

Marco was a target for older boys, they were teasing him, calling him names and often threatening to beat him up if he walked through certain streets, so because of that he would take a longer way to school or back home. What a lonely and demeaning experience that would have been for a young soul! Often they used to follow him on their bikes and throw things at him, like sandwich leftovers, uneaten apples, little stones and twigs made into arrows. He would run with no words able to defend himself. He was clumsy and a sad figure if you looked at him. The other kids would laugh, join in the fun and all together would chant, "Mar-co-li-na si-gno-ri-na." He would run home with a bent head and when asked by elders what was happening, he would say, "Nothing," ashamed to admit that he was humiliated on a daily basis, so he pretended that nothing out of the ordinary happened. These were only understandable attempts to deal with a fundamentally unlivable situation. And while saying his "nothing," he would not say it in a sad voice but answer in a rather cheerful manner.

I heard of some of these incidents but never caught anybody doing it, for when he was with me and Susanne, nobody teased him, they would just give us a certain look and quietly laugh. Yes, some kids feared me, for I was so free to say whatever I wanted to say, plus I had an older brother who was tall, athletic and a bit of a bully himself and for these qualities he was highly respected. All the kids knew I was his little sister, so boys would not dare to say anything harmful about me or about others in front of me to avoid anticipated catastrophe.

Even then I wondered why children were so fond of cruelty. Later I discovered that the human race is inclined to cruelty, how odd, oh, how odd and unacceptable that was for my nature, and I thought that there were unfortunately only two choices: to accept this fact or to fight for a better world. My way of fighting for a better world was to protect the weak and meek and teach them how to get stronger.

Susanne called me out to have a ride on the bike. We came back from school as the summer had just ended and school had started again, because we could not let go of our pleasures so easily. The fig trees were full of fruit, round, dark and heavy with cracks, and we would ride out of the town, lay the bikes on the top of the little hill which was overlooking the olive grove and calm sea in the distance and climb the fig tree; sit there and eat the figs. While we were riding, we took a short cut and we heard shouting and laughing in the narrow ally. As we approached closer, we saw a group of boys led by the street hooligan nicknamed Skunk for his often-dishonest deeds. But what kind of hooligan was he really, I am thinking now, when he was beaten up by an angry, younger girl? When we came closer I let my bike fall on the grass and ran towards them while he was pulling Marco's ear telling him to say, "I am a girl," as he was repeating the same sentence. Marco was as quiet as a little frightened mouse, red in the face, holding back tears as he was holding back his necklace, which the bully tried to snatch with the other hand.

My mind never alternated between neutrality and involvement. The blood ran straight to my head, reason left me at the same moment, the thought of fear never occurred to me, I grabbed the big, thick stick which was lying on the grass and came to the bully and hit him hard on his forearm once. He turned to me and said in a loud, terrifying voice:

"Are you sane, you bitch?"

"Bitch, huh?" and I hit him again on the shoulder.

He screeched, the other boys ran away, Susanne hugged Marco, who was on the verge of tears, and I said:

"I am not afraid of you, you big bully! Are you going to hit a girl?"

And he said:

"A girl? You are as much of a girl as Marco is a boy."

I had no hesitation, I squeezed my wooden stick tighter and once again I hit him across the calf.

He screeched once again, his hair was on his face, all the other boys ran several meters away, but they were still there, very keen to see the outcome. They were hidden behind the houses and some cars, speculating as to how I would get my head alive from this conflict, for Skunk was known as the strongest of them all.

The very same thought had never occurred to me. I was sure that he was the one who had to be concerned about how this conflict would end, not me, for I was made of sterner stuff. I knew I was the winner, for I was defending the weak. I wasn't religious, so I did not think that God was on my side, but knowing that I was doing the right thing, I believed that I had to have extra strength to fight the bully and I was keen to fight with enthusiasm. He was outraged, he jumped closer, grabbed my stick and pulled it out of my hands and as he did it, I jumped on his back like a wild cat and started to pull his hair with one hand and with the other slapping him across the face. To the astonishment of the audience, including Marco and Susanne, the big bully, the Skunk, who was the terror of the neighbourhood, fell down on his knees and started to sob. While he was sobbing, I was still in the tight grip of relentless rage and told him to say:

"I am a girl."

And he was repeating a number of times "I am a girl" while he was sobbing like a little kid. I said to him:

"Go now, if I see you again beating him or bullying him, you will see what will happen next."

He took his bike, sat on it and while riding away, he shouted:

"I'll get you for this, you ... you stinky tomboy...."

We sat on our bikes, Marco behind me with his moist dark eyes and we rode to the outskirts of the town where the figs were the biggest and for free. We sat in the tree and sang the song whose words we could not really understand, and because of this, each of us pronounced the words differently, sporadically correcting each other. Later, many years later, whenever I heard this song on the radio, I would laugh at how funny we were in our attempt to sing the song whose words we could not understand at all.

What happened next was that the entire neighbourhood knew how I won the fight. He said that he would take revenge but he never did. He feared my brother perhaps, or even my temperament, I never knew what.

Susanne and Marco told and retold this story so many times and each time they would add some new details. As myths usually were woven with bits of truth and bits of the free interpretation of narrators, it looked in the end as if I had beaten up the whole group of boys, and they went home with broken and bloody noses, crying loudly.

I was really Marco's hero.

It looked by now that Susanne, Marco and I were members of some exclusive, secretive sisterhood and intruders were not just unwelcome but punished.

This story reached all the ears in our district and my Mother's too, so she said to me that she was disappointed and devastated by the fact that I was fighting in the street, that I was beating up hooligans and she posed the question: what would become of me without any girly manners?

I said to her that I would always do what was just and right. She had swung her head and sighed deeply as if I was one of the hooligans in the street or someone who knew perfectly how to embarrass a respectable family.

When we were a bit older, he would phone me on Saturday or Sunday morning and I would still be sleeping. When I would wake up my Mother would inform me, that Marco rang (she used to call him 'Girlfriend') and said that he was making pancakes for me so when I was ready to come, to give him a call so that he could start frying them, while I was strolling down the stairway to his house and when I got there, they'd be warm. Because of Marco's loyalty, I ate every Saturday or Sunday warm pancakes filled with walnuts and chocolate. Marco would put on some soft music (at seventeen he adored Maria Callas, may I ask now which seventeen-year-old boy adores Maria Callas?) and we would dream together. He wanted to be involved in the fashion world and wanted to go to Milan. For him fashion and Milan were synonyms for freedom.

Years later, he did. His tall, almost perfect body, like a young Adonis, adorned the many catwalks of European capitals and his beautiful androgynous face looked at young girls and boys, who were full of admiration and envy at the same time, from the covers of the expensive, glossy magazines. The time had long passed since he was bullied and was a simple object of ridicule. He said that it looked to him as if among his new friends he was accepted together with his physical beauty and all his faults; his insecurities and possible eccentricity or even perversity, which could be given to him as a descriptive adjective, while one observed his way of talking or the way he walked or dressed himself.

How liberating it was, he said, how liberating.

The mystery of his sensual and tragic (as later became factual) soul could be seen reflected in his moist eyes, often misinterpreted as timidity. Even though I knew him well and from an early age, even though I credited myself with the skill of understanding people's nature, it was never possible to completely penetrate into his inner world to pursue the secrets, which I only assumed came from the depths (of which even he was not aware) of his personality, which was tormented and quite complex when you learn to look through the filter of the moist in his eyes.

While I was with Claude, I wouldn't see Marco so often and when we split up, Marco was again very much involved in my life.

197

Whenever I was sad or moody, he would comfort me with food, he would bake a cake for me, or steal the best home-made wine from his uncle's cellar and we would drink wine and laugh.

Marco never had a girlfriend. Or a boyfriend, either. Marco had me, and Susanne, and to avoid teasing and harshness, he would preferably stay at home, studying, listening to the music or reading books. Once he told me, when I asked him over the phone what he was doing, that he was knitting a scarf and I yelled so loudly that all the neighbourhood could hear:

"That is far too much, Marco! Stop it at once or I won't come! Stop it at once; you really get on my nerves!"

He wanted to explain to me that knitting was a relaxing hobby, plus he could knit the scarf the way he liked it, and I did not want to hear about it at all, I did not want to hear it, all of this was way too much!

I understood then that my duty was not to direct Marco into any direction he did not want to go. That was the problem of the others who tried to tease and criticize him, and I understood that I did not have that right, and in the end, that I did not want to do that. I accepted him the way he was and knowing that in the environment where we lived, to be different was a sin which carried a heavy load. Any difference was not accepted, was laughed at, and the boy with a gentle voice, gentle manners and with an inclination to knit on Saturday afternoon while listening to Maria Callas's voice was not a boy at all.

The problem was not in the question as to whether he was a boy or not, the problem was in the frighteningly low threshold of tolerance towards diversity, and out of that lack of tolerance all other harmful deeds were born. We fear differences; maybe we fear them because we believe that we are missing out on something better? Can it be so? Why was the bully better and more respected? Fear again? What was wrong, again, with being soft and kind? Why was it and why is it often associated with weakness? Weakness only comes when you are unable to express who you really are. For he was a strong boy, I saw that in his smile while he smiled from the glossy pages of the magazines. He was strong to say to this society, "I've had enough of your ways and I am going, all by myself, to find the way which suits me." And he did. He found it and he smiled at all of those who stayed and never really grew, for the bravery and growth was not coming from the known and repeated many times endlessly. He smiled with his beautiful cherry-coloured lips, with his dimples and his moist eyes. Whenever I saw his eyes, whether in a magazine or at my door, all I saw in them was softness and kindness.

And I always loved him. Yes, I did.

He always called me, "My hero," for remembering how many times I would rescue him from the street bullies or shout at somebody, "Look at yourself, you moron," when somebody would laugh at the way he walked or the way he talked.

He came back home only to see his parents, Susanne, and me. He would bring me expensive make-up, which he would get for free, sometimes some expensive accessories, sometimes even books, for he knew that books were to me the dearest and most cherished gifts and possessions.

The citizens of our town could never live without their myth and stories about him. Friendships with people he never knew took on different shapes in local cafes, and young ladies indiscreetly claimed they knew him better than one might suspect. Such is human nature; while he was a young, insecure boy with an aura of feminine softness around him, he was painted as a clumsy, grotesque creature nobody really wanted to know, but when he stepped out of the ordinary life of a quiet town, everybody claimed they knew him, befriended him or rubbed shoulders with him in daily encounters, as always happens to those who distinguish themselves from their fellows, even when it was as simple as being a model in the frenzied world of fashion.

And this world of fashion for him was both a blessing and a curse.

At that time, childhood was behind us and I noticed that he had changed, his soft eyes got a different expression and I could not name it (if I had to name it, I would say that he looked like a victim of his boyish yearnings for independence and some sort of worldly glamour). Later I learned from him that they were coloured by many disappointments, the fraud and greed that followed the followers of fashion, for on their upward climb there are many traps on each step. He was not happy, but he wasn't sad, either, and he said that for the first time in his short life, he lived for himself. I envied him. Not for being part of such a fancy world, but for the fact that he could live his life closest to his conception of himself. On a deeper level I was happy that he finally could be what he wanted to be in his boyish dreams.

I thought it must have been a wonderful feeling, yes, it must have been.

But I never knew if he attained what he aimed for, for more and more often he would say that the world of fashion where he lived was indeed a made-up world, unreal and bizarre, and that this world could not meet all of his expectations.

The last time I saw him, we went to the beach. He put his beautiful, uni-dentified, androgynous head on my lap; he lit a cigarette and said in a soft voice full of nostalgia for lost innocence:

"I wish I could be a little boy again. The one you would look after and protect. You do not know how many times I cried, for I thought that the world

was a hostile place and I was put there by mistake, but having you on my side was equal to having some sort of an angel warrior, if there is such a thing ... you meant everything to me, for you gave me a feeling of self-worth and you supported me in everything. To sum it up: I could be my real self only with you. Thank you; you will always be my hero." He took my hand and kissed it and I combed his ink-blue hair with my fingers and sang the English song which we sang, pronouncing the words incorrectly, in the days of our youth, which was mapped with alley streets, fig trees, cherry and olive trees in the peaceful gulf of our childhood.

I never found the answer to the dilemma about whether or not suffering ennobles one's character. There was an uncertain form of sadness in his eyes (like in the eyes of someone who was constantly wounded) but often he said that suffering did not make him a better person; that there was a hidden wish for vindictiveness when he thought in sketches of his delicate, porcelain past. It was hard for me to imagine him vindictive, for his kind nature could not bear malice deliberately. I believed that his vindictiveness could happen only in the world of his imagination, where he could freely be brave, brutish, cruel, for a few moments, but in the reality where he abided, he could not hurt anybody.

***

When I remembered that story, called to my memory by Susanne's consistent effort to make me remember how fearless a child I was, I said to my Mother:

"Mother, why did you say that I was a fragile child? Why did you say that?"

She said that I was fragile in my emotions and always felt deep compassion for others and I said, "This is a rather noble feeling, isn't it?" but she said:

"You always wanted some sort of justice and fought for it fiercely, sometimes you would be simply exhausted by chasing the wind."

I said, "It may seem improbable then that I was brave when you repeated how fragile I was. It may seem improbable, so do not repeat it ever again, for I know I have to unlearn this statement, yes, I have to unlearn it and I do not know how. I do not know who can teach me this art but if it is just a matter of a simple decision, where must this decision be made? What strength has it and is it of a strong, unbreakable structure? What if it was a fallacy? If I was not fragile but only let my mind believe that I was? Is it so that this belief has eaten my bravery? Just a simple belief? Mother, why did you say I was fragile, a very fragile child?"

My poor Mother shrugged her shoulders and I saw tears in the corners of her eyes. To learn to be really strong, I came closer, hugged her and said, "Sorry Mother, I love you, but I am just struggling to understand who I am, of how many selves humans are made and how often and why we are changing them, whether willingly or not."

My Mother hugged me and said:

"I do not know how I can help you these days, it seems whatever I say is wrong or misunderstood."

She said that she came to nurse me and give me some strength and hope, and I said to her that she carried out her task perfectly. The moistness from her eyes stayed there and I felt guilty yet again, for mothers know the art of making their children feel guilty.

She said:

"I will never repeat it again, it might be that you were fragile; it might be that you were strong and brave. Please, do not ask me all these questions, for I do feel sometimes you are taking advantage of such a difficult situation and out of it you are writing yet another novel."

She was on the verge of tears and I said, "Say no more, Mother," and we sat on the sofa holding hands.

***

As I said before, Susanne's attempts to bring my memories back in order to fight the dark clouds that threatened to consume me completely were consistent and frequent. My Mother told her that I might come next summer with a friend of mine (the plan which never came through because of Erwin's inconsistency in his speech and his deeds) and Susanne told me we would walk together all the narrow alleys, we would take the kids' bikes and ride to the parts of the town which were planted with olive trees some twenty years ago, but were now planted with tall buildings.

That summer, the last one, she took me out to a restaurant. It was the one we used to go to before, and she said that it had changed a bit, but it still had the best and the freshest fish in town. And I told her that I owed her the story about the Other Man, for he came to visit me and I took him to the very same restaurant the week before. She got excited, for she would always get excited when I came with a story she had never heard before. I promised her I would tell the story later when we sat down and ordered our meal.

She came to pick me up and when I saw her, I thought that we were never old to ourselves. She looked to me like a young girl, of about seventeen, just her eyes were a little bit less shiny and the complexion of her skin was

not flawless any more, her hair was still shiny but somehow thinner, espe-
cially her fringe. As always she was dressed with a lot of style but it looked
somehow like a careless look, the touch of youth, and she put on her make-
up, telling me that "the make-up, especially the lipstick, is because of you."

The table was reserved in her name and the young waitress led us to the
table. While she was walking, I was thinking that something in the way she
walked and carried her body struck a chord of somebody uncertain, some-
body I might remember only if reminded.

At the table next to us two men were seated. One I recognized at once, he
was the waiter who served me last week when I came here with my friend and
he called me by my first name as if we were the best of friends sometime. The
other I could not recognize, for I knew that I had never seen him before. They
smiled at me when I looked in their direction and I did not want to ask
Susanne anything about them, for I thought it would be obvious and rude.

When we got our menus, we started to examine them thoroughly and I
did not notice that he had approached our table, and in a quiet and pleasant
voice, he said that if we wished to eat fish, he would suggest snapper as they
were caught today, were fresh, fleshy and very tasty. The rest, he said, was
not as fresh and not as tasty.

Susanne gave him a little nod and he looked at me, addressing me again
by my first name (even though he addressed Susanne by her second name,
calling her 'doctor') and said that I had eaten here a few days ago, so he
said he was pleased that I came back which showed him I liked the food. I
understood that the man was the owner of the restaurant, rather than the
waiter, but all I could say about him was that he had a pleasant voice. His
body and its parts looked mismatched and it gave an impression that his own
parts were at odds and forced to be together. Obviously, he was not good-
looking, and yet strangely, not too ugly.

Even though his voice was pleasant and his intentions were to please us,
there was something peculiar in the way he looked at me, and in the way he
pronounced my name for the second time (for when I was here with the Other
Man, he called me by my name, and I could swear then that I had never met
him either in my life or in one of my dreams).

As he sat back at the table directly opposite to ours, and the conversa-
tions could be heard if talking in normal tone, I did not dare to ask Susanne
about him, but I understood when she lifted her eyes and her chin in his
direction. I started to retell the story about the Other Man, but the version in
which I never waved him goodbye. Instead I sat in his car and he drew me
away into the dream I had been dreaming since I met him. She got excited
and wanted to know all the details and for some bits I said, "I can't tell you
that." She would pout her lips and make a sad expression, telling me,

"Please, tell me, I wanna know," and I would continue with all the details which could be told only to one's best friend. As we ate, we got caught up in that story and some others later on and when we finished the meal, we ordered a cake and asked for the bill.

He, the man who called me by my first name, the one I thought I had never met, brought us cakes and said that we did not have to pay, for it would be his pleasure to treat us with a dinner. I was very surprised, Susanne did not look much surprised, then he looked at me again, calling me by my first name and asking me whether I remembered him. It was some sort of relief for me to know that we were sometime acquaintances, for the look in his eyes was quite disturbing for me. All I said was, *"I am sorry, but I can't remember right now."*

He asked for permission to sit at our table but without waiting for consent, he sat down and said, *"Tony."*

That name did not have any special meaning to me. In my travels to many countries and my life on two different continents, the name Tony did not place me anywhere in particular; neither here, in my hometown, looking at the face to which more was added now, the name - Tony.

Susanne smiled, seeing blankness in my eyes.

They were silent, as if they were waiting for that big revelation which would soon be announced, but I said nothing to the stubby man with a pleasant voice and untroubled eyes.

Then he said:

"Skunk."

When it hit the right place - my awareness - I burst out laughing, and he did, too.

I did not know whether this moment was awkward for Susanne, for we were laughing and she was eating her cake with total dedication.

I said:

"Skunk, the boy I beat up some thirty years ago."

"That Skunk, yes. So you did not forget it."

"No, for you were the first and the only person I have ever beaten, how could I forget such an achievement?"

He said:

"I saw you on television, read articles about you, read your books, I always knew that you were somehow ... somehow ... different, let's say."

"Yes Tony, I was different, for there were not many girls who had beaten up an older boy. Shall I say now to you that I am sorry, for genuinely I am?"

He said:

"We were kids. And I was a bully. I remained a kind of bully for many years, but prison and war, then marriage and kids, had changed me. I bought

this restaurant some ten years ago and directed all my energy into work, people started to appreciate me, maybe for the first time in my life and I liked the feeling. I married a good girl, she used to go to school with you and Susanne, but it took me many painful lessons to get where I am now."

"It is the same for all of us, we all learn painful lessons to make progress on our path, and it is a long road to maturity. Another thing is that the wiser go away with a decent grace. You were the one who walked away."

He smiled an insecure smile and asked:

"Do you keep in touch with Marco?"

"Not as often as I would like to. An e-mail here and there, or I hear from friends about him, but I haven't seen him for a very, very long time."

"When he comes home, he often eats here."

"Do you still tease him, for if you do, I have to be a hooligan again and beat you up right here in front of your family, friends and customers."

We all laughed, Susanne laughed with a mouth full of mud cake.

As we had exhausted the subject and there was really no need to find new ones, we agreed it was time to go.

And there was no way we could pay that bill and while leaving, I said to him that I would come again, for the food was delicious and for free, what more could one ask for?

While driving home, I said to Susanne:

"Why on earth did you not tell me that Skunk was the owner of the restaurant? You knew it, didn't you?"

She knew, but she said she wanted me to discover the story about Skunk. She said that he asked about me at different times, but once again we laughed as we were retelling the story of how I had beaten him up. And I said to Susanne:

"Do you remember, when he sat on his bike, he yelled that he would take revenge ... yet what strange revenge came from him, he treated us with dinner ... what revenge!"

I said to Susanne:

"You see what life teaches us – if you were born as a skunk, if you were brought up as a skunk, you do not have to remain a skunk, you see, we have choices, don't we?" And we laughed again, we laughed and I felt young again.

When we were in the car in front of my house, I said to her that the story of the Other Man was not a complete truth. She gathered her eyebrows together in disbelief and slowly asked:

"What does that mean, exactly - not a complete truth?"

I reminded her of my dubious childhood stories, which sometimes she would even label as lies, but then she asked me what that had to do with the present time. I told her that my so-called nonexistent worlds had a large impact on my reality. I said that in my imagination I had a freedom I could never acquire in the world which I met daily, hence both endings were true, the one where I said goodbye to my friend and waved to him while his car got smaller and smaller in the distance, and the other one was true but was seated somewhere where I freely tailored the plot and its protagonists.

She said:

"Go home and have a good sleep. And find yourself a decent man when you wake up, believe me there are some out there...."

I put my index finger on her lips, kissed her cheeks and said:

"Sleep well, dottoressa," and I walked out into the warm night decorated with a starry sky.

I wanted to tell her that men found me to be too heavy, but she would have had a counterargument, trying to convince me of something I never believed, and on which note would that conversation end? A long time ago I learned that it was better to leave some questions unanswered and some arguments lost.

When Skunk left us alone at the table, I said to Susanne:

"I have beaten up a poor boy and still everybody remembers it, how funny, I have nearly forgotten it. But I would not say I was brave, rather a little bit mad."

"It was all about injustice. About defending the weak and defenseless."

"Our sweet Marco, I was his hero."

"Do you remember when you rescued a neighbour's cat?"

"Honestly, not."

"Oh, c'mon! You've got to remember it. If it hadn't been for your brother you would probably have been beaten to death."

"Really?"

"You really live elsewhere. You are not even living in the past, but listen and you'll remember:

We were strolling down the stairs into the street beneath ours, and we heard loud meowing and loud laughter. There was a fire coming out of the bottle that one of the boys was holding. There were seven of them, all a little bit younger than us, but they were already at the very dangerous age of twelve, real little hooligans, or wannabes. Their eyes shone with malice. Two of them were holding the cat: one had its front legs; the other was holding its hind legs and the one with a flaming bottle was rotating the bottle around the poor cat's body and the cat was shrieking, literally, like somebody who was burning alive.

When we saw it, we stopped for a second. I stopped without intention to act, and you, as always, without having a second thought, jumped down the two remaining steps and kicked the boy who was holding the cat with your fist into the ribs. At once he let the cat's legs and turned to you, but you went to another one and kicked him in the stomach with your fist and I was standing there like a statue. Then one of them grabbed you by the hair and I started screaming, calling your name out and telling them to let go of you, for all of them circled you shouting insults and threats. All I could do was to take a stone and I threw it into the head of one of the boys and I started to run towards your house to let your brother or father know what was happening, but on my way there I saw your brother walking down and I ran to him. In short and confused sentences I told him what was happening and he ran down the stairs as if he was chased by a flaming wind and was there in one second and so strong and tall jumped into the middle. When they saw him, they ran in all the different directions, your brother grabbed one by the shoulder and said:

"Next time I'll burn you alive with this bottle."

I remembered.

I remember my brother told me later that I was really mad; when I told him that I needed to rescue a poor cat from the hooligans, he said that I should have passed by as all others would ... but I could not.

Having an older, strong and athletic brother and being a 'little mad' made me both popular and unpopular among my peers.

But I always wanted bravery and honesty to walk with me.

***

But this episode brought to my memory something that nobody witnessed. It was just my soul that became restless after that incident. It was my first ever encounter with cruelty, or as far as I can remember, the first one. I was about seven years old, standing on the balcony. I remember it was one of the warmer days of spring. April in my hometown was always the most beautiful season for me, for everything was in bloom and new, young leaves coloured my street green. I saw a little bird on the asphalt, maybe it fell out of the nest, but it was so little a birdie and I just thought that I would go out to see how I could help it.

But at the same time as this thought occurred, a little girl, just short of a few months to be in the same class as I was, ran to it. I thought that she would do what I would, so I stayed on the balcony believing that the birdie was rescued already. My curiosity kept me standing there and observing her attempts to help the little bird. The girl gathered the bird in her hands and said something (I believed soft and comforting) to it, and then she threw her hands up, towards the supportive sky and the little bird flew up but only because of the throwing force. It did not have the strength or the knowledge of how to fly yet, so it fell down to the ground. The little girl laughed a cheerful laugh as if she had sent it into freedom from suffering. To be honest, I still believed that the little girl did not understand that the bird failed to fly when she took her the second time into her hands and said something (I believed soothing) to it. The girl put the little bird next to her nose, widened her eyes and said again some words I could not hear, then swung her arms with the birdie in her hands and threw it towards the cloudless, peaceful, but indifferent sky. The little bird fell down with quite a loud thud. The little girl had a strange expression on her face, but it was obvious from her cheerful laugh and the shine in her eyes that this was great entertainment for her. She took the bird again, and I screamed from the balcony:

"Do it again and I will come down and I will toss you up, too, you little idiot!"

I ran down as fast as I could, she ran home.

When I came down, the little bird was dead.

I can frankly say that this was the biggest shock of my life, when I discovered that children could be so cruel as to enjoy the suffering of a living soul. I took the little bird into my hands, pressed it to my chest and sang it a song. I dug a hole and placed the little bird in it and cried. The whole afternoon I was sad and distressed and I remember I thought that I would rather enjoy the company of a little bird than that of a girl, for humans can be crueller than any animal.

That discovery was a very sad discovery for me. Very sad.

*** *

But childhood had to end and with it, my tomboyish behaviour.

When I met Claude, I was already a young lady, with far better manners. Still, a strong instinct to protect the weak was a major trait of my personality. He noticed that and he respected me for it. He thought it was quite a noble behaviour, and because of his thought, I cultivated further my need to be a protector when needed.

I didn't have a need to protect Claude, for he appeared to be brave, honest and kind. When I said, 'appeared to be,' it does not mean that he was not that at all, but the contrary to it. No, he was of kind nature, well groomed, well mannered and had a good but gentle humour. When we were alone, just he and I, we lived in harmony. He appeared to be brave, honest and kind.

But when I met his mother, I understood that she was never pleased with him: she would endlessly criticize whatever he did, and then I saw that his bravery, honesty and kindness were limited by his audience, should I say, I cultivated in him these qualities as he did cultivate some noble qualities within me. But when he was around his mother, he seemed like a little boy who was really not able to think with his own head, or the one whose next move would certainly be the wrong one.

She would foresee unimaginable and unseen catastrophes if he only took a step without consulting her and she would simply roll her big, dark eyes every time when he said something 'out of the ordinary.'

Once, we were invited to dinner at a local restaurant by his friends.

While he had a shower, she was timing everything, how many minutes he was in the bathroom, how long it took him to dry his hair; she made him twice change his shirt, for he did not know how to choose properly, and each time she would comment that we would be late, for he was slow and lazy. He did not argue, for he knew that he would lose the argument anyway, that was a well-learned lesson, but he tried to be quicker, he tried to match the right colours, he tried to dry his hair the way she liked it while she was telling him that he was always late, always clumsy ... and after a long tirade I could not stand it any longer (as always, doing his best was never good enough), so I said:

"Not always! He is not late always, maybe just this evening, but it does not mean always."

She did not even look in my direction, which aggravated my mood. I repeated:

"He is not late yet, and he will not be if only he's given a chance to get dressed and comb his hair the way he wants without pressure or disturbance."

She did not even look in my direction, and that aggravated my mood. I said:

"Since I've known him he has never been late for a date, he's always delivered what he's promised, accurately and punctually."

She did not look at me but at him and said with disinterested passion adorned with little diamonds of motherly sadness in her eyes:

"What will become of you, what will become of you?"

Painful guesswork!

I said to him:

"Say something."

But he did not.

So, I said:

"Just let him be," and I walked out of the house, sat in the car and lit a cigarette. He came after quite a long time, so we were late, as she had predicted. Even though I knew 'what' - I asked him:

"What took you so long?"

He said:

"Do not worry, I rang, they will wait for us...."

"It is not about us, it is about her, isn't it? You are subjected to constant alterations."

He replied:

"Leave it there, just leave it."

"Can't you protect yourself from her attacks?"

He said:

"Please, do not ruin the evening, we will have a nice dinner with friends, just be calm, be happy."

Oh, how easy, how easy. Be calm, be happy, and pretend, just pretend.

What do we do when we are not happy in the world in which we live; with the people we are surrounded with, where firm convictions are required? One of the choices was to pretend that reality was different, that we were not aware of the wrongs, that everything was 'calm and happy'. But this choice separates us from ourselves, or may I say the self takes grand departure and leaves the throne for the one who will accommodate oneself in the 'calm and happy' world created without one's participation.

When I said exactly that to Claude, he said:

"Please, do not complicate things, please do not make it harder for me."

So I did not.

But truly, I never learned the advantage of keeping my thoughts to myself at the critical time. Often injustice would give birth to the emotion of struggling anger in my chest and I would let it out quickly, and later regret it. Regret is often the result of quick anger but I struggled with an idea of injustice and felt like one who had to deliver justice no matter what.

At that time Claude's practice had been to deny the emotions he could not handle, and maybe I learned that art from him when I said to Antonella, "Never mind," or when I went down to Andalucia, believing that emotions could be buried into fine sand and carried to other lands by wind, sand and dust.

When we got there, Claude was called by the owner of the restaurant, for there was a telephone call for him. It was his mother. She rang to remind him that when he was upset and had a late dinner, he would always get sick.

And he did.

She was a perfect prophet and a perfect gardener who gardened in his body with her calculated yet careless hand.

But you know what? She overstepped the territory without my consent and without my conscious knowing, my inner garden started to wither; yes, it started to wither away.

CHAPTER TEN

When She came in, She looked calm. That calmness was obvious in the movements of Her hands, in Her voice and quite a placid smile. Her eyes were focused and when She sat down, She crossed Her legs and stayed seated in this position, like a comfortable and self-assured woman who was accustomed to nothing but leisure and was a stranger to the emotional turmoil and depressive moods, which turned Her against Herself some years ago.

She said with a ring of carelessness, still with a light aura of mystery:

I came to advise you that I'd like to take a little break. May I see you again in two weeks?

"Certainly you may. Are you going somewhere?"

I am going to places where nobody can follow me, not even you. So, to sail and to sink deep down there, I need two weeks and I'll be back, probably with more stories, eventually with more accuracy, or I might be able to separate fiction from reality, the dream from the past and the vision from the illusion, how about that?

He shrugged his shoulders in agreement, but all the muscles on his face stayed relaxed. Before She walked out, She asked him:

Do you think I am a little mad?

He said that a little bit of madness was good, otherwise She probably would not deliver all Her stories and Her dreams, She would not have Her visions and the knowledge how to sink deep down into the depths, where Her stories and emotions were stored in the same compartment and had been mixed with ordinary life events which devalued all that was spiritual there.

She said:

After each novel, Hermann Hesse went to the asylum with total confusion and emotional exhaustion. Not that I put myself shoulder to shoulder with such a genius, but I know what it takes to be a vivisector; I know the torment of the emotions which, even when told time and again, do not lose their strength. While writing I would feel like I was possessed by a mysterious power which was using me for its own needs, and in its hold I would feel as defenseless and helpless as a little bird that was thrown in the air to learn to fly, yet its wings were not adapted to the strong winds. On the other hand, I knew the despair of not expressing myself through my stories, and they would cry within me, asking me to let them go, to let them be told and all the characters were crying loudly to be heard.

Why did I feel others' pain? It looked to me as if we were all connected with invisible, mysterious threads, almost like one organism, so I felt the pain of its parts even when my own body did not hurt. I felt cries that were coming from other eras and eons as they were coursing through the river of our collective memory; as the blood was coursing through my veins. I felt that my own cells were mixed with everything that surrounded me and when others hurt, my wounds would open up and bleed again. I cried with widows and deserted women, with women whose breasts were cut off as Saint Agatha's innocent breasts were cut off, I cried with orphaned children, with a stillborn child and a madman in the sad house. I cried for the weak and disabled, war and rape victims and still I believed all my tears had not been used up.

I felt my husband's pain when his love took a final form of painful disintegration and cried for his pain and with his pain. I felt my Mother's unbearable pain when my breast was cut, when the needles threatened my livelihood, and cried for her pain. I felt another unbearable pain when my daughter's orphaned heart cried quietly every night in my hands, I cried for God and because of him, and felt the pain of his creation, feeling that so much suffering in this world could not be created by a happy and light creator.

I felt Claude's pain when he said, "I do" to a woman he never loved, knowing that he would remain utterly alone with his unbearable sense of betraying himself, and I felt the pain of the Other Man that he couldn't freely love me.

Nicholas's pain, which he tried to drown in alcohol, I felt under the Andalucian sky and because of it, I sat on the steps and talked to him as I would talk to myself when hurting.

I felt Mae's pain as her little boats were mysterious and equally dangerous and threatened to drown her life in the overwhelming ocean of fear. I felt the pain of Marco's almost perfect but feminine abused beauty and the silent pain of Susanne's daughters unidentified pain, and the same pain in St. Yvonne's chest was a demanding guest in my bosom.

I felt the pain of displacement and the pain when nobody writes to you any longer and the same pain of having no one to write to. I even borrowed the pain of great writers and painters and relived it time and again in an attempt to use it all up. Somehow it always came back, as a wounded, half-dead dragon that would attack me with all its might and rage. I felt the pain of the world and at the same time I felt the world was vastly, plainly indifferent to my own pain.

Probably, I would not know how to live without it, how to express myself if not through it and how to relate to fellow humans without it.

My manuscripts were mutilated by it; the pain was the guardian, the plot and the saviour. I was cursed, blessed and purged through it.

***

Even though he was the last person I had written my letters to, I knew that I would never write to him again, but this never prevented me having dreams about him.

I had a dream that he came to my door, one unusually quiet morning when even the birds ceased to sing out of astonishment. It was a soundless morning, and very odd because of this, and I truly was expecting something extraordinary to happen as this strange deafness announced it. In dreams people move differently than in reality, so he was sort of floating, not touching the ground and sat next to me to have breakfast, the very same breakfast as the one we had in Vienna when we woke up that last warm Viennese summer, when we fell asleep exhausted from our passionate and all-consuming dance in his garden.

The Viennese breakfast was brought in by the maid. She came in quickly and left quickly without looking at us, as if she was embarrassed for some reason known only to her. I never liked this woman of oriental looks, for I felt that she was not trustworthy, but when I said that, he giggled rather than laughed, he asked why I should be bothered by a servant. So I wasn't.

It was a rather unusual breakfast. On the big silver tray there were beautifully arranged mouthwatering delicacies: thin slices of the finest prosciutto di Parma wrapped around thin, long, crispy bread sticks put together, in perfect order, next to each other like the best-trained and the best-behaved little soldiers. In between these delicious red soldiers and the squared (all about the same size) pieces of Grana Padano were small forest strawberries, red with little black dots, like the little ladybirds, which I remember I ate only when I was a child. Then there was a long line of caviar running along the silver tray. Its tail curled in the middle of the tray, forming a little inviting hill, and on the hill were olives randomly scattered and they resembled the little black sheep scattered on the unnamed hill, there was a little white hill of goat cheese circled by yet another guard of green olives with red centers, while next to this delicious hill were thin slices of almost transparent parmigiano, which looked like the wings of the butterflies in the herbarium, and among their wings were mixed red and green globes of grapes.

To my astonishment there was the fragola, the sweetest grapes one could find, and when I saw it, my hand instinctively went there, as if it went directly to the hills where I used to pick it together with Susanne, when we used to sneak into forbidden vineyards which we could reach only by riding our bikes. On the big silver tray there were little curled yellowish snails of fine smelling butter, there were slices of mango and pineapple put together on top of each other and on the other side, as a balance to that sweetness, were green sour gherkins, all of the same size, and little dark green capari were mixed with them. The strongest smell came from the freshly-baked French bread and behind the thin slices of bread there were rows of salty crackers, all placed upright, backed up by slices of burgundy coppa adorned with small dots of dark brown pepper. On each corner of the tray there were several little round porcelain dishes with sweet and sour cream and crushed papaya and some chutneys that I had never tasted before. The dearest taste to my palate was the one of codfish pate, which he learned the day before when we dined in the restaurant, which later I heard was owned by the man I beat up when we were young kids. Randomly, without any order, there were fistfuls of blackberries and a few dark red raspberries ... oh, so much sweetness was there that morning when we woke up after the night of the passionate dance in his garden.

And on the edges of the big tray were seated big, blood-red, round cherries, which looked like billiard balls oddly painted, and a few thin slices of pink, smoked salmon.

We started our breakfast with closed eyes at my suggestion, and fed each other with randomly picked delicious bites, trying to guess of what they were made, these flavours mixed together. He said they were made of love, and I said they were made of passion. We did not need the forks, for we took the food with our lustful fingers and licked each other's thumbs and index fingers and he licked my neck, for he said I smelled like an orchid. When I wanted to lick his ring finger, the gold band hurt my eyes, and he took it off and put it in the little porcelain dish with sour cream in it and apologetically shrugged his shoulders. We ate a lot on this Viennese morning and drank nothing, but somehow he said he was drunk, and then I said I was, too, and we laughed as I had never laughed in many years.

He put his head on the pillow and I lined up the little strawberries and the blueberries along his closed lips and then I ate each sweet fruit and while I was picking up the innocent berries, he touched my lips with his, how tender, oh, how tender it was.

When we finished our breakfast, it was already past lunch-time and we were thirsty, for we had drunk only our passion. Then we decided to go out into the warm Viennese afternoon and have a cup of coffee with cream on top of it. We held hands like real lovers do, and we had a twinkle in our eyes, the one which real lovers have, and we talked sweet talk as kids and lovers do.

Now to come back to my dream, which I dreamed several months after that Viennese breakfast; it started with a deaf, soundless morning. I could not hear but only see, and I looked at him standing at my doorstep and holding in his hands an enormous tray with breakfast on it, asking me to let him in. Not only was that morning deaf, but I was deprived of yet another of my senses, so I could not speak, and so, speechless, I showed him in and closed my door which was painted unfriendly to unannounced visitors.

I wanted to ask him when he came and where he found all these delicious bites so early this deaf but generous morning, the same ones which we indulged our senses in before, but he put his index finger on my red with hunger lips and whispered, "All is possible in a dream."
Oh yes, I had forgotten that it was a dream, for it was an identical replica of the other dream and I could not distinguish where it belonged, but when he said, "Who cares where it belongs," I agreed and we started our delicious feast which we both learned together as young lovers do when they together discover the delightfulness of the art of loving.

I took a crayon and sketched a black moustache above his lips, the one Salvador Dali was famously known for, nearly as much as for his art, and when he was about to utter a word, I said that if he talked, he could wake me up and instead of talking, I suggested he could freely, soundlessly kiss me. And he did.
We mixed the kisses with the cherries and the berries, and the cream and the poorly hidden wishes that the dream would never end. But it did.

What woke me up from the replica of the dream in the dream was a telephone buzzing, like a little annoying fly which flew around my head, telling me to give up this elegy which was a longing for romance of unthinkable proportions.

When I answered the phone, my voice was sweet from all the delicious flavours and even more delicious memories brought on my lips from the Viennese breakfast I ate that last European summer.

***

Erwin asked me what I was doing and I said, "Daydreaming," and he said, "How odd, how odd."

I did not expect Erwin to call me ever again, but with Erwin one was never short of surprises. He felt as if he was allowed in God's books to do whatever pleased him, and that was exactly how he felt that morning when he heard my voice sweet from the taste of imaginary cherries. That feeling, that he could do precisely as it pleased him, was especially and generously offered to women. I often asked myself whether he imagined that women were grateful and had a feeling of being privileged, for he called when he felt like calling. I felt somehow that he believed that women could and had to forgive a man for any harm he did to them, deliberate or not deliberate. The women he knew, he said, were foolish and unbalanced and when I asked if I was included in that merry menagerie, he said a firm "No," but I said that I thought I was, for this was the way how he saw women. Deep down, for him, we all were foolish and unbalanced, and probably in the simplest terms, inferior. He talked about love but he had no capacity to love, for his knowledge of love was intellectual knowledge which never touched his troubled heart, divorced as it was from genuine feelings of empathy. He feared commitment and love, as if love was a disease of the weak. He preferred lust, considering it to be a normal need for an adult man, but love, for him, was a trap, and he believed that women gave ridiculous importance to it.

What I understood was that women were instruments of pleasure for him and what exactly kept him attracted to me was my utter indifference to his womanizing ways and my indifference to whether he would call or not. Because of that, at the same time, he loved and loathed me, for all he really treasured was the power he had over women by the way they showed their need for his attention, and he loathed me, for he had no such influence over me. The more he talked about other women, the more I laughed and the more I laughed, his stories became more grotesque and bizarre. What a gift to be given to the writer! What a gift!

Our conversation was short. Why did he say that he did not expect me to travel without him? I said to him that I had travelled without him all of my life, why would he be expecting me to travel with him or not travel at all?

He changed the tone and with it he changed personality, of which he was unconscious, I may say. He said in that new voice that he would like to see me today, as if it was for some urgent reason and when I said that I couldn't see him today, he was agreeable.

But he filled me with astonishment once again: he rang my doorbell a few hours after that conversation. A bunch of flowers was in his hands and a mocking smile in his eyes.

When he walked into the living room, on the table was a big silver tray with delicious food on it. As I usually give names to certain events, I called that morning 'The Replica of the Morning', and he asked if I was waiting for someone. I told him I wasn't, and he asked if somebody was here having lunch with me and I said that I arranged all this food for surprise visitors, and we laughed together. Then I said that I was writing about a particular breakfast morning and wanted to create the exact atmosphere through the flavours, textures and colours.

"Great," said he, "Great," said I, and we were short of words after that.

He cleared his throat and asked me if I was angry with him, for he said that he joked last time he saw me, and as I travelled alone to my hometown, he assumed that I was angry (then repeated again the same phrase he used before) and bitterly disappointed. For a while I did not know what to say, and I was looking at the platter of delicious food to which delicious memories were attached, and after a while, I said:

"You had better not judge."

He said:

"But you judge me all the time."

"I like to know, not to judge. Judgment I leave to you, for you often amuse yourself with sewing sentences onto people's foreheads."

"But it looks it escaped your memory that you wanted to travel with a German man, the one who has known your hometown for the last twenty years. I just stepped aside, for I did not want to interfere with your decisions and choices."

"Look, you made up the story. The German man was somebody I met twice. What do you want me to tell you?"

"I never make up stories."

"You said that the story about your American friend and former girlfriend was a made-up story, you see, you say contradictory things, you make up stories and then you say you do not make up stories. So, make up your mind."

He stood there, hesitant to speak.

He changed the subject. He said:

"We stayed in London for two weeks."

And coincidently, we were in London at the same time, we even arrived the same afternoon. He said:

"We went to Venice," and we were in Venice with my sister exactly the same day.

He said:

"How strange, we could have met each other."

All of a sudden my heart was filled with overwhelming compassion for that man, for I thought how difficult it was for him living in a world of inner conflict and contradiction. There were too many of them and I thought this battle should be exhausting in its consequences. While he was wearing his shapeable mask, he became each time the one he wanted to portray; which one was the real him was not known to his conscious mind, or to mine.

I never understood what he really wanted from me. I never believed that he felt genuine, honest emotions and a need for true friendship or more than that, and for the first time I saw him as a tormented soul striving to find a way for its expression, nothing more, nothing less.

I knew that he could easily change his personalities with his unpredictable moods, but each time when I would see tears in his eyes, it gravely puzzled me, it saddened me. I was so open to human suffering and each time when I saw somebody hurting I would offer understanding.

Like a child caught in a clumsy lie he almost whispered:

"There was no American woman, there were no perverse games in my bedroom, there were no other women, I am a sad, lonely creature afraid of my own feelings. Sometimes it looks as if I am possessed by some hostile entity that makes me tell incredible stories. I would be happier if I could freely and honestly say what I feel ... but I can't. I feel ashamed of my feelings, but if you only knew what is in my heart, probably you would soften your iron will. I have never met a woman with such a strong will, oh, how tormenting it is; you've got an iron will stronger than any man I know."

Quietly, I said:

"Often things are not the way we see them or the way they appear to be. I do not have an iron will, I am not a strong, almost monstrous woman, I am trying to find my way through the maze of betrayal, loneliness, pennilessness, and other turbulent emotions or situations I was exposed to with one simple decision of the man who understood after many years of marriage that he was really not marriage material. I do not suffer less than you do even if I appear to be a woman of iron will. My tears are shed in private, for my daily demands require me to be strong. What would happen to my daughter if I gave in to depression, obvious insecurities and confusion? She is my strength, and if you can learn from me anything, then learn the same: let your daughters be your strength, your reason to carry on, your pride and consolation."

"Will you give me a chance to be your friend again?"

Honestly, it was a very difficult question to answer, plus I really did not know the real reason that stood behind his question.

His speech was never clear, especially when it came to emotions of any kind. Instead, he talked in some sort of signs. In his unusual manner he sought to convey to me the secret treasures of his obviously sometime-wounded heart, but his uncommon way of communicating never let me unlock the signs through which he tried to explain himself. This inability to express and explain himself left him unsatisfied and lonely, unable to ever really know me. Nor did it give me a fair chance to know him. I understood that this frustration was behind his hiding in his garden when I would say something disagreeable. He would not communicate, he would hide, he would make up stories ... but one thing was certain, all his stories were not made up, I knew it. So how could I believe that this sadness of his was a genuine feeling? How could I?

I said to him:

"Let time answer your question," and he quietly walked through the door. When he left, dragging his feet, I must confess he left behind my heart filled with an overwhelming compassion, once again. Even though I could not truly know his real feelings, I believed that with the lapse of time and somebody else's kind heart, happiness would find its way to his heart again. I remembered how intolerable my grief was, but with the kindness of others it softened, and the scar became liquid and transparent, accommodated to the new me, allowing me to write about my Viennese breakfast with delight and joy.

That day I could not reconstruct my Viennese breakfast any longer, so I just looked at the tray with delicious food without any appetite. I was thinking of him the entire day and lots of thoughts were buzzing in my head. I wondered whether there was any way I could help him, but the little voice within me said, "Let it be." But I didn't. As I always liked to draw a conclusion to situations, I wrote him a letter.

It was not so sincere and not so genuine a letter, but all I wanted was to tell him that we were not two people who could give each other sincere joy and pleasure. I expressed my warmest wishes and hopes that he would meet a woman who would be right for him. I took the blame, for I said that I was a troubled soul preoccupied by divine nostalgia for the perfection of the past, for only the past could be tailored with flexible scissors into perfection, or that I was too complicated, or, as he said, "Had an iron will," I told him to ask himself what he really needed, for when he knew he would look more easily for the known. As he said that I had an iron will, I told him that this was obviously something he despised in women, so I recommended to him to look for a softer lady, with a more agreeable character, one who was gentle and dependent (for I was not liked by men for my independence). I reminded him how good-looking he was, how successful in his endeavours, how wealthy and worldly a man he was. I said, "Who would not want a man like you?" I said a few more things, trying carefully to blend facts, good wishes and my need to get rid of him for good, for there was something sinister and sickening in the way he related to me, and if I ever encouraged his behaviour, I tried to say, "I'm sorry."

Well, all this, what I said about Erwin, were just sketches that came to my knowledge and I can't say why I have chosen them in that particular order to portray his sad character, built on tangible confusion. There were bright and light moments we spent together but the other ones prevailed. Thus I concluded that he had this particular personality. Was it enhanced by my painful and occasionally obvious indifference? How can I know that?
I never met the woman with whom he said he had lived happily, so I never knew what good she was able to bring out of him.

When he got the letter the next day, he gave me a telephone call. He said that the letter saddened him gravely and his daughters, too, for he read the letter to them. The last sentence of my letter was that it would be in the best interests of all of us if we did not see each other again. Was it cruel? Was it heartless? Did I make them suffer; for they liked me, they liked my daughter? I could not answer these questions, but you know what, I could not tolerate his moods any longer, his unpredictable highs and lows, his occasional accusations and the inconsistencies in his speech and his deeds. Maybe that was the first time in a long time that I put myself, and my needs, first.

"What was that feeling like?" interrupted the Nobleman, and She said:
It was a healthy feeling. It was the same feeling as the one when I protect my daughter; a feeling of care and love for myself, acknowledging it loudly. And something deep within me started to sing a song, the one I sang when I was a young soul. The song of wonderful freedom. As I was listening to the song, it grew louder and louder and I could see myself on the top of the cherry tree overlooking the placid Adriatic Sea, singing from the top of my lungs to all those who wanted to hear me, including God who was seated next to me while we were swinging with the wind and the cherries swung with us, and the leaves, and the little branches, and the clouds, and the world was swinging and singing with me. I felt as if the world, God and I were one intermingled everlasting reality and I wished that this ecstasy of freedom and of belonging at the same time could last forever.

***

It looked as if among the cherries, the leaves, the clouds and the breeze, I found myself again. While I was swinging, I felt that my soul did not want to be trapped in the cage of my aching body any more.

CHAPTER ELEVEN

Susanne's father was a shrink. One day when we were young, he said to me:

"I am curious to see where you will end up. There is something strong and righteous which leads you without second thought, without any fear."

When I saw him at Carla's birthday, he said he had followed my life story and he asked me if he wasn't right in his observation years before. I said:

"Look at me, I am a broken soul. Maybe I was strong and righteous when I was young, but look what has become of me: I was seriously ill twice, I am divorced but not in a way people divorce, I was deserted as a dry land, as a leper, the money from my books was never given to me and I live in constant fear of the future."

He did not say much but ate his cake. Susanne winked as she usually would when she would indicate, 'be patient.' So I was.

When he finished eating his cake, he took the serviette, unfolded it and wiped his mouth and his moustache, then with the same serviette, he gathered the little crumbs on the table, put them into his hand, got up and went out onto the terrace. Without turning his head, he said:

"Join me."

Like an obedient child I got up and followed him. Without turning my head, I said to Susanne:

"Join us." And she did.

He asked Susanne to bring him his glass of red wine and his pipe. She brought what he had asked for and she brought more coffee for us. It took some time while he was preparing his pipe in a totally devoted ritual and judging by his slow, meditative movements, it really looked as if he had forgotten about us, particularly about what I said earlier. Susanne and I were looking at each other in silence, pulling funny faces. But we did not laugh. In that game we were well trained, for it was one of our dearest games; who would pull the uglier or funnier face and who would give in first and burst out laughing.

He took a few puffs from his pipe and sighed, then sank deeper into the comfortable chair, looking at the sun, which was slowly but surely changing its colour and changing the colour of the sky and the sea. I had known him for so many years and never seen in him more than Susanne's father, who would know everything the best, the one who would bore us with his short stories and parables and never really made us laugh with his peculiar sense of humour. I had a feeling that he would doze off in his chair and I looked at Susanne and lifted my eyebrows but she only shrugged her shoulders. He grew older and the signs of various health issues were written on his sometime-handsome face. Without looking at me, but rather at the last rays of the sun, the first sentence he uttered was:

"I really do not feel any pity towards you and I do not see you as a victim of any great injustice."

"Do you want to say it is all in my head? Did I imagine my illness? His betrayal?"

He did not say anything but he fixed his eyes on the horizon while humming a little song.

When he finished humming, he washed the little song down with the red wine, he cleared his throat and said:

"Suffering, my dear ... suffering alone cannot break the human spirit, don't you know that? You know that humans have survived all kinds of disasters, unspeakable losses and countless injustices. Throughout the history of humankind we survived wars, natural catastrophes, great famines, plagues and 'incurable' diseases, but it never stopped the human spirit from growing and learning, fighting and overcoming what was perceived as invincible. I heard you were ill, but I heard you were cured, weren't you? You want to portray yourself as a martyr, for your husband abandoned you ill and fragile, but let me tell you that he did you a great favour, for who would really want to stay with this kind of a man? Do you want to look at your life as a great problem to be solved or could it be a new opportunity to do what makes you whole and happy? What about your writing? What about Althea? What about the further studies I heard you engaged in again?

What if I tell you that you do not need to repair yourself, there are no mistakes, and all you need to do is to reawaken what is already within you: strength and wisdom? While you are reawakening, do it with love for yourself, for your child, for your family and the rest of us, your closest friends.

When we talk about suffering or pain, what if we discover that pain is beyond our own control? Depends on the angle from which one is looking; if you consider your pain, or to put it differently, your miserable life circumstances as a grand injustice or mistreatment by somebody or life itself, then choices are few - you could feel anger and disappointment, which inevitably leads you toward rage and ultimately to depression. But if you can understand that pain has come with life to all of us, then you will understand the deeper meaning of the pain. Do you remember when you and Sue were in the grip of Buddhism? Buddha said that life was suffering. What that meant to your young, carefree minds I never knew. Look at Susanne, how much she suffers with her children, yet your child is an example of an intelligent, gifted, good-humoured and good-hearted child. What a gift, what a gift!"

He fell silent again and closed his eyes and I looked back into the house and looked at my 'gift' and thought, "What a beautiful gift, how is it that I am not grateful to life when I see her healthy and constantly content? We do take everything for granted without gratefulness to life, is it only that I missed the beauty of it, for my eyes were looking at something else? Is it so that I can shift my gaze at my will and all would be different? Why do I need to explain the causes of my suffering and pain to myself? Do I need to explain it because the pain I felt was so uncomfortable and challenging? Can the explanation of the pain prevent further pain?"

When he got up and went towards the playing children, he said, passing me by:
"Please, do not identify yourself with the so-called misfortunes you have been given, you know better, don't you?"
Did I know better? Did I?
I asked Susanne:
"Do I know better?"
She nodded her head.
We sat down together in the chair her father had just vacated and looked at the ever-changing colours of the mellow sky. She got up, brought a little blanket and covered my legs, then snuggled again next to me and we did not talk for the rest of the evening dedicated to our own thoughts.

That evening my daughter slept at Susanne's and her father offered to give me a lift home instead of Susanne. When we came in front of my family house, he said to me:
"Sometimes in life we need help. Unwillingness to accept the help is not a sign of high intelligence. Please, when you get back home, find yourself a good psychologist, all you need is clarification, somebody who would show you in which direction to go after those turbulent events, which I do not deny were difficult for you. But you've got to find a good one; I would say the best one."

And I did.

***

I said to Susanne that I would come the next day to take my daughter and she said to come around lunch-time.

It was Sunday and she had planned a long, relaxing lunch, which we would enjoy together when I visited.

I could not even dream of a surprise of the proportions they were preparing.

The table was laid outside, under the trees and the vine lines. Heavy grapes were hanging down, almost touching our heads, but they were not ripe yet, as their colour showed to the knowing eye. It was the Muscat, it was to be dark red, almost black when ripe, but the globes were coloured in two colours: green and light red. Just the sight of them made my mouth water, for I knew how sour they were while in these colours, diametrically opposed to the fantastic sweetness at the end of September. But it was just the beginning of August.

Susanne baked the best cakes, but George was the real cook. He knew exactly what I liked, after all the times we all dined together when we were students, earning our first money in the small cafés along the beaches. As Susanne had a house just outside of the city, in a small town with just one church and one medical centre, all her patients were local people and she was never short of the freshest produce from her patients' gardens. Apart from the fresh fruit and vegetables, she was given eggs, chicken, and ham, and fishermen used to bring her lobsters and oysters when they were in season. In their house they had the best home-made wine and smoked cheese.

George went to the fish market that morning and brought a few lobsters and when I arrived, the house smelled of the lobsters and the red wine in which they were slowly cooking. It smelled of coriander, lavender and mint, and above all, the smell of freshly baked bread. All of these rich aromas made my mouth water and made my stomach rumble. Instantly I was hungry and I hurried George to take everything out onto the table, but he said that the lobsters had to be cooked on a low temperature for two more hours. Oh, what a pain!

Besides, he said that he had planned the lunch for one o'clock, so I obeyed, asking only for a few olives and some goat cheese. He did not even want to give me the hot bread, saying that I would spoil my lunch. I felt like a little child in a house of chocolate where purchase was forbidden. I ate a few olives and licked my fingers, only wishing for more.

The wine we drank was red and thick as a horse's blood and it left a black oily rim on the thin, crystal glass. George gave each of us just a few sips of wine so as not to spoil our lunch, and we were looking out for the perfect moment of his absent-mindedness so that we could pour some more.

But he came out, onto the terrace, and took the bottle in, for he said he needed it to pour some more onto the lobsters. We looked at each other in disbelief, then we stood up and went for a short walk through the nearby pine tree forest.

While we were walking and awakening dormant memories, George rang Susanne and told her not to hurry back because we were only disrupting his work and peace, so we stayed and roamed through the forest, occasionally picking yellow flowers whose name I had forgotten.

When her telephone rang the second time, some forty-five minutes later, she announced that George said we could come back, for everything was ready.

While we were approaching from a distance, I saw the kids still bathing in the pool, we saw the table all made up, and I saw a tall man standing next to George with a glass in his hand. He was dark and tall and even from a distance I could say handsome, and I asked Susanne who the man was. All she said was:

"You'll see now."

I still could not see his face but when he lifted his glass, slowly, at the same time precisely and clumsily, I knew who the man was, so I started to run towards him and he walked with a gentle smile on his face and a gentle smile in his warm, dark, almost black eyes.

I hadn't seen Marco for twenty years, but while he was walking towards me, with a smile on his pretty face, I felt as if time had gone back and I thought, "Nothing changes in this world," for we were together again, different yet the same: Marco, Susanne and me, hugging in a loving, tender hug, laughing and crying at the same time.

He could never come without presents, so he brought me a painting of the little fisherman's village where we used to swim or eat pizza in the late afternoons. He brought some books and a golden chain for my daughter and some presents for Susanne's girls.

He brought wine, too, but I said that I would not compromise, for what I liked the best was George's wine, which looked as red and thick as a horse's blood, which would always leave a dark, oily circle on the rim of the glass.

We sat at the table laid out for four. I looked at him freely while his gaze was fixed on my face. His eyes were somehow deeper as a result of a few sorrows he had encountered since I saw him the last time. On the left hand, on the ring finger he had a silver ring, which looked like a wedding band, but in the middle it had three little lapis lazuli next to each other. As always he was dressed immaculately, the way the latest fashion demanded, with a few details like the ring mentioned before, and he had a bracelet made of silver and leather which gave his gentle hand a more masculine look.

But Marco was always a mystery, and I can frankly say that nobody really knew him ever. What I learned that afternoon was that Marco had quit the world of fashion after ten years, for he said it was demanding, immature, greedy, perverse and after all a cruel and brainless world. He said he searched for the deeper meaning but in this environment he could not learn anything anymore, so he left Milan for good and moved to Trieste, where he bought a little house where he painted.

I was taken aback, for I never knew he had a penchant or talent for painting, but he said that he thought that it was not about talent, he just enjoyed painting so much. He said he had made some good investments with the money he earned in the fashion industry when he was paid, as he said, "More than anybody deserved" and because of that he said he was blessed that he could pursue his desire to paint, which had obsessed his mind for a number of years. When I asked him if he sold his paintings, he laughed a little, then he said, "Who in the right mind would ever buy it?" then he stood up and brought the painting he gave me before and said:

"I give them as presents to special friends."

Once again I was pleasantly surprised, for I never knew Marco had such a good talent and his little painting was now even dearer to my heart. He asked me if I remembered that particular beach and the little pizzeria, to which I replied that he made my heart melt. He smiled his feminine smile, his lips still sweet and red as cherries and the way he combed his hair with his fingers awakened some tenderness in my soul.

Marco was quieter than I remembered him and I could not answer to myself why he would be quieter. I had a peculiar feeling that his quietness was the result of some events that left his eyes deeper, his voice softer and his words fewer. But I decided there that I was not going to analyze Marco's every movement or each of his words. I told myself to enjoy this rare opportunity. Every now and then I would notice how bony his hands were, but then I would say to myself that he was always bony. He ate little, drank even less, and he refused to eat the cake.

He said that he did not live alone but that he had a Persian cat he called Princess. We never really knew how he lived in Milan, nor now in Trieste, for any personal question was answered with a little shy smile, or he would say quietly that he always felt himself to be a burden to people, except to Susanne and me.

I often wondered whether we were born with a certain personality or whether really early experiences in our lives are responsible for who we are in the present. Even though he laughed a lot that afternoon, even though the laughter was quiet and often hidden with his hand, I felt as if he was dipped in the vast ocean of melancholy and I did not know when it originated. Was it always there, but I never recognized it, for our characters were still in the making, was it born much later, or was it something newly added to colour him differently?

He did not talk much. Instead, when he talked, he asked the questions and I was the one who talked the most, for I really hadn't seen him and wanted to tell him about my life. He saw Susanne often twice a year, so her life for him was not unknown. But when I would ask him about his life, he would say, "Nothing much," so all the gaps were filled with my imagination. But when my mind touched some possibilities which came from Marco's uncertain smile, an uncertain melancholy fell upon me as if I wanted once again to share his hidden pain, believing that I could protect him from it.

We had been sitting around this generous table for some six hours, and as it started to get darker and a mild wind rose up, he said he'd like to go soon.

Before he got up, he leaned towards me and whispered into my ear:

"Can you walk me to the car?"

And I did.

We walked in silence; I felt as if somebody was walking behind us and had dishonest intentions. I felt as if this invisible somebody was going to stab me in the back. Or maybe stab him in the back. As we walked, our breathing could be heard and I heard vague music in the distance. It was not evening yet but the shadows were longer and darker. Marco opened the door of his car and showed me in. He sat next to me and we looked each other in the eyes. There was something strange in his eyes and if I had ever seen just his eyes without his face, I would never have guessed they were Marco's eyes. I used to love his shiny, dark, eyes, nearly black, as black as the black olives we had left on Susanne's table.

He smiled.

I said:

"Is there something wrong, Marco?"

He shrugged his shoulders.

Then I knew there was something wrong.

I looked at his thin, bony fingers, I looked at his bony face, but he was always slender.

I felt as if I was going to cry without reason. He leaned his head onto my shoulder. I said:

"Don't make me cry, Marco."

And he said:

"Please, do not cry, just hug me."

And I did.

The last time I saw Marco, I was holding his head on my lap and was combing his black hair with my fingers. He was silently smoking a thin, long cigarette.

After a while I said:

"So?"

"I've got cancer." He said it plainly.

I started to cry at once (bitterly, for this word always made me hysterical and I had decided that I would never call this illness by its name) but he said, "Don't."

He asked me not to say anything to anybody, for he said nobody knew but his mother.

I said:

"I can't believe it ... I can't believe ... I can't...."

He said:

"At the end of last summer I got the diagnosis. I felt a dull pain in my back. I thought it was from sitting, because I used to paint for hours. The doctor had examined me and told me to stay in hospital for further examination. The next day I was told that I had kidney cancer. It is now in my ribs, my hip and in the skull. I am going to die soon. I am happy I saw you, that's why I came, to see you, most probably, for the last time."

"Do you take any medications? Do you do anything?"

"First and foremost it is inoperable, it is in the bones. Secondly, I would never have the courage to undergo all these therapies. I follow some alternative therapies, I watch what I eat, I take some natural products, some acupuncture, often I take some homeopathic medicine...." he sighed and continued in a flat voice, "...but I do not know how much good it does me. Anyway, I am still here, I still have enough energy on some days, on some days I am awfully tired, on some days awfully depressed, but I can put up with it all."

I started to cry again, remembering my days in hospital and my pilgrimage there every day after my Mother left.

"Maybe it would have been better if I had never come to see you and disturbed you with this, but I wanted to see you for the last time. I wanted to give you my painting. It is insignificant but I know you will cherish it. I wanted to tell you that you were my only real friend and apart from my mother you were the only person I loved sincerely. Women pitied me and men hated me ... you know why, you know it all ... often I felt like a beautiful but rare animal chased by hungry wolves. All I wanted in my life was to paint, to read clever books and to have a few good friends. Looks like I asked

for little, looks like I got a little, but nevertheless, it was my life and however it was, it came to the end. Thank you for this beautiful afternoon with you and Susanne, you made me feel alive again. Thank you for being my friend, so few people sincerely wanted to be....."

I said:

"Don't talk. Please, do not talk."

Now I laid my head onto his chest and did not want to tell him any words that would sound like consolation. For I knew, in moments like these, no words could sound sincere and believable, I knew silence was the best friend. And in that silence we heard our hearts beating and speaking to each other.

I was crying silently while his eyes were nailed in some imaginary image far in the distance.

I broke the silence and asked him:

"Does it hurt, Marco? Do you hurt?"

A little smile played with his lips like the strings of a guitar. He repeated my question:

"Do I hurt? You know, I have been hurting all my life, since I was born. My mother wanted a girl, because I had an older brother, and all she could do to soothe her pain was to dress me like a girl. I was a pretty child, dressed in the pink outfits she would knit for me and everybody thought I was a girl. I was confused with who I was and I thought I liked all these girly things because my mother made me like them. I never really knew what I liked or what I liked to be, but when I grew older, I understood that my interests, my likings, secret desires and dreams had nothing to do with the way my mother dressed me. I understood they originated from deep inside of me, from my psyche, from my bones, or if you wish, from my soul. I felt trapped in my own body; I was frightened and disgusted on some days. There were days when I would hate my mother for the mistake and injustice she had done, there were days when I would hate myself, for when I looked at myself in the mirror a very strange creature would look back. You know what a misfit I was, you know how kids were cruel and I hid my emotions, I denied my needs, I silenced my voice, I stopped my breathing, I ceased to exist. You were my friend, my hero.

Did Milan bring me happiness?" After the rhetoric question he paused and I did not know if I should say something or just let him cleanse his soul.

"Did Milan bring me happiness? Did the frantic world of high fashion bring me what I was searching for? No. It did not. It brought me fake fame; it brought me money, which in the first few years was spent foolishly on banal things. My girlfriends liked me but they never really cared for who I was,

they just wanted to have a good time, men liked me better but it was the same with them, they wanted to escape the boredom of their lives...."

He paused, then continued with a weak voice:

"*I saw through the world of fashion, I saw through the people, I saw through the world and all I wanted to do was to paint my pain in different colours. I started with little pictures from our youth, some sketches caught on the canvas of my past, then I progressed towards the abstract, where all I wanted was to enjoy the colours. Playing with colours would always free something within me and I would not think about who I was or what was ever wrong with me, I would not think of cunning and brutal abuses in the so-called world of high fashion, where all I had and all I took with me were lies and pretentiousness. If I think about it now, I can say that painting helped me to really face my own pain for the first time. All my life I tried to avoid my pain at all costs, believing that it was too frightening, too disturbing and too deep. I carried it through all my life to bring it to the ultimate altar, the altar of my easel. When I painted, I would not feel the shame, the loneliness, the meaninglessness of my days, I would be the painter and the painting at the same time; I would be whole.*

Years ago I thought that my pain was a mistake; that it could have been prevented if only I had been different, namely strong, so I could avoid it or fight it. I even sought the ones to blame, the ones that caused my pain ... but I understood that we all suffer from pain that is different yet the same. The pain of being human and suffering itself is, and will always be, the thread that will run through the fabric of our lives."

I don't know how long we were sitting there; my head on his chest, his hand on the temple of my head, and listening to his weak voice.

"*It is time to go. Do not say anything.*"

I felt as if I did not want to let him go, as if he was going to meet Death, but while he was with me he was protected from it. No, I knew exactly how he felt and I knew there was nobody who could guard us from Death.

I said:

"*I will ring you while I am here.*"

He said:

"*We are going to Trieste tomorrow.*"

"*Are you not staying here with your mother?*"

"*No, she wants me to be there, for I can paint there.*"

"*I'll ring you in Trieste.*"

I waved and cried while his car disappeared into the evening mist.

My last thought was not uttered loudly but resided in the privacy of my mind: "Can he forgive?"

Was he able to forgive himself and forgive the world? For that was the real malady, unforgiveness.

Susanne panicked when she saw me crying and I begged her not to ask me for the reason.
So she did not.
But she was the one who rang me first to tell me that Marco had passed away in the hospital in Trieste.
They took him home and buried him in the family crypt where his father was buried seven years earlier. Susanne and I cried together while each holding a big bunch of red and white roses, which we silently put on his ultimate abode, knowing that the world was poorer for one gentle, kind and loving soul. Or was his soul freer from the prison of his beautiful body, for the body is anyway only temporarily home for the immortal soul?

After the funeral we were driving in silence and when she stopped in front of my house, her eyes were still full of tears, she hugged me and said:
"Don't go. Don't go there anymore. Your home is here, here is where you belong, come back and do not leave ever again."
But I did.

***

When She left his room after telling him that She needed a two-week break to sail and to sink deep down into the places where nobody could follow Her, I feared where She would go and I feared whether I would be able to follow Her there, for it was a lonely journey and I feared whether She would ever come back, but listen to what She said the next time She entered his room, as if She was walking through the door of a known and placid garden:
It looks like at last I started to form a coherent picture of my life.
You know, my dear friend, that all this time, since I started to remember the episodes of my life and retell them to you, that there was a peculiar feeling that there were two of us, two of me; the one you see, the one who tells the story, the one who shows or does not show her emotions, if you want - the real me, the one you can see.

And there was the other one. The one who could not be seen. The essence of me. The one who would sit next to me and listen without protesting. Just the silent, benevolent observer. The one who gave me the strength and the courage to endure illness, displacement, separation, pain and confusion. The one whose voice I forgot to listen to some years ago, the one I had deserted for thinking that my mind knew all the answers I needed.

She followed me like a faithful servant everywhere; through my pains and my sorrows, whispering in my deaf ear that pain was an illusion, and that my sorrows were illusions. She followed me down to Andalucia and there on the sandy beach of Cadiz's shores I started to hear the fragments of her words carried by the wind. Sometimes I would hear the words and believe that I was really a little bit mad, for nobody was around, just me and the wind ... but she was speaking to me, whispering, but my, at that time, unbearable pain had a life of its own, it had wings and was as appealing as a beautiful, dark-winged lover and it silenced her voice, luring me into its mellow world of nothingness.

And the Nobleman asked, *"So where is She now?"*

She found Her home. All these little selves merged through my remem- brances to form a cohesive picture, one cohesive self. Am I me, for I remem- bered the entire past, including all aspects of myself, or am I me, for I remembered that a human has a soul, not just a mind? For it was my soul sitting next to me like a silent witness, whispering that I am all that: the lover and the loved one, the selfless friend, the betrayed one and the one who betrayed, the unconditionally loving mother and the child who cries for love, the princess and the fraud, the pain and the joy, for to be a human we have to have and experience all these emotions. We have to walk through the valley of the shadows, become the shadow and conquer the shadow in order to awaken to the light of our own being.

Silence lasted.

"So, what now?" Asked the Nobleman

I think now is about forgiveness. I identified myself with the particular forms of misfortune I had been given and the more I identified myself with them, the more I was blinded to the blessings I could encounter daily in my life. I carried the name of my misfortunes and could not separate myself from them, and it looked as if each of them broke me into one of sub-personalities that co-existed but not in harmony. They fought often to find their way or their voice; they were too loud, too quiet, too quarrelsome or too aloof. And being home to such a demanding bunch, my body was at odds, it almost seemed that it wanted to give up, for how could it host so much drama created by different authors and keep the house sane?

When I talked with Marco that evening, I saw him for the last time, I told him that pain was nobody's fault, nobody created it for us, we could neither prevent it nor control it, since it would come as the levante came, unpredictably and unannounced, but what we could do was to find a response to the pain. Even if we found out the 'why', which most likely would never happen, the pain would still be there and there would be a need to respond to it.

I suppose it is the same with fear. We fear the phantoms of our mind. What counts is how we respond to the fear, isn't it so? How can I fear God when I do not know whether God exists or not? Fear of what? Fear of death, or fear of life? Fear of nothingness, a possibility that we will never be remembered, as if we had never really existed? What can elevate the anxiety brought about by the perpetual anticipation of imminent, unavoidable danger?

What could end this endless cycle of pain, fear, disappointment and anger that keeps us imprisoned in our own suffering? Is forgiveness the answer? What are we required to forgive, if it is so? How much do we have to forgive, how often, how promptly? Whom do I have to forgive? Do I forgive the situations or the protagonists? Do I forgive myself because I loved the wrong men or do I forgive them because they were not capable of love? The kind of love I wanted in my dreams. If I do not divorce myself from the people who hurt me, I will be trapped in the eternal dance of suffering with them, and the only way to divorce myself from them is through forgiveness.

I can't carry the responsibility of other people's decisions, but I can forgive in order to set myself free, for every time I think of the pain that was caused by others, it only strengthens the belief of being hurt or being the victim of injustice. It feeds my melancholy and melancholy leads me through the soft and dark landscapes of depression. Depression was brought on by thoughts, by an unforgiving heart.

I had lived in fear since he left. Fear of illness, fear of harm, and fear of the future, but didn't fear alone bring me only harm? What I had done was all I knew at that time, but I isolated myself from the life itself because of my fear. Whether or not I feared my illness, ill luck, pain or death, they are inevitable ingredients of my life. We all share the same feelings, the same pain, the same sorrows and the same happiness.

We do not know the answer of how to live after life's disappointments, but we have to live and that is all. Day after day. I learned to accept my pain, my disappointments, my sorrows, and understood that the dreams of my youth may never come true. All I can say is - let it be. For life is just one gift and all of these ingredients are wrapped in it, and if we have to learn to share, then we can share both our sorrows and our happiness with the same attitude of kindness.

CHAPTER TWELVE

When I met him, I feared him. I feared his piercing, inquisitive eyes. I feared that my necklace of black pearls could be broken and the pearls could be lost forever. I feared letting go of them as if when I let them go, I would lose my identity. I defined myself by my sorrows, by my black pearls. I had woven my stories out of my pearls; I carried them around my neck regardless of their heaviness or the possibility of strangling myself. I was proud of them as one would be proud of a rare gift. I polished them with my tears and could see the events of my life in their dark mirrors. In the end I laid them in front of the man who examined them well, as some sort of very skilled evaluator of deeply hidden, rare treasure.

Where have the fears gone? Where are my fears?

And we agreed, together, that the last chapter of my story should be one of forgiveness. To unburden the soul, to bring it back to where it belongs, I have to learn to forgive. To unburden my heart and allow it to love again, I have to forgive.

When I was lying sick with an aching body, with no strength or energy, he said he had no love to give me. I was unwilling to forgive him his 'unforgivable deeds', but unforgiveness made my heart almost turn to stone and made my soul flee this infertile land.

What was the cost of unforgiveness?

Does forgiveness mean to be courageous but humble? After all, can I see betrayal as a challenge; an opportunity to learn to be a better human being? Or is the meaning of forgiveness to heal one's own wounds and others' hurts?

I knew that forgiveness would ask for all my courage to start that painful journey full of frightening memories, conflicting and confusing emotions, and risky confrontations with unpredictable outcomes.

I have chosen this road hoping that at the other end of forgiveness, when I lay down all of my sorrows, all of my anger and all of my burdens, love will be awaiting me. Love for myself, and pure love for life itself. For unforgiveness separated me from loving life in its simplest form: when joy brings a kind smile to a child, when you utter a word to the worried one, when you feel grateful for the letter from someone who thought about you, grateful for just being alive, able to breathe, walk, talk and greet the new day.

And I asked my Nobleman:
"How many painful lessons do we have to learn before we learn simplicity again?"

EPILOGUE

In order to root out my depression, I needed to go deep down to discover what was chained to my sorrows. I found a vast but frozen sea of tears that never found their way out of my inner realms.

The name of this placid, motionless, almost crystal sea was "Never Mind," for these words echoed when I asked the question, "What was chained to my sorrows?"

"Never mind," it echoed, but on its crystal surface, as if on the big screen, the scene opened and I saw Claude's face, I saw his mother's icy eyes, I saw Antonella's lips delivering the news and I heard my voice. "Never mind," the voice said, "Never mind!"

I looked straight ahead and did not cry, no, I did not.

And when I did cry, I didn't cry enough, for my mind would say that only the weak and the sick cry and I had to be strong and brave, for crying was a shameful shelter, my mind said I had to be strong and proud.

And I was.

Somebody else cried inside of me, and all this vast water belonged to Her, for I obeyed my mind and needed no tears.

The next scene had opened on the surface of the sea and I saw the bent back of my husband leaving our home, because it was not a home of love but of illness, and he said it was about time to find another home. And I was brave, nobody saw my tears, nobody heard my sobbing, for what could simple tears change when love was not the home any longer?

I saw him walking a loud woman, I saw him walking with the young one, I saw him with a short woman with narrow eyes but I didn't cry, for only the weak cry, so I said, "Never mind," just, "Never mind."

In the hospital I never cried, because my Mother came to cry my tears, so I stored mine in the invisible, inner sea, which steadily grew bigger.

I had cried for others but I had not cried for me. I would say, "Never mind" and when I was asleep, my soul would dive into that invisible but real sea, in search of the pearls to undo the process of hardening. And I said to my soul, "Never mind" over and over again and it stopped searching and combing the bed of the sea and when it asked me, in one of my dreams, if I wanted to undo the hardened tears, I said, "Go," and it did.

I remember when I woke up, I felt a strange pain in my chest, as if something was breaking off into sad freedom, for what is the soul without the body, and what is the body without the soul?

When it leaves, it leaves a vast nothingness, meaninglessness, emptiness, an ocean of sorrows, depression.

When I said, "Never mind," when I said, "Go," that was the last time my soul cried next to my dreamless body.

I did not call it back, but rather travelled to Andalucia, hoping that the ocean from unknown shores would wash out his words and deeds.

Without the perception that my soul lived in my chest and in everything around me, in all beings and matter, the world appeared to be cold and meaningless, random and hostile, and these experiences brought on fear and alienation. And when I think of my dreams, I do not know whether they were dreams or if I was carried like a leaf by the wind, for when our decisions are made unconsciously, our life runs unconsciously and we blame fate for our share.

There is not such a thing as fate; because everything depends on which level of consciousness our decisions are made. There is not such a thing as fate, I have woken up to understand the possibility of choosing to respond to life's difficulties and they are only two: through fear and doubt or through love and wisdom. Doubt and fear stood opposing wisdom and trust and led me towards the depths of darkness, but when I understood that I had the freedom to choose, the strength that I was told I possessed grew strong in front of my very eyes. It appears now that the conscious decisions, which are the building blocks of our lives, are a treasure beyond all values.

And knowing that now, I have no memory of fear.

As I was telling this story to my dear friend, the Nobleman, the high tide of my sea was rising and it finally broke and found a way out through my eyes.

I cried my ocean of tears that afternoon, and I cried out the shells and the pearls; I cried out the sand and the little swords that fell from the swordfish heads. I cried out the letters that formed harsh words and reality, I cried out my own unspoken words and deeply hidden emotions. I cried there all the afternoon, for the barrel seemed to be bottomless; this was the first time I cried for myself and I did not cry out of pity but out of compassion.

The Nobleman sat there without a word, only compassion sat in his eyes and I felt as free as someone who was born for the very first time.

When the water, the mud, the shells, the pearls, the swords and the words had all been cried out, the bed of the ocean was vast and empty and I almost thought, "What shall I plant here now?", but from the empty bed of the ocean the shimmering light of love shone upon me.

Now, for the last time, I said, "Never mind," giving all my past, my shells and pearls, to the wind, unchaining every emotion which was chained to my shells and pearls, for there was nothing left and all was washed out, brought to the light of the sun and all my sharp shells, pearls and swords now looked like toys left on the bottom of an empty bathtub.

I was cleansed, not even forgiveness did I need any more, for all was already forgiven even before I came to this existence.

I asked my Nobleman:
"David, what was it all about? Denial?"
And he said:
"Never underestimate the power of denial."

I was ready to remember the times when I was brave and fearless. I was ready, once again, to invite the brave and honest to walk with me.

And here I am, with all the uncertainty that life is. I have learned that if I close my shell and if I close my eyes, life is not going to cease because I do not look at it.
"Never underestimate the power of denial." These were his last words, which echoed in the corridors of my mind, but from the corridors of my mind I sent them into my eyes to remind them to stay open and fearless. I sent them into my heart to remind it to stay truthful to its wishes.

I know that fears will always accompany my uncertainties, but if we listen to the fears and follow them, we are led astray; possessed by them.
We can be aware of our own fears and put them aside and walk into the unknown despite the fears ... then we will walk with the brave and honest.

About the Author

Branka Cubrilo was born in Croatia in1961.

At the age of eighteen she wrote her first novel, I Knew Jane Eyre, and in 1982 it won the Yugoslavian Young Writers Award. Soon after, she wrote a sequel to this story called Looking for Jane Eyre.

In 1992, Cubrilo moved to Sydney and continued to write short stories and novels. In 1999 the novel As a River (Fiume Corre – Rijeka Tece) was published by Croatian publisher Adamic in her native town of Rijeka. The book received good critiques in Croatian and Italian press. After the Croatian book launch, an Australian one followed.

In 2000, the next novel was published, Requiem for Barbara. The book was launched in both Croatia and Sydney.

In 2001, a new novel, Little Lies, Big Lies, was published by the same publisher. This was the first volume of a trilogy called Spanish Stories. Cubrilo had obtained a scholarship from the Spanish Ministry of Foreign Affairs to travel to Andalucia to research the cultural and historical settings of Cadiz.

Cubrilo has written two more novels but she stopped writing and publishing when she encountered serious health issues and the disintegration of her marriage. When she recovered she was able to translate her experiences into a new novel, The Mosaic of the Broken Soul.

Over the last 18 years, Cubrilo has worked as a journalist for various local newspapers in Sydney, writing articles and short stories and conducting interviews. One of her novels was serialized in the magazine Women 21.

Cubrilo also worked as a radio producer, in Eastside Radios Sydney and Special Broadcasting Services – SBS Sydney, where she has produced a number of programs and series, conducted many interviews and written short stories.

Cubrilo now writes in English and is also translating her earlier novels into English.

She lives in Sydney with her daughter Althea.

VISIT

SPEAKING VOLUMES ONLINE

HUGO, NEBULA, EDGAR,

SHAMUS, ANTHONY MACAVITY,

AGATHA, CARL SANDBERG,

ELLERY QUEEN, OWEN WISTER,

SPUR & BRAM STOKER

AWARD-WINNING

USA TODAY & NEW YORK TIMES

BEST-SELLING AUTHORS

www.speakingvolumes.us